TRAITORS

There were few villains Hal Brognola detested more than those who sold out their country, and he didn't give a damn what the reason.

A man chooses a side, sticks with his choice no matter what the challenges, the temptations, the internal conflicts that might have him turn his back and seek what might be greener pastures.

Right then, as he slipped the rest of the sat photos and a copy of Orion's disk into the manila envelope, the big Fed felt a little sick to his stomach. He gave the computer team a last look. They were hard at it, juggling the action—of the coming and certain firestorms—with professional resolve, skill and determination.

And with honor.

For the moment, there was nothing more he could do here, but he had someplace to go in search of possible answers to some dark and troubling realities.

Other titles in this series:

#14 DEADLY AGENT	##47 COMMAND FORCE
#15 BLOOD DEBT	#48 CONFLICT IMPERATIVE
#16 DEEP ALERT	#49 DRAGON FIRE
#17 VORTEX	#50 JUDGMENT IN BLOOD
#18 STINGER	#51 DOOMSDAY DIRECTIVE
#19 NUCLEAR NIGHTMARE	#52 TACTICAL RESPONSE
#20 TERMS OF SURVIVAL	#53 COUNTDOWN TO TERROR
#21 SATAN'S THRUST	#54 VECTOR THREE
#22 SUNFLASH	#55 EXTREME MEASURES
#23 THE PERISHING GAME	#56 STATE OF AGGRESSION
#24 BIRD OF PREY	#57 SKY KILLERS
#25 SKYLANCE	#58 CONDITION HOSTILE
#26 FLASHBACK	#59 PRELUDE TO WAR
#27 ASIAN STORM	#60 DEFENSIVE ACTION
#28 BLOOD STAR	#61 ROGUE STATE
#29 EYE OF THE RUBY	#62 DEEP RAMPAGE
#30 VIRTUAL PERIL	#63 FREEDOM WATCH
#31 NIGHT OF THE JAGUAR	#64 ROOTS OF TERROR
#32 LAW OF LAST RESORT	#65 THE THIRD PROTOCOL
#33 PUNITIVE MEASURES	#66 AXIS OF CONFLICT
#34 REPRISAL	#67 ECHOES OF WAR
#35 MESSAGE TO AMERICA	#68 OUTBREAK
#36 STRANGLEHOLD	#69 DAY OF DECISION
#37 TRIPLE STRIKE	#70 RAMROD INTERCEPT
#38 ENEMY WITHIN	#71 TERMS OF CONTROL
#39 BREACH OF TRUST	#72 ROLLING THUNDER
#40 BETRAYAL	#73 COLD OBJECTIVE
#41 SILENT INVADER	#74 THE CHAMELEON FACTOR
#42 EDGE OF NIGHT	#75 SILENT ARSENAL
#43 ZERO HOUR	#76 GATHERING STORM
#44 THIRST FOR POWER	#77 FULL BLAST
#45 STAR VENTURE	#78 MAELSTROM
46 HOSTILE INSTINCT	#79 PROMISE TO DEFEND

DON PENDLETON'S

STONY

AMERICA'S ULTRA-COVERT INTELLIGENCE AGENCY

MAN®

DOOMSDAY
CONQUEST

A GOLD EAGLE BOOK FROM
WORLDWIDE®

TORONTO • NEW YORK • LONDON
AMSTERDAM • PARIS • SYDNEY • HAMBURG
STOCKHOLM • ATHENS • TOKYO • MILAN
MADRID • WARSAW • BUDAPEST • AUCKLAND

First edition December 2005

ISBN 0-373-61964-2

DOOMSDAY CONQUEST

Special thanks and acknowledgment to
Dan Schmidt for his contribution to this work.

Printed in U.S.A.

DOOMSDAY
CONQUEST

CHAPTER ONE

Whatever the awful truth about the molten storm falling to earth under his command and control, Colonel Ytri Kolinko wasn't all that sure he cared to know. A veteran of the Afghan war and a staunch believer in the Communist dictates of pre-Wall Russia, he trusted simplicity in all its forms, be it on the battlefield or in the high-tech laboratories of his current post. What the eye saw, in other words, the mind fathomed, whether his hand was dipped in the blood of slain mujahideen or held a test tube with microorganisms from outer space. Grinding his teeth as the warning siren blared, he slung the AK-74 assault rifle across his shoulder. Ignorance might truly prove bliss.

Or would it? he had to wonder as he torqued himself to a double-time march, propelled by a heady blend of fear, anxiety and excitement, heard his lieutenants of Command Red Lightning barking for the conscripts and the science detail beyond the steel door to move faster for the transport helicopters. This was his command, his protectorate in this remote and desolate abyss of Tajikistan, after all, the responsibility heaped square on his shoulders to get to the bottom of what had traveled from deep space to previously land in Uzbekistan, Turkmenistan and Kyrgystan. And what was now breaching Earth's atmosphere was neither comet, falling star, meteor shower nor any other space phenomenon identified by Man. If it played true to prior and—what, supernatural?—form, it would not only swamp roughly a dozen square acres, as it had in each of the former Soviet republics, thus forcing a military quarantine, but chances were the event would sear yet another terrifying memory at the sight of human beings...

He shuddered, shoved away the frightening images, cursing the young soldier who allowed the door to thud shut, near smashing his scowl to pulp. Forget the angry albeit sorry fact Moscow had dumped him in hostile country that made his former Chechen post look a Black Sea resort by comparison, the Minister of Defense wanted answers to mysteries that came from another galaxy, perhaps another world, even another dimension, if he believed what his astronomers told him about black holes, shrinking mass and evolving protostars.

Tajikistan, he knew, was marked off by the political and military barons of Moscow as a buffer zone between the Muslim extremists of Afghanistan and Russia, but another image easily leaped to mind when he thought about his woeful post. As Moscow's man in-country, braving the cold, fighting drug traffickers, often engaged in pitched battles with both rebels and narco-thugs—and often both were one and the same—he saw Tajikistan as a vast moat between Afghanistan and Russia, teeming with crocodiles—hungry and poised to devour those who would further erode the moral fiber of his country with the slow white death or outright attacking Mother Russia through terrorism and sabotage.

Prepared to tackle the night's grim business, whatever the case, Kolinko used a bootheel to thunder open the door, barely breaking stride as he swept onto the sprawling helipads.

"Move, move, move!"

He took in the controlled frenzy of soldiers, urged on by his officers as they rushed to board three Mi-26 transports, then spotted the gaggle of spacesuits lumbering for the high-tech cocoon of the custom-built black Mi-14 search-and-rescue chopper at the deep north end. There, a squad of his black-clad Red Lightning commandos lugged the tubular lead containers with fastened vacuum hoses, muled various and sundry metal crates that housed detection and sampling verification ordnance.

As if, he thought, what was streaking for Earth could be understood by finite puny Man.

And Kolinko looked to the heavens, stood his ground, some two thousand feet high on the western edge of the Pamir Range. The scudding gray cloud banks seemed low enough to reach up and grab. Where the billows broke in roiling tendrils, he made out the faint sheen of moonlight, then stared at countless stars twinkling from galaxies both known and yet to be named.

After another few moments of stargazing, aware he was stalling, Kolinko looked back at the compound, briefly wondered if he would return to see its foreboding steel walls, see through to fruition the prototypes of future secret weapons being engineered in its labyrinth. Panning the mammoth complex, north to south, he almost envied the soldiers and science crews remaining behind, nestled as they were, safe from potential lethal doses of radiation or the terrifying clutches of antigravity, deep in the rock-hewn bowels.

Safe, yes, unless the celestial storm changed course and…

At least half the base was burrowed deep into the mountain range that rose from the plateau, the imposing peaks jutting higher, it seemed, forming a natural barrier the farther south they stretched to meet the northern edge of the Fedchenko Glacier, one of the world's longest continental ice river. A final sweep, spying the concrete dome of the observatory looming dead center from the roof where its telescopes—Russian versions of the American Hubble, he knew—monitored the coming tempest, and Kolinko fastened the com link over his black beret.

His team of astrophysicists, he recalled, believed they had pinpointed the core source of the space ore. Give or take a thousand light-years, they claimed its origins in something called the Eagle Nebula, recent but evolving star formations about 6,500 light-years away in a stellar region called Serpens, near the Star Gamma Scuti. Whatever its genesis, for a moment Kolinko wished the observatory a silo, imagined the scope magically morphing into a nuclear warhead, a time-delay fuse that would erupt a thermonuclear blanket, all but vaporizing the extraterrestrial stew.

Kolinko swept back to reality as he felt the icy touch

of rotor wash slashing his face. All set and ready, but for what? he wondered, grunting as he bent his head, forging toward the lead transport chopper.

Watching the first two transports lifting off, he suddenly found something both fearsome and absurd that a simple soldier should be forced to confront, much less explain the improbable and the preposterous. Boarding the Mi-26, he realized he was touching the emblem on the front of his beret and wishing what they were going to encounter was as simple to explain as lightning.

FAYSUD DOZMUJ WAS ashamed of his comrades.

As he cradled the AK-47, watching the caravan of mules and horses from the rearguard, he began to consider how much different he was than his fellow clansmen. One disturbing for instance, he wasn't a terrorist, much less a cold-blooded killer, as many of them had proved themselves to be. The fact he didn't carry a heart pumping with murderous wrath round-the-clock like his cousins for any human being other than Tajik—especially Russians and westerners—left him wondering if he was better than the others, or simply weak. Granted, circumstance dictated the road many of them had chosen, but the circumstance of the desperate poor or the oppressed—as they saw themselves—was a sad and sorry eternal plight the world over.

Always had been, always would be.

The blood of the innocent, he knew, was on many hands here in the Grbukt Pass. Be it Israel, Iraq or Kabul, and as family men themselves, did it not prey on their minds that they had shattered the lives of lambs who only wished to live in peace, perhaps slaughtering children and thus extinguishing future bloodlines? Did they not see that their violence and brutality made them an abomination in the eyes of God? Was there not one even half-righteous man among their lot?

And how did they see him? As a coward, always making himself scarce when an ambush was in the wings, having never fired a shot in anger against their hated Russian oppressors?

Shucking the heavy wool coat higher up his shoulders, he shivered against the icy wind that howled like a thousand banshees, or the giant hairy *almasty*, he thought, the man-thing rarely seen but often heard baying from the black depths of mountain forests. He side-stepped another pile of dung steaming in the snow, thinking this was the last time he would follow his cousins when they hired themselves out as drug mules for men, he knew, who clearly had no regard who suffered, directly or indirectly, from the evil they peddled, as long as they lived on, rich-fattened swine indulging their every vile transgression.

It wasn't the long and dangerous drive by truck to the border, picking up something like two to three tons of heroin from Afghan warlords and their corrupt Russian counterparts each trip. The consignments were paid for in advance, their tribal leader, Ghazin, having won the trust of Russian gangsters long ago to deliver the cargo to designated rendezvous points in the Pamirs. Nor did the grueling three- or four-day march on foot when they were forced to abandon their vehicles in exchange for pack animals to trudge out the final leg of the journey bother him. Hardship was an accepted way of life for the Tajik.

Rather, it was his fear of God and the dreaded loss of eternal Paradise that disturbed him to no end, his heart and soul burdened by the weight of guilt, far exceeding, he imagined, the combined load of burlap sacks now being hauled out of the gorge. Way beyond the earthly consideration of a few paltry American dollars, by which he could feed a family of seven during the coming months, his conscience admonished him that what he did was wrong in the eyes of his Maker.

No more.

This was his last journey for the Devil, aware that what he did only enabled the spawning of evil, that was gain of illicit money to advance the slaughter of lambs.

He was trudging up the rise, searching the forested high ground, wondering if any of his cousins could forsake this wrong and find redemption before it was too late, when the animals began crying, shuffling and bucking against their burdens. The line lurched to a sudden halt, his cousins cursing the beasts as the braying and snorting rose in what he sensed was panic. He was wondering if the animals were spooked by the sudden arrival of the two giant black transport choppers as they appeared, hovering over the tree line of the high plateau, Ghazin on the field radio, confirming, he assumed, the helicopters ferried the Russian gangsters, when the sky erupted in a brilliant white light. Something inexplicable happened next to the helicopters, Dozmuj watching, shocked, as what appeared like a web of blue sparks began shooting, dancing around the hulls of the choppers. A heartbeat and one of the choppers was thrown into a whirling dervish, then propelled, it seemed, by the shroud of blue lightning, aimed on a course to smash into the heart of the caravan.

Whether it was instinct or some haunting premonition of doom he'd gnawed on since the border, Dozmuj knew something far out of the ordinary was blanketing the sky.

Terror then gripped him as the animals burst in a pell-mell scatter off the trail, his cousins shouting, torn between chasing after the beasts of burden and staring, frozen in fear, at the heaven's spread of dazzling—

Fire?

Dozmuj backpedaled, the assault rifle slipping off his shoulder, falling to ground as his mind tried to conceive that he bore witness to a vast sheet of white fire blossoming but rolling like ocean waves in a great storm across the width of the sky. And it powered the heavens above into instant day, as if the sun had burst through the celestial blackness, light so piercing he was forced to shut his eyes, afraid for a moment he was blind.

When he opened his eyes, he found the world on fire, the seeing all but beyond any belief.

Shouts of panic flaying the air and animals braying loud enough to further warp his senses, Dozmuj turned away and ran.

"PULL BACK!"

For all of their—what was to him—incoherent physics babble, it hardly explained the blue lightning shooting from the comm and tracking station amidships the transport chopper. More conjecture than anything else, the best his science people could come up with by way of explanation was that the storm of space lava created a supercharged electromagnetic field. Highly charged alpha particles, the most powerful of ionizing agents, the way he understood it, were in the process of fusing, splitting deuterium nuclei as they collided, but somehow creating antienergy in the process. One of the end fantastic results was that the ore emitted EMP—electromagnetic pulse—similar, but vastly more powerful in ways they couldn't yet explain than those produced by a nuclear blast. Had he believed in God, angels or even an afterlife, he might have agreed with his scientists when they referred to the phenomenon as Heaven's Vomit.

The pilot didn't need to be told even once, Kolinko roaring the order again, though, through the cockpit hatchway just when the bird was thrown to a steep dip to port. He tumbled to the floorboard, his soldiers falling from their stations in a thrashing heap of limbs, Kolinko still fearing the fire in the sky would overtake them. As opposed to arriving on-site after the three previous showers, this was the first time he'd been eyewitness to the falling space matter. Cursing the horrifying unexplainable, he hoped it would be his last, but he wasn't about to see his choppers bathed in celestial soup, sure to send them crashing to earth.

Jumping to his feet as his pilot straightened the chopper, Kolinko marched to the door, hollering for one of his men to pull the plug to their monitors from the battery-powered generator. He was just in time to find the two black Mi-14s—drug ships, he suspected, taking the high ground and waiting on the Tajiks to climb up the trail from the gorge—erupt into fireballs that defied any blast he'd ever seen on the battlefield. It was all lightning and blue flame along the plateau, two giant, sizzling orbs that appeared like electrical charges gone haywire, blinding-white explosions touching off, one after the other, inside the spheres, the jagged streaks seeming to gather renewed angry force, as if whatever energy they consumed from the doomed birds inside the blue furnace fed their unearthly power core.

It was the rolling molten tidal wave in the sky, though, that commanded his full and terrified attention. Patching through to his other flight crews, he confirmed them engaged in evasive maneuvers, all of them falling back in southerly vectors at top speed.

Kolinko watched, squinting against the brilliant sheen as the molten rain washed over the forested plateau, then pounded a path down the gorge. With nowhere to run or hide, he saw the sea of molten stew drench man and animal. The Tajiks and their Russian end purchasers were little more than criminal scum, but Kolinko wondered, just the same, if they died quick, or slow and in great pain as they drowned in the ore.

"IN TERMS OF PURE scientific theory, as defined by Isaac Newton and Einstein, the laws of gravity and inertial mass being proportional to gravitational mass—G-Force—this shouldn't even exist. Alpha particles, if that's what they even are, will yield their energy quickly, but whatever the particles, they are fusing, multiplying and growing in mass and strength, creating in the process what I can only describe as…antimatter?"

Kolinko bared his teeth, stepping toward the hastily erected work area. He found himself growing exasperated to the point of boiling anger, what with their lack of plausible scientific explanations, but realized, under the circumstances, he needed them more than they needed him.

The good news was that the laser field, a reverse electromagnetic barrier, as he understood it, held back the undefined particles that created this purported anti-gravity. With the extended poles rising forty feet high, laser beams interlocked at the speed of light, the abominable stench of sulfur was held in check, but the unreality of the moment was still there for his eyes to behold. Unable to look at the frightening spectacles farther down the gorge and just inside the laser wall, he watched his eight best and brightest, still donning hazmat suits, while striding closer to the banks of monitors, his science detail having informed him the lethal doses of radiation were cocooned behind the bars of blue laser light and presently dying off at an inexplicable rate. Only flaring back to life, fusing together again, they told him, at a speed faster than light, mounting in hyper-strength, though giving off no measurable radiation! Impossible, he decided, would be the most preposterous understatement he'd ever heard. Moscow would never buy it.

Geiger counters, he saw, were hooked into a radiation monitor, the clicks no longer audible, but Kolinko stole a read on the digital screen just the same, confirming he was in no danger of coming down with cancer in the near future. The last problem—no, the last nail—he needed was another Chernobyl in what was, essentially, a militarily occupied Russian protectorate. His own anger and mounting fear fusing like those particles they mentioned, Kolinko looked at their dark baffled faces inside the bubbled helmets as several of the geniuses filled test tubes with white crystals collected from the ground near the field station, then mixed them with a clear liquid. With syringes, they extracted the concoction, squirting drops on Petri dishes, sliding them under microscopes.

"It makes no sense at all how this could be happening."

"But it is happening, Comrade Bukov!" Kolinko snapped, forcing himself to not even glance at the figure no more than twelve feet in front of him to confirm the terrible truth. Should this happen again, he dreaded, and in a heavily populated area…

Kolinko keyed his com link, scoured the skies with an anxious search. When informed by his flight crews that soldiers were now on the ground and securing a wide perimeter, erecting more laser walls, he turned back to his scientists. Two of them were hunched over the control panel of a solid aluminum cylinder they called a gravitational wave detector. When he saw them shaking their heads at each other, he nearly erupted, aware the mystery was only growing as they appeared to understand less with each passing second.

"I want answers, and within the hour, do you understand me, Comrade Bukov?"

"Then we'll need to return to our laboratories for further and more accurate testing, Comrade Colonel. I am thinking this substance will first need a laser burst of at least a hundred picoseconds…"

"Picoseconds?"

"Measurements of trillionths of a second, done in a laser fusion chamber, therefore determining, if we are lucky, if these nuclei of atoms initiate fusion on their own, which, I already fear, they do."

"You fear? What do you mean by that?"

Bukov went on as if he hadn't heard the question. "Beyond that I am afraid that what, or part of what we are looking at, judging the previous samples and testing is an ongoing, unexplained fusion-fission reaction, but far more fusion than fission."

The enormity of what he believed Bukov implied left Kolinko speechless for a long moment. "You are telling me that what is inside this force field is…that what came from deep space is…"

"Yes. We are perhaps looking at the possibility of a thermonuclear explosion. Developing critical mass as we speak, from, as you said, the far reaches of the galaxy."

Kolinko swallowed his terror, wondering how long he could keep this from Moscow. The truth, of course, would get buried, but if Tajikistan was wiped off the map in a nuclear mushroom cloud with its unknown origins from deep space, there would be no way to hide it from the rest of the world. There would be international outrage. There would be sanctions. There would be much threatening noise, to say the very least, from the Americans. There would be fallout, and clear up the Ukraine, depending on the prevailing winds, with thousands, perhaps hundreds of thousands dropping dead in their zombied tracks from radiation poisoning so high it would be off the charts of gigajoule and human-sievert measurements. There would be…

Numb, he was about to turn away, return to his chopper, when he found Dovkna pulling his visor away from his microscope. "What is it?" he barked.

Dovkna muttered something, shaking his head.

"Speak!"

Dovkna pointed a rubber-tipped finger at the crystallized rock formations on the ground, where the snow was still melting to puddles, a faint trace of sulfur still lingering in the air. "This white substance?" he said, and paused.

"Yes?"

"It's sodium chloride."

"Salt? You are telling me, comrade," Kolinko said, throwing an arm at what was at the deep end of the pass, "that those men were—what? Turned into pillars of salt from outer space?"

Dovkna nodded inside his bubbled head. "That is precisely what I am saying."

Kolinko staggered back a step, then froze, aware of the pleas and pitiful cries he'd up to then forced deaf ears to. Now, his mind tumbling with questions and fears holding no foreseeable answers or solutions, he stared up at the Tajik rebel, hovering some twenty feet in the air.

CHAPTER TWO

Nuclear power was a disaster begging to happen. Off the top of his head, he thought of Three Mile Island and Chernobyl, the most notable of grotesque nuclear reactor accidents, or the ones at least known to the world at large. Where they were concerned, he pictured—from an educated guess based on experience and access to classified intel—their reactor cores blew, most likely, due to incompetence, quasi-ignorance of the volatile nature of fission reaction under extreme stress, and the brazen zeal of self-proclaimed genius in search of the next quantum leap, that bold but proved foolish notion that Science Man adhered to the belief they could learn more about nuclear power through trial and error. Tell all that, he scoffed to himself, to those dying in protracted misery under radioactive clouds that were most likely still spreading to God only knew how far and wide.

Madness, he decided, and for what? All in the name of progress? The advancement of civilization or global annihilation? Either way, Man may prove someday to be his own worst enemy, but he hoped he wasn't around to see it, though his three children might. No tree-hugger or global-warming doomsayer, he was an ace Stealth pilot of two Gulf wars, in fact, who'd churned up whole square miles of earth into smoking craters where not even a dandelion could sprout in the next foreseeable generation. But he still believed Man either took care of Mother Earth, or Mother Earth would take care of Man. That in mind, nuclear-powered submarines and battleships, he weighed, were nightmare scenario enough, but easily dispensed with as far as cover-ups went. Scuttle the works and the truth sank to the bottom of the ocean, where only a few in the loop were the wiser.

All those potential catastrophic voyages, but vessels chugging along over vast stretches of empty ocean?

No sweat.

Try flying, he thought, a supersonic fighter jet with a nuclear reactor's guts cored with U-238, meant to torque up the yield of Pu-239 to keep on giving the gift of record-shattering speed and hang-time. Talk about flying Armageddon, but the doomsday potential for such a craft, he knew, hijacked and commandeered by the enemies of America, was less than zero.

At least for the immediate future.

Still, the more United States Air Force Major Michael Holloran pondered the facts as he knew them, considered what was housed, aft in their superbird, the more he believed he harbored some dark bent toward suicide. Or was it simply his nature, he wondered, a hyperachiever in his own right, pushing the limits of personal reality and talents to the edge, a middle-finger salute to fate to dare force him to stare into the abyss, face his own mortality? Certainly, he knew, whatever drove him to chase the next figurative or literal horizon had cost him two marriages, rendering him a man alone now among the gods of ultratech, transcended in some way beyond the norm he couldn't quite define, but could surmise he wasn't sure he liked all that much, given what he knew.

Get a grip, he told himself. He had a job to do.

They were sailing along at supersonic speed, Mach 5 to be exact, eighty thousand feet and change above the Canadian province of Saskatchewan, bearing down on the U.S. border; ETA a little over three minutes and counting. With what he knew lay ahead, those anxious thoughts began whispering louder over everything that could go wrong, near hissing, he imagined, like the highly flammable pure oxygen being pumped into his helmet. This was, after all, the maiden voyage of a classified prototype and ultrafighter jet that shouldn't—and officially didn't—exist.

Three years earlier a celestial mystery had fallen to the continental U.S., and it now powered the craft. And lent it properties far exceeding the narrow prism of Man's understanding.

Thus, lack of knowledge about unknown properties and alloys—and he knew whatever the truth was being jealously guarded from those who now bore the task of flying the thing, as in himself and his copilot—should provide fear enough for him to reconsider the sanity of all involved.

For instance, the reinforced glass—if that's what it even was—was as classified as the fuel that could propel them to Mach 10, more than three times faster than the now-retired SR-71 Blackbird, which had previously owned the world's speed record of plus Mach 3. Officially—sort of—the fuel was classified as supergrade JP-7, the juice that kept the Blackbird aloft and a streaking black blur beneath the heavens. Why, then, was it pumped into the wings from a massive lead-encased tanker by hazmat suits in a hangar guarded by both armed sentries and batteries of surface-to-air missiles and M-1 Abrams tanks? Or was the answer so obvious…

The visor trapped the sound of his own grim chuckle.

In practical working theory, he knew they shouldn't have even gotten off the ground, but the superjet and its power source defied all laws of aerodynamics, nuclear physics and gravity. Whether or not the reactor was a prototype, for instance, scaled down to near-dwarf stature in comparison to the mammoths that powered nuclear plants, it was still housed in a steel container, wrapped, in turn, by thick concrete walls. Therefore, the tremendous weight alone should have created drag enough to virtually snap off the tail.

Oh, but there were answers, he knew, as unbelievable as they might sound.

Yes, perhaps they believed him, in the dark and blissfully ignorant, those black-suited DOD superiors, their armed goons and aerospace engineers contracted out by Lockheed, but he'd caught on the sly the floating rumors. Since no secret was really ever such, he'd come to know that what they referred to as "the Divine Alloy" was a molten ore of some type from deep space. Whatever the unknown substance, he knew it was blended somehow with carbon-fiber laminates and aluminum and titanium, stem to stern on their ultratech ride. Likewise, cockpit and reactor housing were coated with the Divine Alloy. Which, believe it or not, made the superjet, code-named Lightning Bat, lighter than air, but able to withstand all the mass, thrust and gravity that Earth could pound mortal flesh with, once the shield was activated prior to takeoff. Moreover, their shield, sealed inside by the alloy, converted the cockpit into some vacuum of space, spared them G-force that should have crushed their insides to pulp. Rendered weightless by the Divine Alloy, they would have floated to the ceiling, pinned there, if not harnessed into their seats.

Holloran checked the instrument panel. All green, all systems go, he found. Comprised of intricate supercomputers, once the codes were punched in, he knew from two years of 24/7 training and virtual reality flight simulators that technology did roughly ninety percent of the work. From speed to navigation, down to calibrating the payload in the fuselage, Lightning Bat nearly had a mind all its own.

So why did that disturb him?

It was just about time, he knew, checking the digital readout to countdown, aware their audience was anxiously waiting back at Eagle Nebula, ready to monitor the test flight via camera link-up, once Lightning Bat descended and leveled out within a hundred miles of the area in question.

He was about to look over at Captain Thomas Sayers when he glimpsed something flash across the cockpit shield.

"Did you see that?"

"What the hell?" Holloran wasn't sure what it was, but he would have sworn blue lightning had just streaked past Lightning Bat's tapered nose. They weren't low enough for any bolts of lightning, no storm systems to factor in, according to their Doppler radar. A shooting star, then? Meteor fragments?

Sayers repeated the question over the com link, Holloran staring up into the infinite black of the cosmos, when blue light jagged, but flashing this time, he believed, from inside the cockpit. Or did it shoot from the instrument panel? he wondered. After too many sorties in combat to count, having seen flying "things" he had more than once been warned by nameless spooks to never speak of, he wasn't one to push panic buttons. But he felt the hairs rising on the back of his neck just the same, instinct warning him that something was either wrong or about to go south.

"Check all of our computer systems, Tom," he told his copilot. "A to Z."

"Roger, sir."

"While you do that," he said, wrapping one black-gloved hand around the side-arm controller, while tapping in the access code to the electro-optical navigational computer, "I'll start dropping us down and prepping this puppy for its big audition."

Holloran hoped he sounded confident, relatively gung-ho to the younger man, but he'd been dumped on the receiving end of too many SNAFUs to not trust his churning gut.

"Protostar Eagle Nebula Central Command to Lightning Bat Alpha. We are confirming your altitude and speed. Four thousand feet and holding steady, but you will have to decrease your speed to well below subsonic. Give us four hundred, Lightning Bat Alpha, and we can track you with visual confirmation."

As the pneumatic doors hissed shut behind him, Gabriel Horn found he was just in time for the big show. The ground control station of Eagle Nebula wasn't exactly the sprawling network of NASA's command nerve center, he knew, but there was eyes-only supersophistication enough here to warrant all hands signing blood pacts for a black project so secret only a dozen men in Washington were aware of Lightning Bat's existence. And, as head of Special Action Service, it was his duty to make damn certain all knowledge here either stayed under the compound's roof or went to the grave with these people.

In that exclusive realm, however, there was critical mass, and building beyond the Eagle Nebula nest.

Easing up on their six, his rubber-soled combat boots padding silent as a ghost over sheer white concrete, Horn counted twelve aerospace brainiacs. The Chosen, he thought. Or the damned, depending on how well they held their tongues in check, though in his experience, considering at least three of the Seven Deadly Sins—pride, greed and envy—a couple of them, maybe more, would find a nasty and mysterious fatal accident in their futures. He could always count on the worst in human nature.

They appeared little more than shrouds at Horn's first glance, white lab coats casting off a sort of glimmering hue as the fabric, woven out of nylon-silk, seemed to reflect light from the workstation with its running bank of monitors. Com links tying them all to Lightning Bat Alpha, their voices were a mixed babble to his ears as they relayed instructions to Major Holloran, confirming this and that.

Showtime.

Horn ignored the Air Force colonel boring daggers into the side of his head, focused instead on the cameras as they locked in on the arrowhead-shaped fighter jet. Briefed as thoroughly by Eagle Nebula's commanding officer as he had expected, Horn knew the test flight was now monitored by four, long-range camera-fitted Black Hawks and two prototype Gulfstream SBJs. The supersonic executive jets, customized for military purposes, had the sleek Stealth hybrid covered, fore and aft, with the only variant being altitude at each end. To cover the fireworks, the Black Hawks were ranged around the compass, hovering now over the blast area.

All set for bombs away.

When the payloads were launched, gun cameras in the guidance systems of each nose, he knew, would track their flight paths, speeding bullets, near skimming U.S. government-owned prairie of North Dakota, until impact flashed obliteration then oblivion across the screens. Four payloads all told, he thought, what were technically cruise missiles, streaking at low altitude for the mock-ups, powered at subsonic speed to target by jet engines. Digital contour maps, born from radar and aerial and sat imagery, told the computer navigational systems in the warheads where to go.

Predestined supertech boogie-woogie.

Only these mothers of annihilation, code-named the Four Points, Horn knew, housed a series of thermal cluster bombs, eight to a package, two more inside each eight. As he did the math, recalling the computer graphics outlining the blast radius, he pictured smoking craters—or dozens of raging infernos—eating up something in the combined neighborhood of four to five square miles.

Sweet.

Welcome to the war of the future, he thought, aware that if this test run was successful, the empty wastelands of Nevada were next up, and in for a whole other galaxy of big bangs.

As Horn glimpsed Colonel Jeffreys moving his way, he pulled the pack of Camel unfiltered cigarettes from his pants pocket, stuck one on his lip. Clacking open his Zippo lighter and torching up, spitting tobacco flecks then dragging deep, he saw the head aerospace genius, Dr. Benjamin Keitel, glaring his way.

"Hey! Are you nuts? There's no smoking in here!"

Horn washed a dragon's spray of smoke toward Keitel, the man flapping his arms like a headless chicken, a couple more of his comrades jumping into the act. The geek was squawking out the virtues of nonsmoking to Jeffreys when Horn blew another cloud in his face and told the colonel, "Maybe you want to remind Dr. Frankenstein here who's really in charge?" He ignored Keitel's diatribe, adding, "Maybe you want to inform him I don't exactly hand out pink slips at the end of the day for insubordination?"

"Get back to work," Jeffreys told the aerospace engineer, who muttered something to himself then returned to his monitors.

Horn stared ahead, puffing, as the good colonel

scowled him up and down. He could almost hear the man's thoughts. Beyond the shoulder-holstered Beretta 92-F, if not for the white star emblem over his heart on his blacksuit, Jeffreys could pull rank.

"If I were you, I wouldn't be so free in issuing implied threats like that, Mr. Orion," the colonel said, layering disdain on his code name like a curse word.

"Well, you're not me."

"And I pray every night that blessing will continue."

"Really?" Horn smoked, bobbed his head, got the message, hoping the day came when Jeffreys crossed into what he liked to call the Black Hole. "Fear not, Colonel. I'm not about to turn my quarters into a torture chamber," he said, then, looking at the two female engineers, smiled and added, "or a rape room."

"You son of a... Don't you have some business to attend to, regarding an AWOL and, may I add, critical employee of this program?"

"We're working on it. Something this sensitive, Colonel, it takes time," Horn said as Jeffreys moved into his personal space.

"Time better served if you were, I would imagine, out there as point man in the hunt."

Horn was searching for some threatening reply when he caught the change in tone from Keitel, questions hurled from his work bay, edged with concern as they were snapped into his com link. The SAS commander took a few steps forward, sensing a problem as he peered into the monitors where the executive jets mirrored Lightning Bat. The air became lanced, he felt, with rising panic as he saw what he believed were blue flames—or sparks?—leaping from the black ferrite-painted surface of the fighter jet, dancing next, nose to tail, there then gone. What the hell had just happened? he wondered, Kietel barking the same question to Major Holloran. Lightning Bat's coating, he knew, was meant to absorb radar radiation, standard for any Stealth fighter to render it near invisible. Only he was privy there was more to the fighter jet's body, from nose to swept-back Delta wings to tail, than earthly alloys.

Jeffreys banging out questions, Horn rolled up Keitel's back. And clearly saw what looked like blue lightning shooting from the cockpit.

"Lightning Bat Alpha!" Keitel nearly shouted. "You are nowhere near the targets."

"Why are the bomb bays opening?" Jeffreys demanded, checking his watch. "They're way ahead of their scheduled launch!"

Horn heard Keitel gasp an oath as he saw the missiles lowered from their bay by the robotic arms. "Lightning Bat Alpha, respond!" he hollered, eyes darting from a digital readout to the play-by-play screens, snarling next as he pulled the com link from his ears, static crackling through the room like a string of firecrackers. "Colonel," Keitel said, eyes bugged to white orbs, "all Four Points are recalibrating their targets!"

"What? How?" he demanded, flying up on Keitel's rear. "Where?"

Horn was crowding Keitel and Jeffreys when he heard Holloran patch through, the panic in the major's voice loud and clear through the static. "Ground Control, come in, dammit! We have a colossal and definite problem!"

Keitel looked about to vomit, sounding on the verge

of hyperventilating as he tapped the keyboard on his computer. As a digital grid map of North Dakota flashed onto the monitor, Keitel paused, staring in horror at the blinking red dots. "Oh, God, no. This can't be happening!"

"What?"

Keitel turned to Jeffreys, his face ashen, and told him, "All four missiles are recalibrated to strike civilian targets."

"SWITCH TO MANUAL override!"

Targets Engaged flashing in red on the head up display from the holographic image illuminated by laser light on the inside of his visor, Holloran stifled the urge to smash his fist into the instrument panel.

"I can't," Sayers told him, his fingers flying over the keypad that would shut the targeting computer system down. "Dammit to hell, it's locked up!"

Holloran swore under his breath. This was the next-to-ultimate nightmare scenario—four cruise missiles with cluster bombs set to launch and take out civilian targets—as he heard ground control telling him what he already knew.

The two of them were on their own.

Do something!

For all the four-digit Einstein IQ between them—there was nothing Eagle Nebula could do on its end. Short of blowing them out of the sky with a SAM—and he wouldn't put it past them—there was one other option, he knew, waiting now for those three dreaded words.

Initiate Fatal Abort.

From the beginning, no ejector seats, no self-destruct button had been designed for Lightning Bat. There was good reason for that, he knew, fully accepting from the onset the twisted reasoning that IFA meant finding a vast and wide-open stretch of nothing and slamming Lightning Bat to Earth. A suicide ditching, a fireball spewing radiation, but hopefully nowhere close to a populated area. Or, at worst, only a few souls hopefully still wandering around outside Ground Zero, until Eagle Nebula could ferry in the hazmat platoons while soldiers quarantined God only knew how many square miles around the compass.

Holloran switched his HUD to the inside of the cockpit shield, wondering why some systems worked and others were—well, acting on their own, rebelling, as if they had willpower, defiantly commandeering the vessel. He grabbed the side-arm controller, hoping to God if he could throw the wings to a quick dip, forty-five degrees, port and starboard, the missiles might impact on what was empty prairie. Provided, of course, he got the timing right, but with everything else unraveling…

The stick was jammed!

And the blue lightning came back, leaping from the instrument panel, as Holloran found their own retractable cameras lower from each side of the hull's underbelly amidships, zooming in on the two robotic arms lowering their payloads.

Targets Engaged freeze-framed on the shield.

Holloran cursed, rechecking the new calibrations, locked in still, he discovered, ground control screaming in his ear as the payloads fanned out into crossbars on their monitors.

Covering north, south, east and west, two on an arm, one frame hung a few meters lower than the other, and for the sake of what was now doomsday clearance. Just as they pulled the damn things up on their computers, he knew, they were held for the moment by titanium clamps, talons that would release them at any second as he watched the numbers fall to single digits on his readout.

Holloran stared at the vast prairie, looked to a long, sweeping horizon that seemed to run straight into the setting sun. They were still some fifty miles from the Badlands, Holloran certain, or rather praying, they were as empty as the lunar landscape he knew them to be.

"They're going to fire, Major!"

And Holloran watched in helpless rage and disbelief as four cones of flame shot out beyond the stabilizing fins. The missiles released and went streaking away on four points of the compass.

GROUND CONTROL, Horn knew, was an obscene misnomer, and by galactic degrees in this case. There were no command guidance systems, at least for this initial outing, to depend on laser beams to pin down the targets to within a few meters, steer and keep the missiles locked in to impact. No passive system, either, meaning they homed in specifically on infrared radiation, as in heat-seeking the likes of auto or jet engines—or warm bodies. The Four Points were their own Alpha and Omega, relying solely on active systems, which was radar already engineered into the missiles, their guidance computers flying them on, unstoppable and untouchable, to vaporize the targets. Keitel was in the process of pointing this out to Colonel Jeffreys, they were little more than limp baggage on this end.

"Sweet Holy Virgin Mother of…"

"I'm afraid we are way past any hand of God, Colonel."

"Don't get smart on me, Keitel! Where are those missiles fixed to strike, mister?" the colonel rasped, clear to all now he realized he had become a master of the obvious by rattling off questions he already had the answers to from double-digit briefs.

The good Major Holloran seemingly all but forgotten for the moment, Horn watched as Keitel slammed in a series of numbers on one of his readouts, then hit his computer keyboard, informing the colonel he would bring up the targets on the wall. Looking past the workstation, Horn stared at the project's emblem, thirty feet by twenty, painted on the stark white wall, dead ahead. The Eagle Nebula, he recalled, was a bright cluster of young evolving stars, but a massive gas formation, still condensing though not nearly thermonuclear enough to shine like Earth's sun. Imaged by the Hubble Space Telescope only as recently as 1995, the dark nebulosity was more widely known among the deep space stargazers as "the Pillars of Creation."

Keitel flashed the digital wall map of North Dakota over the emblem, framing four red circles, then enlarging the targets with a few taps on his keyboard.

With one ear, chain-smoking now that all the PC air was cleared, Horn listened to the colonel shout a litany of questions laced with orders, but he was more intent, fascinated, in fact, by the sight of the gun cameras framing in real-time the prairie sweeping below. Again, Jeffreys demanded to know the new targets, what might be the number of projected civilian casualties, railing next at Keitel to initiate some sort of abort action.

"It's too late for that, Colonel! The damage is already done!"

"The hell you say. You people created it, do something to uncreate it! Or we are all in a world of hurt none of us can begin to even fathom!"

Horn smiled around his smoke, enjoying their sweat and panic, these pompous asses who often looked down their noses at him, a wolf among sheep who held the power of life and death. The snooty broads, too, often thinking they needed some R and R with a real man who could launch them into some deep space they couldn't begin to get from their wonder toys. Maybe soon, figure the ladies might need a comforting shoulder to lay their distress on. Hope sprang eternal, and now on more fronts, he knew, than in his loins.

The gathered herd here didn't know it, but he had his own plans.

He listened to Keitel's ominous report. It looked like the Fort Berthold Indian Reservation was slated for one big bang, Jeffreys groaning as he heard the guesstimate for dead and maimed Native Americans. If there was any good news to be grabbed from this vision of hell, it appeared the westbound warhead would detonate on some rancher's spread near the eastern leading edge of the Badlands. On that front, Jeffreys barked for numbers on family members, Horn now sensing the colonel was on the verge of fainting as the virtual reality of the body count kept on piling up in his churning desk-lifer mind, higher, he imagined with a puff and grin, than every piece of shredded document or deleted CD-ROM he was probably the first blast away from racing to. Another ranch on the Four Points' feeding frenzy, but far larger in terms of cattle as imaged by a satellite parked over the state, was up for some more cluster dusting. Finally, there was a town, population twenty-six, but one of the geeks informed them at that hour the saloon was a big-ticket draw, Horn filing the man's name away, wondering how he came by that information. When Horn caught the town's name, another grin tugged at the corner of his lip.

Little Big Horn.

It was most definitely cover-the-assets time before some twenty-first-century scalping got in full swing, he knew, perfectly albeit horribly understandable, given that more than careers were at stake.

Talk about Black Holes.

Already, though, as he saw the watching eye on the Black Hawk closest to one of the civilian targets framing what was a row of small wooden buildings on a barren stretch of plain—assume Little Big Horn—the solution to the grim problems of the immediate future was shaping up, and in sweet accord with his own dreams. Funny, he thought, how a little patience and fortitude could find destiny smiling when a man decided to stand his ground.

As the Black Hawk closed to monitor the coming inferno, Jeffreys reached a level of near hysterics, ordering Keitel to fall to Plan IFA.

"You're kidding, right? Unless you want to order Major Holloran to crash Lightning Bat out there, and with what's going to happen if they do, do you really want to explain one more nightmare than we already have to deal with? You do know what's on board that craft? You do know what fuels that jet?"

"I'm fully aware of the gravity of the situation, mister!" Jeffreys fumed, Horn again believing he could read the man's tortured thoughts, what with all that gyrating body language and panic like neon signs in the eyes. Damage control, without question, time to place the SOS to DOD, the Pentagon, get the blame game cranked up, heating to thermonuclear critical mass, but in all directions other than his starched uniform.

Horn heard Holloran shouting from Keitel's com link, the hooked-in intercom likewise now blaring the major's voice. But he was locked on to the monitors, worked his spectating view between the gun camera and the Black Hawk relay.

And it happened, but far more spectacular than he could have imagined.

The gun camera winked out first as its cluster avalanche slammed into what Horn believed was the broadside of the first building in a Little Big Horn replay of that fateful and very gruesome day for the white man, but with total annihilation here for all present, indiscriminate of race, sex and age.

Complete and absolute obliteration, Horn saw, boiled like the smoke and fire of the Apocalypse, straight for the Black Hawk's relay.

Just about all done, he knew, except for the cover-up.

Apparently, Horn found, Jeffreys had seen more than enough, the colonel wheeling, striding for the exit. A finger flick of his smoke, arcing it across the room, and he was marching hard for the intercept. Barking for Colonel No-Stones to halt, Horn grabbed him by the arm as the doors hissed open.

"Get your hands off me," Jeffreys warned, wrenching his arm free.

"Listen to me, Colonel, and hear me but good. This fiasco, which, technically, falls under your responsibility, has a solution."

"Solution?" He paused, the jaw going slack, the dark look betraying thoughts he knew what was about to be dumped in his lap. "No..."

"Yes. Now, you want to make some phone calls. I'll give you a number you're already aware of to someone who will, in no uncertain terms, inform you that what just happened lands square in my department." It was Horn's turn to breach personal space, as he put himself nose-to-nose with Jeffreys, and said, "The next words out of your mouth, Colonel, better be what I—what we all—know we need to hear, or, 'sir,' there could be more for you to dread than testifying before a bunch of fattened calves on the Hill. Oh. I see I have your full attention."

"I'm listening."

"Okay. Now, if it makes you happy, here's what I propose to do...."

CHAPTER THREE

Aaron Kurtzman wondered what it would be like to walk again. Maybe it was the ten cups and counting of coffee he'd consumed, all that tar floating in enough sugar to wire a small army, electrically hyper-charging the caffeine-soaked thoughts off on grim tangents best left alone. Maybe it was working through the night at his computer station, by himself, for the most part, locked up in his head, most of the world sleeping, including some of his comrades and co-workers at Stony Man Farm, though he couldn't say for certain. Intensely private, he was not a man to dump emotional baggage on others, wear suffering on his sleeve or to cast blame like a human storm raging about until the misery was spread sufficiently to the four corners of the globe, but the thoughts and feelings were there, just the same, and he couldn't deny them.

At that predawn hour, staring at the monitor of his computer, he suddenly imagined himself out of the bowels of the new-and-improved Computer Room, removed from this trapping of time and space, free, unconfined, able-bodied. And there he was, up top, strolling the grounds, sans wheelchair, the barrel-chested, powerfully built titan he recalled from the ghosts of years past, that Big Ten champion heavyweight wrestler of the University of Michigan, a young lion. Breathing in the cool, crisp air of the Shenandoah Valley of Virginia, he imagined, sun on his bearded face, drinking in the lush greenery of the Blue Ridge Mountains, unshackled from the shell that imprisoned him. He pictured himself on a leisurely jaunt, down a wooded trail, maybe a dog by his side for company, he'd always had a fondness for German shepherds....

Enough, he told himself. No, it never hurt to dream, he thought, or to pray even for a miracle, as long as he didn't get mired in self-pity, one of the worst of human failings, in his mind. Rather, if it be the will of some Divine Force beyond his finite understanding... Maybe someday, some other time, space or dimension, beyond the physical constraints of Earth, there would be a new and improved Aaron "The Bear" Kurtzman.

Leave it at that.

There was work to do.

Head of the cyberteam, the think tank of Stony Man Farm's Computer Room—the nerve center for intelligence gathering that kept the warrior machine rolling in the trenches of the world's flashpoints, overt or black ops—was his realm. As such, Kurtzman went back to tapping in the next series of access codes on his keyboard.

They were alphanumeric codes and bypass encryption, what he tagged "circumventors," the sum total faster and far simpler than any software program he'd previously created, though this one was designed for more than hacking. The FORTRAN, or formula translation, was part of his Infinity program, the server software managing and sifting through data from interconnected systems at light speed, until only the critical information he sought was framed on his screen. The client-servers were never the wiser he or one of his team had just broken through about three firewalls, stolen whatever buried cybertreasures, then rebuilt those walls after a lightning and untraceable bolt back to Stony Man mainframes. Whether they changed their passwords on a frequent basis or not, on the client-servers' end, Infinity was the cryptographer's answers to all mysteries of the cyberuniverse. Those faceless, nameless clients almost always came from any alphabet-soup intelligence agency within the United States and the world over, likewise any military or law-enforcement agency mainframes Kurtzman needed to access.

He wasn't sure what it was about the news report he'd been watching in a corner of his monitor since last evening, using the remote on his keyboard to snap through the local and national cable networks, but something disturbed him about the images of reporters being ushered away from what was clearly a large area quarantined by armed soldiers. Initial reports cited some natural disaster, or so the reporters were told by military spokesmen, belonging to what branch, though, no one knew or was allowed to say. Speculation had body counts mounting by the hour, but these nameless spokesmen were denying any such rumors. He heard about meteor showers, or something or other unexplained that had fallen from space. Each new report sounded flimsier than the last. He smelled cover-up, a brittle conspiracy ready to unravel with a good swift kick.

And the Smoking Gun and Infinity programs were hard at work, he saw, alphanumeric codes tumbling in the top left-hand corner, as his labor of love raced out to those far reaches of the cyberuniverse to cross all pertinent I's, dot the t's of truth that not even the brightest award-winning journalist could uncover. Every shred of data from all U.S. intelligence agencies, black-inked or otherwise, was correlated with daily news reports, written or televised. Once any paper or station's Web site dot.com was filed away into Infinity—Smoking Guns's memory, the two programs became their own investigators. Between that and the sat imagery they burglarized from the satellite parked closest to the area in question—AIQ—in this instance North Dakota, and classified documents regarding military black ops and their installations within the state, Infinity did virtually all of the work for him. At the moment he was left with more questions than answers, but felt something far beyond space phenomenon had turned four separate areas in southwest North Dakota into what appeared to him on the imagery as smoking craters his trained eyed told him were the result of aerial strafing.

He was wondering how far and how to pursue it, when he became aware his partner at this early morning hour had cranked up his CD to that kind of fuzzy contortion blasting out of his headphones that should have rendered Akira Tokaido deaf.

Kurtzman wheeled sideways, Tokaido bebopping his head in rhythm to the tune. He held his arms out, caught his teammate's eye, and said in a loud voice, "What the hell, huh?"

Akira, still bopping, looked at Kurtzman's mouth and said, "I can hear you just fine. You said, 'What the hell, huh?'"

"Okay, smart-ass. Do you think you can get to work while you're getting all wet in the eyes over that blaring duet?"

Still bopping along, Tokaido's fingers began flying over his keyboard. Kurtzman saw his monitor split into two screens. "What am I looking at, Akira?"

Two more images crowded the number on Kurtzman's monitor to four.

Tokaido killed his CD. "Clockwise, top to bottom. A major Russian weapons factory in the Pamir Range of Tajikistan, the usual we know about it, they know we know, and the beat goes on. We check it with some of our own sources, I'm sure they'd verify there's more going on under the roof than your basic WMD alchemy, the floating rumor out of spookdom's black hole being they're engineering superweapons of the future. Next, for your viewing pleasure, what I believe—and since the DOD, NSA and Pentagon files I accessed had so many black deletions regarding this base I discovered at great length tagged as Eagle Nebula, thus you can safely assume black project—is our version of the Pamir weapons factory. Is East meeting West, both sides dreaming up the future together regarding superweapons? Don't know, but I think it's worth looking into, in this humble whiz child's often overlooked opinion."

Kurtzman made a face. "Cut the crap or I'll take away your CDs."

Tokaido paused, considering something, then went on, "Whatever they've engineered inside the walls of Eagle Nebula, however, is what I think either crashed or burned up what Infinity calculates is roughly two square miles and then some of scorched earth that makes the Badlands look arable."

"And you know this, how?"

Kurtzman watched as Tokaido further enhanced the imagery and he saw what his partner was referring to.

"Where there's smoke, Bear... Now, the four areas the media is being pumped by the military to claim were hit by something from outer space are actually the results of cluster bombing. I compared those images through Infinity's war-gaming, and they jibe. Blast radius, destruction pattern, spiral all the way down to the intensity of the fires, which indicate thermite payloads were used. These AIQs, I have confirmed, were civilian targets. From the body count, or what you can make out on your screen, gives you an idea of how nasty this could get if it's going to involve a cover-up."

Kurtzman weighed the enormity of what he heard then saw, tallied at least a dozen bodies, or what looked like the remains of such, on one of the AIQs. "A test run, you're telling me, that went awry?"

"I would hope it wasn't done on purpose."

Kurtzman flashed Tokaido a scowl. He began chewing over the current mission of Phoenix Force, which was, more or less, still on the drawing board. At present, they were bivouacked at the American air base in Incirlik, Turkey, while the cyberteam at the Farm kept digging for clues about rumored supertech weapons being smuggled to Iranian extremists, somewhere along the Iraqi border, further in the process of attempting to put together pedigrees and place names to the faces of bad guys in question from their ultratech lair.

Kurtzman began to suspect he saw a pattern emerge, some connection, or so he believed Tokaido alluded to, between the death factory in Tajikistan and weapons-hungry jihadists. Was there more? Such as connecting the dots somehow to this Eagle Nebula black project? It wouldn't be the first time, he knew, someone on the home team had sold out to the other side. Able Team was standing down, Kurtzman checking the digital clock at the bottom of his monitor, aware Hal Brognola, the man who headed the Sensitive Operations Group, would be arriving at his office at the Justice Department shortly. He needed to run his suspicions past the big Fed.

"There's more, Bear, only I'm not sure how this fits, if it does…only…well, it's just a feeling," Tokaido said, and Kurtzman watched as four more sat images flashed onto his monitor, blurring the previous pics. He heard Tokaido mention the three names of former Soviet republics, then told him the last image was shot by NASA. "Remember that story CNN ran a few years back about a purported NORAD quarantine of an area in the Colorado Rockies that was supposedly hit by some type of…well, what was described by an eyewitness as 'alien space matter.'"

Kurtzman knew he was looking at a full-blown military quarantine in each of the AIQs, complete with soldiers, choppers, makeshift work areas of equipment he couldn't define, but manned by spacesuits. All told, he knew it spelled disaster area, civilians Keep Out, perhaps at the risk of jail time or worse.

"I do," he told Tokaido. "It ran one time, as I recall."

"NASA officially reported the Colorado incident as the result of a meteor shower. But ask yourself when was the last time you saw a hazmat detail gathered around a meteor, or stone fragments thereof, and with what appear to be radiation detectors?"

"And something tells me you got hold of classified documents that state otherwise."

"Off the public radar screen as 'unexplained extra-terrestrial ore of unknown origin and substance.' And that eyewitness?"

"I bet you're about to tell me he vanished off the face of the earth."

"There was one brief follow-up story, but the star witness was nowhere to be found."

"Next you're going to tell me NORAD, or whoever this Eagle Nebula, has iced down the bodies of little gray men with grasshopper-shaped heads and huge black eyes."

"They're actually a sort of off-white, but with a gray-ish hue. Hey, stranger things have happened, Bear, when it comes to the military wanting to keep unexplained phenomenon, whatever the truth and the mystery, all to themselves."

No truer words, Kurtzman thought, could his cyber buddy have spoken. He reached for the intercom to start sounding off his suspicions.

CAMERON DECKER was sure he was dead, about to meet his Maker as he believed he opened his eyes, but was forced to clamp them shut when the blinding white light stabbed him clear through the brain, a lancing fire.

No, this wasn't heaven, he was in way too much pain for any eternal bliss, his body throbbing with knifing twists, scalp to feet. Gingerly he touched the side of his head, just to be sure he was, indeed, still on earth, probed the bandages wound around his skull. Why did he feel as if he was floating on air, though, his head like a balloon set to burst, both sensations bringing on the nausea? The last moment he remembered was…

A vision of hell on Earth, to say the least.

He saw himself being hurled through the air, far away from his ranch house, fractured pictures of recall slowly groping their way together. One minute, he had been dragged from the kitchen where he was preparing dinner for his bed-ridden wife, alarmed by the shrill barking of Custer. Even in the twenty-first century cattle rustlers were still alive and on the prowl for prime heads of choice beef, and it wouldn't have been the first time some thieves had come through his spread and loaded up a trailer. The Winchester 30.06 in hand as he'd shucked on the sheepskin coat, grumbling his way out the back door, his normally stoic German shepherd dog going berserk, straining to break free of his chain. Spooked by what, he couldn't tell, but his cattle were agitated as hell, his horses snorting from the barn, all in a lather. He'd heard that animals had some sixth sense, though, a built-in radar that warned them of mass atmospheric disturbances, and it wouldn't be the first time that beastly extrasensory perception had foretold him of a sudden thunderstorm. It all looked like another red sundown over the prairie from where he stood, but there was "something" in the air. He could feel it. Something he thought he heard like a whistle, or those incoming rounds he remembered from Korea, the cattle stomping around the pen in a fury next as he walked…

There was an explosion, out of nowhere, or rather, a series of blasts that sounded as one, but with each ear-splitting trumpet of thunder there was no telling as his senses were shattered. Before he could fully assess the moment, glimpsing in horror his home and his parents' home of eighty-five years being uprooted and blown away like so much fertilizer in a twister, he was sailing, dumped, last he remembered, facedown inside the cattle pen.

Now…

He thought he was going to puke, groaning, as he dared to open his eyes. He was getting his bearings, found himself dressed in a white smock like a hospital gown, squinting into the shroud of white light that seemed supernatural in a way he could only describe as some waiting room—Purgatory perhaps?—between Heaven and Hell, when a voice called from the glow, "Mr. Decker? Can you hear me?"

A hard search, adjusting his vision, and he spotted a lean shape in black, straight ahead. The figure was blowing smoke through the light, sunglasses so black and fat they looked more like a visor. Between the combat boots and the pistol in shoulder holster, any hopeful notion the man was a doctor evaporated. Had he landed, though, in a hospital? The light alone was spooky enough, but there seemed to be no walls surrounding him, as if he were in some vast empty space, with the white shroud, bright as the sun, going on forever. Calling him? he wondered, wishing he didn't feel so sick to his stomach, that feeling of being disembodied chilling him to the bone, warping his senses.

"Who are you? Where am I?"

"You can call me Mr. Orion. And you are in protective custody for the time being."

"Protective…what the hell is going on? What happened to my ranch?" He tried to stand, but rubber legs folded, collapsing him back into his seat. Groaning, the room spinning, he said, "What's wrong with me? What have you done to me…"

"Minor burns from the incident, a few cuts and contusions, Mr. Decker. We gave you a shot of morphine for the pain, patched you all up… You'll be good as new in a few days. As for your ranch and all your cattle and horses—they are no longer standing."

He felt his stomach roll over. "And my wife?"

"Your wife, Allison, Mr. Decker, was dying of breast cancer and emphysema. We'll, uh, just call the incident where she is concerned a blessing in disguise. No, belay that. You being a devout church-goer and all, think of her passing as simply an act of God, that she now rests in eternal peace."

Anger cleared some of the sludge away, this Orion character slamming his nose with one smoke bomb after another, speaking of his wife's death as if it was nothing more than some near-miss highway crash he ought to be making the sign of the cross over. "Why, you rotten… I want to know what happened and exactly who you are, mister, or I swear…"

"Relax, Mr. Decker. Do you really need to bring on number three heart attack?"

Decker froze, the man reciting more of his medical history, with doctors' names, dates of operations, down to length of each recuperation. Was that a smile? he wondered, this Orion talking next about his two sons, matter-of-fact, how they had turned their backs on what they called Nowhere, U.S.A., riding off to chase the wind of whatever their dreams in the big cities of Chicago and New York. Putting him in his place, playing mind games. But how did he know so much?

"I'm here to help, Mr. Decker, but only if you wish to help yourself. First of all, let us be clear, what happened to your ranch was the result of a meteor shower."

"That wasn't no rock falling from the sky that leveled my ranch and killed my wife. Those were explosions. I'm guessin' some sort of missile or rocket."

"As you might well believe that's what you think you saw, being as you were a decorated veteran of the Korean War, having seen more than your rightful share of combat. And I salute you for your service to the country, sir."

"Stick all that noise, and I don't need to think about nothin'. I know what I saw. I'm bettin' you're military, work for the government. Something screwed up with you people, and now you want me to shut my mouth about what I saw. Let me tell you, friend, out here, we may be just dumb cowboys to you people, but I got no love for your Big Brother."

And the faceless smoker knew all about that, too, the threats of bank foreclosures on his property, the audits and subsequent liens that drove him into bankruptcy, the suits from Washington offering to buy up his land, claiming they could cut him a break on what he owed if he grabbed the brass ring of his last stand.

"You seem to know an awful lot about me," Decker snapped. "Whether or not much of this is a matter of public record, you don't understand me at all."

Another wave of smoke and Orion said, "No, it's you who don't understand, sir. Here it is, and this is a one-time, nonnegotiable offer. Between property value, including livestock, what would be your projected future earnings for the next five years and your wife's insurance policy, we are prepared to write you a check in the amount of three million dollars, nontraceable, nontaxable funds. Death certificates have already been made out for both your wife and yourself, only you, sir, get to relocate, all expenses paid, until you get set up in someplace far away from North Dakota. Washington, all your medical bills and those banks you so detest? Your debt is erased, officially you become the man who was never born. Think about it. New name. New identity. You could be sitting on a beach in Hawaii, sipping mai tais and playing with the local hula-hoop talent by tomorrow. If I were you…"

"You ain't. No deal. I'm walkin' outta here and goin' straight to the county sheriff."

"Is that your final answer, Mr. Decker?"

"First and last."

"Suit yourself."

It was too easy, Decker's instinct stirring, the old combat senses flaring to life, telling him something was wrong. He saw the glowing tip of the cigarette fall to the floor, eyes up, but the faceless Orion was gone, vanished, as if the light had swallowed him up. No sound of any door opening or closing to betray an exit, he was rising when he heard the electronic whir, looked up, thought he saw the ceiling part. A black hole yawning into view, barely perceptible as Decker squinted into the light, he heard machinery grinding to life, from some point beyond the white halo, deep in the dark void. If he didn't know better, it sounded like a threshing machine was cranking to life. What the…

Warning bells clanged in a brain muddied by dope. He cursed whoever'd shot him up, limbs unwilling to respond to a rising sense of fear when the noise shrilled into what he was now certain was a wood chipper, and a damn big one, unless he missed his guess. He ventured a step forward, trying to get his sea legs, when the first gust of wind blasted around him like the gathering onslaught of a twister ready to rip across the prairie. Fear began edging toward terror, thoughts racing, as the wind strengthened, suctioned up and through the tunnel in the ceiling. What was happening became inconceivable, a nightmare he was sure, but here he was—all alone, no one knew he was even still alive, that he was dealing with the almighty hand of Big Brother who could do whatever he wanted and get away.

The cigarette was sucked up, flying past his eyes, the invisible force of a great vacuum swirling around him now, tugging arms and legs. The chair went next, shooting into the black hole, followed a split second later by a sort of screeching metallic grind.

And it dawned on him what was about to happen, horror setting in, the unholy racket of machinery torqued up to new decibels, spiking his ears, as he heard his cry being swept away into the white light. He tried to forge ahead, but the wind seemed to root him to the floor, the ground beneath like magnets daring him to walk, and far worse than any mud he'd ever slogged through more than half a century ago. The scream was on the tip of his tongue, but he knew the sound of terror would be lost to all but himself, if even that, as he was sheared naked by the cyclone, the flesh on his face feeling wrenched up, as though it was being blasted off bone, the twister sucking the air out of his lungs.

Oh, God, no! he heard his mind roar as he was lifted off his feet, levitating for a moment before the invisible strings began jerking with renewed violent force.

And he burst a silent scream into the wind, arms wrenched above his head, as he rose toward the black hole.

IT WAS A MOMENT, about as rare as a Nellie sighting in Loch Ness, Hal Brognola considered when he felt himself about to be scourged by depression. Or was it something else, he wondered, and far more insidious as he weighed the few facts as he knew them? Self-doubt? That what he did perhaps, at best, only pounded a small dent toward making the free world a better, safer place? That the only real solution, he morbidly thought, was kill 'em all, let God sort 'em out?

And dismissed that as soon as the first whisper of fatalistic pessimism filtered into his head. No way could he look himself in the mirror if he lived without principles, he knew, briefly angry with himself for even entertaining such notions. To doubt his duty, first of all, would be tantamount to death. And to undercut the fact there were good people everywhere—who only wished to live in peace and harmony, raise families, do whatever was right, whatever it took, no matter how tempting it was to turn their backs and go through the easy and wide-open gates of hell—was the first step toward becoming what he'd spent his life fighting.

Troubled, nonetheless, sifting through grim thoughts, the Man from Justice stole another few seconds, staring out the window as the Bell JetRanger swept over the Blue Ridge Mountains. When was the last time, he wondered, he had actually enjoyed the pristine view of those forested slopes, free to observe the rising sun spread the arrival of a new day, free to relax, not burdened by the weight of the nation's security?

He couldn't remember, and maybe it didn't matter. By nature or destiny—and he wasn't sure where the line blurred—he drove himself with the task at hand as hard as the day was long, grimly aware the wicked did not rest in his world. Beyond that, he was committed to the duty of defending America against its sworn enemies, from within and beyond its borders. On that score, it was an endless battlefront, he knew, forever expanding, as far as he was concerned, another roster of monsters always rising up to replace the evil dead, and often before the smoke cleared enough to see the next blood horizon. Or to pin down the next threat to God only knew how many innocents.

And it was a changing world out there, he reflected, evolving darker and more sinister by the day. Weapons of mass destruction. Suicide bombers. Suitcase nukes. Whole nations harboring, training and financing the murder of innocents. Supposed NATO allies, France and Germany, for example, doing business in the billions of dollars in the shadows with a former tyrant who used murder and torture and rape as an entertaining pastime. Forget any goodwill toward all men, there were mornings, like now, he wondered if the whole world was just going straight to hell.

He stood and went to the scanning console set on the small teakwood table. It was roughly the size of a notebook computer, but with attached fax and what looked like a microscope, Brognola finding his access code had been relayed to the Farm's Computer Room, confirmed and framed in white on the monitor. Initiate Phase Two flashed, and he took a seat. IPT, he knew, was part of a trial run to upgrade security, establish identity one hundred percent, thus save time and keep the blacksuits from rolling out of the main building, or find the antiaircraft battery painting incoming aircraft.

The retinal scan was first, Brognola placing his right socket against the scope's eye, depressing the send button, grateful high-tech refinements didn't produce any flash that would leave him squinting. Right thumb rolled over the ink pad, then placed on standard-size, white bond paper, he punched in the numbers for the secure line, faxed it to Kurtzman. Tapping in a series of numbers to activate the system's scrambler—Go illuminated in green on the monitor's readout—he spoke into the miniature voice box.

"This is Alpha One to Omega Base Home. Confirm Voice Test Analysis. All tests initiated, awaiting your confirmation. Out."

While he waited, Brognola eased back in the bolted-down leather swivel chair. There was a gathering tempest out there, and only direct actionable response, he knew, would hold back the barbarians before they tore down the walls of civilization.

FORMER DELTA FORCE Colonel Joshua Langdon took the smaller of black ferrite-painted aluminum steamer trunks by the nylon strap handle as soon as the ninety-foot-long inflatable boat scraped sand. Known to his men and the attached three-commando unit calling itself Tiger Ops as Commander X, he allowed the others to jump over the side first, splash down in ankle-deep, blue-green water. Five altogether, two commandos each to a steamer trunk the size of a body bag, the odd man out he knew as Capricorn Alpha Galaxy Leader, hands empty except for an HK MP-5 subgun, and they were on the beach, seconds flat, hauling the high-tech loads—one of his troops likewise burdened with a hundred-pounds-plus of folded camo netting on his back—deeper into the lush tropical greenery. A GPS module in the hands of his one of his commandos, steering them down a path to erect their base predetermined by satellite shoots, he followed Capricorn Alpha Galaxy Leader to shore.

Home sweet home, at least for the immediate future.

A quick search of the beach, black wraparound sunglasses shielding eyes from sunlight that beat off the emerald-green waters and white sand like imagined glowing radiation, and the ex-Delta colonel found himself alone with the Tiger Ops leader. Setting the trunk down, shucking the slung HK subgun higher up his shoulder, Commander X checked the screen on his handheld heat-seeker. Sweeping the perimeter, he found six ghosts in human shape, with much smaller thermal images flashing across the screen. He took a moment, listening to the gentle lap of waves on the beachhead, the caws of wild birds from some point inside the ringing walls of greenery on the coral island roughly the size of a city block.

"Almost paradise, huh? Nothing personal, you understand, but it kind of makes me wish I'd brought along my own little Eve."

Commander X glanced at the lean figure in tiger-striped camous, the Tiger Ops leader working on a smoke, clearly not all that inclined to do much more than profile, opting to leave the grunt work to others, while drinking in this Eden and maybe picture romping naked through the lagoon with his own vision of the mother of mankind. Something about the leader troubled Langdon, but he couldn't pin it down. The guy had shoulder-length, salt-and-pepper hair and a nappy beard as opposed to his own buzz cut, clean mug. Langdon noted the military bearing, decided there was more mercenary—or buccaneer, in this instance—than a current or ex-serviceman or intelligence operative performing his duty for country and God. Likewise, it was unclear who the Tiger Ops leader pledged allegiance to, even why he'd been assigned to assist him on what was a satellite relay station somewhere in the Maldive Islands.

Langdon saw his two men hustling down the beach to retrieve the rest of the steamer trunks. As they splashed down, he turned, looked at the anchored Interceptor Gunboat. The skipper, he knew, was one of his people, and the inshore patrol craft, on loan, presumably from the CIA station chief in India, would stay put until he green-lighted the man to pull away for surveillance duty. Langdon ran an approving look, stem to stern of their gunboat ride. Two Deutz MWM diesel engines, top speed of 25 knots, a range of 600 nautical miles, with a forward 12.7 mm machine gun, and he had no doubt about the ability of his troops manning the ship to fend off trouble, alert them to any incoming surprises. They worked for the same people, he knew, his men having been culled from various special forces for both their proved martial skills and high-tech talent, signing the standard "training" contracts that swore them to a lifetime of secrecy. Halfway around the world from Omega Base, they would be able to reach the Farm as if they were but a few yards away, once the fiberoptic comm station was set up. As for his Tiger Ops comrades...

Well, in this age of the media and politically stamped "new war on terrorism," every intelligence, law-enforcement agency and military arm wanted to muscle itself in for a piece of the action. Langdon, like the people he represented, wasn't in it for money or the glory. Truth was, he—like anyone who worked in the shadows for the Farm—was nowhere to be found on any official record.

He stole another moment, staring off into the vast Indian Ocean, getting his bearings. They had departed from Cape Comoros on the southern tip of the Indian subcontinent, pushing out, south by southwest, where the Lakshadweep Sea flowed into the Indian Ocean. The Maldives were comprised of a chain of twenty-six atolls of 1190 islands, only 200 of which were inhabited, and none of which rose more than ten feet off the water. Most of the islands sat, more or less, on the equator, and for this stint plenty of bottled water was required to get them through the long, hot days. Call their position somewhere in the vicinity of 400 miles due west of Colombo, Sri Lanka.

"Shall we get to work, Commander?"

Langdon heard the soft whine of battery-powered drills working on tent pegs. Hoping the man was inclined to do more than catch a tan and daydream about some island girl, Langdon skipped the remark as the Tiger Ops leader turned and strolled away, slinging his HK around his shoulder to free his hands for another cigarette.

ROBERT FIRE CLOUD was angry and scared.

For what he guessed was ten hours or more now, he had been watching them from a safe distance. Hidden in a gully in the hills north of what used to be his home, and the white eyes government-built-and-paid-for houses of his neighbors, each time one of the black helicopters—three in all for the moment—lifted off and swept the prairie near his roost, he took cover deeper in his hole. Who they were, he didn't know, but assumed they were white eyes soldiers, between the choppers, the submachine guns, black uniforms and matching helmets.

What he knew was that four homes had been blown off the face of the earth. Only now were the fires of brilliant white beginning to lose their anger and intense glow. When the wind blew his way, he caught the sickly sweet whiff of charred flesh, the memory of neighbors and friends burning deep his anger each time his nose filled with the stink. His home, little more than a two-room shack, may be just a glowing cinder, but he was thankful he lived alone.

His neighbors hadn't been so blessed.

Granted, the edge of hot anger had dulled some during the course of the past few hours, after the few first bodies had been dug out of the smoldering piles by men in spacesuits, dumped in black rubber bags. Now that it was clear some horrific accident had befallen Crazy Horse Lane, he wasn't sure how to proceed, where to run, who to go to for help. The county sheriff, John Mad Bull, would be passed out, too hung over to do anything even if he woke him at that hour.

So he watched the spacesuits use long metal poles to dig through more rubble, extracting bodies or what was left of men, women and children who shared this lonely stretch of the Berthold Reservation. His closest neighbors were six to eight miles in any direction, but surely, he thought, they had heard the tremendous series of explosions? Or had the same fate befallen them?

Again, he considered his own good fortune, felt a flush of shame on his cheeks, thinking himself lucky as opposed to the dead. If not for his nightly ritual at the Crazy Horse saloon…

He was stone-cold sober now, but began thinking about the bottle of Wild Turkey under the seat of his pickup, a few down the hatch to get his nerves and the shakes under control. The longer he watched them, he wondered if the white eyes soldiers spotted him, would he use the G-3 assault rifle, bought at a gun show and converted to fully automatic, stand his ground, go down in some blaze of glory. After all, he thought, he was believed to be direct blood to Crazy Horse. Only the white eyes had him outnumbered fifty or more to one. A 40-round detachable box magazine would hardly take down more than a few, considering he saw gunships armed with machine guns in their doorways.

He had to do something, even if it was wrong.

One of the gunships made the decision for him, as it lifted off, veering in his direction. As if it knew he had been there all along.

He stood, hunched, and worked his way down the gully, as fast as limbs swollen with the sludge of liquor would allow. Beyond his heart thundering in his ears, the assault rifle growing heavy in hands filling with the running sweat of the night's drinking, he heard the insect bleat of chopper blades bearing down from behind. After what he'd seen, what was to stop these men from taking him prisoner, or killing him? Or was he being paranoid? He didn't know, wasn't about to freeze where he stood. They were still white eyes with guns.

Stumbling out of the gully, he hit level ground, running for his Chevy pickup. Out of nowhere, the light flared, fear seizing him as he was framed in the white umbrella, heard a voice boom from a loudspeaker, "You there! Halt now and throw down your weapon!"

The command was delivered, not only with anger, he thought, but with menace. He was turning, snarling as the light stabbed him in the eyes, to split a brain throbbing from exertion, when he became aware he was lifting his assault rifle.

Then the machine gun roared through the light. He felt numb flesh absorb the first few rounds, the impact jerking him halfway around before hot emotion and the desire to die standing on his feet seized him. Rage that these white eyes soldiers would slaughter him without further warning erupted what he hoped was his best war cry. He held back on the G-3's trigger as the big gun thundered, chopping up his flesh, spraying hot blood on his face. He was dead on his feet, he knew, seconds from floating away to the next world, but Robert Fire Cloud only hoped his death and whatever had happened to his neighbors would be avenged.

CHAPTER FOUR

Hal Brognola watched the War Room's wall monitor as Aaron Kurtzman took the remote and clicked on the bearded, turbaned face of what he suspected was the bad guy of the month.

"The Sign of God, Rafiq Namak…" Kurtzman began.

"The what?" Brognola exhorted.

"That's what Ayatollah means, sign of God. Only this cleric has anointed himself Grand Ayatollah, and it appears he's looking to muscle out all the competition, from drug and arms traffickers to rival mullahs, all the way to the president of Iran, who, as far as moderates go in that part of the world, is about as rational as they come."

"Meaning, can we say, 'he wants to be chummy with Uncle Sam,'" Brognola interjected.

"Up to a point, but only as long as he can keep the country from being overrun by Pizza Huts, rap music, satellite television that pipes in western entertainment while kissing up to the hardliners behind the scenes. The president of Iran, as we all know, isn't the real power that keeps either the oil pumping or the radicals frothing at the mouth and chanting 'Death to America.' He's a puppet, in truth, toeing the line between bringing his country into the twenty-first century and appeasing the radical clerics.

"According to our CIA intelligence skims, there's been another in a long line of internal power struggles between rival clerics for the choice seat at the head of the extremist table. Right now, it looks like Namak has fairly fitted himself to wear that crown. He has his own and not-so-small army of radicals, including some of the most dangerous and vicious intelligence officers, ex-SAVAK thugs, a mass following of politically indoctrinated Revolutionary Guards who do his bidding, which is pretty much offing the competition or who are so cruel and barbaric they could have given Saddam's sons a few lessons in torture. He's done pretty good for himself, if you factor in his last known five or so years of opium and heroin proceeds coming across the borders with Afghanistan and Pakistan, cutting himself in a for a nice chunk of change for safe passage and warehousing. Then there's his version of madrassas, about twenty schools, our intel cites, only far more radical than anything in Saudi Arabia or Pakistan or Egypt, and which he runs across Iran in every corner, with hand-picked mullahs who give new meaning to the word extreme. Pretty much the usual brainwashing of angry impoverished youth being groomed for future martyrdom, only these students, some as young as seven or eight, are being shipped out to blow themselves up wherever Namak aims his 'kill all Americans' automatons.

"Considering he was born with a silver spoon shoved down his vitriolic anti-West yap—the son of a father whose father brokered himself a sweet deal during the early Anglo-Iranian Oil Company days—Rafiq was educated in Europe where he apparently forgot all about the strict tenets of Shi'a Islam, his reputation being one of a free-spending, drug-using playboy, who, so the rumor goes, had some peculiar tastes in sexual games. Word from spook city is he spent a few years in the late eighties and early nineties ingratiating himself to the CIA, the NSA, DIA and whoever else might help him climb the ladder of success while he lies, backstabs, generally plays both ends against the middle in a high-wire act that apparently left a whole lot of wreckage—spell dead American intelligence operatives."

"Meaning," Brognola said, "his former friends are now his enemies."

"Or may still be his pals, if what is rumored churning out of the spook mill pans out and he's handing out the ready cash to the buzzards of the day. What he wants, publicly stated, is one united Middle East under Shiite control, and he's starting with Iraq, lighting the powder keg of resistance. Beyond that, engineering mass killing sprees, who knows what his end game really is? He's made plenty of enemies, no question, there have been several assassination attempts, but he seems blessed by that weird dark light that always sees his ilk live to savage another day. He uses body doubles to keep trigger-happy rivals guessing, never known to be in the same place for very long. Sometimes you see him in robe and turban when he makes an appearance before the adoring mobs. Other times a three-piece suit, or he sports tiger-striped camous when he ventures into the desert to check out one of his three known training camps for the youngbloods. There are claims by his followers that he can see the future."

"Do tell."

Kurtzman grunted. "Apparently he's not bashful when it comes to touting himself an oracle of Mohammed."

"I'll venture a wild guess here, but his psychic powers predict terrorist attacks."

"He's been right on the money, at least the where and how of it," Kurtzman said, cocking a grin in Brognola's direction. "The body counts are a little off, but with each attack, whether in Israel or his favorite killing ground, Iraq, the crowds go wild in Tehran. Lately he's been hitting the airwaves over there with predictions of total annihilation for the Great Satan, a 'conflagration from God that will wipe America off the face of the earth in a storm of fire the world will never forget.'"

"Blowing smoke?"

Kurtzman shrugged. "Hard to tell. How far along Iran's reprocessing plants are to make weapons-grade plutonium and uranium, we don't know, but we know of at least two factories of WMD that are well on their way, and believed to be loosely controlled by an influx of Namak cash. We do know that he calls his organization of fighters the Army of Armageddon, and with radical ties all the way to Lebanon where, it's believed, he wants to establish a power base. And, yes, in order to jumpstart his war of annihilation, presumably starting with Israel while he torches what he can in Iraq."

Brognola gnawed on his cigar, perused the intel

packet Barbara Price had handed him earlier. During the brief pause, Brognola noticed that the Stony Man Mission Controller seemed unusually quiet, but the lady was a pro, no problem listening with one ear to the brief while she scanned the monitor of her battery-powered laptop, combing through the grim facts as he'd received them late last night from his nameless source in Shadowland. Likewise, Kurtzman had his own notebook computer, having already downloaded the CD-ROM to his hard drive, hooking the modem that would allow him to frame pertinent data direct from both computers to the wall monitor.

"This," Kurtzman said, clicking the screen to frame what looked like a typical artillery shell, "is SPLAT. Special Purpose Laser Anti-Tank."

Brognola waited as Kurtzman broke the screen into four quads. He saw a tracked vehicle, a UAV that looked suspiciously like a CIA Predator, and some sort of delivery system, complete with radar screen, the background appearing to be a stone hovel.

"During a U.S. special ops raid on a stronghold believed used by Namak along the Iranian-Iraqi border, these were seized, along with blueprints and instructions strongly suspected of having their origins somewhere far outside the Mideast realm."

"Any ideas on who's looking to help pile up the body count with SPLAT?"

Kurtzman sipped from his mug, frowning. "There was some talk, the French were mentioned, but we think it's a smoke screen to deflect blame. Since France was dumped in the crapper on oil contracts in Iraq, however, they have been schmoozing the Iranians. I'm not one to jump on the PC bandwagon, so I don't mind saying they're a sneaky, backstabbing lot, with a whole lot to hide in some shady dealings with Saddam, but I don't think they have the balls to start dumping off ordnance that could be used against Coalition Forces in Iraq, though they most likely have this technology. That aside, there are no markings, serial numbers and such that we know of on the ordnance, which leaves suspicion enough to go around it could be Germans, North Koreans or Russians…"

"Or someone on our team."

"It's happened before, as we all sadly know. Now, as for SPLAT, it's the next step in laser-guided artillery and its sister version for short and intermediate range missiles. Laser guidance has been tried in the past where field artillery is concerned, but there's a few refinements on SPLAT. Thermal, or heat-seeking guidance systems have been upgraded, for one, the use of sophisticated super microchips installed in computer systems, developed, in part, from the U.S. Navy's Sidewinder AIM-9D. You can see the tracked vehicle with eight launch rails, I'm told twelve to twenty more shells, or short-range missiles, can be stored in ready-access pallets. As for the shells, they range anywhere from 85 mm to 155 mm. On the short-range or intermediate missile range…"

"I bet you're going to tell me they can be fitted with chemical or biological warheads. Or tactical nukes."

"Not only that, but they can, ostensibly, hit their target down to within a few meters. Gunner in turret mount, he aims the projectile using GPS. The tracking signal processor feeds into the computer optic link using Global Positioning Satellite. Point and fire."

"And the package can be guided in by an Unmanned Aerial Vehicle."

"Yes. All things considered, Hal," Kurtzman said, "it's a quantum leap in laser-guided field artillery, vastly improved for bad weather and night operations."

"Range?"

"Unknown. But, say for the sake of argument, you go with intermediate-range missiles, using this delivery system and rocket fuel…"

"You could hit Tel Aviv."

"With your eyes closed."

Brognola grunted around his cigar. "And we're thinking Namak is beefing up his Army of Armageddon with SPLAT?"

"And/or arming foreign fighters across the border in Iraq," Kurtzman said. "And if he has UAVs at his disposal to guide the projectiles to target."

"Which bring us to Phoenix Force," Brognola said. "What's its status?"

"They're ready to move when you give the green light," Kurtzman said.

"To link up with our Tiger Ops allies," Brognola muttered. "And I use that word 'ally' with great reservation."

"I know you tried to get the Man," Kurtzman said, referring to the President of the United States, "to cut Phoenix loose on its own, but with the instability of the area in question near and along the Iranian border, and with no telling how many enemy combatants they may be facing, a few extra guns may not hurt."

"The jury's still out on that, Bear. For one thing, you can't dig up any background on who these Tiger Ops are, which agency cuts them blank checks from who-ever's slush fund. I hate having our people working with and inside lurking shadows who may have dubi-ous agendas. Especially since we don't know who is funneling SPLAT and whatever other high-tech ord-nance to Namak and thugs."

"I concur, which is another reason I thought we'd run with the satellite relay station. In the event Phoenix needs backup on the ground, Barb worked it out with the CIA station chief in India to have them a Gulf-stream fueled and ready to fly to the battlefront on a mo-ment's notice. Not only that, but with the weather predicted to be nothing but tropical paradise, clear skies for the next two weeks, any satellite imagery relayed to us from them will be in crystal clarity. With the fiber-optic camera mounts Phoenix will have on their person, our guys can monitor the battlefront for them, live and in color, cyberspace directors, if you will, on the bloody stage. Likewise we will get relayed images, but they will be time-delayed by about three seconds."

Brognola watched as Kurtzman snapped on the vast Indian Ocean, enlarging an area southwest of the sub-continent's tip in the Maldive Islands in red.

"Emerald Base Zero," Kurtzman said, "confirmed they are set up and ready to begin sweeping the Iran-Iraq border with the first available satellite they can park over the AIQ. What I did was provide Commander X and his team with a software program—Ghost Dreams—which will create a ghost satellite of the one they park in space. That way, whoever's on the ground monitoring that eye in the sky will think it's still orbiting, will even have 'ar-tificial imagery' relayed to the station."

"And, once again, our blacksuits are running the relay station in a joint effort with Tiger Ops, who will be watching the backs of their own guys," Brognola said, then paused, watching Price. "You know what I'm thinking? It looks like these Tiger Ops have been running around in Iraq and maybe Iran for some time now, that they have in all likelihood established contacts on both sides of the fence."

"And you suspect some or all of them may be sleeping with the enemy?"

"If they are—and like you said, Bear, it's happened before—Phoenix will get the thumbs-down from me to take them out, and I don't care how highly touted they came to me from the President. I may be liaison between the Farm and the Oval Office, but I won't play anybody's fool when it comes to putting our people in harm's way. Barb? I gather you've found something I received from my Shadow Man that's grabbed your eye?"

"Perhaps, but I'll need to make a phone call or two to some old contacts of mine at the NSA. Before you arrived, Bear, Akira and I were kicking around some ideas about this 'incident' in North Dakota. It smacks of a military test gone wrong. In this instance, terribly wrong. Our sat pics show civilian casualties, full military quarantine, denials being issued to whatever press can get close enough before they're driven back. From the facts given to you by your source, I'm thinking there's a strong possibility…well, your source states this Eagle Nebula is creating superweapons of the future, including, as unbelievable as it may sound, flying war vans that can be fitted with state-of-the-art hardware. Moreover, he hints that maybe a few loose cannons are selling whatever the supertechnology to our enemies." She tapped her keyboard, framing a fighter jet on the wall monitor. "That is Lightning Bat, allegedly the prototype super fighter jet of tomorrow. With its swept-back Delta wings and arrowhead configuration, it appears just like an F-117 Stealth, only with quantum leap variants. According to your source, it has a top speed of Mach 10. To go ten times the speed of sound, your intel alludes to some type of super combustion ramjet, using air for fuel."

"Only, Lightning Bat is powered by a nuclear reactor," Kurtzman added.

"Which I find damn hard to believe. You have the problem of the tremendous weight of a reactor alone, for one thing, all that steel and concrete housing," Brognola said. "You're releasing huge sustained amounts of energy, which is basically heat, I believe, producing what is steam to keep a turbogenerator going strong. You've got to keep the reactor cooled by water..."

"We believe it's done at high altitudes," Kurtzman said, "by air pumped through vents to cool the reactor. Somehow, we don't know how, but they've purportedly done it at Eagle Nebula, weight problem and all. Problem is, the single greatest fear and why no aircraft before now has been propelled by nuclear energy should be the obvious crash landing in a heavily populated area. Depending on how much uranium or plutonium is used, you would most definitely have a Chernobyl to deal with."

"And we're thinking Lightning Bat's test run," Brognola said, "was a belly flop, and that they've got radioactive clouds spreading over half of North Dakota?"

"No," Price said. "We're thinking its payload was launched by some sort of computer malfunction. Or by direct sabotage."

"And these payloads are suspected to be?"

"Conventional cluster bombs," Kurtzman said.

"And your man in the know," Price added, "claims the bomb bay can hold nukes, and that a nuke test run is on the drawing board for Nevada. Cluster nukes, he calls them, one designed to go off after the other in varying outreaching circles of obliteration around the compass. The payloads are lowered on something like a crossbar, which allows for a simultaneous launch of four warheads, north, south, east and west. Whatever happened out there I think warrants investigation. And if weapons or technology is being hijacked to be sold on the international black market…"

Brognola nodded. There were a lot of blanks that needed filling in, and if there was one type of savage he detested it was a traitor wrapped in the Stars and Stripes, selling out for money or twisted ideology, it didn't matter. Treason, he believed, deserved the ultimate rough justice.

"Okay, what's the status on Able Team?" Brognola inquired.

Price cleared her throat. "Carl and Gadgets," she said, referring to Carl Lyons and Hermann Schwarz, two of the three commandos of Able, "are in Chicago."

"Let me guess. R and R," he offered, "tearing up the town. Gentlemen's clubs, all-night drinking binges and the possibility I may get a phone call they need bail money."

"How well you know our prodigal sons," Kurtzman quipped.

"Yeah, well, there may come a day they'll rue when Daddy hangs up the phone. So, what's the story on Rosario?" Brognola asked, meaning the third leg of the team, Rosario Blancanales, sometimes referred to as the Politician.

"I arranged to have him sent to Vegas," Price said.

"I didn't know he was a gambler."

"He's not," Price said, and tapped her keyboard. "He is."

Brognola looked at the wizened face on the wall monitor. The eyes were hidden by dark sunglasses, a mane of snow-white hair flowing to the shoulders of his aloha shirt.

"That," Price said, "is Ezekiel Jacobs, the creator of Lightning Bat and its purported nuclear-powered capabilities, among other superweapons systems, as confirmed by your source's intelligence. An Israeli national, he was educated in the States, then disappeared for a number of years after a brief stint with NASA. The NSA says he worked for the Russians during that missing time on a space program to someday see man travel deep space. Apparently a number of his theories, travel at light speed using controlled bursts of fission reactions, was a little too radical for the NASA crowd. He begged for funding to create what he called the Dynamo Matrix Program—again deep space travel at light speed—raised a stink, was fired by NASA and, it appears, sold his services to the Russians. He's considered a genius, however, in the field of aerospace engineering and physics."

"And he spends his free time at the slot machines?" Brognola said.

"Blackjack. He can count cards so well he's been banned from several casinos. Now, apparently, he's switched to dice just so he can get through the front door, or not end up in an unmarked grave in the desert."

"So what's Pol doing out there?"

"Helping an old friend from his Vietnam tour," Price answered.

"Come again?"

"He was reluctant at first to go into much detail, then I pushed him when he asked about me arranging a classified flight out of your office, so he could take whatever hardware he needed, thus, as you know, bypassing the usual boarding inspections. If I overstepped my authority, Hal…"

"No need to apologize, it isn't like I have to go to Congress for a blank check or have to explain myself to a bunch of senators. And I'm sure you had good reason, and that you're about to drop a bomb on me about Mr. Jacobs here."

"Pol's buddy is a private investigator," Price said. "For whatever reason, and I gather the reason is that there is some degree of danger involved, the friend enlisted Pol's help."

"Called out of the blue?"

Price shrugged. "I gather they've stayed in touch over the years, as a lot of vets of that war probably have. Anyway, the PI, he lives in South Dakota, near the ranch where Jacobs lived with his wife, and one day recently up and vanished. Being as he's been known to hole up in Vegas before, she contacted this investigator who, in turn, called Pol."

"And the danger is?"

"Russian intelligence operatives," Price said. "Pol confirmed his PI buddy believes Jacobs is being courted by the Russians. Not only that, but Pol told me Jacobs had a classified job at a remote North Dakota installation that required he work there, four days on, four off."

"The Eagle Nebula," Brognola said, watching Price nod. "So, we think we've fallen into some snake's nest and by accident or by way of the accident or sabotage by our own military? And we have more riddles than answers, and we're thinking there could be homegrown traitors clear from North Dakota to Iraq?"

"Pretty much the usual," Kurtzman said.

Brognola worked on his cigar. "Okay. Barb call Carl and get those two to North Dakota, but have Pol stay put in Vegas for the time being, see what he digs up or what may fall into his lap."

"You'll want Carl and Gadgets looking into Eagle Nebula? As what, part of some special task force from the Justice Department?"

"Complete, if I can get it, with a presidential directive that gives them free and ready access to the base and to question whoever's in charge there," Brognola said. The grim note in Price's voice and the wry glint in her eyes not escaping him. "Oh, yeah, I know. Lyons isn't big when it comes to smearing on the gentle diplomacy. But, if they're hiding something out there, covering up a disaster that involves civilian casualties, I'm counting on his crocodile style to flush out and chomp down on some raw meat. The perfect pit bull for the job," Brognola added with a grim smile.

EZEKIEL JACOBS HELD his Russian benefactors in contempt. Assuming they were either current or former Spetsnaz commandos or ex-KGB, perhaps even tied to some criminal organization, this ignorant rabble who lived by the sword and were enslaved by all the animal inclinations of such didn't have a clue how to handle themselves when in the presence of genius—or women—much less understand the fine point that living well was the best revenge.

"This is what we are throwing away good and very large sums, may I add, Comrade Jacobs, of money on? A computer graphic of an American Stealth fighter? Charts of chemical equations and numbers and physics babble?"

And there it was, he thought, pulling back his flowing mane of snow with one hand, staring at Boris Rustov on the other side of the coffee table as the Russian glowered at the specs on Lightning Bat, his black ferret eyes nearly bugged out with profound confusion and anger over mathematical equations that only a few in his elite stratosphere could even begin to comprehend. Clearly this barbarian was blind to the creativity of pure genius that was as close, he thought, to the Divine as Earthbound Man could get.

Ah, but why must he suffer fools gladly? Then again, why not? A few more days and playtime was over. For the moment he figured he was as close to heaven on earth as he could possibly ascend. One look out the massive window, and the constellation of neon out there on the Strip beckoned him the world could be his, but for one more roll of the dice, another few hours at the blackjack table. From his six-hundred-dollar-a-day suite on the north corner of the Bellagio hotel-casino—all the trimmings of two giant screen TVs, whirlpool, fully stocked wet bar and room service with all the frills, complete with ladies of the evening—he could drink in the glittering diadems of Caesar's Palace, the Barbary Coast, the Flamingo Las Vegas, Imperial Palace.

The 3000-room ultraresort was a marvel of flamboyance, he thought, grabbing up a fat chunk of real estate where the old Dunes was perched on the southwest corner of Flamingo and the Strip. Considered one of the most expensive hotel-casinos on the planet, it featured Italian gardens, a twelve-acre lake, showroom, water shows, with a few hundred million in art displayed and spread around all the heavenly opulence. The best news of all was that families with children were strongly urged to seek accommodations farther up the Strip, high rollers only to walk through these pearly gates. Granted, he was still mid-Strip, in the thick of the hustle and bustle, traffic and noise a near 24/7 nuisance, but there was no reason to venture farther north where the common folk—low-rollers—wasted their paltry sums in grind joints.

From behind his dark Blues Brothers sunglasses, Jacobs watched the Russian scowl, looking him up and down as if he were some sideshow freak. Jacobs crossed one pajama-wrapped leg in white silk over the other, smoothed out the robe in matching color and fabric, brushing a fleck of tobacco off the Playboy bunny monogram on his left breast. Believing he could feel the steam building in the Russian's primitive brain, sure

Rustov's blood pressure was ready to shoot off the monitor, he turned to Cleopatra, his companion. He watched her with an approving eye, as the striking Asian beauty slinked up to the couch to deliver him another brandy.

"Thank you, my dear," Jacobs said, twirling the drink in his snifter, then patting the seat beside him. And he thought Rustov would erupt as she dropped her luscious flesh, barely concealed in the leopard-skin one-piece, bottom thrust his way, snuggling close to genius, all purrs and caresses. Breathing in her exquisite fragrance, he felt the stirring of heat in his loins, then the guttural bark of his Russian visitor soured the rising mood.

"There is a limit to our generosity and a bottom to our money pit. Explain yourself now, Comrade Jacobs."

Jacobs took his smoking pipe, tamped down a fresh snootful of tobacco. "Six million million miles," he said, smiling. "Three hundred thousand kilometers or 186,000 miles per second. Mass, force, space and time."

"You find this amusing, comrade?"

"The first was the measure of a light-year. The second was the speed of light. The third is part of an equation whereby I explain how to shrink mass, while heating a hydrogen core for controlled bursts of a thermonuclear explosion that would allow for travel at and beyond light speed."

"You are trying my patience to its limits."

"So I see." Jacobs puffed, sipped his drink. He took the remote box, snapped on a James Bond movie behind the Russian thug, wondering if he could replicate or refine one of Q's high-tech toys, but saw the scene and already knew that he had. If he hadn't, he knew the

Russians wouldn't be here now, waiting on him, hand and foot, frothing at the mouth, impatient to get on with business, surely entertaining violent fantasies of what they'd like to do to him if he weren't regarded as the Holy Grail to their superiors.

"What you see, Comrade Rustov," he said, speaking now in fluent Russian, "as a typical Stealth fighter jet is, in fact, the war bird of the future, created by my own hand, and for which your country came to me and agreed to my demands in order to—one—not only engineer a version of Lightning Bat, but—two—deliver to you my considerable expertise in likewise building weapons and weapons systems that far surpass your incomprehension of me and my creation. What you failed to understand and thus give me a chance to become immortalized beyond the likes of Albert Einstein is that Lightning Bat was one, perhaps two, steps away from being able to send man into deep space at the speed of light through my sweat and labor. Which requires nuclear propulsion, of which I installed in Lightning Bat and was in the process of designing for a prototype spacecraft."

"You are talking much but telling me nothing of what I wish to know."

"Ah, I see. You think I throw you a crumb with those computer printouts on the table. You want to know where the good stuff is kept." Jacobs tapped the side of his head. "Nearly all of the treasures of the mysteries of the universe, comrade, are locked safely away in here. Regarding my continued health and happiness, I will lead you to all pertinent documents and data in due course. After, of course, I have enjoyed what was agreed upon as one week of R and R in Las Vegas. That leaves me at present with three days to suffer your scowling and barbs and demands."

Rustov leaned forward, an edge to his voice. "You may feel genius should be granted all the perks and privileges it demands, while we, the common peasants should bow and scrape before you, but I would be very careful how you speak to me, Comrade Jacobs. Your continued happiness is really of no great concern to me."

Jacobs blew smoke across the table. "It damn well better be, Comrade Rustov. Your life depends on just how happy I am." Jacobs watched the gunsel, thinking he could almost read his mind as his thug's brain churned over at the rate of drying concrete, searching for some response that would save face.

"Three more days, then it is I who will dictate the agenda."

"Until then…if you would be so kind as to order up some breakfast for myself and Cleopatra. Eggs over easy, I like my bacon juicy with fat, not irradiated to shoe leather as it was yesterday. Make sure they understand that. If I discover you are cutting budget costs by stiffing room service on the tip, I will be most unhappy."

Rustov chuckled as he stood. "Perhaps you are unaware, believing myself and my men only your ignorant lackeys. While you sleep with your whores, we cracked the mainframe on your laptop."

Jacobs felt his heart flutter. "That was most unwise, since you should treat my privacy like you would my happiness."

"We know about the Web sites, your e-mails to your

former colleagues in my country. Should you not deliver as promised, we believe they have sufficient expertise to assist us."

"Sufficient, in this case, will not cut it, Comrade Rustov. Further, you seem to forget I worked at Compound Zero-159-A, and that these former colleagues of mine could not complete work I left unfinished when the money dried up. Now. Are you going to respect my privacy and see to my continued happiness, likewise see to it that my pockets are deep when I leave for the casinos or do I contact your superiors and tell them the deal is off? And inform them it is because you are uncooperative cheapskate with a considerable chip on his shoulder?"

Rustov smiled, bobbed his head. "We will continue the arrangement, Comrade Jacobs, as you wish. Only bear this in mind as a gambler. When your marker is called in, you had best pony up."

"The threat implying it's a big desert out there?"

Jacobs watched Rustov, the baboon wearing his stupid grin, as he turned and walked for the foyer, barking at his four gunslingers to fall in. Grateful when he was alone, he draped an arm over Cleopatra, pulled her closer, and said, "I certainly hope that little bit of unpleasantness didn't ruin your mood, my dear."

"YOU THINK YOU CAN TAKE IT easy on the liquor, Slim, while we're sailing along at a hundred miles an hour and five hundred feet off the ground?"

"The name's Rupert, son. And I don't care what that tin badge you flashed me sayin' you're with the Justice Department, this is my plane, and I been flying since you were but a mere itch in your daddy's sac. And unless you wanna arrest me for FWI and land this bird yourself, you might want to lose that nasty attitude of yours—Mr. G-Man—sir."

Carl "Ironman" Lyons was in a foul mood as it was. It was never a happy day when he was snatched off R and R, duty calling or not. No, it wasn't so much he was being bosom-nuzzled by a beautiful dancer way more than half his age when he got the call from the Farm to put his pants on, as it was the hangover now pulsing wardrums through a swollen brain that was sorely tempting his sand-papered tongue to mollify the old prairie buzzard for a shot of whiskey if only to help pull shot nerves together. At the moment, fear of flying took on a whole new meaning for the leader of Able Team.

As if flinging his scowl an invisible middle finger, the old-timer lifted the bottle and took another haul, then took his free hand off the wheel and lit a smoke. Lyons looked over his shoulder, found Hermann "Gadgets" Schwarz had a half-cocked grin aimed at the old geezer.

"My buddy thinks you're a real hoot, Rupe," Lyons growled.

"That a fact? Well, he wants to do some back-seat flying I ain't opposed to helpin' him step out the door neither. And I don't believe in carryin' parachutes when I hit the friendly skies."

"You're a real piece of work, Rupe, a real dinosaur, but I kinda like your style," Lyons said, faced front, and began scanning the prairie through his field glasses.

"That's Ru-pert, Mr. G-Man. You want I should smack you upside your hard head?"

"I'd rather spare myself the shame of getting brained by a guy four times my senior."

"You need to lose that smart mouth, you know that, sonny?"

"I'm working on it, one day at a time, you know. Just keep heading northeast toward Gladstone. And try and hold her a little steady before I start tasting my nuts."

Lyons left Rupert to muttering and bouncing the bird between pulls of Wild Turkey. Schwarz, he knew, was getting the video cam ready to start filming whatever it was they were there to see. Destruction of private property, presumably, with a classified military-aerospace installation to the east responsible for the mayhem that was being kept buried in the closet. Plan of attack? he thought. Soon enough he figured to encounter the flying cavalry once old Rupert breached restricted airspace, only Rupert didn't know that yet. To say they were off to a less than auspicious start, with Pol gallivanting around Las Vegas with some war pal turned private dick...

How the Farm had even found Badland Tours on the map to begin with was a nagging mystery that only fueled the fire in his brain. The closest post to any sign of civilization in Slope County in southwestern North Dakota, the Gulfstream had landed at Rupert Baynard's private airfield, as arranged by the Farm. That was if Lyons could even call a graveyard of rust bucket twin engine Pipers and Cessnas and gutted choppers an airport. They had ditched their gear in a backroom at what Lyons figured passed for his home-office, doling out enough cash for both a week's room and board and Rupert's skills as a pilot, and Lyons would bet the old buzzard wasn't even FAA-certified.

The plane itself resembled an old Dakota C-47, Lyons recalling four or five bullet holes he'd seen scarring the portside fuselage before he climbed a ladder that nearly buckled under his boots. Beyond that, the bucket of bolts shook and shimmied, and from what Lyons could tell there was nothing but blue skies, no wind blowing across the prairie below that should find the craft damn near bucking like a gored bull. Not only that, but it felt as though his seat wasn't fully bolted down, seeming to list to starboard when he shifted his weight, and the port radial engine mounted in nacelles belched black smoke when Rupert cut back on the speed even a hair. If that wasn't bad enough, Lyons saw that a few of the instrument gauges didn't even work, the glass coverings cracked.

"I'll be damned. That's Cam Decker's spread, or what's left of it. What in the…"

What was left, Lyons saw, was charred ruins, as they flew over a few dozen carcasses, impossible to tell if they were horse or cattle, burned as they were beyond recognition. Rupert began spouting off his anger and outrage in a string of four-, ten- and twelve-letter expletives directed primarily at the new breed of Washington bluebelly, stating he knew the government was testing out new weapons in the area and was sure they were to blame for what happened to the Decker ranch. Which left Lyons somewhat amazed and wondering that he'd even agreed to the Farm's request to allow two special agents from the United States Department of Justice to violate his airspace and claim his digs as a temporary base, though a sizable cash contribution to Badland Tours was clearly the acceptable peace pipe.

"You have any clue as to what happened out here last night, Rupert?" Lyons asked.

"I live alone, I ain't got no TV, no radio. My closest neighbor is old Cam and his wife. Since you people got my phone number somehow, I'm thinking about disconnecting that."

Lyons scoured the black lake of destruction for any sign of life, but found none. "You might want to make that 'was' your closest neighbor."

"Was? You telling me you think they're dead?"

"Agent Schlitz?" Lyons called over his shoulder, using Schwarz's handle of Special Agent Henry Schlitz. "You get any of that?"

"What wasn't jumping off the lens when Rupert hit all that turbulence."

"That wasn't no damn turbulence!"

"Hey," Lyons rasped at Schwarz, "didn't you hear the man say he doesn't like smart-asses?"

Schwarz flashed the Able Team leader a wry grin. "My humble apologies."

"I did hear somethin' about strange explosions when I was at the diner this morning."

"And?"

"And nothin'. Seems these skies have been swarming with black helicopters all night long, or so I heard. Someone even said a whole town near here was blown to smithereens, but it don't seem no one cares to confirm that rumor."

"An entire town, you're telling me, gets wiped off the map and nobody goes to check on their neighbors?"

"Got the area cordoned off, way I hear it. Military keeping everyone gets too close away, and at the barrels of machine guns."

Lyons spotted the red butte, the flat vista of brown mesa rising just beyond. A few more miles, according to the Farm's intelligence, and they'd hit the restricted airspace of Eagle Nebula. As they were soaring over the mesa and Lyons spotted all the sat dishes bubbling the rooftop of a low-lying but massive concrete installation, ringed around the compass by razor wire, it dawned on Rupert he'd been duped.

"Hey! This is restricted airspace!"

He was cutting the wheel when Lyons ordered, "Keep it straight and stick to our scheduled course."

"The hell you say! That place, I heard, has antiaircraft cannon! You want we should get blown out of the sky?"

"Nobody's going to blow us out of the sky."

"No, sir."

"I'm paying for this ride, Rupert, and this badge and gun," Lyons said, patting the bulge beneath his black windbreaker where the .357 Magnum Colt Python was shouldered, "state that as an agent of the United States government I can go wherever I damn well please whenever I damn well want because I am duly authorized to do just that."

"You gonna pull that piece on me, mister? You gonna shoot me? Can you fly this bird?"

"I'm asking you to cooperate."

Rupert grumbled through clenched teeth, but stayed the course. They weren't but another two hundred yards closer when the Black Hawk gunship seemed to drop straight down from the sky, about a quarter mile, dead ahead. Rupert began cursing when the gunship hovered in a holding pattern, swinging around so the M-60 door gunner had a clear line of fire.

"We've got two more bogeys, gentlemen," Lyons heard Schwarz inform him. "And their door gunners look like they've got itchy trigger fingers."

Sure enough, Lyons found they were blocked in by two more Black Hawks, port and starboard, M-60s looking so close he could spit on them.

"You piloting the aircraft!" a disembodied voice boomed from what Lyons knew was a loudspeaker. "You are in restricted airspace of the United States government! You will land the craft immediately or we will force you down! Wave, if you understand!"

Lyons watched as Rupert waved at them with a middle finger. "I don't think that was too smart, Rupert. By forcing us down they don't mean a gentle escort with a ticker tape parade waiting on the ground."

"All right, all right. I don't know what the hell I let you get me into, but if I lose my plane on account of—"

"Relax and do what they tell you. Just get us on the ground in one piece," Lyons said.

As Rupert waved he understood, minus the bird this time, Lyons reached behind, grabbed the nylon safety harness. As he tugged forward he heard fabric tear, and came back with a hand full of shreds which he displayed to Rupert with a scowl, reconsidering that fat swig of Wild Turkey.

CHAPTER FIVE

Colonel Boris Rustov was no man's flunky, genius or whatever. He was Spetsnaz, first and last, and as such he knew the word alone was enough to send ice walking down the spines of adversarial warriors the world over.

Nothing less than the heart of a lion, he knew, the balls of a bull elephant could fashion a Spetsnaz commando.

Thus it was a source of stung pride, more or less, that found a warrior of his vaunted and stature viewed by a pampered, self-indulgent think-tank as a monkey to his organ grinding. Perhaps he was touted by the GRU as a genius who—if he was so inclined to believe the propaganda—could propel their country light-years ahead in both high-tech weapons and its space program, leave the competition to choke in the afterburning dust of what Moscow hoped was a new-and-improved version of Lightning Bat, but Rustov knew something Jacobs did not.

Secrecy and duplicity was the way of the Russian, after all.

Yes, the Israeli national had been granted an advance of two million U.S. dollars, though Rustov had informed him only half that much was presently available in the coffers—to be doled out as he saw fit—and to much squawking, flapping of arms and threats that fell on deaf ears, though the man clearly didn't want to bite the hand that fed his vices. And yes, much to his own burning chagrin, the smug bastard was to be catered to, every whim indulged, no matter how obscene or distasteful, no matter how dangerous to the task at hand if he became sloppy drunk, made a spectacle of himself in the casinos, or was rousted by security at the blackjack table for counting cards.

Three more nights, he thought, and the arrogant worm would see the gravy train slide to a screeching halt.

Boris Rustov was under orders to torture the esteemed Dr. Jacobs if he didn't fully cooperate after the allotted R and R.

First, extract the vital information his country sought, or the whereabouts to whatever key documents he had stashed, and Rustov was sure he could crack the egghead with a mere backhand slap or two across his arrogant face. After that, it would be up to him how he chose to dispose of the problem. And the mere notion he might end up having his way with Jacobs, deciding on how long he would prolong the man's suffering before killing him in any number of gruesome and dehumanizing ways…

It fairly made his mouth water in anticipation.

"If you want me to stay, that will be another five hundred dollars. Per hour. Two thousand if you want me for the whole day."

He caught the whore staring at him in the mirror, curled up under satin sheets, hugging them tight to her supple figure. Pulling on his trousers, he felt her eyes wander the length of torso cut by far more than rippling sinew. For a moment, he allowed her to stare at flesh that looked more armor than muscle, wonder in perhaps fear and awe at the sight of so many scars and the dead purpled flesh of bullet wounds from so many distant battlefields so many lifetimes ago. Slipping the black turtleneck over his head, he realized she was asking him to decide how much he enjoyed her company, though judging the uncertainty in her eyes figured she'd rather return to the safety of urban cowboys or johns in suits who used her while tasting parole from nagging wives, squalling brood and the drudgery of suburban life.

He snapped on his watch. "Why not."

"Why not, what? One hour, or the whole day, sport?"

Diplomatic immunity, he considered, came catered with plenty of its own perks and privileges. Weapons, for one critical matter, the heavy artillery housed under the very roof of his adjoining suite, with caches for ready access in sedan rentals. As for circumventing the normal channels—arranged with inside assistance from the American State Department—he and his fifteen commandos had carte blanche to carry concealed weapons. Breaking laws, though perhaps short of mass murder, was another star in the plus column. And by dangling the sore issue of dwindling funds over the greedy swine's head, outright lying about the other million, there was thus plenty left to skim for his own joy and happiness.

He peeled off two thousand in hundreds, U.S., flipped the wad on the bed, noting how closely she watched him shove the rest of the currency back into his pants pocket.

"Typical American whore," he muttered in his native tongue.

"I'm sorry, but I don't speak Russian, comrade. But that didn't sound very nice."

"It wasn't meant to be."

She retreated deeper inside her silken shroud when he pinned her surly look in the mirror, thinking he'd just as soon kill her, take back his money and use her body again. He was heading for the door to his master bedroom, slipping into his shoulder rigging, when he heard the knock. A check of his watch, twisting the knob, and he knew by now the Israeli swine would be in the casino, the Asian call girl on his arm while he played the high roller. It was a little soon, and he'd capitulated by handing off forty thousand for the good doctor's buy-in stake, so he couldn't imagine he should be whining for more money, or just yet.

He found Vladimir Kruchenov on the other side, the chiseled hawk face looking dark with concern.

"My apologies for disturbing you, Comrade Colonel," he said, using Russian as prior the order when an important or critical matter needed to be discussed. "But the desk called me as you had requested them to do if someone came asking about our guest."

Rustov listened to the details. It was just this moment he had been on war footing for since arriving in Las Vegas. Apparently, Jacobs had been tracked down. From the description his lieutenant gave him, it hardly bespoke of a consummate professional. Cheap white sports jacket. Cheap white shoes, looked like they just fell off the shelf at a discount store. Wrinkled aloha shirt with half-naked island girls, flamingos and palm trees. Black sunglasses, profiling and cracking wise, or like he was Hollywood royalty incognito. Reeking, so the deskman further stated, of whiskey fumes and smoking like a dragon wherever he spread his sunshine. Rustov had the picture.

Only he knew what sort of individual guarded the lair of the Eagle Nebula, and was the interloper coming to them, disguised as a low-rolling bum better suited for a grind joint up the Strip…

A clever ruse? One professional, easy enough to single out if the description held up, luring them into an ambush? Whichever it was, it was time for one side to either raise or fold their hand, as the good doctor might say.

He told Kruchenov to alert the others, wait for him in the living room. "I will be gone for a while," he told his playmate, opening the top drawer of his dresser, then fishing the sandwich bag out of his briefcase.

"For how long?"

"As long as it takes." He tossed the bag on the bed, disgusted by her as the sight of all that white powder instantly changed her from surly bitch to demure cat. "I know how much is in there, and I expect to get my money's worth out of you between that ounce-and-one-quarter and my two thousand. Be here when I return."

"No problem, comrade. I'll just entertain myself."

"I'm sure you will," he snarled, shutting the door behind to leave her either wondering what he just said or how long she could ride the Russian Gravy Train.

Rosario Blancanales had no problem admitting he was a gambler, but the risks he undertook were worlds apart from the frenzy of the gaming pits he'd seen since his boots touched down at McCarran International. As an Able Team commando and Stony Man warrior, he put his life on the line each time he waded into the blood-soaked trenches where he battled the enemies of national security, or defended the right to pursue life, liberty and happiness wherever humankind wished to live in peace, but were devoured by the cannibalistic forces of terrorism, despotism, organized crime and all the criminal ills that fell in between to spread a cancer of misery and despair.

What he did was a matter of honor, duty and principle.

No lust for more money than to suit basic needs, carry his own weight. No limelight in which to take a bow before adoring throngs. No worldly gain of any sort for placing his head on the chopping block, other than perhaps the occasional curt acknowledgment of a job well done—he was only human, after all—by comrades and colleagues who undertook either the same risks or were committed to the same task behind the front lines. Here in Vegas, around the clock, though, in something like thirty-two casinos rising or plopped down along the seven-mile stretch they called the Strip, with a million or more souls, he'd heard, crammed into the downtown arena at any given time that was designed for 300,000 capacity, the air wherever he trod was hypercharged with the electricity of raw greed.

And this was the fastest growing city in America.

It was the start of his second full day in Vegas and already he had a bellyful of the human appetite to grab more, and often just for the sake of grabbing while hinging it all on a wing and a prayer. Also known as the Politician for his ability to reach into the hearts and minds of friend and foe alike, he found his thoughts troubled that so many came here to spend so much of what they really couldn't afford to lose, in reality short-changing responsibilities and commitments elsewhere. On the other end of that tainted rainbow, the few who could squander so much and not miss it in their never-ending quest for more were either blind or didn't care that a huge, sweltering chunk of humanity worried whether or not they would eat that day.

Welcome to the human race, he supposed. Viva Las Vegas. How long this bout of quasi-depression would last, he couldn't say, but reckoned his dark mood had more to do with his current stint than feeling as if he was some alien from outer space that just stepped off the Mothership on the South Lawn.

Walking out of the coffee shop with his five-dollar cup of java—having been promptly and curtly informed when wandering into one of the casino's restaurants in search of a breakfast buffet that he needed at least a six-month reservation in advance just to eat and had to be a guest of the hotel—he bottom-lined the difference between himself and the madness he found swarming everywhere he set foot. Grateful, but sad at the same time for all those racing around here to chase a vapor, he was keenly aware a truly elite few knew what he did, why, and who he really was.

After a check of his watch, wondering what was

keeping his Vietnam pal turned private investigator, he gave his opulent surroundings a search, grabbing a piece of marbled turf as the early morning throngs swept past. The Bellagio, he had to admit, was light-years from any grind joint where he and his buddy were holed up at the Stardust, farther north up the Strip. A man could get lost in here, he figured, the hotel-casino more like a cathedral where he needed a day-long tour guide just to get his bearings. What with its boasting of showrooms, numerous restaurants, shopping mall, sprawling casino, botanical gardens, it also came advertised hanging thirteen original Picassos somewhere in all this ostentatious gaming basilica, the sum total of all this grandeur billed by the bigshots, he figured, as the crown jewel of Vegas. Out front, there was even a man-made lake with Italian village theme park, complete with dancing fountains...

If he felt way out of his league, at least in terms of being a warrior with simple needs and solid contentment for what was real and honest, then he was reasonably certain his Nam buddy believed he had arrived, that the Bellagio was built expressly with one Eddie Parker in mind.

And there it was, he thought, another dagger thrust into his grim mood, twisting to open his bleeding soul a little more, this time in regards to his friend.

Blancanales looked down the wide-open space of corridor he believed led to the front desk. It was a hodgepodge of humanity swirling around him in all this glittering acreage, as he searched for his former Black Beret pal. Cowboys and business suits, blue-haired retirees, Japanese and German tour groups, giddy on the high alone of being in Vegas. James Bond pretenders in tuxedos marched for the gaming pits with drink in hand and well-heeled women on the arm, often in lockstep beside the Bermuda shorts, espresso and sandals crowd. All told, it was a melting pot of class, culture and attire, clear the bottom line was the size of bankrolls and not wardrobe.

And there he came, a rolling neon sign spouting a smoke stack that fairly parted the sea of humanity. Blancanales noticed a little extra bounce in the white-shoed step, but couldn't be certain if that meant good news in their quest or the first of many double whiskeys to mark the new day in a town that never slept.

Sad, he thought, recalling a young soldier, an eighteen-year-old kid scared to death like the rest of them back then, but finding the warrior stuff it took to fight and survive, as compared to what he saw now, a lifetime later down the winding road of life. Where it went wrong for Eddie he couldn't say, but he was a full-blown alcoholic now, teetering on the edge of self-evisceration. It might have started with that "Dear Eddie" letter from his high-school sweetheart who wrote to tell him she was marrying his best friend while he was knee-deep in blood, leeches and rats, as worried as hell when Charlie might come screaming out of the jungle any second, AK blazing. Or it could have begun with something far more insidious, far uglier that scarred the souls of a lot of men from that war.

For whatever the reasons Parker's life had clearly gone into the toilet. Between two divorces, getting "retired" from the Chicago police force, he had then relocated to North Dakota. There, supposedly, he'd run his own private investigation agency—Parker Probes—claiming he drummed up most of his business using his own Web site on the Internet, but alluded to some trouble with Uncle Sam, and Blancanales could add two and two on that score. As for the current client in question, Parker told him she was a lonely lady friend whose husband was a philandering "bigshot rocket geek," as his buddy so stated with all the compassion of a hovering buzzard licking its beak while its meal breathed its last.

This was only the second time he'd seen Parker since the end of the war, though they'd kept in touch over the years via the phone. They did their nostalgia thing at the Wall the first time they'd gotten together, but hashing over war stories wasn't a priority, then or now, and for that Blancanales was grateful. Not only did war stories in his experience require an extra-large shovel with each retelling, but what they did when they were Black Berets would have put a whole new spin on what a messed-up, murderous fiasco that war was, lending credence to the outrage of the liberal crowd who didn't go but had been out there on the protest front lines. There were memories, granted, and Blancanales heard the ghosts on the verge of howling to life as he watched Parker close on his roost. The Black Berets, by and large, had been an assassination and sabotage arm of the CIA, and not even the Company wanted to know they existed. A lot of nasty behind-the-lines action, sometimes deep into Laos or Cambodia to hunt down Vietcong officers, often using torture, sometimes razing villages…

The ghosts were best left in the past, he decided. For

him, there was always another war. For Eddie? Well, he wondered if Eddie hadn't brought the memories home, using the mistakes of the past—distant and more recent—as a crutch.

Whatever the case, as Parker beamed and puffed, Blancanales wrestled with a decision, dubious to the point of despondency they'd find the man if they stuck to his buddy's game plan. Which was to troll the casinos, staking out the pits, dropping a few bucks, here and there, just to pry the suspicious eyes of security off them long enough so they could move on to the next happy gaming ground in one piece. As for security misadventures in the event of a Parker or quarry-related problems, Blancanales had his bogus Justice Department credentials stating he was Special Agent Ray Blanco, which meant he was authorized to carry the Beretta 92-F in shoulder holster beneath his black windbreaker. As for Parker's .357 Magnum pistol, well, he claimed he was licensed in the state of Nevada to carry a concealed weapon.

If not for the Farm informing him that his jaunt to Vegas was, on the surface, turning out to be more than some freak coincidence, he would bail right then, friend or not.

A noseful of whiskey fumes, Parker then streamed a halo of smoke around his head, a winning smile on his blotchy, swollen face. "He's here." Blancanales felt his jaw go slack, Parker's grin widening as he added, "That's right, so you can lose the constipated look. How did I do it, you ask? Good old-fashioned detective work. You see, before you start a gig, you need to ask the right questions, you've got to know your man in other words, but this comes from years of doing this. See, I knew his favorite hangouts coming in, his fair wife having shown me past credit card receipts for starters. Yesterday, we stake out at Harrah's, Caesar's, the Mandalay, Bally's. Struck out, yeah, I know, and I maybe ran up the expense account a little on drinks and at the craps table, but you've gotta keep the faith. Rocket Man's here." The grin holding, Parker raised a clenched fist and shook it. "It's all in the karma, the attitude. You gotta believe in yourself."

Blancanales shook his head, chuckling. "You call blowing eight hundred bucks on dice and whiskey a little padding of the expense account?" Blancanales said, fairly certain Parker believed squandering someone else's hard-earned money on drinks and gambling could be written off, possibly even for reimbursement by Big Uncle.

"Come's with the job, lighten up, will ya? We're in Vegas, Sin City, might as well live a little while we're working. Hey, I'm getting five hundred a day plus expenses and I offered to cut you in, but you shot me down. And this is a milk run. Once more, you sure you don't want in for half?"

"One more time, Eddie. I'm doing this…"

"Yeah, yeah, I know, as a favor. But you might want to rethink all this Good Samaritan nonsense. The old lady's going to be loaded when I serve this joker papers of notice of divorce. Payday, a fat one. You could be in, easy money…"

Blancanales scowled. "Eddie."

"Okay, okay. Back to my 'Sherlock' routine. The old man, I knew where to look, he's a mid-Strip clown, good buddy, I already know this from the missus, see. The Bellagio was my—our—next obvious pitstop."

"Let me guess. You showed his picture at the front desk, made a bunch of noise?"

Parker frowned. "You make that sound decidedly unprofessional."

"But that's what you did?"

"Okay, that's what I did. But the kid's eyes, hell, they were like neon lights I mention the name, show him the picture. And I snuck a look back and he was on the phone no sooner I was walking away, lighting up another smoke."

"Unbelievable."

"What is?"

"As for professionals, Eddie, remember you telling me how your lady friend was paid a visit in the middle of the night by some very scary-looking men in black habits and military buzz cuts and that she was positive were all carrying weapons and all this right before Rocket Man blasts off into the black hole? How they spoke to each other in what you told me she told you sounded like Russian?"

"And? What's your point?"

Blancanales sipped his coffee. "I'm thinking, Sherlock, those were Russian spies. Maybe black ops. Trained, cold-blooded killers, probably ex-Spetsnaz or KGB."

Parker chortled around his smoke. "Russian assassins. You've been reading too many Tom Clancy novels."

"Trust me, Eddie, I know something about this. I bet they came to nab this Jacobs character, or offer him outright a bigger salary to come to work for them in the Motherland. Follow me here, before you shoot me down, tell me I'm full of crap. One, I know for a fact he speaks Russian and has lived in Russia, and that he works on cutting-edge black projects."

"And you come by this wisdom, how?"

Blancanales kept his cool, aware his friend had no idea of who he worked for, what he really did, how the Farm could gather information on anything and anybody that few in the world could access. "Didn't we discuss this last night in between your sucking down a fifth of Jack Daniel's and snoring loud enough to have me levitating off the bed?"

"Refresh my memory. And when did you get to be such a smart-ass?"

Blancanales heaved a breath. "This guy's either a high roller or is dying to be one. He's a gambler, that's a sickness like any other vice that takes control of a man's every breath."

"How come I hear a note of criticism in that?"

"Listen to me. If he's here, I'd wager the money you're getting for your so-called milk run, he is being sat on, even courted by Russians. He's turned, gone to the other side, they more than likely used his gambling addiction to reel him in. Worse, whatever classified project he was working on back in North Dakota, the people he left eating his dust are none too happy. They, too, are trained pros. Which means they know his habits. They know where to look. They want to find him, they will. Which means I expect pros to show up, if, in fact, he's here in town."

Parker looked grim, then put on a brave face. "Which translates into what?"

"Trouble. Which means we might get thrust right into the middle of a high-stakes game. A shooting war sort of game where the only winner is the one left standing."

"You really know how to put a damper on a man's hopes and dreams, you know that."

"Just trying to be realistic. Before you—and me— get into something from which there could be no turning back."

"Damn."

"You can say that again."

"Well, all this prophecy of gloom and doom has made me thirsty. Let's go find a bar or one of those little chippies walking around with a tray."

Shaking his head, Blancanales was deciding to hang in there one more day, two tops, falling into the slipstream of Eddie's nicotine afterburner, when he spotted them. One look at the grim quartet rolling for the intercept and Blancanales knew the cavalry had arrived.

"You two. Stop."

"Who the hell are you clowns?" Parker retorted.

The foursome fanned out, Blancanales noting they moved with purpose, forming a tight circle, human sharks blocking them in. Professionals, no question, Blancanales reading the hard looks behind the sunglasses of combat or predatory men who had come under fire more than once. And they looked itchy to reach for the bulges beneath their black jackets. As for Parker, the Able Team commando noted the look and tone of war footing, hoping his friend didn't start shooting off his mouth.

"Lose the cigarette, Comrade White Shoes, and follow us."

The one sounding off the orders had a slight accent, but Blancanales was taking no pleasure in being right about Russians, sensing a turn coming for the worse. It did, when Parker gave the Barking One a look, wreathing his face with smoke. Blancanales groaned when his friend added, "No problem, pal. Open your mouth and say, 'Aa-ah.'"

The goon on Parker's right flank ripped the cigarette away and tossed it on the marbled floor.

"Hey, assholes, my friend here is a special agent with the United States Department of…"

Blancanales saw it coming, let it play out. Sometimes, he figured, letting the worst course of action unfold—in this instance taking it on the chin—could open doors the opposition wanted to stay closed. The grim question he asked himself, as a Russian goon buried a fist deep in Parker's gut, doubling him over, and he was staring down the barrel of a Makarov pistol was, Would the two of them live through the next hour?

"We will explain on the way, my curious comrades," the Barking One said, snatching Parker by the shoulder. "I will take your vehicle, assuming it is close by."

Blancanales decided to brazen it out. "You damn well better hope you can explain," he quipped as the coffee cup was slapped out of his hand and he was relieved of his side arm.

"By the way, I love the white shoes, my curious comrade."

"Up yours," Parker wheezed as he was manhandled ahead.

LYONS FOUND they landed in a vast, space-age complex, after what he guessed was a three-story drop down the elevator that first required retinal scan, voice and fingerprint analysis followed by an access code punched into a keypad. That, he knew, ended the possibility for a return trip for some late-night intrusion. Not even Schwarz, with all his technical expertise and gizmos, would be able to crack that nut.

Hemmed front and back by two HK-subgun-wielding guards in black helmets with visors, they were marched down a corridor so white it hurt the eyes, but something told Lyons there was a reason for the supernatural effect, though he'd be damned if he could figure it out. Oddly enough, considering the ultra-classified nature of black ops compounds, they had been allowed to keep their side arms after an inspection of their credentials up top, followed by an escort call to an undetermined individual. Where they had taken Rupert, he couldn't say, and their two automatons didn't seemed inclined to answer any questions.

As they passed the thick bubbled glass overlooking a massive hangar, he slowed the pace. He couldn't even begin to count the work personnel, but rough-guessed it in the neighborhood of a hundred-plus bodies as he panned left to right. There were two big Stealth fighters that appeared to float on fat girder-like objects he believed were called spars. There were wings, tails and dark bubbles he figured for cockpits hung on more girders. He spotted a wind tunnel, a flight simulator in one corner. In the opposite corner was a sprawling network of computer bays. But the question he was eager to ask whoever the Eagle Nebula commander was, Why, if they were working on Stealths, did everyone down below require the cumbersome shells of hazmat suits, no exceptions? According to the Farm, the work force here was handling radioactive material meant to shoot Lightning Bat to super Mach speed. If that was the case, why then were there no stacks up top to release the heat generated by nuclear reactors? Say, though, they had created a scaled-down version of a reactor, did the waste simply get dumped in the grasslands or the Badlands?

"Let's pick up the pace, chief. This isn't some sight-seeing tour."

Lyons tossed the rearguard a look, thinking he'd been taking crap off guys since landing in the state, first Rupert and now the robot. He was on the verge of making a statement the Ironman way, when he heard air hiss, saw a door slide open to his left flank. The point man stood by the door, bobbing his insect head they should enter.

Inside, Schwarz on his right wing, he found what looked like a small office, Spartan except for a couch, desk and a computer station. The doors were hissing shut behind, and Lyons found they were alone with a man who was frantically downloading information of some type from his laptop, eyes locked on the monitor.

"The cup."

Lyons wasn't sure he'd heard Schwarz's tight-lipped muttering correctly, until he turned and watched his Able Team comrade mouth the words. He knew what Schwarz wanted now, found it crazy enough to suit him. More than likely they would be treated with all due contempt, sent packing ASAP, never learning a damn thing anyway. And the computer man looked desperate enough to cuff and stuff for nerves alone. Whatever was on the CD-ROM figured to answer most, if not all, questions.

The steam rising from the oversize cup told Lyons there was enough hot lava to do the dirty deed. "And you might be?" Lyons queried, gathering momentum; found his timing couldn't have been any better as whatever was being downloaded was saved, the screen going blank.

Lyons thrust his hand up, bowling the cup in the direction of his target. The desired effect was instant, Lyons sure the computer whiz would draw his side arm and shoot him on the spot as the superheated puddle landed in his lap.

Bull's-eye.

"You stupid son of a bitch!" he shrieked, flying back from his swivel chair, slapping at his crotch and hurling more expletives.

"Hey, sorry about that, pal," Lyons said, though choked down the chuckle when he spotted tears of rage and agony pooling in the bugged eyes, the man hopping around, showing off creative variations for the F-word. "Hey, I said I was sorry. Accidents happen. Let me get you a towel and help you with that," he added, the man looking at him as if he was stone-cold insane. "I hope you don't have any lady friends on your dance card tonight. That looks like it hurts."

That unleashed another round of berserker cursing. As the man danced and screamed, then fired up a cigarette, apparently in hopes of killing his pain, Lyons looked over his shoulder, found Schwarz easing away from the laptop with attached modem, throwing him a curt nod.

"I'm Special Agent Carl Lincoln and this is—"

"I know who you are, goddammit! And if you think you can just waltz onto restricted United States military property and start snooping around—and I don't give a damn if you have a presidential directive or not—I will personally rip your balls off and feed them to some rancher's horse! You violated about ten laws already that I could have you arrested for and detained! You breached restricted airspace, which, in case you want to know, I could have ordered you shot out of the sky! And if you think I'm going to stand here and tell you, A to Z, what is going on in this facility, you're more stupid than you are a clumsy fucking oaf!"

Lyons stepped up, put an edge in his voice. "You finished?"

He got himself just barely under control, smoking with a fury and clouding up half the room.

"You got a name?"

"Orion, that's who I am to you."

"I see the white star on your chest as opposed to those billowy clouds with stars for emblems that the others wear."

"Pillars of Creation. That's the Eagle Nebula. And this star means I created the universe here as you see it."

"Sounds like your world already crashed."

"What?" he snarled, Lyons sensing he'd touched a nerve.

"Something went wrong out here last night, Mr. Orion. There are reports of civilian casualties, of a cover-up, of, in general, a clusterfuck that, if true, you will be held accountable for."

Orion took a few moments, smoking, gathering his composure. "First of all, the situation is under control. Yes, there was an accident involving an experimental aircraft. There was some property damage, but any rumors of civilian casualties have no foundation."

"Then you wouldn't mind if we go talk to the natives?"

"Do whatever you feel you have to do. The worst of what you'll find is that anyone whose property was damaged will be amply compensated by the government."

Lyons could sense Schwarz in a hurry to leave, before Orion finally doused the fire in his crotch and stepped up to his computer to discover the theft. "In that case, we'll have a look around the areas in question, call Washington and see how they wish to proceed. And our pilot?"

"He's being questioned."

"And why is that?"

"Because that's the way it's going to be done."

Lyons cocked a mean smile. "I want him released when we walk out of here. And you will not confiscate his plane. Or I will fly in the biggest damn armada of gunships, with more Justice Department, FBI agents that you won't have enough hardware to kill them all until you are cuffed, stuffed by yours truly and shipped pronto to Leavenworth where you will vanish for the rest of your natural life, sans memoirs, sans movie deal, maybe sans personal pride and respect, if you get my drift."

Orion seemed to soften his tone, bobbing his head. "This is how it is, Agent Lincoln. Since he breached restricted airspace, we are running a background check on him. We will uncover every skeleton in his closet, we'll know when and how often he even takes a dump. If he is not a licensed pilot, and I somehow don't think that old whiskey head is, we will make sure he understands he is not to fly within ten miles, around the compass of this facility. If he chooses to disobey, if he gives me any crap at all…it looks like the three of you are walking back to his airfield."

"That's how it's going to be, huh?"

"You can leave here anytime."

"No guided tour?" Schwarz piped up.

"Not unless I have a directive from my superiors at the Pentagon, then the Department of Defense, who in turn will have to get permission from the President of the United States. That could take some time, hell, it could take months, you know how the wheels of bureaucracy turn in Washington."

Lyons had seen and heard enough. "You want to let us out of here?"

"The door has a sensor."

"Have a nice day. We'll be in touch. So, you might want to have someone give us a number, radio frequency, something."

"How about I call you about that tomorrow? You have a cell phone I assume?"

Lyons rattled off the number, then wheeled and headed out the door. He could feel Schwarz holding his breath, worried himself an alarm would start blaring any second, guards swarming over them, shoot to kill. With any luck, Lyons believed Mr. Orion would be more concerned about checking his groin for third-degree burns and easing the pain than his computer, long enough for them to fly off the grounds.

"That went real well," Schwarz muttered.

Lyons picked up the pace as the two guards materialized to his right and pointed the way. "Better than I expected, actually. Nothing else, I got to let off some much-earned steam."

"Stay as you are, Agent Lincoln, don't ever change or it would break my little heart."

"You don't have to worry about all that nonsense."

BLANCANALES HOPED for the best, but somehow feared the worst. He always knew, as a Stony Man warrior who put it all on the line every time he stepped into battle, a bloody, violent end was the only guarantee he could expect. That was fine, no problem going down, toe-to-toe in combat.

Acceptable, if that's how it had to be.

Being executed, though, left gall in his mouth, a gut clenching with hate and anger, a bitter torment he was being cheated a warrior's due.

They were driving south on I-15, far away from all the neon and bright lights and swarming humanity of Sin City, the Able Team commando sandwiched between two Russian goons in the back seat of the sedan. Blancanales was certain two lives were minutes away from being snuffed and dumped in the bleak Nevada desert to join the ranks of God only knew how many mobsters, cheats and big losers who couldn't ante up and had been executed out here to never be heard from again. With tension coiling his whole body, he felt the muzzles of their Makarovs digging into his ribs when he breathed, his heart jackhammering in his chest, as he weighed his options.

Slim to none.

Two more Russians had joined the foursome on the way to Parker's car, a picture of his friend sweating out the toxins framed to mind, as he was likewise hemmed in between another pair of goons in the back seat of a beaten-up, rust bucket Camaro convertible that had seen its best days a quarter century ago. Much like his friend, he compared, but hoped the old warrior spirit still lived in his heart, aware he, at least, would go for broke before he stood his ground and took a bullet through the brain.

"Do not even think about lunging for one of us," Blancanales heard the hardman on his left warn, the muzzle jabbing deeper into his ribs as they began jouncing down a dirt strip, heading deeper into the desert where no eyes could watch from the interstate.

And the lunar hills, Blancanales decided, looked as dark as his mood felt. Another half mile or so, eating the Camaro's dust, and they jerked to a stop. As the door opened, the Russian hitter sliding out and hauling him along by the shoulder, he saw Parker spill from the Camaro. The Barking One kicked him a couple of beauties in the ribs. Two goons grabbed his friend by the shoulders, lifted him off the ground, spun him like a top and smashed his face through the driver's window. Apparently one battering ram facial wasn't good enough, as they hauled Parker back and drove his face into the door with a resounding thud, the Camaro shuddering on its chassis, blood spraying to the dirt.

Blancanales had seen enough. A few more times using his friend like a rubber ball off the Camaro and they wouldn't need to shoot him. And despite the warning, he was ready to spring on one of the hardmen, go for the fences or strike out.

Hearing Parker wheeze and groan into his act about serving Jacobs with notice of divorce, Blancanales felt the barrel of the Makarov slam over the back of his head. He was hitting his knees when the kick to the jaw laid him out on his back, the blue sky doing a funny ballet dance in his eyes. Somehow he rolled onto his side without getting another wingtip to the jaw when he saw the Barking One rip the papers from Parker's jacket.

"You must think you are clever, my comrade with the cheap white shoes and the smart mouth," the Barking One growled, two of his goons holding Parker up, one of them unable to resist driving a shot into his breadbasket, which Blancanales was sure would bring up some of his friend's spleen or leave him pissing blood for a month, assuming he lived. Then the Russian tore the papers, shoving them into Parker's mouth, one of the goons laughing as he clamped a hand around the throat to keep the choke hole open.

Blancanales was rising to one knee, skull chiming, fear and adrenaline launching him at the nearest goon, his fist shooting up with a terrible life of its own, piledriving into a sac. The goon sang out like a million and one slot machines, Blancanales hoping to hell he'd just crushed the family jewels to dust, certain he would be shot before he reached the Makarov dumped at the shrieker's dancing feet, but if this was it...

His hand was inches from grabbing up the weapon when the kick speared him deep in the gut, flipping him onto his side.

"Move again, I shoot you!" he heard the other Russian shout, but found he was concentrating more at sucking wind back into starved lungs than paying much attention to threats. "Justice agent or whoever, I do not give damn!"

He took a shot of spit to the face as they both stepped out of range. Blancanales glimpsed the Russian holding himself, all bared teeth and wincing feral hate and rage, sure he was going to get one through the brain anyway, then it dawned on him what was going to happen. A beating, a warning, brutally plain and simple, but as to why, he could only venture a guess. It was because he carried a badge. Maybe ship him back as their punished and humiliated trophy to other Justice agents they feared were looking for Rocket Man. Impossible to read the moment with much certainty. And there was hope still they would simply read Parker the riot act, send him on his way to the nearest emergency room.

"The wife will get no divorce, because our special guest, Comrade Doctor, will be leaving America forever in three more days. No divorce, no money for her. Life is tough like that, but extend her my sincerest apologies when you go and try to collect your fee for your abysmal failure. Should you attempt to find him again in one of the casinos, I will bring you both back here and shred you like divorce papers you are eating, my good comrade with the cheap white shoes."

Blancanales watched as the goons jacked Parker to his feet, bounced his face off the hood then tossed him clear to the other side, the laughing hyena making a grand gesture of washing his hands of the problem. Blancanales flinched at the first pistol shot, but found the Barking One emptying rounds into the portside tires, then blasting out the windshield before he finished off the floor show with a round through the radiator.

"You, Justice Man."

Blancanales watched the Barking Man roll up, the Makarov low by his side. If he could just get his hands on the smug bastard...

"We have full diplomatic immunity against any and all crimes committed on your soil. I could kill you now and get away with it, but I have decided to be charitable and let you live. Return to your comrades and display yourself and your friend, let them see that a beating is as good as it will get if they attempt to find us. Should they think they can arrest us in Las Vegas, there will be much bloodshed. Many innocent people could and would die in that event."

Blancanales found it hard to believe he spoke the truth, but if there were traitors in high places covering for the Russians...

Stranger things had happened in his day.

Blancanales groaned, wobbled to his feet as doors thudded shut and the sedan reversed out of there, spewing dust in his face. Staggering ahead, he called his friend's name, fearing the worst as he rounded the back end, air and steam hissing in his ears.

And Eddie Parker chuckled through his punishment, struggling to lift himself before slumping against the wheel. He shook glass out of his hair, grimacing as he pulled a sliver out of his cheek, let the blood flow off his battered chin. "Is this where you say, 'I told you so'?"

Blancanales bent over his friend, checking his injuries, hoping as bad as he looked...

"Eddie, we need to get you to a hospital. You could have a gasket set to blow in your brain."

"No way. A couple shots and I'll be good as new." He groaned, spit a glass sliver off his lip and said, "So much for the milk run, huh, good buddy. Now what?"

Blancanales gave that a long moment's grim thought, feeling every muscle and joint aching and throbbing, scalp to toes, as he turned and watched the sedan vanish down the trail. "Now, Eddie...now we do it my way."

CHAPTER SIX

Hal Brognola listened to the sitrep as Lyons snarled, loud, crystal-clear and angry enough to chew uranium-depleted bullets, over the Computer Room's intercom-linked satellite relay. Apparently their reception at Eagle Nebula had been less than friendly—no real surprise there, Brognola thought—Lyons quickly filling in the details how Schwarz purloined the CD. The encrypted data was now being shot at light speed from Schwarz's computer to Kurtzman's, likewise Tokaido having access through some new modem link. Brognola knew better than to ask how it worked, unless he dared to endure thirty minutes of jargon that would leave him reeling and inhaling a pack of Rolaids. Listening while Lyons finished his report, growling how he wanted to go back and kick some heavy ass—since they were threatened to not fly over any area cordoned off by guards, thus handcuffed from grilling the local population—Brognola chewed on a cigar. He scanned the faces of Price, Kurtzman, Tokaido, Carmen Delahunt and Hunt Wethers. All grim, all steely business and, like himself, he was sure they were wondering how to proceed.

However it shook out on Lyons's end, Brognola suspected it was going to go very badly for someone from there on. Carl Lyons had no problem stomping all over toes, official or otherwise, bulldozing walls, generally making himself a human typhoon pain in the ass.

Well, Brognola thought, that's why he'd sent him to Eagle Nebula in the first place.

"It's an alphanumeric encryption, Carl," Kurtzman said. "Pretty basic by DOD standards, but with a few wrinkles I've never seen before. Akira and myself will be able to break it, but I think we'll need, say, two hours tops. Give or take."

"I would strongly urge haste, Bear, if you consider this Orion character will probably make a move on us when his crotch cools off and he finds his precious data was lifted under his tirade. In other words, we're sitting ducks here at Badlands Tours."

"Understood…hold on. I'm starting to piece together bits and snatches of the puzzle already."

Brognola stepped closer to Kurtzman's workstation as Price, com link on, moved up to where Delahunt and Wethers were monitoring the Phoenix Force front in eastern Iraq via satellite imagery from an NRO spy eyes parked in space thanks to Emerald Base Zero. As of yet, no action there, he knew, but Phoenix-Tiger had established themselves, with the help of a presidential directive, to be granted all cooperation and consideration from the commander of Base Leviathan, a Coalition Forces compound east of Baghdad. Presently, as he tuned in to the mission controller's side of the conversation, David McCarter, the leader of Phoenix Force and Jim Block who commanded Tiger Ops, were grilling two Iranian prisoners. Solid intelligence, he knew, was more often than not the key to opening the door to victory in battle. From the sound of it, the prisoners had—or claimed to have—information on the current whereabouts of Rafiq Namak. What they needed over there, Brognola knew, was actionable intelligence before they brought out the heavy artillery. Near misses wouldn't cut it on the Iraq-Iran border, one of the most dangerous places on earth where western faces didn't last long unless they were willing and able to go the distance.

"Carl," Kurtzman said, "it looks like this Orion has his attention turned toward Las Vegas. For how long he's been looking that way, or what his plans…"

"Vegas, again," Lyons rasped. "I hope my good friend is having a nice time out there."

"He's dropped off the radar screen, Carl," Brognola said. "We've tried to contact him, but no luck."

"Maybe he met a showgirl. I know he's not one to piss money away on games of chance where the odds are all stacked with the house. Unless he's become a card counter in his downtime I wasn't aware of."

"Somehow, I doubt that," Brognola huffed, aware Carl "Ironman" Lyons was geared up to kick down some doors. But he wasn't in the mood for verbal sparring with the former Los Angeles detective. Pieces of the puzzle were trying to fit and the big Fed could feel some critical mass building, but they needed time in the Computer Room to come up with some answers, leads, anything that would clue them in to the opposition's agenda. And time, Brognola feared, seemed to be on the enemy's side right now.

"Okay, then what? Saying that maybe he and this PI pal of his actually found the AWOL genius?"

"Or it could be," Brognola told the Able Team leader, "someone found them looking for Jacobs. It disturbs me, what with us knowing Eagle Nebula is so classified it doesn't show up anywhere in our search of intelligence and military mainframes. Let's call them the black hole of spookdom, but somebody has obviously cut them a blank check and wants this outfit buried deep, and even from the light of Capitol Hill scrutiny. To me, it all smells of some high rollers at either the Pentagon, DOD, the NSA or whoever's umbrella they fall under and who has, off the books, made them the Alpha and the Omega of classified projects involving cutting-edge technology that we're only now just getting a peak at, but don't have a clue as to how it works. We think it shouldn't work, only we know it does."

"This Lightning Bat, the mother of all fighter jets."

"And other weapons or weapons systems they may have on tap. Okay, so Jacobs has flown from the Eagle Nebula nest, and as such he took with him invaluable information that can be sold to this country's enemies. And this head spook, Orion? You can believe he wants his superstar back on the team…or else."

"You're implying a hunting expedition was shipped out from Eagle Nebula? That Pol may be hung out there on his own against black ops gunslingers who have a license to kill?"

Brognola went to the coffeepot, his gut churning

with tension. "That's exactly what I'm thinking. But I want you to sit tight until we hear from Pol."

"And if Orion shows up here with a goon squad asking about his CD?"

"Lie to him," Brognola said. "See how he handles himself knowing full well you and Gadgets are the thieves."

"You're the boss," Lyons said. "We'll just sit here in limbo for the time being, but call back the second you find out what's going on with Rosario. I've got a bad, sinking feeling about Vegas, Hal, and something tells me Pol needs our help."

"You'll hear the second we know something," Brognola answered, and felt his stomach roll over, somehow concurring with the Able Team leader's dire assessment.

In his experience, the big Fed had learned the hard way no news from the front lines was often bad news.

BLANCANALES TOOK the shards of his secured cell phone from the ripped pocket of his jacket and tossed it on the ground. Score another one for the Russians. Good enough, he determined, there would be another round, even if he had to chase them clear to Moscow or wherever, and may God have mercy on their rotten souls because he sure as hell wasn't about to forgive and forget this drubbing. And if his buddy succumbed to his injuries...

Keep going, he told himself, one foot in front of the other. Focus. Swallow the pain and anger, use it for fuel.

There was no point logging the miles they'd trudged—or in Parker's case, limped—across the desert, before hiking up the side of the interstate, eating dust and exhaust fumes half the morning or more. Hitching a ride from a Good Samaritan was obviously out of the question. Considering the shape they were in, even the most compassionate heart, he figured, would have passed them by, what with their clothing nearly shredded off their backs, bloodied and grimy with sweat and dust, head to toe, so he really couldn't blame any motorist who didn't want to get involved. The grueling slog, every yard earned with sweat and pain and raw determination, with the sun rising higher to pound down like the anvil of hell, and Blancanales wasn't sure his pal was going to make it back to civilization.

With Parker's arm draped over his shoulders, Blancanales shuffled them into the parking lot of what looked like a diner. About all he knew was they were south of Vegas, the first line of casinos shimmering in the distance. McCarran International was due east, as the big jets seemed to thunder close enough to rattle his bones, though Blancanales understood that was only a delusion of pain, the buzz of adrenaline and the wardrum of his heart in his ears.

"Hang in there, Eddie. I'll find us a ride back to the Stardust."

"I'm hanging, but who in their right mind," Parker groaned, "would be crazy enough to let us track blood and crap all over their car? Plus, I've already puked twice and I'm afraid number three gusher is coming on."

"For a hundred bucks or so I'm sure they'll overlook it."

"I'm just about broke, Rosario. But you cover it, I

can put it on the expense account, or maybe I call Mrs. Rocket Man, have her wire us a few bucks."

Blancanales was too tired, busted up and angry to argue about how foolish his friend sounded.

"Kinda like the ancient times we shared, huh, Rosario? When you humped me, shot to shit, out of the jungle. About a thousand or so Vietcong chasing us all the way to the Huey... Remember?"

"I remember. We made it then, Eddie, we'll make it now. Hang tough."

Blancanales gritted his teeth against another wave of pain, the ghost of the memory of what was one of the longest, bloodiest and most frightening nights dancing through his mind, howling once, then flying away to its dark tomb, sealed for the moment.

Parker moaned, becoming heavier with each step Blancanales hauled him across the lot, and from the way in which he slurred his last words, he was sure his friend was becoming delirious, certain he was, at best, dehydrated. And if only because Jack Daniel's was the only liquid he ever seemed to put in his system.

A well-heeled couple emerged from the front door. Blancanales was hopeful for all of two eye blinks, about to ask for help, when they took one look at two zombie slabs of raw hamburger and beelined it for their BMW, gone in seconds flat. Worst case, he was thinking he could call a cab, when a cowboy stepped into view. He studied them for a long moment, Blancanales reading something in his eyes, then he whistled a note that struck the Able Team warrior as sympathetic.

"You two need some help?"

"Would appreciate a lift, if it's not too much trouble," Blancanales said. "The Stardust. Up the Strip."

"I know where it is."

"I can pay you."

"Keep your money, friend. Looks like the two of you had a tough enough morning already without some stranger taking your money."

If you only knew the half of it, my Good Samaritan, Blancanales thought, and lugged Parker ahead. He hoped his pal at least had the decency to keep gusher number three on hold, when Eddie piped up, "Say, partner, you wouldn't happen to have a bottle of booze in your car, would you?"

"YOU IN OR OUT, big time?"

"He's out."

Boris Rustov scowled at the boxman, daring him to say otherwise as he took Jacobs by the arm, jacked him hard enough away from the craps table to send the dice bouncing like lethal stones toward the stickman. The Asian whore began squawking loud enough to match the doctor's whining, then one of his men grabbed her elbow and growled into her ear, "Shut your mouth this instant or I will personally throw you out into the street."

"What is the meaning of this!" Jacobs snapped.

When they were out of earshot of the pit boss, Rustov snatched Jacobs to a grinding halt, eliciting a delicious cry of pain from the Israeli swine. He knew he was wearing the face of the perfect Spetsnaz killing machine, Jacobs paralyzed and silent, as meek and humble as he would ever hope to see the man outside of being strapped to a chair with electrodes attached to his balls.

"The meaning, Comrade Doctor, is that you were tracked here to the Bellagio. Ah, I see I have your attention. Now, if you wish to finish your stay in this city, you will move to whatever accommodations I decide upon, even if it is that grind joint you so detest. Or we leave Las Vegas now. Well?"

Jacobs took a long moment deciding his fate, then nodded. "A grind joint it is, if that's what you wish, comrade. May I take Cleopatra with me, however?"

Rustov appreciated the new tone of subservience. "If it will keep you obedient to my wishes, you may."

"I shall be the picture of humility from here on."

"We shall see, Comrade Doctor," Rustov said.

He lifted Jacobs a couple inches or so off his feet, just to make certain he understood how serious he was, then shook and shoved him ahead.

GABRIEL HORN WANTED to smash the computer on the floor, stomp it into a million pieces. Instead of launching into a pointless tantrum, he chuckled. He should have seen the ploy for what it was, but the pain had blinded him, nearly driven him to his knees, and even long after the two supposed Justice agents had left the grounds. Smart, though, the big one, Lincoln, playing the clumsy fool, while he hopped around, shrieking like a banshee, certain his sac had all but been burned off.

And he had let them just waltz out of the most secure installation on the planet with information so devastating…

There would be one attempt at the sort of damage control his operatives had undertaken with a few of the more outraged citizens of Slope County, but he was already looking beyond North Dakota. What he had done here would never be excused, rationalized, justified, much less forgiven, if the light shone through the darkness he had spread over the grasslands. He had murdered the rancher by his own hand, could assuage his guilty conscience, yes, that he had attempted to make the man see reason, but he had also ordered the executions of at least a dozen American citizens. Whatever remains were uncovered from the Indian reservation, the town and both ranches, whatever civilians his men had outright executed, were loaded into choppers, brought back to base where they were tossed into the grinder-incinerator, the ashes then taken and spread over the Badlands.

All in the name of national security.

Not to mention his own.

It was no secret to him that this was not the first time American civilians had been executed because they had trespassed on restricted military areas cordoned off, clearly marked with the warning that lethal force was authorized by the United States government on intruders. Somehow his situation seemed grotesquely different—thanks in no small part to the media sharks—even though he had been sanctioned by the shadow movers and shakers who actually ran the nation, dictated the future of not only the country, but could decide the fate of the world. The President of the United States, he knew, was little more than a figurehead, a puppet, in truth, jerked, albeit in ignorance, on the strings held by the shadow government. And there was more than one shadow in supreme authority who not only had the access codes, but fingers poised on the buttons of multiple mega tonnage thermonuclear…

But what rational, honest, voting, patriotic citizen, he thought, could ever believe that was the truth and nothing but?

Yes, he could stand up in front of some Senate committee and shout how the catastrophic test run wasn't his fault, but part of his job description from the start had been to clean up messes, no matter what they were, what the circumstances. And there was no textbook in his world that stated in no uncertain terms how that was to be achieved.

Just get it done.

The pneumatic hiss alerted him that Grogen had arrived. While his second in command stood at attention, he lit a cigarette, rocking in his swivel chair. For a moment he pondered the future he had helped set in motion long ago. Had it not been for the failed test run, the wholesale destruction of public and private property, the top brains of the Eagle Nebula program selling out to the Russians, he could have funneled more merchandise through the pipeline. It galled him now that fate had thrown him a bean ball that would cut the profit margin by perhaps a third or more.

Well, it looked time to grab the bull by the horns, see what happened.

"We're bailing."

"Sir?"

"I want you to round up Alpha Squad," Horn said, putting an edge to his voice that should leave no doubt. "I'll give you further orders once they're assembled."

"Sir, but Colonel Jeffreys…"

"He'll be but a bad memory in a few minutes. You do understand what's happened?"

"Yes, sir."

"You do understand that if we do not correct the situation we may lose our entire investment with our Middle East people?"

"I do, sir."

"Then what are you waiting for? Carry on."

He barely heard the "Aye-aye, sir," as he turned toward the computer, fighting off the onslaught of depression, a feeling that would leave him thinking he was the loneliest SOB under the stars. Even if they cracked the encryption, it would do them little good. They could march in a battalion of law enforcement, shut the place down, for all he cared.

It didn't matter.

He was already gone.

"EDDIE, I REALLY WISH to God you'd let me take you to a hospital."

"No. I either make it, or I don't. I been through worse shit than what those Russians laid on me, and you know it. So don't talk to me about any hospital again."

"Suit yourself."

"I will. And besides, I still got a job to do."

Shaking his head, Blancanales watched his friend sprawl out on the bed, Parker taking a deep pull from a fresh bottle of whiskey, of which he seemed to have an endless supply of in his duffel bags. He had no time to play mother hen, went and squatted over his war bag. It was tamperproof, wired to unleash two canisters of acid that would melt its contents to a puddle of molten slop within seconds if it was opened by hands other than his own. As he pulled the small black box out of his jacket pocket, thumbed the button, the red light flashed on.

Score one for the good guys.

He disengaged the canisters, unzipped the bag. Delving beside the heavy artillery, he pulled out the sat phone. He could have gone down to the Stardust's lobby to place the call to the Farm for complete privacy's sake, but Blancanales didn't think Parker was going to last another few minutes. If his friend was going to die, he would rather he didn't die alone, though that, in and of itself, was a strange concept.

Everyone died alone.

"You want some music?" he asked, if only to muffle the sound of his own voice.

Parker choked down another swallow, coughed. "That'd be nice. My Sheryl Crow's greatest hits should already be in the box. Punch number eleven."

"Oh, Eddie," he said, but did as he asked.

"Oh, Eddie, what? I'm a sad sorry sack of shit? Maybe I am. Fuck 'em. Fuck 'em all."

Blancanales looked at his friend for a long moment, the strangest, saddest thought dancing through his mind that maybe Eddie Parker would, in fact, be better off dead. "I have to make a call."

"You're excused."

"Hey, don't get an attitude with me, or I'll walk out the door."

"Sorry. Go make your call."

"Thank you."

Blancanales went into the bathroom, shut the door. He punched in a series of numbers that would secure the line, waited until the automatic scrambler kicked in, and hit SEND. Moments later, the beep told him he'd connected.

"It's me," he said, knowing the Farm had a voice analysis box hooked on their end of the transmission.

A few moments later Hal Brognola said, "We've been worried about you.

"And with good reason, as it turns out."

LYONS NEARLY ERUPTED when Brognola confirmed his worst suspicions about Blancanales being on the firing line and against some long odds.

They were in the Gulfstream's cabin, Schwarz at his computer console, receiving the decoded data, both on his screen and over his com link, from Kurtzman and Tokaido. One ear tuned in, Lyons listened to Schwarz jabbering back and forth with the cyberwizards, and the Able Team leader stole a moment to give those two an invisible salute. They had cracked most of Orion's Sphinx Riddle in record time. That was the good news. The rest of the intel rolling in indicated they were in for the fight of their lives, up against both the supposed good guys and some unknown Russian hitters.

"We need to get out there, Hal, forget Eagle Nebula. We'll never get back in there anyway. And the murdering sons of bitches who are in charge of the place are, or have already got a hit squad on the move for Pol and this private dick buddy of his." Lyons stormed, aft to cockpit hatch, felt as if he was two inches off the carpet as adrenaline burned through him like wildfire, the sat phone shaking in his fist. "Now you're telling me the Russian Mafia or Spetsnaz is sitting on the genius, kicked the crap out of Pol and his Nam buddy, claim full diplomatic immunity even if they kill cops and the ballsy vodka-swilling Russki SOBs actually told him they were sticking around Vegas as if daring him to take a swing back at them. Unbelievable, this is unfu—"

"Are you finished?"

"Finished? I haven't even started to fight."

"Settle down and listen."

"I'm listening."

"It's already taken care of. Get in the air as soon as you can. Vegas is still one of the crime meccas of the country, despite all the nonsense they try to peddle the Mob no longer owns the town. The Justice Department can land a classified flight at McCarran anytime it wants. You're cleared. Gadgets will be given the authorization code to pass on to your pilot."

Lyons listened as Brognola laid out some more details, logistics and such. Then Lyons heard Brognola's own dark suspicions, which grew out of Orion's CD.

"You're telling me," Lyons said when Brognola wrapped up his brief scenario as he knew the facts, "this Eagle Nebula may be selling the superweapons and weapons systems of the future to Islamic extremists? Maybe even unloading Lightning Bat or the technology to build one?"

"From what Bear and Akira determined, there's a pipeline that's been established but they haven't yet determined where or how the weapons or the technical knowledge is being moved. It would be too risky, assuming there's some honest, God-fearing patriots on the premises, for this Orion to simply fly it right out of Eagle Nebula, but stranger things have happened, and we don't know the end purchasers. They think there's a pipeline through sister offices in both Chicago and Montreal. Like I said, they should know more in another hour or so. We know Orion knows Jacobs is in Vegas. From what Bear tells me, he has a state-of-the-art computer trace network that can scan hotel registries, trace credit cards, and it looks like Jacobs was using a preferred escort service and Orion was also running a scan on their computer."

"I would imagine the last would be an all-cash deal."

"This is the computer-credit-card age, Carl, only street hookers operate all cash."

"I wouldn't know about that."

"Anyway, it seems Jacobs was his to hand over to the Russians for a fat payday."

"Only the Russians decided to cut him out of the deal."

"Given what we know, that's a safe assumption. And, by the way, I have enough, judging from what we have on sat imagery, to shut Eagle Nebula down through the Justice Department."

"So there was a cover-up, with civilian casualties?"

"I have the dirty pictures in my hand to prove it. I have work to do, so get to Vegas."

No sooner had Brognola severed the connection when the pilot called back, "We've got a bogey, gentlemen, coming in fast and hard from the east, about two miles out."

"I wonder who that might be?" Lyons quipped. "Gadgets, say goodbye and grab some artillery.

"I want this bird," he ordered the two-man blacksuit flight crew, "out of harm's way. Run it a good mile out of here but don't take off unless I tell you to." As the pilot copied, the turbofans firing to life, Lyons marched for the war bag.

"Come on, Gadgets, shake a leg. We're not getting spruced up for a night at the titty bar here."

"I'm coming. Hey, and didn't you tell me Hal said to just lie to the man?"

"Forget that. After scalding the good Orion's balls, I don't think he'll be in the mood for conversation," Lyons said, and tossed Schwarz an M-16 with fixed M-203 grenade launcher. "Do not hesitate, if they open fire, to blow that bird the hell out of the sky. And what's your problem anyway?"

"No problem, if you think I have cold feet. I would rather not get bogged down here or blown off this junkyard when Pol's in trouble."

"I agree with that, but I don't think they'll just let us jet on out of here into the sunset knowing we have the disk."

Schwarz caught two clips and two warheads. "And you don't think they're not in contact with other warbirds in the area?"

"Bring 'em on. Just grab a few more 40 mils on the way out the door if you're that worried about it. Listen, these assholes are bad news, traitors to our country. By now they figure we know that." Lyons hauled out his SPAS-12 autoshotgun, hung a bandolier of 12-gauge man-eaters around his shoulders, pocketed three frag grenades.

Schwarz snatched two more 40 mm grenades from the war bag and followed Lyons out the door.

IF HAL BROGNOLA thought about it long enough, it would have ripped his guts apart, might even have shaken his faith in the good fight.

Traitors.

There were few villains he detested more than those who sold out their country, and he didn't give a damn what the reason.

A man chooses a side, sticks with his choice no matter what the challenges, the temptations, the internal conflicts that might have him turn his back and seek what he might think greener pastures on the other side of the tracks. A man chooses a friend, becomes considered a loyal companion through the building of trust and respect, and woe be unto him who betrays that friend. And in the end a man—Everyman—chooses God or the Devil.

Right then, as he slipped the rest of the sat photos and a copy of Orion's disk into the manila envelope, Brognola felt a little sick to his stomach. He gave the computer team a last look. They were hard at it, juggling the action—or the coming and certain firestorms—with professional resolve, skill and determination.

And with honor.

For the moment there was nothing more he could do here, but he had someplace to go in search of possible answers to some dark and troubling realities.

With Price already alerted to his missing time, the big Fed walked out of the Computer Room.

CHAPTER SEVEN

Hermann Schwarz wondered if there was a special clandestine factory not even the Farm could dig up in their cybersearches where the black helicopter was manufactured. There had been numerous reports over the years by civilians claiming to have come into direct contact with the flying beast when they had either wandered by accident or deliberately breached classified military installations. They stated they were descended upon, out of nowhere, by this frightening winged shark, men in black fatigues jumping out—or so the rumors went—faces invisible behind black-visored helmets, HK subguns forcing them off the premises, or else. Area 51 leaped to his mind, first and foremost, but he had personally encountered this armed pterodactyl in black ops compounds other than that infamous Spookland in Nevada. He could never decide if it was a Black Hawk or an Apache, or a little of both, and not that it mattered. With pylons fitted with Hellfire missiles, what he suspected was a 20 mm chain gun in the turret and door gunner manning one mother of an intimidating Gatling gun...

It was a definite major worry, this destroyer of worlds, and it would have to come down first. Or their tickets would be punched before they capped off the first few rounds.

The aircraft graveyard, in his estimation, would either lend them cover and concealment or aid and abet the enemy if they chose to leapfrog from wreck to wreck. How the old-timer had accumulated so many skeletons of Hueys, JetRangers, Piper Cubs, Cessnas, Beechcrafts and other makes and models he couldn't even begin to identify, since they were little more than rusty shells, was beyond him. Then there were wings, rotor blades, half cabins, engine blocks strewed from the old guy's dilapidated shack to the south, clear into the northern prairie. Throw in a dozen or so battered hulls of Chevy pickups, Cadillacs and various and sundry other older model vehicles to the east, and he was looking at a maze of metal and piled tires where either side could lie and wait in ambush, if they chose to do so.

In short order, Schwarz would discover if this dead sea of machines would be a help or a lethal hindrance.

Hunching behind the wing of some long dead and forgotten aircraft, he watched six men in black fatigues and black-visored helmets, armed with HK submachine guns, hurl themselves into the dust storm, roughly a hundred meters east. They broke off in three-man teams, north and south, armed wraiths that melted on a dead run into the first line of ruins.

The black pterodactyl lifting off, Schwarz watched his target as it climbed for a bird's-eye view of the wasteland, then hovered. If the flying Goliath was, in

fact, a bastardized version of the Apache, it would prove
no small feat to bring it down, and he wasn't all that sure
his twenty-first-century slingshot would do the trick.
Four rounds, one of which was an incendiary projectile,
already down the chute, and he knew he would only get
one chance to play David. Mentally he mapped out his
attack strategy, and it hinged on a number of factors, one
of which was a whole lot of luck. Figure the skin was
boron armor, the flying sorcerers in the cockpit sealed
in Kevlar, and he feared the leviathan would simply absorb a 40 mm round, shrug it off as little more than a
mosquito bite and keep on flying.

Or shooting.

Which meant he had to dump the first round or two
into the belly of the beast. Hit the tail rotor next, drive
a missile into the hollow mast, the hub arms linking the
blades…

A voice suddenly boomed from the dragon, "You
two out there! You have exactly ten seconds to throw
down your weapons and hand over the disk!"

Ultimatum time.

And Schwarz couldn't see Lyons just giving up the
goods.

LYONS HAD THE URGE to bellow, "Nuts," but kept his
mouth shut and eyes peeled, ticking off the doomsday
numbers in his head.

Eight, seven…

Hunkered behind the starboard nose of a gutted Jet-
Ranger, he scanned the southeast quad, caught two of
the three hardmen he'd already spotted veering to outflank him, as they lurched between two twin-engine

Cessnas, both tipped over, braced to list on engine blocks, resting on three-quarter broken wings, for whatever the bizarre reason. SPAS-12 cradled and ready to start blasting any second, he scoured the graveyard, panning nine to one o'clock, but no sighting of the odd man out. One shooter left for a charge up the gut, while he trained all attention on the rolling twosome to his right wing? It made sense, or at least that's the call he would have made. Smart money then warned him the other threesome was going for a wide sweep, north by northwest, rolling to lock their half of the pincers down on Schwarz. The last, but certainly least of his grim concerns, was that the crew of the warbird would most certainly have its positions painted on heat sensors. With the foot soldiers tied into the flyboys via com links, it was a grotesque understatement, he knew, to say the two of them had their backs to the wall.

Four, three...

As for simply handing over Orion's disk?

Damned if he did, damned if he didn't.

That in mind, he broke down the side of his standing armor, the massive autoshotgun leading the surge, just as he heard the heavy metal thunder of the Gatling gun erupt, the hull of concealment thudding like a million wardrums against the barrage, the JetRanger shuddering so violently it seemed as if the wrath of the lead tempest alone would tip it over, flatten him. Charging to intercept at least the two hardmen he knew were bringing it on, Lyons hit the tail end, crouching—and got lucky.

Lyons squeezed the autoshotgun's trigger, pealing out a burst of 12-gauge doom at the hardman veering for a Huey, the guy caught out in the open, already spun full his way, his subgun chattering for all of two heart-beats. The distance no greater than ten yards, the Able Team leader caught him flush in the chest, dropped him as if he'd been slammed to ground by a wrecking ball.

One down, but if Schwarz couldn't nail that door gunner...

The world around him seemed to burst apart from the thundering fusillade of the Gatling gun. His senses shattered all to hell, Lyons was panning the skeletons of aircraft, rolling ahead, when he glimpsed the dark blur in the corner of his right eye.

And knew he'd never make it.

Snarling, as fear and adrenaline fused, instinct shouting at him it was over, Lyons was whirling toward his own extinction when the hardman's stomach burst open in a gory detonation of blood and chewed entrails.

And, lo and behold, Lyons found Mr. Badlands Tours standing, tall and proud, behind the fallen eviscerated sack, a smoking pump shotgun in his fists.

"Think you can say my name right from here on, sonny?"

Lyons wanted to shout he owed him a case of Wild Turkey, but Rupert was already in flight, darting behind another twin-engine wreck. The Able Team leader was surprised at how fast the old-timer moved, but there was killing left to be done. Congratulations were on hold, for damn sure, and that was assuming the flying dragon or the hard force didn't finish them all off before the party.

SCHWARZ KNEW the ground troops were coming, but he stole a few critical seconds, holding his position, hop-

ing to get a clean shot at the door gunner who was pounding away at what the Able Team commando knew was Lyons's position to the south.

"Come on, come on, you bastards!" he growled, his angry words swept away by the Gatling's rolling thunder, silently urging the enemy pilots to swing around, just a few more feet to starboard was all he needed.

Finger curled around the trigger of the M-203, he tracked the warbird as it began sailing his way.

Come to Papa Schwarz!

He was gauging the distance, aware he'd have to aim high, factoring in the downbeat of rotor wash when the dragon swung around, opening the window to its fifty-fifty demise.

The blanket of rolling lead ripping through the twin-engine plane but a few yards to his side, shredding fiberglass as if were nothing but paper, Schwarz tapped the M-203's trigger. As the storm hammered down, obliterating the top half of his wing-shield in two eye blinks, he was up and running. Spying the zigzag flight of the missile out of the corner of his eye, he hit the edge of an engine block—and flinched as the belly of the leviathan blossomed in a blinding white firecloud. He figured he was blessed, at least for the moment, by the gods of war, knew the hellbomb had impacted ceiling, belching its fiery payload over the door gunner. If his luck held, that firestorm would puke its way straight into the cockpit, vaporizing the flyboys where they were harnessed.

The door gunner flailing, swathed in flames; he was in swan dive when Schwarz dumped another 40 mm round down the M-203's gullet.

Lyons skidded to an abrupt halt on the fire side of a Piper Cub to watch the sky roiling on fire. He threw Schwarz a mental salute, but the beast was far from slain. The door gunner crunched up on the ground, cooking now in white phosphorous, and Lyons was grateful the Gatling menace at least was erased.

Another fireball punched into flames dancing out the doorway two shakes later, more sound and fury for those flyboys to contend with, if they were even still manning the helm. It was a beautiful sight, Lyons had to admit, the dragon spinning halfway around, trying to beat it out of there, when number three explosion sheared off the tail rotor and four plowed into rotor blade hubs, all but ending it. The dying leviathan thrust into a whirling dervish, Lyons checked his six, then dashed for a Huey, dead ahead, vectoring north to link up with Schwarz.

He reached the nose end of the chopper just as he spotted two hardmen bull-rushing his position, firing subguns on the run. Dropping to a knee, Lyons cannoned off a round, but the 12-gauge decimator scored only the top edge of an engine block, the hardmen flinging themselves to cover beneath a flying shroud of metal and sparks.

Lyons glimpsed the doomed warbird spiraling to the east, slated for a crash-landing he knew would rock the world of all combatants, and worse. Assume a full tank of fuel, Hellfires maybe getting touched off, what with rocket fuel to boot, and he figured the big bang was set to burst on this stretch of North Dakota.

The hardman duo lurched up, triggering long bursts,

oblivious, or so it seemed, to the conflagration to their neighborhood. Rounds spanging off metal, Lyons was throwing himself for deeper cover when the dragonship plowed into earth, unleashing thunder and what he figured would be two or three fireballs of Hindenburg dimensions.

IT WAS ALL coming to a fiery end.

Schwarz was trading 3-round bursts with his adversary when he knew the aircraft cemetery was about to be hit by a volcano of fire and a flying tempest of lethal shrapnel that could well encompass an acre or more. East, the dragon was whirling, engulfed in flames, thirty yards or less behind the enemy who seemed more concerned about something other than the coming firestorm sure to consume him. The hardman kept retreating for the cover of a Beechcraft, snarling out his pain and anger when Schwarz took out a chunk of shoulder, wild return fire snapping lead hornets past his ears. He gave chase for another two or three yards, sighting in on his own dicey salvation—a row of engine blocks—squeezing off another triburst of 5.56 mm lead as the gunner weaved in backpedal, then rolled around to the far side of the aircraft.

And the world beyond his enemy exploded like the wrath of God.

Schwarz hit the deck, covered his head as a series of dirigible-size explosions, sounding to him like the end of the world, tore apart his senses. He rode out the shock waves, the ground seeming to ripple beneath his prone figure. Feeling superheated wind rushing over him, he dared to glimpse the flaming pterodactyls sailing overhead, pounding through skeletal targets to the west, with more comets of debris ripping apart a twin-engine Cessna, stem to stern, as if it was made of nothing more than aluminum foil.

With the sky raining fire and trash, his face feeling as if it had been exposed to the core of the sun itself, he looked up over the engine block and found the Beechcraft little more than a memory.

BEN GROGEN STOLE a second to curse Horn. He recalled the brief—done in rather glib fashion for his money—that his commander had given before shipping them out on what he assured them was a task on par to guaranteed sex from a fifty-dollar hooker. No body armor required. No backup units, maintain radio silence. They were going after two G-Men, standard issue, and an old buzzard who stayed juiced on whiskey around the clock.

Light work. Cakewalk. No sweat.

So where was Horn? he raged to himself, as what felt like half of North Dakota was going up in flames behind him.

Going to Las Vegas.

Whoever the opposition, Grogen, ex-Delta, knew combat men when he saw them. These bastards were no Justice Department agents, as Horn claimed. Not that he gave a damn anymore, since the tide of battle had turned in the opposition's favor, the SOBs wielding firepower no G-Man he knew of packed. One of those so-called standard issues flung himself around the Huey's nose, banged off another round from the mammoth SPAS-12.

Grogen was up, hosing down the Huey's nose with a long burst of HK fire, then glanced at the chopper's open doorway. Blue skies over the prairie showering them with flaming meteors, he stole a critical heartbeat to bark for Paulson to go through the Huey's door. Which meant, hopefully, the SPAS man would retreat south or west, or Paulson would drive him toward the tail.

Where he'd be waiting to wax the not-so-standard-issue.

They broke in a full-bore sprint for the Huey, Grogen veering hard for the tail, HK poised to mow down whatever moved in front of him. Out of the corner of his eye, he saw Paulson bound up through the doorway, vanish—then heard the mighty peal.

And Paulson was flying back out the doorway, HK subgun stuttering a few impotent rounds, a sinkhole the size of a basketball gouged in unprotected chest.

Grogen cursed the standoff. If he didn't know better, he would have sworn Horn had simply marched them all to their deaths.

One on one now, he was thinking, braced to go under the tail, hurl himself to the other side, shooting...

Then he heard the autofire blister the air, a microsecond before he spied a shadow roll up on his blind side, the other G-Man eating him up with his M-16, as he felt hot lead tearing through his ribs.

AFTER A QUICK SWEEP of the hellzone, they confirmed the sixth kill. There was a seventh body, and it belonged to Rupert Baynard.

Lyons stood over the hardman sans right arm below

the shoulder, half of his left thigh nothing but ragged flesh sheared to the bone. No sense checking for a pulse. He then looked at Rupert's empty stare, five holes riddling his chest, shotgun still clutched in one hand. Whoever the old-timer really was, whatever his life had been all about, Lyons would never know, but suddenly found himself wondering. What he'd first seen was a sad, lonely old man, a broken down drunk, a reclusive enigma living out in the middle of nowhere, but he was sure there was more to his story than that. A vet? WWII? Korea, maybe? Did he have children? Was he a widower? Whatever he'd been, Lyons now saw a stand-up act who had saved his bacon.

A warrior.

"Come on, Carl," Schwarz urged quietly. "We need to get the hell out of here before the cavalry arrives."

Lyons nodded. "You know something? I kind of liked the old guy. I really did."

He saw Schwarz flash him a strange look, as if seeing him for the first time, then walked away.

"THEY ARE A PARAMILITARY ARM for classified or black projects. Their recruitment and special training is every bit as classified—Eyes Only—as the projects they guard. They are mostly Special Forces, Delta, with some regular infantry among their ranks, all of them sworn to secrecy and under the threat of death, and they will act to preserve national security, no matter how incredible or atrocious the circumstances. I believe you've seen this before."

Indeed, Hal Brognola had. As a general rule of thumb, the Justice man shied away from direct dealings with spookdom, if at all possible. In his experience, the truth—if it came at all—was a jumbled assortment of fact, speculation, need-to-know and misdirection from Spookland. Spookland too often had its own agenda, and it usually involved a power play where entire countries could be moved around at their whim, like pieces on a chessboard, according to which nation had whatever it was they wanted at the moment.

Tyrannical bedfellows came and went, murderous, oppressive regimes rose and fell according to the interests and the dictates of Spookland, and when it all went to hell—as it had in Iraq—they ran for cover, often dividing the blame between those who had served them on the front lines, while hanging certain politicians out there as public whipping boys. Geopolitics and the Stars and Stripes aside, there was often the money factor tossed into the equation, where a salaried representative of the U.S. government had ready access to slush or "black" funds, ostensibly meant to purchase intelligence, in-country operatives, arms, troops and so forth. Be it oil, narcotics, nuclear proliferation, a so-called "friendly" country's strategic location to an enemy nation state, Spookland was always there to aid and assist, give counsel, break bread. More than once, he'd seen Spookland go for itself.

Spookland was not to be trusted.

As usual when meeting a shadow source with dubious intentions, Brognola felt uneasy with the setup. But three of the Farm's blacksuits were close by, stationed in the SUV, HK subguns ready for any threat, whether bodily harm or the fact the Invisible Man knew something about the Farm he shouldn't and was prepared to go the blackmail route. In that case...

Brognola had rules about security, too.

He was in the well of an oversize black van, facing himself in a one-way mirror, hunched on a bolted-down swivel chair. The fact they had agreed to rendezvous at an underground garage in Crystal City left Brognola briefly wondering if the individual on the other side of the glass worked at the Pentagon, given its close proximity. Of course, Langley was a short chopper ride away and the NSA was…

It didn't matter. He would never know, and he didn't need to know.

They had traded intel packets via the wheelman, and Brognola found himself looking at the blueprints for Lightning Bat and other weapons systems. "I would say that what happened in North Dakota would certainly rank as an atrocity."

The voice on the other side of the glass came out of an intercom, garbled, sounding slightly robotic. "It was most unfortunate, but there are people working right now to rectify the situation."

"By rectify, you mean kill civilians who won't take payoffs? I suppose you're going to tell me they were simply collateral damage?"

"This has happened before, the military testing weapons or a classified aircraft goes down, and in some farmer's wheat field. Only not to this extreme, considering we know there's a body count Eagle Nebula may not be able to sweep under the rug. Regrettably, the press is onto the scent, but they will be dealt with in a timely fashion."

"Go deaf, dumb and blind, you mean, or else?"

"Understand, the people I represent had no hand in

this mishap, but our office has had knowledge of Eagle Nebula for some time, as you know from the first package I delivered. We have operatives on the inside, watching the watchers, you might say. And we have suspected there were those inside the facility who are, shall I say, 'readjusting' certain manifests."

"Meaning, they're selling the store. Who's the lucky end purchaser?"

"Our first choice is Iran. Given the situation in Iraq, with Tehran looking to muscle radical Shiites to the forefront and take control of the government, we have been able to trace shipments of weapons from Eagle Nebula to the Iraq-Iran border, where there has been direct delivery to extremists. The other problem we have is the Russians. In that package is another round of satellite photos of a compound in Tajikistan, one of the largest weapons-producing factories the Russians have. For our amusement, they play it off as an aerospace facility, and as far as that goes, the Russians, we believe, have a modified version of Lightning Bat already— only they are set to arm it with tactical nuclear warheads."

"What's the connection between the Russians and Iranians?"

"The Russians want the Iranians stirring up the hornet's nest in Iraq. They don't want American occupation so close to their back door, plus they don't want to see control of all that oil falling directly into our hands, nor for that matter, do the Saudis. You know how it goes. The Russians say one thing but mean another, the Motherland forever paranoid, forever xenophobic. The arms race never ended, in truth, it's only been elevated. Naturally both sides pretend it's all warm and fuzzy for the world forum…anyway, with the Russians being cash-strapped they're looking to unload WMD, and the Iranians are willing to fork over whatever Moscow's asking price. Chem. Bio. Nuke. They're also willing to sell certain technology, blueprints for weapons systems and such, but they don't quite know how to modify or engineer into their Lightning Bat version what is being called the Divine Alloy."

"The what?"

"It's all in the package. Four separate incidents, complete with sat imagery of an ore that fell to Earth in areas that were instantly quarantined by the military on both sides. And which has strange properties no one can explain. Now, our side managed to engineer this ore into the skin of Lightning Bat with the help of the individual you already know as Dr. Ezekiel Jacobs. Apparently this alloy shields a pilot from G-force—how, no one seems to know. Further, coating the nuclear reactor with the ore makes it light enough for two men to be able to pick up and carry."

As usual, when meeting with one of his shadow sources like this, Brognola couldn't help but wonder how much they knew about the Farm and its own black ops. The way it was always left—intelligence being doled out with hints of retribution against the enemies of national security—told him that someone somewhere knew something they shouldn't, but that they had decided to pawn the dirty work off on the Farm.

Or pass the buck.

"There is a situation developing in Las Vegas that could become so volatile as to maybe topple the present administration," the robotic voice informed him.

"I don't follow."

"Barely we do at our office. Suffice it to say, we suspect there is an operation about to be undertaken with two objectives in Las Vegas. One—a snatch of Dr. Jacobs by black ops, to be sold to the highest bidder. Two—Las Vegas may become a testing ground for both revolutionary small and large arms."

"Come again?"

"Let's just say what happened in North Dakota would all but be forgotten should a large American city become a litmus test for high-tech weapons."

"A killing ground, you mean?" Brognola said, and felt his blood boil. "And you suspect all this and you're sitting on your hands? Let me guess. The traitors you've been watching are operatives hired out by your office?"

"It's something out of our control."

"Which means you're looking to cover your assets."

"There is a political animal to consider."

"Bullshit. You start running around, murdering American citizens, using them as test subjects…"

"We are not the ones doing all the killing."

"Shut down the facility."

"It isn't that simple."

"Political considerations and all that."

"It's a little more complex than that, but yes, there are mitigating circumstances to weigh."

Brognola shook his head. A check of his watch and he hoped by now Lyons and Schwarz had landed at McCarran. He wasn't sure why the Invisible Man had held back on him with the first batch of intel, or perhaps he was hard at work himself, uncovering the sordid truth in bits and pieces. If it was true, however, what the Invisible Man foreshadowed…

Why, didn't matter.

Stopping the genocidal litmus test did.

"If there is nothing else…I believe you have all you need with you for the present."

Brognola gnawed on his cigar. "I'll be in touch," he concluded, and piled out the door.

As he retraced his steps for the SUV, the spook van reversing out of there, vanishing around the corner in seconds flat like the ghost ship it was, Brognola felt sick to his stomach. He hoped to God the Invisible Man was wrong, even stringing him along about Las Vegas being some murderous testing ground for weapons.

If he wasn't…

God help us, he thought, picking up the pace for the waiting SUV.

CHAPTER EIGHT

"Let's go nail us some Russian ass, old buddy. It's pay-back time."

With great reluctance and trepidation, Blancanales had agreed to let Parker tag along for the hunt. Now he worried he'd made a colossal error in judgment, sure Carl Lyons would not be pleasantly surprised at the unannounced invite. It wasn't that he doubted Parker's martial talents—rusty and whiskey-sodden as they might be—nor his determination in tracking down and confronting the opposition. Rather, he feared rage and hate would consume his friend when the shooting started, thus endangering both noncombatants and his teammates if he acted with unprofessional reckless abandon.

Too late now.

Three hours ago, when word had come from Lyons that he and Schwarz were en route for the Vegas showdown with both the Russians and some black ops headhunters from the Eagle Nebula who were likewise interested in putting Ezekiel Jacobs on the international job market, Blancanales told his friend he had to cut him loose.

That the Jacobs problem—and all problems related to—would be handled by the Justice Department.

And that's when Eddie Parker came alive, kicking and screaming.

A shower, a change of clothes and draining another half of a fifth of whiskey maybe put an artificial spark back into him, but Blancanales noted a subtle, even ominous change in his friend. There was a fire in his eyes, brightening and more hungry with each passing minute, a neon light that warned the Able Team commando Parker was at the edge of the abyss, didn't care who went down as long as he carved out his own pound of flesh. Dangerous, and foolish, yes, but he capitulated when Parker stated he would follow him, find the Russians with or without his help, and may God have mercy when he did, because he was as far from a forgiving mood as Pluto to Earth.

Better, then, to have his angry, half-soused, vengeance-fueled buddy within arm's reach than rolling up on their rear when the curtain went up.

And up it was going, if he judged Lyons's mood correctly.

So he handed off the Uzi submachine gun with special swivel rig, five spare 30-round magazines in 9 mm Parabellum. Parker then asked for and received the .45 Colt in stainless steel, three extra clips, all of which he snugged in the waistband of black slacks held up by an alligator—or facsimile thereof—belt. He produced a knee-length, checkerboard-dotted coat from one of his duffel bags as he wrapped himself up, lighting another smoke off a dying butt, Blancanales wondering if Eddie didn't swipe his clothes off the rack of a circus clown's dressing room. White shoes freshly spit-polished, now sans blood, dust and vomit, the final touch to the new Eddie Parker was a gold crucifix, hanging proud and glinting on the open chest of a wrinkled tiger-striped silk shirt. If nothing, his friend, Blancanales thought, was as consistent in bad taste as he was obsessive-compulsive in all areas pertaining to self-indulgence.

The music box, at least, was cranking out fresh country, Martina McBride's greatest hits, according to Eddie, who kept playing the same damn song, as if psyching himself up for the battle sure to come.

Blancanales checked the loads on both Beretta 92-Fs, slipped them into shoulder rigging, butts out for a cross draw, then slipped on his windbreaker. He zipped the HK MP-5 subgun in the war bag, ready to break it out when they had a clear fix on the enemy, the arsenal rounded out with plenty of spare mags and a mixed bevy of grenades.

Time to go.

Parker had already checked them out of their room, but Blancanales found him standing in the doorway, empty-handed except for his bottle and smoke. He gave Parker's bags a look on the move, then said, "What about your stuff, Eddie? I don't think you're leaving your music box as a tip for the maid."

Parker polished off another third of the bottle, flipped it on the bed, then, blowing smoke, slipped on a new pair of shades, as grim as hell. "I won't be coming back here."

And he was out the door, coat flowing behind him like a cape.

Already gone.

Blancanales felt his stomach sink as he listened to the music, picturing the future ghosts that would haunt him, assuming, that was, he survived Las Vegas.

"LET'S GET DRESSED for the big show, ladies!"

Fixing the last glob of C-4 to the underside of the comm station, setting the time delay for two hours, Bo Heller watched his team as they moved for the port wall. Six of the best commandos in any man's army— all Delta with plenty of grim experience in the Iraqi killing fields—they hauled the black leather trench coats off hooks, single-file, slipping them over shouldered Beretta 92-F side arms. The gate to the eighteen-wheeler rolled up, the ramp went down, the engine on the oversize black van "special" revving to life. War bags grabbed up next, Heller hefted the leftover body bag, told Paul Rocker, "I believe this one's for you, big guy." With a grunt, the Goliath ripped more than two hundred pounds of hardware and ammo out of his hands as if it weighed nothing more than a beer bottle, hung it over his massive shoulders.

Heller stood back as four of his commandos piled into the van, Jackson priming the gate and aft wall with plastic explosive. The best shooters money could buy, and they were all riding into the future, he knew, what was the next quantum leap in fighting vehicles. The classified rig had U.S. government plates and, like their Department of Defense credentials, the whole smoke screen would lend them free and ready access around town, the law of DOD in the name of national security stating to any cop or security goon who didn't like the looks of them that they were licensed to carry concealed weapons. But the ruse would work only up to a point. The war van special cost, or so he overheard, something like ten million dollars, with two more battle rigs housed in the second tractor-trailer, ready to rumble. Soon enough, he knew, Sin City would get a taste of all this high-tech fire and thunder, and God help any cop stupid enough to get in their way. Another sixty miles or so down I-15 and Vegas was about to become ground zero, compliments of the latest in Uncle Sam's inventory of high and low-tech weapons. Of course, there was an AWOL aerospace magician to bag, but they had him tracked, thanks to the genius cavorting with the same escort service.

And Heller knew the Russians weren't going to just politely hand him over.

No problem. It was going to be a really big show, he thought.

Welcome to Las Vegas.

He marched down the ramp behind the war van, slipping on his shades as the desert sun and heat slammed him in the face.

"Let's rock and roll, girls!" he flung at the rest of the team as they trooped down the ramp on number two eighteen-wheeler.

"Viva Las Vegas!" he heard one of his soldiers call.

Indeed.

Heller claimed the shotgun seat of the lead war van, and they were on their way, into the future.

"COME HERE, you."

Blancanales followed Lyons to a private cubbyhole

in the Stardust's lobby, leaving Parker near the front doors, girl-watching, smoking and contemplating his bleak future. One look at Lyons and Blancanales knew the Able Team leader was ready to turn into a pit bull. He did.

"Do you know what I'm thinking about doing to you right about now?" Lyons snarled.

"I can be sure you're not thinking about giving me a big old hug."

Lyons grunted, took a step back. "You're starting to sound more and more like Gadgets every day. Like a smart-ass."

"Let me explain."

"By all means."

And Blancanales quickly pitched Lyons the same argument he'd gotten from Parker.

Lyons huffed and growled and shook his head, throwing Parker dagger eyes. "So, if I don't bring him on board, he'll just muck up our play on his own?"

"That's about the gist of it. And what would it hurt? This way, I can keep an eye on him."

"We're a team, Pol, we don't take on wannabes, and I sure as hell wouldn't recruit some guy looks and smells like he needs about a fifteen-day stint in detox anyway."

"He's my friend, for one thing."

"Right, Nam buddies and all that."

Blancanales put some steel in his voice. "Cut me a little slack here, Carl."

"Very damn little."

"I think he's earned the right for some payback. Give him half a chance, you'll see he can perform when the heat's on. He's stand-up, you have my word on that."

"He looks like he's been run over by a Greyhound bus and dragged for twenty miles. I'm not even sure he can stand on his own two feet much longer."

"He's tough, if nothing else. He'll make it on his own, trust me."

"And in that getup the bad guys will see him coming a block away—oh, I forgot, you two have already been introduced to them so I guess stake and stealth are down the crapper." Lyons cursed. "Okay. He's your responsibility, and this is a one-shot deal. Don't ever pull a stunt like this again. He screws this up, and he'll have to answer to me—and I won't go easy on you, either."

"Understood."

Lyons brushed past Blancanales, aiming his anger at Parker. "Barker, is it?"

"That's Parker, chief."

"Whatever. You follow my orders to the letter, got it?"

"No problem. So, what's the plan?"

"The plan is to find some Russians and try to get this Jacobs away from them without having to turn some casino into the West Bank or Fallujah."

"I somehow don't think that's going to happen."

"Well, this time, Parker," Lyons snapped, "if it hits the fan, they'll be throwing bullets and not punches."

"I'm game."

"You're game, huh."

"I've put my head in the lion's mouth before, pal."

Blancanales watched Lyons flash him a look, then the Able Team leader bulled out the door, elbowing his flight through two Japanese Elvis impersonators.

"Is your buddy always that surly?"

"Shut up, Eddie."

KAHMUD NURIJ BELIEVED he was living out every freedom fighter's dream, and he wasn't about to squander his chance to fulfill this holy obligation. When he thought about it for even a few moments, he believed it was his just due, fulfilling a destiny long ago preordained, and by the Prophet himself. He was, after all, Nizari Ismailis, descendant of the blood of a long line of Iranian assassins whose legacy was known and feared throughout the Islamic world. In truth, there were those in his village who believed they could trace their unique ancestry back to the end of the tenth century, where the political-religious Islamic movement waged both overt and covert war against the Iraqis and Syrians. The end game of that bloody struggle more than a thousand years ago was to proclaim a caliph, successor to Mohammed. He had found his savior in the Grand Ayatollah.

And he had arrived at the gilded portal of a great destiny.

It had taken time, thirteen months to be exact, waiting on all the right—or bogus—paperwork to be delivered, landing finally in New York City, unaware of the exact nature of his mission, but wondering if his task would rival 9/11. Moving across the country then with all due caution, he communicated with the others via predetermined mail drops, before linking up with the sleeper cell in Las Vegas, his contact filling in the blanks once it was determined he wasn't compromised. But with his training in the camp back in his homeland, the imams stressed patience, faith in God and loyalty to jihad every bit as much as learning tactics, weapons, demolitions. And back in his village in Iran, the Grand Ayatollah had blessed him with a sacred mission.

He was about to bring jihad to the Great Satan.

It confused, even made him anxious, at first, that his contacts in America were infidels, but the Great One had assured him the enemy was betraying its own, that his mission involved the hands-on field testing of a new weapons system. Where the infidels were in it for money, he was prepared to act out on behalf of God, proud that he'd come this far, ready to plunge a sword of vengeance into the Great Satan's heart, and on America's own soil.

And he was watching the one who called himself Orion about to give him a crash course in SPLAT.

They were in a canvas-covered transport truck, far out in the desert, hidden from watching eyes, he hoped, in a narrow canyon. Hunched next to Orion, he watched as the American's fingers flew over the computer keyboard. A detailed grid map of downtown Las Vegas, what he knew as the Strip, flashed up on the monitor. While Orion listed the targets for him, Nurij stared at the stainless-steel cannon, the rack of 188 mm shells. Two other grim hardmen had already hauled the aluminum crate out of the bed, assembling, he assumed, the drone that would fly over Las Vegas. Equipped with GPS and laser sights, the small UAV would home in on the targets, the shells with microchips in their warheads steered by the magic of the man's computer link to the drone. Four missiles, about twelve feet in length, were chained to the wall, and he assumed the delivery system was the bulk beneath the tarp outside, the rockets ready to be dumped into pods at a moment's notice, sent streaking for preset targets in Las Vegas. What their explosive punch, he didn't know, but was sure they weren't there to take up space.

"Assuming," Orion said, "you like what you see, I can begin arranging delivery at the end of our business here. You're going to need detailed instructions on how the system operates, but I have a CD ready to hand over, and I have operatives on your end who can likewise give you further instructions in the field. Assuming I receive the price I'm asking for."

"The final decision regarding money is not up to me."

"Right, but your people are going to have to deliver half down before I start shipping the goods. The first batch was a good-faith gesture on my part, but from here on money talks."

"I will inform them as much."

He watched as three separate targets were painted red, Orion informing him each shell and missile had a gun camera, with the UAV likewise equipped with a television monitor. Thus they could sit here and watch Las Vegas go up in flames and anarchy, live and in color.

God was truly great.

"What you're buying," Orion said, "are basically upgraded artillery shells, but with laser and thermal sights. They have time-fuse settings that can be programmed by computer."

"Heat-seeking missiles?"

"You could say that, only a lot more sophisticated than any round you could pop off from a tank. Artillery is meant to provide fire support for combat infantry."

"I am aware of that," he said, anger flashing through him that this infidel was suddenly talking to him in a condescending tone.

"You have three branches of specialized artillery. Coastal defense, antiaircraft, antitank. We're looking to unload a variety of cargo, make you the ultimate tank battalion from Allah, my friend, and I'm telling you not even a bunch of Abrams M-1s will be able to match your strength once you're armed with SPLAT. I can get you chem, bio, even nuke, but that's down the road. Now, the shells, when fired, will open wings and stabilizing fins, minicruise missiles, if you will. The computer does all the work for you, just punch in the coordinates according to what the software program tells you, and you're ready to start blasting."

"When does it begin?"

Orion checked his watch. "As soon as I get the call from my man. Let's say we step outside and send the UAV on its way."

Nurij followed the American operative, his heart racing as his eagerness mounted. It was truly a blessing from God, he decided, poised as he was to burn down— or a portion of, at worst—what was the infidel mecca of vice. When he thought about the evil that raged across this land—gambling, pornography, drugs, and all manner of ills in-between—he had to have been truly sent by the Prophet, a cleansing flame to consume the infidels. They were spawning their evil around the world, he thought, occupying Islamic nations, importing their transgressions and vices, contaminating Muslims who were weak of faith. It had to be stopped, and he was just the warrior to carry the torch. Start the fire small, he thought, then let it grow as his own righteous fury burned brighter, until someday perhaps he had his finger poised on the button of the suitcase from God.

He was Nizari Ismailis, after all, and he had a special destiny to fulfill. Las Vegas was only the beginning of the coming Islamic firestorm, he was sure of it. All he had to do was keep the faith.

HEAVEN SENT ESCORTS was tucked near the corner of Flamingo and Paradise Road, right next door to And the Angels Sing Wedding Chapel. With a slew of hotels, casinos and inns catering to the grind crowd, Carl Lyons figured one Teddy Showers was never hurting for business, the Able Team leader wondering briefly if what was essentially a pimp also doubled as a chaplain. Prostitution was, of course, legal in Vegas, but according to an FBI file on the proprietor, he had Mob connections that had business booming beyond the stratosphere, an elite clientele that included famous names, ranging from politicians to movie stars. The Farm, he knew, had tracked down the aerospace wizard's favorite whoring haunt, cracking Herr Orion's codes that betrayed a vast knowledge of the seedier underbelly of Sin City. This was far from Ezekiel Jacobs's first trip to Vegas, and Lyons couldn't help but compare him to a dog returning to its own vomit, a creature of bad habit whose arrogance was about to find him netted, cuffed and stuffed. With Schwarz working together with Kurtzman and Tokaido, the dirty trail ended—or began—at a grimy little stucco building not far from the heart of Glitter Gulch.

Lyons had a head of steam, a full plate to contend

with or choke on, the least of his headaches being factor unknown in Pol's PI buddy who was now sitting with Blancanales in the Justice Department van with comm and tracking station. He'd relented, against his better judgment, allowing Pol to plant his Nam buddy on the team. It was a definite first, admitting a total stranger into their exclusive commando arena, but Blancanales had made a couple of good points. The last worst-case scenario Lyons needed was this Parker character traipsing into their play when they went toe-to-toe with the Russians, or the Eagle Nebula goons, or found themselves caught in the cross fire of both.

And Lyons suspected the clock was ticking. The Farm's logic dictated that if they knew the whereabouts of the AWOL genius-turned-traitor, then Orion and his gunslingers were either on the way or already making inroads in a death march toward the Russians.

Gadgets on his heels, Lyons went through the front door, in no mood for haggling, lies or bullshit.

There was a blonde behind the reception desk who, at any other time, Lyons would have made a pitch to, but now demanded, "I want to speak to your boss."

"And you are…"

Lyons flashed his Justice Department credentials. "Trouble, depending on Teddy."

"Sir, I can't just—"

"Get him, front and center now, cupcake, or I will have more cops, more FBI, more of my agents swarming this dump and tearing this place apart looking for dirt, then I'll personally place a phone call to Teddy's boss, one Don Tony Cabrone of the Cabrone Family, and tell him Teddy's turning himself into the witness protection program and he's squealing like the stuck pig he will be and Don Tony just shot to the top of my shitlist."

The ruckus, Lyons saw, brought forth a fat guy with a bad perm, white sports coat and enough gold dangling on his hairy chest to pay off the debt of many developing countries.

"What the hell is going on here?"

Lyons produced a picture of Ezekiel Jacobs, along with thrusting his Justice Department badge in the pimp's face. "I understand this man has a fondness for your girls. He may have sent some guys with funny accents, as in Russian, who paid for your services. I need to know where he is. And don't lie to me."

With odd facial spasms, Teddy Showers seemed to think about something, weighing the pros and cons, no doubt, Lyons believed, of cooperating with the Feds as opposed to answering to the boss why he bent over for G-Men in the first place.

"I can make life very miserable for you, Teddy, if you don't tell me where this man is."

"I believe you, sport. Okay, okay, I don't want no trouble with the Justice Department, I run a legit business here...."

"Where is he, Teddy?"

"Okay, yeah, some Russians came by this morning. They moved from the Bellagio, but they're real close, if I recall right. Arrogant pricks they are, throwing around muscle, know they're talking trash about me in their language, and they're still holding on to one of my best girls."

"I forgot to bring my violin, Teddy."

"Relax, will ya, just let me check the computer."

Lyons flashed Schwarz a mean grin. "See how easy that was."

Schwarz returned the look. "Yeah. You're a real diplomat."

BO HELLER WAS in no mood for sightseeing, but the juices were racing, adrenaline floating him along, it seemed, light as air on rubber-soled, combat-booted size 13 wides. He took in the raucous surroundings, but admitted to himself he was relishing the circus atmosphere of street musicians, celebrity impersonators and the teeming multicultural masses streaming in and out of the casinos. From Fourth Street to the Plaza Hotel on South Main he already knew Fremont was foot traffic only, one big rolling party.

No sweat, their joyrides were close enough to bring the carnival to a screaming halt.

Point man, eyes wrapped in dark shades and lugging his war bag, he led the trench coat procession, six shooters trailing in pairs, with Rocker bringing up the rear, com links to a man. The hustle he found swarming four blocks of Fremont seemed to only throw more gasoline on the fire in his belly as he caught a few strange looks from passersby, alien creatures in the spotlight as if the eight of them were headlining musicians with a gig on tap at one of the finer hotel-casinos.

Only this was their killing ground. And once they vacated town, Las Vegas would never again be the same.

Perhaps the whole country, he suspected, would go into another 9/11 tailspin.

Not his problem.

Under different circumstances he might have found the 1400-foot-long, ninety-foot-high vaulted matrix that canopied the coming blocks vaguely interesting, but this was business, and he wasn't inclined to bring a camera. Then there was a symphony—Beethoven or Wagner, he couldn't say which, if either—blasting from speakers somewhere, the music matching in beat, though, the futuristic light show that left the senses reeling in awe and wonder, bedazzled.

Nice touch, all things considered.

He liked marching into battle with music and lights.

Killing civilians, if it came to that—and he could be sure a few platoons of Sin City's finest would come roaring up in their faces—didn't trouble him in the least. He had shed his blood for his country, he thought, and collateral damage was simply a fact of war. He was owed. Once upon a time he perhaps believed in all that patriotic fervor, how sad it was when the innocent were killed as well as the guilty in battle, nursing a sort of jingoistic pride as a young soldier, fighting evil in the name of God, country and flag and all that naive rubbish. Only cold, hard reality—and more than once staring down his own mortality—had a way of making a fighting man see the light.

Money.

And why not? he figured. As far as he was concerned, America had changed for the worse. Time to grab his own brass ring, jump off the sinking ship of the United States of America. At the moment, he didn't need to get bogged down in his head, wrestling with about a thousand-and-one politically incorrect scenarios that had seen him clear out more than one bar from sea to shining sea. If some cop or civilian popped up in their gun-sights, they were just some cash on the hoof. And if the genius bit the dust in the process? Well, their com-mander in chief had stated that was no big deal, either, as long as the Russians didn't have their talons dug into him.

He swept past a billboard proclaiming Don Rickles Live at the Aladdin, felt a twinge of regret he wouldn't be able to catch one of the last great comic acts, then he hit the doors to the targeted casino, Jackson holding open the way into the lobby.

Showtime.

It was a moment of high drama, not to mention the hour of truth, so Heller marched in a few yards, pulled up to a sudden halt, his troops fanning out on his wings, with Rocker lurching a couple of feet forward, the Go-liath bobbing his head at all the sound and fury and light.

Scanning the wide-open, sprawling glitter, rock-and-roll thundering clear down the banks of slot machines and toward the gaming pits from the sound of it, he spot-ted them. Two buzz cuts with earpieces and throat mikes, they wore long, oversize black windbreakers, big bulges telling him they toted shouldered hardware, with duffel bags at their wingtips, sure to be chocked with the heavy artillery. For a moment Heller watched them watch him, as they babbled on, somehow holding the smile in check.

Russians.

Bingo.

And he marched ahead, his shooters falling in behind for the really big show.

CHAPTER NINE

"They are here, Comrade Colonel. And they are coming your way."

"Proceed as ordered."

Boris Rustov rekeyed his com link, alerting the others in the casino to the gathering storm. They would know when it began, passing on those exact words, supremely confident of his team's lethal abilities to roll back, annihilate the enemy. Of course, the security detail would come running when the shooting started, naturally believing the casino was being robbed, the Las Vegas police not far behind, their SWAT perhaps leading the charge. First, the American operatives, the heavier firepower on reserve for law enforcement, once they were clear of the casino. Beyond that...

Nothing about combat was ever guaranteed.

Feeling the electric sparks of prebattle jitters and adrenaline surging fire through his veins, he looked at Vuknovta, threw a nod to the blackjack table over his shoulder where the good doctor appeared to be winning big for a change, then vectored for the far edge of the upraised bar, trench coat sweeping in a broad flourish as he flew up the steps, hit the landing.

Perhaps the enemy believed them careless or stupid Russian peasants, he thought, hiding out in the open as they had, but this was precisely the moment he had been craving. In fact, before he even touched down on the chartered diplomatic flight at McCarran International he knew black operatives from the Eagle Nebula would force his hand in Las Vegas. It was his brazen manner—leaving clear footprints of his flight and the whereabouts of the esteemed swine's sanctuary for the enemy to track them without much effort—in which he had hoped to lure them to a showdown, thus eliminating rabid dogs who might later come snarling on his heels. Be it Vegas, Moscow or Tajikistan, he knew the opposition would not rest until they cornered him. American operatives, in his experience, were predictable, hemmed in, by and large, from the constraints of the Geneva Convention, international law and order, politics and their own sense of fair play and morality.

Rustov knew no such boundaries, fearing them foolish to the extreme, capable of getting a man killed when he least expected it.

Regardless of how the game of espionage was played out the world over, there was really no such living creature as a secret in the world of black operations, not in this day and age of supersophisticated electronic intercepts, military satellites that could trace a man's footsteps in crystal-clear telemetry, phone taps, parabolic mikes with laser enhancement that could virtually hear through walls, and so forth. Then there was the human factor, rife with so many faults and flaws it was too often egregious to the point of instant transparency, and he considered himself a true master when uncovering then using a man's weakness to work for him.

Once he knew of Orion, detailed some of his background with the American Special Forces—a man more mercenary than military, it seemed—he had made his power move, procuring the services of one of his enemy's operatives who wasn't satisfied with his paltry government salary.

That operative was right then sitting at the opposite end of the bar, nursing a drink, an identical twin in black sports coat and crew cut seated next to him. Which one had aimed the guns his way didn't matter.

Rustov had chummed the waters and the sharks were circling.

As Dlynka and Petrov raked in their own black bags and descended the landing to take the battle to the enemy, Rustov, one hand toting his oversize duffel, began marching down the length of the bar. One look across the vast expanse of gaming pits and he spotted them. They were marching in a skirmish line, fanning out the deeper they advanced into the casino, eight shooters in garb he might have found semicomic had their intent been any other than to kill him, his men and seize Jacobs.

No time like the present, he decided, and dug out his Makarov pistol for all to behold. The twins were turning his way, a female gasping from somewhere at the sight of the weapon, when he began squeezing the trigger, pumping one round each into the side of their heads, spraying the lavender wall behind them with blood and muck, driving them off their stools to dump them on the carpet in a tangled heap of spasming limbs.

PRIORITY OF KILLS was insignificant, and that was already green-lighted, straight from the top. That in mind, Paul Rocker couldn't have been happier with his gargantuan part, eager to grab centerstage, start the rock and roll.

He had done his time for his country, in both Afghanistan and Iraq twice over, above and beyond the call of duty, as far as he was concerned. There may be those over the course of both military and civilian life who considered him a sociopath, misfit, loose cannon, given a few incidents regarding Taliban prisoners that were swept under a magic carpet of special ops see no evil, and like that. Then there was an ex-wife, the bitch-whore somewhere on the prowl across America, most likely warming the bed of some other dupe, and who he was pretty sure might agree with superior officers in a regular grunt's army he required daily visits to a shrink. The problem wasn't him, the way he saw it, it was the rest of the world beyond his command and control. Hell, he was fine as the day was long, especially when wading onto the battlefield, guns blazing, but try adjusting to civilian life and he was amazed he'd never done hard time. So he had reinserted himself into Gulf II after that disastrous failed marriage, the simple truth hitting him like a bullet square between the eyes that he didn't fit into normal society, where he walked, a lion among the sheep and hyenas.

And when it came to hunting men, he knew better than to trust anyone appearing to be simply sitting on the sidelines. He had seen boys, no more than, say, seven or eight, hurl themselves at his fellow soldiers, wrapped in explosives, blowing themselves up in the name of Islam or some such nonsense, while taking out half a squad of real fighting men. There had been women, too, shedding croc tears, who would shuffle up to them, looking set to bow and scrape before hauling out an AK-47 or a hand grenade hidden beneath those eerie *burqas*. There were so-called Iraqi police—trained by his own hand, no less—who would no sooner take a few bucks American as a starting salary, then run to the militants and plan ambushes against Marines.

The hell with it. Trust no one.

Kill them all.

Like the others going the distance along with him, he had long ago turned his back on the Stars and Stripes. Whatever the politicians, the brass mugging for cameras at some White House press conference and all Americans under the bootheel of whatever the current 1600 Pennsylvania Avenue regime's bootheel thought the flag and the Constitution stood for—liberty, freedom and justice for all—was a B-52 load of rhino dung. Too many soldiers, he knew, had given too much for too little, in every way, pretty much tossed aside and forgotten, left to fend for themselves, often sans an important body part, floundering about in a spoiled, self-indulgent society at large that didn't give a damn about their sacrifice, one way or the other.

Greener pastures now spread in front of him, paving the way to a future of his choosing.

A few of the playbabies at the closer tables began gawking in his direction as he set down the massive bag, zipped it open in a piece of turf semiringed by partitions and billboards advertising rock bands and comics now appearing all over town. He glimpsed Millerton on his right wing, as his eyes for the blindside produced an M-16/M-203 combo, his comrade standing tall, scouring the immediate vicinity for security.

Quickly, Rocker went to work, fastening the thick canvas straps around his neck and shoulders first, as he felt a hush settle over the crowd in front of him. What lay beneath was a thing of beauty, no question, and he stole a heartbeat to admire its stainless-steel length and girth. Engineered at Eagle Nebula, the Gatling gun was classified, not yet on any legitimate manifests or legal markets for sale. Known to him simply as the M-2000 Revenger, the four barrels were capable of spitting out up to 5000 12.7 mm rounds in a minute flat, depending on how fast the man handling the monster could burn through fat-box magazines holding 250 flesh-eaters apiece. Muzzle velocity zipping in at just under 4000 feet per second, these special rounds alternated between armor-piercing and full-metal jackets tipped with fulminated mercury. In other words, when he hit flesh, he knew the unlucky number would nearly burst apart in front of his eyes.

Crapped out.

Ammo pod snapped into place, cocked and locked for grim business, he heard the pistol shots, then saw two bodies kicked to the floor of the bar at the far side of the casino, the shouting and panic unleashed in grim earnest. The opening thunderheads trumpeting the call to arms, Russian opponents were getting it together in swift course, he saw, assault rifles and machine guns flying into view, the Ivans spreading far and wide for a standard outflanking maneuver.

Time to rock.

And Rocker hauled out the Gatling gun, grasping the control handle, finger taking up slack on the trigger. A peek at Millerton, as he heard the stutter of weapons-fire, and he found his fellow warrior hard at it on the giving end, already bowling down two brown-suited rental cops with a lightning sweep of M-16 autofire, slamming their flailing scarecrow forms into a billboard, spraying ZZ Top with red gore.

"Viva Las Vegas!" He laughed.

Then found the gaming throngs frozen deer for two heartbeats in his grinning pan of the killzone, before he hit the trigger to a roar of shouts and screams, and bellowed, "Elvis is in the building!"

THE DEALER WAS FLIPPING him over yet another face card, this time to a ten of clubs, when Ezekiel Jacobs sensed the commotion.

Only moments ago he had felt keen relief and gratitude when Rustov finally peeled himself off his back, but another thug had stepped up in his parting shadow, planting himself nearly on top of his Italian loafers. But something was happening all over the casino, as he felt sudden tension in the air. For reasons he couldn't quite fathom, he felt his mood deflate from euphoria over an unbeaten streak he was finding next to impossible to believe—his cash was trash—with anxiety rapidly on the rise as he saw the grim pall harden the dealer's face, certain then he just heard a woman scream something about a gun.

And the shooting erupted, leaving no doubt he was trapped in a whole galaxy of feces.

The Gold Eagle Reader Service™ — Here's how it works:

Accepting your 2 free books and gift places you under no obligation to buy anything. You may keep the books and gift and return the shipping statement marked "cancel." If you do not cancel, about a month later we'll send you 6 additional books and bill you just $29.94* — that's a saving of 10% off the cover price of all 6 books! And there's no extra charge for shipping! You may cancel at any time, but if you choose to continue, every other month we'll send you 6 more books, which you may either purchase at the discount price or return to us and cancel your subscription.

*Terms and prices subject to change without notice. Sales tax applicable in N.Y. Canadian residents will be charged applicable provincial taxes and GST. Credit or Debit balances in a customer's account(s) may be offset by any other outstanding balance owed by or to the customer.

If offer card is missing write to: Gold Eagle Reader Service, 3010 Walden Ave., P.O. Box 1867, Buffalo NY 14240-1867

NO POSTAGE
NECESSARY
IF MAILED
IN THE
UNITED STATES

BUSINESS REPLY MAIL
FIRST-CLASS MAIL   PERMIT NO. 717-003   BUFFALO, NY

POSTAGE WILL BE PAID BY ADDRESSEE

GOLD EAGLE READER SERVICE
3010 WALDEN AVE
PO BOX 1867
BUFFALO NY 14240-9952

Get FREE BOOKS and a FREE GIFT when you play the...

LAS VEGAS GAME

Just scratch off the gold box with a coin. Then check below to see the gifts you get!

YES! I have scratched off the gold box. Please send me my **2 FREE BOOKS** and **gift for which I qualify.** I understand that I am under no obligation to purchase any books as explained on the back of this card.

▼ DETACH AND MAIL CARD TODAY! ▼

366 ADL D749   **166 ADL D747**
                                              (MB-05R)

FIRST NAME	LAST NAME

ADDRESS

APT.#	CITY

STATE/PROV.	ZIP/POSTAL CODE

7	7	7	**Worth TWO FREE BOOKS plus a BONUS Mystery Gift!**
🍒	🍒	🍒	**Worth TWO FREE BOOKS!**
🔔	🔔	♣	**TRY AGAIN!**

Offer limited to one per household and not valid to current Gold Eagle® subscribers. All orders subject to approval.

He heard Cleopatra shriek in terror as the gaming universe around them erupted into a stampede of players, pit bosses and dealers, with security guards swarming the area out of nowhere, the sounds of gunfire blowing in at him, it seemed, from all directions. For what felt like the longest few seconds of his life, Jacobs was paralyzed by the sight of some behemoth in black at the far side of the casino, wielding the most mammoth machine gun he'd ever seen, its barrels spinning and blazing, the storm raking anything and everyone in its path with utter decimation. He glimpsed other dark-clad specters with automatic weapons on the surge, blazing a lead tempest with indiscriminate but all due haste, taking out both pit bosses and players.

"What the—"

Imploring a God he hadn't prayed to since he was a boy to spare him, Jacobs hit the floor, daring to look behind, searching for Russian salvation he hoped was every bit as bold and lethally talented as self-advertised. Wall-mounted televisions and shelved liquor bottles exploded in a wave of glassy detonations, sparks hitting the air like myriad shooting stars. He saw bodies, riddled with ragged holes, spiral off stools, bounce off the bar front or tumble over the rail, some armed, he believed, but most of the victims clearly just innocent bystanders. He thought two, maybe three, of his Russian handlers, howling like madmen and holding back on the triggers of assault rifles, shooting at God only knew what, were getting chewed up in the barrage, falling hard next but firing on. Aware he'd all but forgotten about his two-grand-a-day whore, he looked up, flinching as chips and wood slivers slashed off his face.

And found Cleopatra sailing away, her chest a sea of red, spuming the air in her wake with a crimson mist.

FROM HIS FIREPOINT near the edge of a partition between the casino and the sports betting annex, Heller saw two, hopefully three, Russians scratched off the roster with the opening rounds.

Bingo.

Gadsen thundered away on the opposite end with the black ferrite-painted Eagle Nebula shotgun special in 12-gauge, the ex-Delta commando pumping the crank handle just in front of the attached rotating cylinder holding twenty rounds, sweeping the floor, nine to three o'clock while booming out the war cries. Heller spotted a trench coat bulldoze through the stampede. Dead ahead, the Russian bulldozer was knocking bodies this way and that before he rushed their firepoint, AKM blazing. Heller squeezed the trigger on his MP-5, caught the Ivan with a rising burst of 9 mm Parabellum rounds that mangled him, crotch to sternum, then launched him back in a jig step where he crashed down on a craps table, arms and legs flopping out the final nerve spasms. Return fire from several converging points gouging out chunks of plaster above his head, slugs grazing his scalp, Heller whirled for deeper cover.

The betting line on his opposing number was heavy odds in favor the Ivans would neither retreat nor seek the nearest exit. Smart money already told him they would leave they way they came in.

Through the front door.

So far, Orion's intel looked to be on the money.

As the action out on the floor seemed to skyrocket

to new and greater ear-shattering crescendos with every howl, scream, grunt and burst of weaponsfire, Heller spotted three, then four, brownsuits—two with pump shotguns and two wielding old M1 carbines—charge from a corridor that looked to run adjacent to the betting windows.

The sports bettors were already in full flight, though one hero, Heller found was barreling toward him, hurling a beer bottle, snarling oaths that were vacuumed up into a soundless void by all the hellish racket. Glass shattering over his head, Heller hit the subgun's trigger from a knee. He tagged the hero with a crimson figure eight, suspected the SOB was either drunk, crazy, some angry sore loser or just plain stupid—and he didn't give a damn which, since the rental cops were already unloading weapons—and blew him over a lounge table, elbows and legs taking food, beverage and ashtrays with him on his tumble to the carpet.

Digging into a pocket and fisting a frag grenade, Heller fell back as rounds peppered the partition, inches above his head. He was hollering at Gadsen but found the commando was already in a 180 pirouette, the Eagle Nebula special pounding out three peals across the lounge, all but erasing any house advantage for the moment. A brief burst, firing the MP-5 one-handed, waxing a brownsuit off his feet as two more security guards with gaping holes in their chests were hammered into the betting windows, and Heller knew he had to raise the stakes.

Any second L.V.P.D. would crash its way onto the party, and he hadn't marched in here to simply fold his hand.

Not a chance.

Gadsen dusted number four rental with a disemboweling blast, and Heller primed the frag bomb, stood and hurled the steel egg across the lounge. They were screaming and racing from behind the barred windows when the lethal loaded dice bounced up against the wall and blew its fiery payday. Two eyeblinks of the smoking ruins, glimpsing shredded greenbacks as they fluttered in the whirlwind of dust and debris, and Heller flung himself around the edge of the partition.

He knew the targeted casino's layouts from Orion's faxed blueprints, suspected the Russians would make a power move toward the escalators.

They were, or at least in the process of advancing in that direction.

The one he knew from intel pics as Rustov, he saw, was vaulting on top of a table, a black machine gun with twin cylindrical barrels in one hand flaming downrange, a fist full of their hi-roller's sports jacket dragging Jacobs behind, then down to cover between the next line of tables.

The Russians were leapfrogging, he found, toward his troops, digging in behind the craps and baccarat spreads, lurching up, triggering a mixed arsenal of AK-47s, -74s, AKMs. There was an odd Ivan out, hosing the roulette wheels—where a few of his troops were hunkered and returning fire—with an RPK-74 light machine gun.

As detailed by Orion's intel, Heller looked up and saw the glass canopy stretched the length of the vertical-running gaming pits.

High time, he figured, to flush out some Russian rats.

And began raking the mirrored ceiling with long bursts of subgun fire.

RISING OVER THE BACCARAT table, sweeping the RPK-74 submachine gun special, left to right, at least one operative downrange flung back into a roulette wheel under his barrage, Rustov was forced to kick Jacobs in the ribs when the swine grabbed at his leg, hollering something unintelligible. He fired on, shouting at his human cargo to be quiet and stay down, when he glimpsed the ceiling shatter in a rolling wave. And he flung himself to the deck, eating carpet a heartbeat before the avalanche came down, Jacobs shrieking in his ear as glass sheets that felt as heavy to Rustov as the gaming tables, pounded their cover, hammering his head and shoulders. Perhaps he had underestimated the enemy, overlooking the possibility the gaming pits could become their deathtrap, an opponent now hitting them with a glass meteor shower, no doubt looking to drive them from cover, dancing out in the open, end of game. No question, the opposition was determined, professional, prepared to go the full distance, and Rustov begrudged them a moment of admiration.

Planting a boot in the middle of Jacobs's back, Rustov lurched up, firing. Eyelids slitted, as slivers kept raining and pelting his face, he ignored the waves of hot pain where needles dug into his scalp and face, his fusillade churning up a bank of roulette wheels. He glimpsed a black-garbed figure, M-16 washing a hail of bullets over the poker pit, the enemy flinching, listing to the side, dropping out of sight behind the wheel, as Rustov believed he scored flesh.

His weapon of choice was produced in the Tajikistan compound where he hoped to dump off Jacobs, only that particular triumph looked light-years removed. The Eagle Nebula, he knew, hadn't cornered the black ops market on specialized prototype hardware. Handed out to only a few in Spetsnaz, those who had proved their mettle in combat, time and again, the latest in hardware could pump out 800 rounds per minute, each 5.54 mm round muzzling at 900 meters a second. Two drums fixed to the RPK-74, each one storing fifty rounds, four more cylinders swelling the pockets of his custom trench coat, but Rustov began to wonder if he'd brought enough firepower, once he factored in the police, sure to either barge into the casino or form a perimeter around the building, ready and waiting to unload.

Worry about the present crisis, Rustov told himself as he fished into a coat pocket and pulled out an RGD-5 hand grenade.

THE GLASS MOUNTAIN FALLING on their heads did virtually nothing to take the steam out of the Russians. Instead, Heller found them popping up, triggering longer bursts, slot machines and video poker banks getting blasted to sparking garbage as two of his troops fell back in the direction of the escalators. Looking more enraged than ever, the Russian opposition seemed oblivious to lethal sheets of glass shrapnel still dousing the arena, two, maybe three, of the Ivans, he spotted, now pitching grenades, aiming the explosive baseballs for his right flank. He was darting, pillar to post, vectoring to link up with his left wing, intent on a broad sweep to the rear of his fighters, when the war blitzed up to what he sensed was a point of suicidal abandon.

Time to call in the heavy artillery, he knew, and palmed his cell phone with secured line, slipping the com link off his ears. Gadsen on his six, pumping out 12-gauge thunder, Heller saw Comrade Light Machine Gun—or what was left of him—sailing over the baccarat expanse, as Rocker's Gatling leviathan all but shredded him to red pulp and gristle. The sight of little more than ground-up tatters of trench coat mesmerized him for a dangerous moment, as Heller spied what looked a severed forearm, sheathed in leather, twirling like some gruesome baton through all the smoke and flying trash. As he hit Send, hoping to hell and back his troops had the sound judgment to run for cover, a triburst of fireballs obliterated the bank of roulette wheels.

As the din raged on, and the Russians, crouched and firing, pumping swarms of projectiles into the churning smoke and directing relentless autofire on down to where Rocker had once stood—and what the hell had happened to his biggest gun?—Heller patched through to Orion.

"We are engaging the enemy, sir!"

"So, I hear."

Heller felt a flash of anger over their commander's cavalier tone, but Orion's role was no less important. "Feel free to fire at will, sir! No L.V.P.D. sighting as of yet, but you can be sure they are en route."

"You'll be fine. Hang tough. And our star?"

"Still on the planet, sir, but the Russians still have him."

"Negate my original order. He is to be taken alive, and at all costs."

"Sir?" Heller said, forced to shout as he saw Rocker rise from a pile of rubble to his two o'clock, shaking off debris as the Gatling thunder began pealing again, two craps tables vanishing in front of his eyes under the 12.7 mm onslaught, thinking he glimpsed Rustov flinging the genius of the millenium to the floor.

"I may have a prospective buyer. You copy me, soldier?"

Heller gnashed his teeth, angry he was ordered to put the lives of his men at further risk for a monumental task that bordered insanity or certain suicide, considering the Russians were clearly hell-bent on going down to a man before giving up Jacobs.

"Aye-aye, sir."

"Carry on. Help is on the way."

Heller was up and running toward the slot machines, patching through to his team, shouting the new order. He was forced to repeat the dire warning to get Jacobs alive and in one piece when he heard the outbreak of gunfire beyond the slot machine banks, followed by a thunderclap, which signaled a new round of grenade tossing. Dashing ahead to exit the gaming pits, as both warring factions kept spraying each other with extended salvos from across a no-man's land of ruins and splayed corpses of both fighters and noncombatants, he saw bodies sailing off the escalator, thrashing out of the boiling fireball for their swan dive. Another batch of figures was tumbling down the steps, a cowboy hat flying out of the avalanche, as the human bowling balls in tattered brownsuits appeared to mesh in a bizarre tangle of arms and legs before they rolled up at the bottom.

Son of a bitch!

Yet more Ivans upstairs, at least two hardmen he was aware of, and they were hosing the positions of his people with autofire, covering the fighting withdrawal of their own, shooting down over the rail.

Heller fed his subgun a fresh clip and gave chase. Whatever the stakes, he knew the ante was upped, and neither warring side would dream of bluffing their way out of this hell.

KAHMUD NURIJ TENSED on the edge of his seat, but felt the jolt of gleeful anticipation now that the big event was moments away from becoming his vision of bliss. The glittering lights of Las Vegas filling his eyes where the drone relayed the image of towering rows of hotel-casinos, he felt the smile break over his mouth, as Target Search blinked in the upper right-hand corner of the screen, Orion working the keyboard with a fury.

The American had set up another monitor on the metal table, this one with a split screen, numbers scrolling in one corner as the countdown to target one ticked off. Now they both saw what the drone and the gun camera in the first 188 mm shell framed, Nurij dividing rapt attention between the American's computer and the real-time Vegas auditioning of SPLAT. With the drone on course for its second flyover, he knew it was cruising at an altitude of five thousand feet, its fiberoptic eye panning the Circus Circus, Algiers, Westward Ho, Stardust, the Marriott, the Las Vegas Hilton hotel-casinos. Wondering which would be the first to feel the lightning bolt of destruction, Nurij nurtured his euphoria, heart racing, mouth dry. If only these shells were packed with a chemical or a biological agent, he thought, forcing himself to fight back bitter disappointment, choking down a shout of outrage. No, if only he could get his hands on just one missile with which to wreak nuclear devastation! Ten—no, a paltry fifteen—kilotons and he could have wiped Las Vegas off the wicked face of the Great Satan, nothing but a radioactive crater left where the infidels cavorted in their bastions of evil!

Target Accessed!

It was actually happening. So far, the SPLAT technology appeared to work so well, it was as if the hand of God guided the projectile, steering it with divine will to rip out the heart of his enemies.

He couldn't wait to inform the Great One of what he witnessed.

As yet, though, he received no detailed instructions on how the system operated, other than Orion explaining what set of keys he punched on his keyboard, to what end. When the first shell was launched, the American explained the computer could actually select a target while the projectile was still in flight, that he was able to steer the drone on his end, tap in whichever target codes he had already programmed into the software, altering its course, if he so desired. Nurij knew the shell was sailing along at plus three hundred miles per hour, the northern end of the Strip zooming into view now, the Sahara rapidly enlarging to what seemed life-size, swelling the screen next, in fact, the hotel-casino with its roller coaster blurring out as the projectile streaked on for its final leg, a rocket ride aimed straight at the target's facade, gathering yet more speed, it seemed, then—

Impact!

He smiled from the heart, staring at the gray flickers where half of the second monitor had winked out. Confirming Target Hit blinked in the corner of the magic computer.

Not missing a beat, Orion worked the keyboard, his fingers flying like a master pianist.

"McCarran."

"What's that?"

Nurij bent closer to the American, ran a tongue over dry lips. "I said, the airport—can you target a jetliner, one that is preparing to take off? Can you bring one down?" he asked, watching Orion's monitor as the drone zeroed in on the Las Vegas Hilton, a red triangle framing the hotel's facade, the entire structure then shrinking in a machine-gun-fire series of zoom-ins, before a green window flashed around what he believed was an area just above the lobby.

"I can, but I'm not. When you buy it, you can call the shots. I don't care if you use it to blast the White House or the Capitol to smoking dust. But this is more than an audition, friend. I have men under fire right now and a plan to stick to. Not to mention we can't hang around here forever, even if we are miles from the highway and any outpost of civilization."

Disappointed but understanding the situation, Nurij saw Target Search, then Accessed flare into the corner, Orion keying his com link, telling his gunnery mates outside, "Fire number two, gentlemen."

The sonic boom near the transport jolted Nurij. If the American was worried about the noise of cannonfire alerting anyone within miles, he showed no sign of concern, all grim business as he stared into the monitor.

"When can I try it?"

The American bobbed his head as Nurij saw the shell's gun eye gobbling up a vast stretch of desert, leveling out, on course. "Let me fire off two more right quick, drop one of my cruise specials into the convention center, and I'll give you a shot."

Nurij smiled as he saw the distant skyline of Las Vegas shoot up into view, growing larger by the nanosecond. A cruise missile special, he thought, on the back burner but ready to plow into the convention center. How many infidels were inside the building? How many would die? He could hardly wait to man the SPLAT's helm, grab his moment to shine, and for all of Islam. This, he thought, was more than a dream come true.

This was as close to Paradise on Earth as he could ever hope to find.

CHAPTER TEN

Carl Lyons didn't have any official military service on public record like Blancanales and his PI pal, not that it mattered to him. A former Los Angeles detective and now a Stony Man warrior, he had seen more than his share of combat and dead bodies, not to mention firing shots in anger more times than he could count. As leader of Able Team he often mapped out tactics and strategy—seeking counsel, of course, with his two comrades and the Stony Man team—and he was grimly aware that almost without exception, when the bullets started flying and men were bleeding out all over the place, battle plans went straight to hell.

This time was no exception.

Hard truth be told, there were too many unknown variables to weigh beyond fleeting consideration, not without getting brain lock, careless or reckless when he jumped into the shooting gallery. Start with Parker, untested as far as he was concerned, not a clue as to how the private dick would hold up under fire, what his combat moves, or if he would even follow orders, all of which was a recipe for potential disaster. Then there was no clear fix on enemy numbers, positions, opposition hardware. Problem number three was cops, innocent bystanders, security detail to factor into the murderous equation. Their Justice Department credentials may well prove as worthless as cheap cracker box tin, if the law started getting ground up in the battle zone, especially with the kind of hardware they were lugging into the casino. With the exception of Parker, they were webbed and harnessed to boot, the three of them weighted down with grenades, spare clips beneath their knee-length, black nylon windbreakers, commando daggers, big and sharp enough to filet a white shark, in shin sheaths, just in case all else failed. There was the war van, parked several blocks away, meaning if the enemy here, by chance, made the street or a getaway vehicle rolled up...

Why piss and moan, he decided, over what he couldn't change. They were late for the bloody horror show as it stood, judging the utter bedlam that consumed Fremont and the surrounding streets, screams of terror flaying his ears, sirens wailing in the distance, cops sure to be bulling up their six anytime. Leading the charge into the stampeding herd of terror-crazed civilians, his M-16/M-203 combo clearing a narrow path as runners spotted then veered sharply from the weapon, he heard the blistering retorts of gunfire, the muffled crunch of what he suspected was a grenade blast somewhere in the building, beyond the casino's front doors.

There was no way, he knew, to play it other than a charge straight up Broadway.

No sweat, they'd all been to Hell and back before.

Schwarz on his left wing, wielding a match for his M-16/M-203 squad pulverizer, Blancanales and friend picking up the rear, Lyons hit the door, surged into the pandemonium. One sniff of the air and Lyons caught a noseful of cordite, blood, loosed bowels and bladders. It reeked as if the gates of Hell had swung open in his face, but the senses didn't stop reeling there. Homing in the autofire dead ahead, he swept past the walking wounded. The cries of the innocent, the sight of several men and women bloodied and hobbling all over the casino, both enraged and sickened him.

And he spotted the enemy. Payback time.

Russian or American black ops, it didn't matter. The shootout was still in full-tilt boogey, Lyons knew, and, though they were late, the big plus was hitting them from their blindside.

Starting now.

They were firing down into the lower level, three hardmen covering for a chorus line of black-leathered, armed figures, six total, now bounding up the escalator. Advancing, the Able Team leader recognized the human prize, neck-locked in a goon's arm, Jacobs getting hauled up the escalator like a sack of groceries, thrashing and screaming God only knew what.

Lyons held back on the trigger of his M-16. Streams of weaponsfire chattered on both his flanks, the quad-bursts joining to converge into one lead meat grinder that ripped into the backs of the trio, flung them into a convulsing 180 dance step before they toppled.

Hope, then, the four of them could roll up the enemy without much fanfare vanished in the next moment.

The hardman using Jacobs as a shield balked as he

looked toward the new combatants, his focus seeming locked on Parker and Blancanales. He shouted something in Russian, what sounded to Lyons like a curse, then his troops began unloading autofire, shooting from the hip, shuffling for the cover of the slot and poker machine arcade but not before their barrage ate up a few low-roller jackpots.

Bullets snapping past his ears, Lyons flung himself behind a slot machine getting shot up to ruins. He glimpsed Parker, then Blancanales two shakes behind his pal, racing past—and where the hell were they going, charging straight into the guns like that?—as sparks, glass and coins sprayed the air around him in a minivolcanic eruption, a blast of all this shrapnel slashing off his skull. Battle plan? he thought. What battle plan?

The killing game here had just spiraled down to another circle of Hell, with no end or winner in sight.

"YOU'RE ON."

Arthur Donemus gave Vance, their wheelman, a thumbs-up. "Rock and roll, hoochie-goo."

As the proud albeit anxious savior for the rest of the team, he was moments away from field-testing the prototype, six-barreled Gatling gun, "liberated," he knew, from the Eagle Nebula's weapons factory for the operation. Only this monster of death and doom, the Leviathan MX-60, pumped out 60 mm grenades, created by war-gamers in their think tanks back in North Dakota, he heard, with the express purpose of reducing entire city blocks to rubble, thus paving the way for advancing infantry to mop up any shell-shocked rabble still staggering. The link-belt feed special from the mammoth stainless-steel weapon's pod could spew out something like 600 projectiles per minute, with selector switch for single shot, 3-round bursts or full-blown automatic hellfire. With a range of 3500 meters and each missile capable of streaking at 400 meters per second, that was more than plenty enough distance, velocity, and not to mention big bang for the latest in techno bucks.

He didn't think he'd need to burn through the whole bin of three hundred rounds for a dozen or so police cruisers, but the action was only just heating up, no telling, with the Northern Strip now getting slammed by 188s and Eagle Nebula cruise missiles, just how large the legal army would swell before evacuation. And getting clear of Vegas was still in serious doubt.

Killing cops might have bothered him had there not been a six-figure payday waiting on the other end, but what could he do? His orders were clear. Arrest was unacceptable, especially in light of the fact he had plans to retire somewhere in the South Pacific, but dreams of island girls giving him hummers on the beach while he sipped mai tais all day long were on definite hold.

Business first.

He barely heard the electronic hum beyond the shouts, screams and blaring horns as the war van's ceiling parted and he rose on the platform toward the spotlight. Under different circumstances he might have admired the red tint painting the twilit dome above Sin City, staring, an awestruck tourist, at the umbrella of glittering diadems crowning Vegas.

Only he was no Johnny or Jane tourist, but he was damn sure taking the biggest gamble of his life.

Anarchy, he heard and saw, had swept like Noah's flood through all of Glitter Gulch, engulfed the surrounding blocks all the way down to his fire point on the corner of Las Vegas Boulevard and Carson Avenue, the masses running pell-mell for their lives to clear the combat zone, or stuck in traffic, lying on horns. Eagle Team One, he knew, was already engaged with cops to the northwest on South Main Street, with ET3 the roving backup unit, to be called in only as an emergency, its primary task to evacuate Heller, his team and the genius. That so many stand-up acts, battle-hardened men who had never known anything but tough to the extreme were fighting, killing and dying for one geek slob whose only concern was the gaming tables and scoring his next broad.

Screw it. He was getting paid a handsome sum, and not to question the moral or legal consequences of the operation.

He was on stage, no question, as he saw the first of four cruisers, sirens wailing, lights flashing, attempting to navigate a boulevard choked with snarled traffic. Another three cruisers, with a SWAT van pulling up the rear, jerked to a halt. Picture perfect, he thought, the uniformed cavalry figuring they could make the Great Vegas Shootout at the casino far quicker on foot.

Rats in a barrel. Cash on the hoof.

They were barging out the doors when Donemus lined up the lead car in his gunsights. What the hell, he thought, and flicked the selector switch to full-auto.

Squeezing the trigger, the opening rounds chugged

on, vaporizing two cruisers off the bat. The fireballs blossomed brighter and bigger with each sonic boom, fiery clouds intercoursing with every new roar to consume man and machine, gutting and shredding vehicles, flimsy tin cans. There was recoil and smoke, as expected, and he was forced to aim low as the spinning barrel demanded to rise. He began raking the line of cruisers, stem to stern, fighting to keep from being hypnotized by the sheer gargantuan power of the army-slayer he wielded. He lost count of the blasts, but glimpsed shredded uniforms and sheets of wreckage flying away so hard and far he believed they'd end up plastered all over the facades of Fitzgeralds and the Four Queens casinos a block away, maybe some ground hamburger and debris sprinkling the steps of the court house on Third Street.

"Bogey at two o'clock!" he heard Vance shout over the com link.

Laying off the trigger, squinting against the rolling wall of fire, panning the carnage for maimed or wounded but only finding a row of sprawled meat, he looked at the radar screen fixed to the platform. Sure enough, there was a blip, and heading his way, due north.

Swinging the barrel, he lined up the chopper, glanced at the small digital readout. The computer system gauged range and elevation, likewise factored in the possibility of wind-altering trajectory, then made the adjustments for him, while calculating the bogey's speed as he tapped in the code for Target Accessing Data. That done, he looked up, gave the chopper some lead, according to the readout, then fired away.

And scored three, perhaps four or five, bull's-eyes, all but lighting up the sky with a supernova they might have seen clear to Reno. It was impossible to tell how many hits, since the ball of fire, roiling out so large and brighter than all the winking diadems of Vegas, seemed punched away by the sheer force of the conflagration. The flaming shell appeared to hover next, then it dropped in a spiral of black smoke and winging debris, floating for impact, he saw, with the Lady Luck casino.

He sat, able to drag a moment's breath now, mesmerized as he scanned the flaming lake in front of him. Movement then to the rear of the garbage heap, spotting two SWAT commandos limping out of the smoke and flames, and he unleashed Leviathan, sealing them in their explosive tomb.

RUSTOV COULDN'T believe it. The private investigator with the cheap white shoes and comrade had come back for more punishment, and they had brought two extra guns to the party. Where there were four new combatants, he had to suspect more reinforcements in the casino, or en route, especially if the comrade of White Shoes was, indeed, with the Justice Department. If that wasn't bad news enough, he knew the black ops would fly into the arcade any moment, blasting away with indiscriminate savagery. With his rear then sealed off, and the way out the front door blocked by two commandos with M-16/M-203 combos, capable of wiping them out if they so desired…

Down to six shooters, including himself, Rustov barked at his commandos to form a perimeter, cover him, front and back.

"This is madness, Rustov! We'll never get out of here alive, and even if we do, the police—"

"Stop your whining!" Rustov snarled, wadded up a handful of Jacobs's hair, then jamming the muzzle of the subgun in his lower back as he thrust him forward. He checked the lane between the slot machines on either flank. Clear. But for how long? With the sudden end of weaponsfire, he listened to the moans, the pleas for help of wounded or terrified gamblers from somewhere in the vicinity, ears tuned to any sound warning him of an enemy advance.

"Give it up, Ivan! You're not going to make it!"

Rustov hissed at Jacobs, "Be still and stop whimpering or I will shoot you dead on the spot."

There. Three rows down, he spotted the big commando, crouched on a knee, the muzzle of his assault rifle visible as it poked around the edge of a slot machine. Suddenly another commando sprinted across the lane, grabbing a perch behind the next bank of machines directly opposite his comrade, matching assault rifle drawing a bead.

"Listen to me, whoever you are!" Rustov shouted. "We are walking out of here, or I am prepared to kill Dr. Jacobs!"

"So kill him."

Startled then angered by the grim nonchalance of the commando, Rustov shook Jacobs when he cried out, sniveling something about the love of God.

"Too many people, a bunch of whom I'm assuming were completely innocent, have already died and for just this one asshole. You can have him."

A bluff? Rustov wondered. Heart thundering in his

ears, sensing movement to his left, he was turning his head when he spotted White Shoes advancing toward him. The big stainless-steel handgun was already aimed his way, Rustov believing he could read the fire in the eyes, burning through the dark sunglasses. He heard the anticipated gunfire erupt from behind, was in the process of swinging his human armor toward White Shoes but knew he'd never make it. It flashed through his mind how odd it seemed to know he was dead on his feet, how wrong it was that some drunk in a stupid-looking checkerboard longcoat would punch his ticket. He heard the gun thunder, thought for a lightning nanosecond he could actually visualize the bullet streaking toward him before impact doused the lights.

BLANCANALES HURLED HIMSELF behind the slots as a Mountain Man in black rushed around the pillar and cut loose with the mammoth Gatling gun, a weapon that was all fire, smoke and blistering rounds of pure steel-jacketed lightning bolts. He gave it brief consideration, as the slot proved flimsy cover, obliterated to a sparking dungheap within a few heartbeats, that Lyons had been right. Assuming he survived, he could expect a thorough reaming out by the Able Team leader. But why blame his buddy for bull-rushing the Russians now? And to what end? Right then it was every horse for himself to whatever the finish line.

Only all bets were off, and it was every shooter for himself.

The roaring tidal wave sweeping on, Blancanales pictured the behemoth rolling to come up on the rear of the Russians. With the beast he commanded, the Ivans didn't stand anything other than a hope or a prayer, if that. The Gatling gun against their assault rifles and subguns? Talk about killing a mosquito with a sledgehammer.

Circle back, then, he decided, and come up on their blindside.

It sounded like the only game under the roof, Blancanales jumping to his feet, forced to cover his own twelve and six, as he scanned and retraced his steps, when the worst of the shooting erupted about two or three rows down.

Where he'd last seen Eddie Parker.

He hugged sparking garbage cans, on the move, coins spilling in his wake, steel and silver rubbish winging off his skull. MP-5 subgun leading the way, Blancanales caught a man in black whirling around the corner, blew him off his feet with a lightning bolt of 9 mm Parabellum manglers to the chest.

One more bad guy waxed, but how many left standing? He'd know soon enough, and sensed it all winding down to a bad end.

THERE WAS NO BACKGROUND music, no roaring crowds to cheer him on, no admiring female in the audience to groan and flinch each time he took a hit. This, Eddie Parker knew, was it.

The sight of their leader—half his skull blown away and sprawled at their feet—swung their rage and gunsights toward his death march. He bulled into the blistering wall of lead, triggering the Colt in one hand, sweeping the Uzi in the other, left to right. Ignoring Jacobs, as he crabbed his way then ate carpet when he

claimed a cubbyhole in the slots to ride it out, sniveling, Parker thought, like the cowardly turd he was. The
P.I. cannoned off two more .45 ACP rounds, the subgun blazing away but riding high and wide. One Russian was dropping, though, bellowing something, his
AKM still hosing down the slots and hurling yet more
shrapnel into the meteor shower of coins and glass.
Parker felt the first few rounds tear through him, maybe
the ribs, the upper left side of his chest. What did it matter? Little more than bee stings, since he was fairly a
walking mummy anyway, formaldehyded as he was by
whiskey, adrenaline and rage, but he would be down and
out in the next few moments.

The end.

So be it.

Something happened next as he felt another round
bore through his shoulder, throwing his aim off, the .45
slug blasting out a jackpot of coinage at his feet.
Whether it was the hard truth he would die here—but
on his feet, by God—or the sum total of raw anger and
bitter pain he'd both endured but inflicted on scads of
humanity over the years of a sorry life glared for all the
world to behold all his faults and flaws, failings and foi-
bles seizing him in the final few seconds...

But it was there, that collage a man glimpsed of the
life he'd led, shooting at light speed through his mind,
a living entity, it seemed, and right before he cashed in
the chips—or they were cashed in for him, as was his
doomed case. The unholy racket strangely enough
began to fade to a blissful evanescence, even as he believed he heard autofire break out from some point to
the rear—or was it the front or both?—of the Russians.

From somewhere deep in his mind, as he felt himself pummeled into, then driven down the slots, with what looked like half the arcade downrange obliterated to smoking trash mounds, Russians getting dismembered and eviscerated to dancing slabs of gristle, he saw his mother.

And there he was, locked in a closet for the thousandth time, the old man, drunk again, screaming for him to stop crying, while he beat his mother senseless to near dead. Mama, by God, finally got sick and tired of the abuse, so the firemen had to come that one day, put out what was left of flames that had incinerated the sorry bastard.

He felt another two or three rounds drill him, left side of the chest, spinning him, the Uzi stuttering but from light-years distant it sounded.

Rolling on, falling back, but aware he was still on his feet.

And what was his life all about?

A high school dropout, three tours of duty, two of which came after the Dear Eddie letter, and he'd spent his Nam time trying his damnedest to get himself killed, take the medals and stick it. Love just didn't look real promising after his sweetheart dropped the bomb—and maybe anger was simply disappointment in love, but he'd been known as a thief of hearts more times than he could count. Two failed marriages to his discredit, he counted his blessings there were no children tossed into the nightmare.

Leaving nothing behind that was remotely worthwhile, not even flesh and blood to remember him, sorry SOB he was.

Floundering as a private investigator, committing the same mistakes that had gotten him kicked off the police force, ruined countless relationships. Gambling. Alcoholism. Chasing skirts. What was his problem? What had he been looking for all these years? Love in all the wrong places, simple as that? What was he? A failure—like father, like son?—wanting to be more than what he was, but not really sure what, wondering why he was so weak and if he'd ever change his ways.

A wasted life, or was it? He'd know all too soon enough.

May God have mercy.

He was falling now, no fighting gravity and the constant barrage hammering away, eating him up. Tasting the blood on his lips, wondering why and how it went so wrong all these years, he felt the weight of the crucifix on his chest, the floor seeming to open up and swallow him as he heard the air leave his lungs in a guttural belch.

"Hail Mary…"

LYONS FOUND IT TOUGH to swallow that one man—and a traitor, to boot—was the root cause of so much death and destruction. No single human being, he thought, had that much talent, that much money, that much to offer to bring on the kind of murder and mayhem raging still in front of him, the body count sure to pile up to the damn ceiling at the rate it was going. And Jacobs was unarmed, sure to not even jump in and fire off a few shots in anger or even save his own sorry butt, just sit tight and ride it out while everyone else did the shooting and the dying, not to mention however many innocents he was sure got ground up already between the warring factions. Talk about injustice. Talk about madness. Talk about evil. Oh, there would be an answer, and Lyons intended to get it, no matter what.

Motivated by cold anger to wax the enemy and get his hands on the genius for the mother of all throttlings, Lyons made a wide and hard circle around the behemoth with the Gatling man-eater, using slots for cover, stare fixed on the massive weapon. The hardman, though, seemed more interested in cutting the Russians to ribbons while blasting slots all to hell, enjoying his work, standing tall, man and monster roaring on. Lyons figured he had his blindside all to himself, unless one of his teammates nailed him first. Doubtful, since they sounded engaged elsewhere with the latest batch of men in black fatigues.

He hugged the line of slots, sweeping his flanks with the assault rifle, closing on the big killer's six, the Gatling thundering on, the sight of the mayhem he wreaked breaking him out in a fit of laughter. The devastation unleashed on man and machine, bodies and appendages vanishing in front of his eyes in gory red cloudbursts, told Lyons armor-piercing bullets or some sort of explosive-tipped rounds were being hurtled toward the doomed at a rate he didn't even want to consider.

Ten feet, nine.

Lyons drew his Colt Python as weaponsfire faded.

Four feet.

The Gatling gun spun on, silent now but breathing smoke clouds over the strewed carnage. Chuckling, the SOB stood there, admiring his gruesome handiwork.

"Elvis...has left the building!"

Lyons let him have his chuckle, raised the handgun as the hardman was turning, clearly now sensing a presence on his back. "I never did like that guy," he growled, and pumped a round between his eyes.

"EDDIE!"

Kicking through a bed of change and glass, Blancanales crouched beside Parker, gripped by anger over the sight of his friend sprawled and bleeding out. The sounds of battle and the wounded crying out for help floated around him, seemed to weigh him down with his own grief. He stared into his friend's eyes, calling his name again, letting him know he was there. It was over, Blancanales knew, as he saw the light fading in his friend's eyes, shock setting in, no way to tell with all the blood how bad or how many times he'd been hit. He couldn't be sure, as a renewed din of weaponsfire erupted from the direction of the front doors, but he thought he heard Eddie praying, a bloody hand wrapped around his crucifix.

"Eddie, don't die on me, dammit! I'll get you help."

"Forget it," he croaked. "Tell me…did you get the rest of the Russians?"

"It's in the works."

"And those other…clowns…"

"We're working on it."

Parker grabbed Blancanales by the shoulder, blood gushing from his mouth. "You've been a good friend…even when I…didn't deserve one…I'm going home to Mama."

"Eddie!"

"God help me," Parker groaned, and died.

And what was a man's life? he suddenly wondered, guts clenching, brushing the eyelids shut. Did he ever really know Eddie Parker? Or did he never really want anybody to know him? What demons tormented him, drove him to self-destruct? Strange how he really never got to know his friend beyond the war, never learned about his life prior to Vietnam, or what his dreams, troubles, hopes, Eddie always acting out as though something was haunting him to the point of madness. Or did anyone ever really know someone else to the core of their soul?

God help Eddie Parker, indeed.

Glass crunching, Blancanales rose, subgun swinging toward Lyons, who was keying his com link, barking, he assumed, at Schwarz. On the march, the Able Team leader then snatched Jacobs off the floor, practically hurling him in his direction, the feet of the man so many had died for bicycling air.

Lyons looked down at Parker, silent for a moment. "We need to vacate, Pol. Gadgets says a few hostiles made the street, and he has them on the run. Only it sounds like all hell's going to break loose on us once we hit the doors. There's big trouble everywhere on the streets and surrounding blocks, complete chaos for some reason. This whole town is an uproar, and I get the impression it's about more than what happened here."

"He was my friend, Carl."

"I know that. May he rest in peace, but we need to boogie."

Blancanales gave Parker another look, then saw Lyons shake Jacobs as the Able Team leader asked,

"Did you get the Russian SOB who had this one here in a headlock?"

"No."

"If not Schwarz or me…"

Blancanales rose. "Eddie got him."

"Your buddy then might have saved this jerk's life."

But he couldn't save himself, Blancanales thought, turned and fell in behind Lyons.

CHAPTER ELEVEN

Kahmud Nurij thought he might hyperventilate. With every 188 mm shell or the so-named Eagle Nebula Cruise Missile Specials guided by computer navigation system then slamming home to target, his heart raced faster, his blood ran hotter, his breathing amplified in his ears until all other sound was wiped out. In fact, he was so excited by what the drone televised in real time he lost track of how many casinos and hotels had been hit.

He was mesmerized by the sight of the convention center—or what was left of it—as the drone panned the North Strip. It looked as if two, maybe three or four direct hits had nearly razed the building to little more than smoking rubble by the cruise missiles, or angels of vengeance and death sent from God, as he thought of this glorious technology that could advance the cause of jihad. Better yet, the infidels—whoever had survived, and the fact there were any survivors at all disturbed him for a second—appeared to limp, run from the ruins or collapse from terror or injuries in their tracks. He couldn't be positive of how much longer or how many more shells or missiles were ready to launch, since Orion—grunting now on his satellite phone—had lapsed into grim silence. Nurij knew they were on the clock, and no matter what desolate piece of real estate they had staked out, Orion had informed there were more military bases and classified installations than could be counted. With the destruction they had rained on Las Vegas and a body count certain to be in the thousands, it wouldn't be long at all before the skies were swarming with search or attack helicopters and fighter jets.

So he watched the monitor, trying to drink in all the destruction he saw, as if it were sweet wine warming his belly. He gave silent but fervent praise to God for allowing him to live long enough to see this demonstration—no, to be the one who would deliver this weapons system to the Great One. Unless he missed his guess the Circus Circus, the Westward Ho, Stardust and the Marriott Suites hotel-casinos bore massive gaping holes in their facades, bodies, he saw, strewed all over lots, in the street, some crawling and clearly crying out for help, the North Strip lit up by the flashing lights of emergency medical vehicles, fire trucks, police cruisers.

Utter ruin and chaos.

Victory.

"We need to pack it up. The demonstration's over."

Nurij looked at Orion, disappointed, but noted the change in his expression and voice. Something was wrong, so he decided not to push his luck. He was sold on SPLAT.

Orion began tapping the keys, working with a sense of urgency and anger that Nurij found disturbing.

"What are you doing?"

"The grand finale," Orion said. "The drone? It's packed with five hundred pounds of plastic explosive, all wired to an impact fuse. I'm putting it into freefall, nosedown, but telling its computer what to hit."

"And the target?" he asked, glimpsed Orion throw him a funny look. "May I pick it?"

"No time for a crash course. This area is going to become hot soon with more fighter jets and helicopter gunships than you've ever feared to see in your wildest nightmare." Orion scowled. "We get caught here with our pants down and this kind of ordnance, they'll shoot us on the spot. To answer your question, the drone is going to rip out the heart of the Desert Inn Country Club."

"If only we had more time, if only we had more missiles."

"Right. Well, when your people buy it you can stroke yourselves each time you blow something up."

Nurij wasn't sure he cared for the tone, a hint of contempt in the American's voice, but he—jihad—needed the man. "You said five hundred pounds. Is there capacity for more?"

"I can deliver one with a two-thousand-pound limit. And, I know what you're thinking. Yes, it can deliver chemical or biological agents."

"How much explosive was in each cruise missile?" he asked, heard the weight, and thought he would keel over from giddy joy.

"That's nearly twice what's in a Tomahawk. Show's over. Let's move out."

Nurij watched as Orion shut down the notebook computer, closed it up. He wanted to watch this grand finale but the American was barking at him to get up and get out. "We will buy it."

The computers stashed in a duffel bag, he saw Orion pin a dark look on him as he stood.

"After the time, sweat and money I dumped into this audition, I would damn well expect so."

HERMANN SCHWARZ had three hardmen on the run, but with all the chaos swirling around him, runners darting all over the street and sidewalks, a whirlwind of bodies and noise, he couldn't risk cutting loose with autofire, chopping down civilians. And Trench Coat in the lead had already grabbed human armor on the way out of the casino, blasting him back to cover for a few critical heartbeats. Their game plan to grab Jacobs from the Russians backfiring in their faces, Schwarz knew they were leaving Las Vegas.

Not if he could help it.

Between sirens, blaring horns, screams and what sounded like rolling thunder from some undetermined point, the din alone was enough to rattle the senses, but Schwarz pushed on, bulling his way through a pack of civilians as he pounded down Fourth Street.

Another block of full-bore sprinting and the carnage and destruction he spotted filled his eyes. He balked at the sight for a second, then kept running, gathering steam, enraged, but aware now why no cops or SWAT had made the casino battleground. Other than some type of grenade launcher that could pump out more than a few rounds in seconds flat, he couldn't imagine what had turned those cruisers into crushed tin.

Special Eagle Nebula ordnance, no doubt.

They appeared to angle for a waiting oversize black van when Schwarz went for it. Squeezing the trigger on his M-16, he cut the legs out from under the slowest trench coat, the hardman screaming, toppling. Lyons might not like it, after the slaughter they'd manage to live through, with Pol losing a good friend, but he wanted a songbird.

They needed answers as much as enemy blood.

He closed on the van, twenty yards or so out, when the side door flew wide. The two trench coats forgot all about their comrade, going for themselves, a black-clad figure in the doorway shouting at them, waving his HK subgun. As he kicked the shotgun with its attached cylinder from the hands of his prisoner, a blast flying high and wide for the lights of Vegas, he spotted the stainless-steel cannon with its cylindrical barrel. More Gatling gun specials, plucked, he could safely assume, from the Eagle Nebula.

Time to give them a taste, he thought, of their own big bang.

They were jumping through the door when Schwarz tapped the trigger on his M-203, watched it zigging on for easy paydirt. One hellbomb was enough for the job, as it streaked through open door, impacted on the far wall, but Schwarz stole a moment to watch the fireball incinerate all aboard, the blast lifting the van off its wheels, a mangled figure dumped to the street.

"YOU WANT MORE OUT OF me, I want a deal. Full immunity, the whole sweet cherry pie."

Carl Lyons was sick to the point of murderous rage by the facts as he so far had them, but he had a prime target at his mercy to taste the wrath he felt set to blow.

They were in the black surveillance van on loan from the Justice Department. Blancanales had the wheel, jostling them as best he could through the jumbled maze of vehicles fighting to get off Dunes Road for Interstate 15, the landmark that was the Palms Resort and Casino looming at one o'clock. But to Lyons it looked as far away and unreachable as those famous Eagle Nebula "pillars of creation," and just as they were ready to blitz up the rear of the last enemy war van. According to the prisoner, their black ops leader had told the roving van to bail but to stick to the escape route, south down I-15, everybody was on their own. Van three, or so their prisoner said, held the last of the troops standing. Responsible for so much murder and mayhem, the worst traitors he had ever engaged, Lyons wanted to nail them so bad...

In pursuit, and with Lady Luck willing, soon enough he'd get his shot.

Headset on, Schwarz had the comm and tracking station all to himself in the back, providing Lyons with minute-by-minute updates and play-by-play as he juggled police, FBI and military frequencies. Already he verified the last war van was bogged down in a traffic jam on I-15. Spotted by a police helicopter, state police and FBI had erected two barricades down the interstate. One blockade was penning back traffic, hoping to lock the war van in long enough for the authorities to swoop down. Number two barricade was four miles farther south, just in case the murdering bastards blasted through number one, or maybe veered off for the desert. They were close, a few short miles, at best, but not near close enough, Lyons thought as he heard the blood pressure thunder into his ears.

Because Schwarz had also informed him of what appeared a terrorist attack, which was why half of the state's population, it seemed to Lyons, was fighting to get the hell out Vegas. With the city under siege, the skies now screamed with fighter jets, buzzed with helicopter gunships. Since they were likewise armed and dangerous...

They were in this to the bloody finish line, win or bust.

Lyons glanced at Schwarz who was scrolling numbers to all police, FBI and military frequencies in the area. The software for this unique brand of eavesdropping, he knew, was created by Kurtzman and Tokaido. Listing whatever frequencies they needed to break into for instant communication, Lyons knew they would have to contact the authorities if—no, when, he determined—they engaged the last round of blacksuits. The way he heard it from Schwarz, Vegas authorities believed both artillery shells and cruise missiles had blasted up the North Strip to what he imagined was a version of Baghdad during the initial shock and awe of Gulf II. The body count was undetermined, since huge chunks of everything from the convention center to hotels and casinos had dropped the roof on occupants. Why Vegas? he wondered. In a terrorist scumbag's mind, why not? To what end lay siege to a city, waste so many innocents? Again, why not? But Lyons suspected there was more going on behind the scenes than mass murder. And who was behind what would surely go down as the worst attack on American soil? Well, he had his suspicions on that front, too. Worse, for the moment, at least, how many more terrorists or Eagle Nebula black ops were on the prowl, ready to fan the flames of the anarchy sweeping Vegas? Say they vanished into the wind, where then did their scheme of mass murder go after leaving Las Vegas? He needed the truth, and fast.

And Lyons had Mr. Mark Knudsen of the Department of Defense sprawled under his crouch. He gave the credentials another scowl, already told by his prisoner they were bogus, and flipped them to the floor. The tourniquets he'd fastened around both the prisoner's thighs would, he hoped, stem the bleeding out long enough for him to get more information. As for Jacobs, he was cuffed and on his ass, told to keep his mouth until spoken to. And with his stare locked on the .357 Colt Python in the Able Team leader's hand, everyone's favorite aerospace genius, quaking and looking set to piss himself, was so far complying.

Lyons saw Blancanales attach the strobing red light to the roof, a siren blaring to life before he began bucking them ahead, aiming for sidewalks, any opening he could find. He dropped the muzzle of the handgun on Knudsen's forehead, kissing him square between the eyes.

"You kill me, you have squat."

Lyons thumbed back the hammer, heard Jacobs gasp. "Spill your guts or your brains. You talk and it pans out, I will go the extra undeserved mile for your murdering ass and pitch your deal. Two seconds for you to decide."

It took half of one second. "Okay. There's special ordnance, state-of-the-art cruise missiles and artillery shells. What was dropped here was part demonstration for a potential buyer and a means to cover our escape."

Lyons clenched his teeth. "And this buyer?"

"The ordnance is being funneled to Iran, or maybe it's already there, I don't know. The guy you want, his name is Gabriel Horn, but he goes by Orion."

Lyons pulled the gun back. "We've met. I dumped coffee in his crotch and stole his disk."

Knudsen stared at Lyons, the look betraying his reputation preceded him. "You?"

"Me, the clumsy Justice Department flunky. Now, you were saying…"

ALLAN GIVENS WAS STOKED on fear and adrenaline. He was prepared, however, to field test the Eagle Nebula war van, discover if it could perform as advertised by the Einsteins who'd created the urban fighting vehicle of tomorrow, or die in the attempt. Nerves on edge and talking back at him, he didn't like it, truth be told, but there was no other way out he could see, as they were dogged by an Apache gunship on their rear, with F-16s somewhere in the vicinity, according to both his copilot, Turnbull, with Winters sighting fighter jets to the west from the rear window.

Weight, thrust, lift and drag, the four interdependent forces for flight, he knew, that would get them up and stay up. Three phases for takeoff were ground roll, transition, climb, with the craft under constant acceleration, until velocity brought on the lift and drag, then pitched up to sweeten the angle of attack. Thrust first, he told himself, one small step at a time. He punched the red Start button, flipped two-thirds of the dashboard over, revealing the computerized instrument console that would either see them lift off into the twilit horizon or…

"Strap in, gentlemen. Winters, lose the big gun and shed our armor."

He glanced at Winters in the rearview glass. Working his control panel, Winters opened the back doors, the mammoth Gatling gun rolling out on its electronically controlled plate, dumped off and quickly lost in a cloud of dust. Givens then worked the computer's keyboard, scanning to find if there was now sufficient loss of weight. As he hit a rut in the desert floor, fought to keep the wheel from being ripped out of his hands, the screen informed him he was just under the weight limit where the force of gravity would not pull them down, keep them grounded. He released the Divine Alloy anyway from their miniature tanks, lined in the paneling, stem to stern. The numbers dropped so low, he was more than confident liftoff would be no problem, as long as he fed the computer the right codes. In fact, he would have sworn he felt the vehicle wanting to rise on its own, nerves snapping at that sensation, then wrote it off to the hard drive he was shooting them over the desert.

Givens glimpsed their faces one last time. They may be wound tight with anxiety, but wore the brave faces of seasoned pros, not squawking about the danger, knowing the score. Whatever had gone wrong back in Vegas, all hands cut loose to escape and evade…

Ancient history, as Givens rode them on into the cutting edge of the future.

They buckled up. As the seconds ticked down to the moment of truth, Givens became even more grimly aware this was no daily training routine in a flight simulator, where computerized virtual reality claimed the damn thing could perform as engineered, or a bunch of geeks standing around, testing the Eagle Nebula in a wind tunnel, slapping one another on the back.

This was the big one. Or the big bang, since he knew exactly what fueled this rocket ride, though it was classified, so implausible a mixture...

They said it came from outer space. Had he not worked security detail at Area 51 he would have scoffed off such a fantastic absurdity.

Gripping the wheel so tight he thought he heard his knuckles crack, he briefly thought about what fueled the war van. Since he wasn't a bona fide pilot, military or civilian, some of the specialized and complex aerodynamics escaped him, but he had nailed down the computer system—like a champ—which, supposedly, would do all the work. Still, he shuddered at the thought of failure, a crash landing at takeoff, for instance, though it would be quick, if nothing else, all lost in a fireball of possible supernova dimensions. Kerosene when wheels touched earth, he knew, but the fuel system converted over for flight by a mixture of solid rocket fuel, spent radioactive fuel from a thermal reactor and a dose of the Divine Alloy. This earth-meets-the-stars brew mixed with compressed air injected thrust through classified prototype "ramjet boosters," housed now, port and starboard to the stern, slated for release from their pods any moment. Once they were skybound, miniturbofans would suck in the air, hit the compressors and back to the combustion chambers...

Well, in theory, just like a big jet airliner.

He kept jouncing them over the rough terrain, parallel to the interstate. As he motored past the barricade, he spied a few uniforms staring their way, more than certain a few of those watching eyes of the law would attempt pursuit.

No problem.

Givens knew they had an ace in the hole, looking in the rearview, a moment's admiration for the 500-pound thermite vaporizer in the bomb bay, just beyond amidships. It was modeled after the Maverick AGM-65 for precision-guided, air-to-ground, but when Winters had intercepted the police ban, another plan of action had banged to mind.

One more roadblock, he knew, four miles and counting.

"Get that 500-pounder ready, Winters, for manual release. I'll tell you when."

The big bang, he knew, was gripped in tongs attached to a steel cable hung from the ceiling. Timing was critical, between takeoff and bombs away. If they weren't climbing well clear of ground zero from the barricade they would be toasted to ash.

Cutting back on speed, he rolled up the short incline, flew into a short jump over the edge, touched down with a jolt, then leveled out on flat highway. Smooth sailing for a few more miles, he thought as he released the wings from their housing that humped up the floorboard two feet or so, giving Winters full clearance to open the bomb bay. The tail rose next, two panels beside it falling away, morphing the war van as close to streamlined configuration as it would get.

In the distance he spotted the line of cruisers, lawmen ready and waiting for a sight they could tell their grandchildren, assuming, of course, they somehow escaped the Big Bang.

"This is it, gentlemen," he said, and released the ramjets.

SAILING OVER THE RISE, Blancanales hammered them down on the interstate so hard he nearly dumped the van on its side. Lyons heard Knudsen—or whatever his real name—groan at the jarring impact, Jacobs bleating out something unintelligible while Schwarz barked at the two-man Apache crew they were Justice Department. Lyons heard him pass on the same code that granted landing clearance at McCarran, throwing in the registration number of their van, shouting at them to check it out pronto between expletives, and woe be unto anybody who took it upon themselves to blow them off the interstate.

The Apache, he saw, hunched in the gap between the seats, streaked past, soaring down the highway. Something, he thought, going right for a change.

Or was it?

Blancanales pressed the pedal to the floor, held the vehicle at an even 100 mph. They sliced the gap in a lightning-bolt hurry, Lyons figuring they were two hundred yards behind the enemy and closing when—

He blinked, then stared hard enough at the war van to feel his eyes bulge.

"What the— Pol, am I suffering from combat stress and hallucinating?"

"If you are, then I am, too. But those are wings and that's a tail."

"Is it possible? They're going to fly over the barricade and into the sunset?"

"You'll have to ask Jacobs."

Later on that, Lyons thought, frozen by the fantastic sight, but angry they were more than likely going to lose their chance to mop up, as he saw two cones of fire ignite from the back end of the war van.

GIVENS GROWLED as the G-force wanted to crush him straight through his seat, the air sucked from his lungs so hard he was sure various body parts would fly from his mouth. Two eyeblinks and they were rocketing at 500 mph, shooting even faster next, straight at the barricade. They were on automatic, and with the computer in charge of control surfaces Givens heard his mind savagely curse for the Bernoulli effect and attack angle to kick in, urging airflow over the wings to get them off the ground before they plowed into the roadblock, incinerated.

It was only a blur, but he somehow made out figures scurry in both directions off the interstate, sprinting for cover.

And he felt them lifting off, would have laughed out loud if he could get the clamp off his throat.

"THEY'RE GOING to do it!"

Lyons couldn't believe it, as he silently echoed Blancanales's disbelief. He felt Schwarz and Jacobs pressed up against his back, then instinct warned him the Apache wasn't going to allow the most impossible feat of technology he'd ever witnessed to become reality.

"Hit the brakes, Pol!" he shouted as he saw the first

few rounds from the gunship's 30 mm chain gun rip into the roof.

GIVENS FEARED all along it was too good to be true.

It was, he discovered, as the roof above was sheared off by a barrage of 30 mm rounds. He figured the Apache was nearly on their bumper and just above, judging the chain gun peals.

And he knew it was over.

Out of the corner of his eye he saw half of Turnbull's skull vanish, the control panel eaten up to leaping sparks and ruins beyond recognition. The force of the heavy metal barrage pounded them back to earth, Givens paralyzed, jarred to the bone by the sudden touchdown, then the combination of speed and raining storm propelled them on, aimed straight for the heart of the blockade. He thought he heard Winters shout, but the words were swallowed up by the chain gun's thunder, then lost forever by impact which, in turn, ignited the Big Bang.

"BACK IT UP, Pol!"

They were well below a hundred yards from ground zero when the Big Bang erupted, and Lyons feared the raging expansion of the universe in his eyes would reach out and incinerate them. The blinding flash alone stung the eyes, but Lyons slitted his lids as the whirlwind of white fire, he glimpsed, devoured anything standing in that hell on Earth. His head slamming off the driver's seat next, both tires and Jacobs screaming in his ears, Schwarz eating leather beside him, the meteor shower began slamming the roof. Digging his hands into the edges of the seat, he was sure his fear was about to be realized as something very large with giant carnivore teeth and growing rapidly came winging toward the windshield, propelled, it looked, straight from the eye of a rolling wave of fire.

"Duck, Pol!"

Blancanales, foot mashed on the pedal to keep hurling them back, threw his head and shoulders down to starboard as the windshield vanished in a spray of glass. A superheated rush of wind seemed to rip the air out of the Able Team leader's lungs as glass razored the air, clipping ears and scalp and debris and God only knew what else thudded the van, stem to stern. There was a jolt, a rending of metal, as more jarring impacts and shock waves pelted the length of his body. An eternity later, it seemed, he could breathe again, Blancanales easing off the gas as the comets stopped threatening to crush them all in a metal coffin.

Squinting, he stared through the hanging fangs, ignored the raw sensation of a face that felt sunburned. The blast furnace was still expanding, consuming, what looked a cyclone of wreckage and mangled scarecrows falling to the ground. He then spotted two sedans Pol had played bumper cars with, front ends smashed and spewing steam, settled on the side of the highway. Figures in dark suits stumbled out the doors.

"Dear God…"

Lyons turned on Jacobs, saw the man busy patting himself down to make sure all body parts were still there. Resisting the urge to slap the sellout at the center of this universe of death and mayhem, he checked on his teammates, then Knudsen. He found they were all still on the planet, as one last giant's foot stomped off the roof.

"What we just saw," Lyons snarled at Jacobs, "is it possible? A flying car?"

Jacobs nodded. "It better be. I designed it." He paused, fear growing in his eyes. "But you need to evacuate this area immediately, full quarantine as soon as possible."

Lyons felt his heart skip a beat. "I'm almost afraid to ask, but I bet you're going to tell me…"

"Yes. There was a radioactive mix in those fuel tanks."

CHAPTER TWELVE

"Yes, sir, Mr. President…. Understood, sir…. You can be assured it will be done."

Hal Brognola was placing the receiver back on the red phone when Barbara Price walked into the War Room.

"The Las Vegas police are not saying at this time whether it was a robbery or a ruse meant to deflect the attention of the authorities away from the horrific series of bombing attacks on the North Strip, what initial but unconfirmed reports are stating was an artillery barrage or land-based cruise missiles that are believed to have been guided by an unmanned aerial vehicle, and that was spotted by several eyewitnesses before it struck the—"

Brognola felt sick to his stomach as he muted the wall-mounted monitor, both angry and tired from watching all the cable news channels. He knew the bloody score from the grim inside, as he clenched his jaw, shut his eyes, Price giving him a moment to compose himself. The big Fed felt as if he'd just taken about

101 body blows, all of them knocking the wind from his lungs. Where in God's name did it all go from there? he wondered. No sense, he then told himself, in grieving or raging over what he couldn't change. The living would bury their own in due anguished course. What the Stony Man team needed to do from here on was turn up the heat. The gloves were off, and that came straight from the Oval Office.

Rough justice.

"Hal?"

Brognola chomped on an antacid tablet. "What do you have?"

"Carl is, uh, to use his words, 'bogged down in a pissing contest with the FBI and an undetermined arm of the military.'"

Brognola scowled. "Meaning they're stuck in Vegas until the Hand of God from the Oval Office gets them cut loose."

"They're under something of a cloud of suspicion since they were in the casino, helping to shoot the place all to hell. And since they 'somehow bagged Dr. Jacobs and an enemy combatant,' according to the FBI field supervisor in Vegas, they have a lot of questions to answer, and he doesn't care if they're with the Justice Department."

Brognola rubbed his face. "Son of a—"

"Between FBI agents, state police, SWAT, L.V.P.D., then the security guards working the casino, many of whom were police officers moonlighting second jobs, or former cops, they lost over a hundred men and women, and still counting, depending on the wounded. I can understand the problem on their end, especially in light of the fact we have Americans committing mass murder against other Americans, but it needs to be resolved."

Brognola felt his guts twist with hot anger. Those lawmen, he knew, never stood a chance against weapons in the hands of American intelligence operatives turned traitors meant to slaughter small armies with small arms. Add civilian dead and wounded, with the body count sure to rise once they began to clear away the rubble...

If September 11, he thought, had torn the guts out of the nation with grief, outrage, anger and a demand for vengeance, well, this was even worse in his estimation. This attack was the result of an inside job by men who commanded authority over and were supposed to protect national security. If that came to light, the horror that had shelled Vegas could very well undermine all authority, push the country to the threshold of anarchy. Yes, there would be cover-ups, with some of the snakes in question certain to slither off into their holes. There would be an endless parade of press conferences, explanations, rationalizations, official heads on the chopping block...

Politics wasn't his concern, though the fiery backlash was certain to scorch the Justice Department. He—the Stony Man team—had a monumental task set before all of them. The bottom line, however, was to hunt down and nail those responsible.

No mercy.

Whatever it took.

"I'll handle Vegas, or I'll have that supervisor's job before I hang up on him," he told Price. "Is Jacobs and this black ops killer still in Able's possession?"

"On Carl's tight leash. But both want—"

"A deal. Full immunity. Relocation to Hawaii to ice the cake, I'm sure."

"You know how it goes."

"Damn straight, I do," Brognola growled. "The bad guys get caught, more blood on their hands than Saddam and King Herod put together, and they want to turn in everybody short of Saint Peter, tell you the sins of everybody including their grandmothers. The Man didn't come right out and say it, Barb, but as it stands, the only deal on the table is life or death, talk or die. When I free up Carl, he can go ahead and tell them they can have anything they want."

"You mean, lie to them?"

"Why the hell not? Depending on where this ends and how it ends, I'll decide whether they hang or go into the witness protection program. Has Jacobs or the other one said anything we can use?"

And Brognola listened to the full, grim rundown.

A radioactive fuel mix blown over the interstate when a supposed flying war van nearly lifted off the ground but ended up a fireball in the law-enforcement barrier. That Jacobs—master hacker that he was beyond being the architect of Lightning Bat, SPLAT and other high-tech war systems—discovered the head of security at Eagle Nebula had been smuggling special ordnance on bogus manifests to a trans-shipment point in Chicago, complete with classified schematics, access codes on SPLAT delivery systems. Destinations—and there was some confusion on Jacobs's end why it was going down this way—were split between Iran and the Russian weapons factory in Tajikistan, but that Gabriel

Horn had a falling out with Russian black ops who took it upon themselves to buy his services. Further, Jacobs suspected a giant wood chipper in what was tagged "the White Room" at Eagle Nebula, meant to demolish scrap metal or ordnance that had been tested and failed, had also been added to the compound in the event Horn needed to grind up a few employees engaged in pillow talk or seeking self-aggrandizement.

"That amounts to government-sanctioned murder," Brognola stormed.

"Not necessarily. At least, not the government we see and the public is aware of."

"The shadow government?"

"We've seen it before, and we know it exists," Price said.

"The good news," Brognola said, "the Man gave me full authority to shut down Eagle Nebula. Everyone there is considered under arrest. Guilty until proved innocent." Brognola shook his head. "The media loves its conspiracies, and this one, I'm afraid—the truth about the shadow government and cover-ups that reach to God only knows where—will go down in the history books."

"Unless the White House steps in and—"

"Sweeps it under the rug? Not after the fiasco in North Dakota that got this particular avalanche rolling. What else did the boy aerospace wonder have to say?"

"Jacobs believes what was used in the Vegas attack were special cruise missiles, a version of the Tomahawk, but made lighter when they're coated with what he called 'the Divine Alloy.'"

"The space ore from Colorado."

"Right. Claims, depending on how much an object is coated with, this extraterrestrial alloy will make said object as light as air."

"Which accounts for how a van can fly?"

"Or how two men could pick up a 3000-pound conventional cruise missile. A source of mine informs me the state police found the launch site, about forty-five miles northwest of downtown. There was a military transport, government issue—empty. And an eight-cell launch pod on a towed tracked carrier. In the general area, the remains of two eighteen-wheelers were discovered. Blown up when the occupants vacated."

"So, the bad guys defending national security just drove in a small army, covered most of their tracks, except I gather they didn't care if the launch site was left for the world to behold?" Brognola nearly bit his cigar in two as he felt the boiling anger shoot the blood pressure into his ears. "Like they were proud of what they'd done?"

"Other than perhaps this Horn and whoever else was at the launch site, Carl believes they took down all enemy combatants, both Eagle Nebula black ops and the Russians."

"With their full diplomatic immunity."

"We're going to need to clean house at the State Department."

"Goes without saying. What about this Knudsen?"

"Not talking."

Brognola sounded a grim chuckle. "These guys. If I had my way, and I might still get it, I'd string them up by their… Anything else from Jacobs?"

"He says the Russians have a version of Lightning

Bat, but that it needs some fine tuning. We know the Russians have samples of the space ore, but from his understanding they don't quite know how to apply it to Lightning Bat. It gets worse, or so he suspects. The Russians in charge at this Compound Zero-159-A are looking to put certain weapons and weapons systems, bastardized versions of his own work, or so Jacobs claims, on the black market. He thinks the Iranians were at the head of the shopping line."

And the plate, Brognola thought, runneth over with problems and enemies.

"Beyond that, Jacobs won't say any more."

"I guess he thinks he talks we'll just pat him on the back and give him another week's all-expenses-paid trip to Vegas?" Brognola heard the simmering anger in his voice as he told the mission controller, "Send a team to Chicago to pick up those two. Bring them back here. I will personally interrogate them."

"Done."

"What's the status on Phoenix?" he asked, and saw a dark expression shadow Price's face.

"There may be a situation on their end."

Brognola sat on the newest knot in his stomach, cigar poised near his lips. "A problem, you mean?"

THE PROBLEM was Tiger Ops.

Given their previous dance step, David McCarter sensed more confrontation on the way between himself and Jim Block, the leader of Tiger team.

The list of nagging concerns was short, he thought as he stretched out in a prone position along the lip of the wadi, M-16/M-203 combo fanning the predawn darkness below, and for that he figured he should be thankful. Red flag number one. Block had a way of interrogating prisoners in a manner that fairly stated he'd rather wipe himself with the Geneva Convention. Granted, there were times when the Phoenix Force leader understood certain extreme measures need apply on a prisoner when lives were unquestionably at stake. Various and sundry means of degradation weren't part of McCarter's agenda for extracting information. Back at their joint base near Baghdad he had nearly hurled himself into full-blown knuckle-dusting on the issue, but, lo and behold, the simple threat of pissing on the Iranian prisoner's face loosened his tongue. Only, their prisoner blathered on about four hostages the world at large already knew about, sketching out in detail precisely where they were being held. Block, however, wasn't interested in rescuing the three American journalists and a freelance Canadian writer who had been snatched near the Iraq-Iranian border, where their captors had brayed to the West—through al-Jazeera—how they would soon begin executing the hostages unless all American forces withdrew from the entire Middle East. No, Block, humanitarian that he was, wanted to bypass the lair, leave the hostages to their fate, move on to the border town of al-Namak for the big showdown.

Red flag two.

McCarter, on the other hand, knew if he did nothing to try to free those hostages he wouldn't be able to look himself in the mirror again. A lengthy and heated argument ensued, but Block relented, begrudging that the Iranian lair was on the way to al-Namak, anyway, so what the hell.

So there they all were. Ten miles from the Iranian border, give or take, ready to trample the snake's nest, only Block once again had his own ideas on how to proceed.

Hence another boil that needed lancing.

Red flag three.

Mr. Block had vanished with his five-man team to the north, stating they would circle wide of the cave in question, sweep the perimeter in that direction for any roving sentries, all hands going for it, when Mr. M—McCarter—and company were in position to the south. Block barked that twenty minutes should do it.

Briefly, the ex-SAS commando gave it angry consideration how this potential fiasco had come to pass. Only a few days ago, the President of the United States had green-lighted Phoenix Force to headhunt one of the world's most wanted terrorists, the Grand Ayatollah Rafiq Namak, who was smuggling arms and insurgents into Iraq, bagging western hostages, with rumors from the intelligence mill he was purchasing high-tech weapons and possibly WMD from an unknown source from depthless vats of pilfered oil and drug money. Then, as had happened to him in the past in the war on terror, some bureaucrat or fat-cat honcho at DOD or the Pentagon had stepped in, burned the Man's ear until Tiger Ops was attached to his hip.

SNAFU on the horizon, McCarter was certain.

Working with unknown commando commodities, the Briton knew, was courting disaster, not to mention sudden death for either himself or his teammates. He could eat up his thoughts on how wrong it was, but Brognola had been told Tiger Ops was in with his people or they were out of the game.

So be it.

With his night-vision goggles, exposed flesh daubed in black cosmetics, weighted down in full combat harness and webbing, with pouches stuffed with spare clips and grenades, McCarter saw two figures in hoods emerge from the cave, AK-47s slung around their shoulders. They gave the wadi a rather nonchalant inspection both ways, north and south, then busied themselves smoking. Then the Phoenix Force leader scanned what sat imagery—provided by Emerald Base Zero in the Maldives, and thus another potential X factor dumped in his lap—detailed were two trails leading to the mouth of the cave. There, he spotted Calvin James and Rafael Encizo, hunched and shadowing on for position, M-16/M-203 combos leading the two silent green ghosts.

According to the Iranian prisoner, they could expect to encounter anywhere from six to ten militants hunkered down inside, armed with AKs, two RPGs. The prisoner—on a CIA list of Iranian fighters believed working closely with the hostage-takers and who had been bagged by a special ops team while en route to deliver cash, some weapons and a videotape of the next round of demands and the dwindling timetable to the first hostage execution to an imam in Basra—claimed to have been inside the cave. No mines, no boobytraps, his brothers-in-jihad believing they were protected by the sheer remoteness of the region so close to the Iran border.

McCarter wasn't about to take him at his word. Which was why Gary Manning had already turned loose the spider cam, the big Canadian having already positioned himself so close on the right wing of the sentries, he could almost reach out and slice their throats with his shin-sheathed commando dagger. T.J. Hawkins, wielding a Squad Automatic Weapon, was perched behind Manning, covering while the big Canadian watched the digital readout on his screen, crunching numbers for his teammates.

A look in Manning's direction and the Phoenix leader believed he made out the shape of the spider cam on the crawl. McCarter held his breath as the silent, black-painted baseball with legs moved past the sentries, undetected as they worked, all business on their smokes, and on its way into the cave. Outfitted with state-of-the-art sensors, the microchip was engineered specifically to allow the spider cam to navigate its own course, over or around any object obstructing its path. With a miniature camera that could roll in all directions, Manning could watch everything it saw on his handheld monitor, the digital readout capable of gauging distance from its point of release, measurements, dimensions of the cave.

Taking it all in, live and in color, from a spider's POV.

McCarter gritted his teeth as Block patched through on his com link. "I thought we agreed to maintain radio silence until my men were in position and I called you?"

"Those sentries won't stand there all night, Mr. M. My sniper is in position and ready to pull the trigger."

Incredible, McCarter thought, the bloke wanted to bullrush in, guns blazing, without solid intel on the layout and numbers. Almost as if he didn't give a damn whether the hostages survived the coming engagement. Or was it something else?

"My men are right on top of them. Two quiet pops," McCarter said, referring to the sound-suppressed Beretta 93-Rs James and Encizo carried, "at arm's length, then dragging them away is the better part of discretion instead of your man maybe blowing them back into the cave."

"My sniper can shoot the fly off a bull's ass at three thousand meters, Mr. M, and at four hundred feet he has them kissing close in that scope of his."

A pissing contest.

"My guy takes them down, then your team moves in, my guys right on your six."

And yet another question mark. Block seemed to want his way or the doorway, but he was allowing McCarter to lead his troops into the eye of the storm, taking all the risk, while Tiger Ops picked up the rear. Almost as if…

He wanted them out of the picture? Whatever the case, McCarter was too professional to squawk about being the first one through the door. The job needed to get done, sealed in blood, and it didn't matter in the final analysis who did it.

McCarter dredged up enough patience to keep his voice calm and low. "Listen to me, mate. I sent in a special package that will give us a firm read on the cave's layout and a fix on numbers."

"What package? Hey, are we on the same page here? 'Mate.'"

Obviously not, McCarter thought, but said, "Give me another ten minutes."

"Set your watch. Ten minutes, then my sniper goes to work. Agreed?"

"We'll try it your way this time."

Golden silence.

Ten minutes, he thought, and began navigating his own course to link up with his teammates, ready to lead the charge into the belly of the beast.

ALI KHOROSAB was eager to begin executing the hostages. When first capturing the infidels—after ambushing their meager security force of five guards in a village near Basra where they had ostensibly been searching out imams for a story—he had already determined he would kill them, one by one, film their executions. The videos would be delivered by an elaborate web of couriers, none of whom would ever lay eyes on each other due to arranged drop sites. When the final courier was within shouting distance to al-Jazeera he would place a phone call to the station, informing them where the package could be found.

Film at six.

That they were noncombatants didn't bother him in the least. They were pawns, nothing more, nothing less, to be used as a warning to the Great Satan to leave, not only Iraq, but all of the Middle East. From the outset, though, he had never expected the Americans to simply fold up their tents and go home, tails tucked between their legs like the mongrel dogs they were. Quite the contrary, he hoped they defied his demands.

Four less infidels, he thought, only made for a better world.

AK-47 in one hand, he fingered the ivory hilt of his *jambiya*. Which one would he behead first? he asked himself, looking at the four hostages sitting in front of him, terrified to even glance up at his black-hooded face. Most assuredly it would be one of the Americans. Save the Canadian for last, then, hopeful he could fan the flames of animosity between the two countries, not that their petty squabbling over how to handle international affairs in regards to Muslims made any difference to the jihad. Diplomacy was little more than international bickering between fools too weak to stand their ground and fight, he thought, certainly no match at all against the power of the sword. But any friction he could create between western countries might further erode their resolve to fight, see them drop their guard, perhaps someone of proper authority accepting a bribe to let a certain container ship dock in one of their ports, or allow a suitcase of suspect origins and content pass through customs.

He let his stare burn over them, pleased when he thought he saw one of the Americans squirm against his rope bindings. For several days, they had sat there, shrunken into a grim acceptance of their fate. No questions. No complaint. That angered him, since he much preferred them whimpering, pissing themselves even as they begged for mercy, imploring him to be set free. Or they should patronize him, at least, espousing the virtues of Islam, how they understood his position, professing how they would write his story for all the west to hear if only he cut them loose. He had considered inciting an argument between them over who should be sacrificed to spare, free the rest, but he was growing tired of both the game and their every breath.

In Farsi, he told Ahmadah to set up the video cam. It was time.

He was ready to choose when he spotted an object crawling around the corner, then toward him, a shadow on the periphery of the generator-powered light. Peering, he took a step toward what he believed was a spider, only he'd never seen one shaped like a—

Ball with legs?

He felt his guts coil, instinct shouting at him that it was no spider, not one that he'd ever seen in that part of the world. As he nearly ran toward the object, Khorosab spotted the small but glassy eye in front of the orb.

"WE'RE MADE. Forty-three feet straight, sharp left. Five shooters eight feet down."

McCarter hung back a second as Block's vaunted sniper proved his lethal talent, even if his scope framed the hoods, he imagined, so large and lifelike he could reach out and rip them off. The SSG 3000 in .308 Winchester ammo was the killing piece of choice, he knew, as two quiet rounds from its sound suppressor dropped both sentries, one shot to the hood, down and out on their backs, limbs twitching out the final nerve sparks. The cave and its jihadists mentally sketched, the ex-SAS commando wheeled around the corner, sweeping the big comb-blaster around, finger taking up slack on the M-203's trigger. He had already hashed over the party-crasher with his own troops and barked, "Fire in the hole!"

A gentle squeeze of the M-203's trigger and the 40 mm flash-stun grenade chugged away as he aimed for impact where the wall began to curve left. Forty-three feet, he considered, a quick dash under normal circumstances, but in this instance it seemed like a mile—or an eternity for someone. He was considering the short list of backfires to his opening strike—when the cave downrange blew in one million candlepower and a concussive thunderous din sure to rupture some eardrums and blind fanatics into staggering dummies.

And the big Briton was sprinting for the finish line, assault rifle pointed toward the boiling smoke, searching for live ones, as he zeroed in on all the commotion, militants howling and cursing around the corner.

Getting closer now.

There was a split second of darkness, McCarter ready to drop the NVD goggles in place, then the gods of war smiled on his plan, a backup generator humming on the auxiliary light. James and Encizo hugging the opposite wall, Manning on his six and Hawkins with his SAW out and ready to eat fanatic flesh, McCarter gathered steam, cutting the distance quick.

And began shooting into the belly of the monster.

They were rocked senseless perhaps, but McCarter heard two, maybe three, assault rifles unleash blind sweeps. He went low across the corner's mouth, M-16 set for 3-round bursts, dropping one fanatic with his opening volley. He took in the hostages, rolling and shouting on the floor, on the fly before he hit a knee against the far wall, lending his troops clearance to join in the slaughter. Two black hoods were grabbing at their ears and eyes, he glimpsed, with two jihadists firing away with AKs, their rounds going high and wide, ricocheting off stone above his head. The tight confines of the cave trapped the eruption of four M-16s unleashed in unison, the SAW in Hawkins's hands like the sonic boom of relentless cannonfire. By the time two or three Tiger Ops pitched in with HK subgun chatter, the last militant was blown off his feet.

McCarter gave Encizo and James the nod to make sure the dead stayed that way. He spotted the bullet-head of Block, HK subgun leading his tiger-striped march, his troops hanging back, waiting on their commander to take charge. James, he briefly watched, was working on the hostages, stunned and scared witless, several of them crying out either in pain, shock, terror or all three. James and Encizo had to shake the hostages, mouthing, "Americans," before they began to calm down.

"Mr. G," McCarter told Manning, "radio one of our Black Hawks in here to evacuate the hostages."

Block stepped up. "I can't spare any of those birds now. Not with Namak just across the border. We're going to need all the air support we can get when we hit that town."

McCarter walked up to Block. For a second the Phoenix Force leader would have sworn the Tiger Ops leader looked disappointed he was still breathing. "Listen to me. If you don't get your act together now, I will call back to CENTCOM and inform them what a major hemorrhoid in this operation you and your people have become."

Block took a menacing step forward, nearly in McCarter's face.

The Briton glanced at the hostages. "And would you want these fine journalists here to know just how much you cared about their futures?"

Block stood his ground, considered something, then

barked at his teammates, "Take care of the hostages and get them outside for evacuation.

"Look," he then told McCarter, softening his tone, throwing in a soft chuckle as if there were some big misunderstanding, "you did good here."

"This was no audition for your approval, Block. And myself and my men aren't here for your appreciation or anybody's applause." McCarter told his commandos to check the hole for weapons cache, any documents or other intel to be secured. He was brushing past Block when the Tiger Ops leader grabbed his arm.

"Look. Maybe we just have different ways of doing business, but we're fighting for the same thing."

"Are we?"

"The last I knew we were. We've got the big one in the wings, so let's say you and I sit down and draw up a plan we can both agree on."

McCarter found himself trusting Block less the more the man talked, tried to convince him it was suddenly one for all. They were outfitted for covert war, down to the black cosmetics, webbing and gear, but something disturbed the ex-SAS commando right then about the tiger stripes.

"Whatever you say, Block," he told the Tiger Ops leader, and walked away.

CHAPTER THIRTEEN

Josh Langdon knew there was a little over two hours time difference between Emerald Base Zero and the code-named Hot Zone on the Iraq-Iran border. And the new day breaking over their tropical relay station, with the cawing of wild birds and the smell of salt in his nose, didn't bring good news.

Quite the contrary, he discovered, as the NRO satellite they had parked over the area in question framed a sight he hadn't expected to find, but was glad to be on board now as the one who had stumbled over it. If the Farm had seen it, a red flag would have flared in the upper right-hand corner of his monitor. No flag, as of yet.

"Do you see that, sir?"

He looked over at Commander Z hunched over his monitor, nodded as he clicked his mouse to enhance the imagery. "Indeed, I do, soldier. Relay it to Omega Base," he said, then sat back in his metal chair. "Get confirmation they are in possession."

"Aye-aye, sir."

There was no such animal, he knew, as perfect intelligence or the perfect satellite. Weather, cloud cover, other atmospheric disturbances were factors in concealing troop movements, and no satellite he'd ever heard of could see through walls of classified installations where WMD could be manufactured. Military satellites, as advanced as they were, either often missed such red flags, or someone purposely turned a blind eye. Considering the landmass of Iran alone, the Islamic country ate up something like 1,650,000 kilometers. That was three times, he thought, the size of America's favorite NATO ally, France. In fact, Iran was as large as the U.K., Switzerland, Italy, Spain and France slapped together. Not all of it was barren desert, either, land sprawled naked for the eyes in the sky to monitor. The Zagros Mountains in western Iran formed God's natural wall to Iraq, the devil's playground where they now searched for clues as to the whereabouts of Namak's training ground believed to be funneling all the chaos across the border. Desert smack dead center, nothing but mountains rising like a fortress around the rest of the country.

Not someplace he'd pencil in on his vacation itinerary, given, too, western faces—despite the hype from Tehran's tourist center—were about as welcome as the plague.

And it was understandable how what now just popped up on their monitors could be missed up to that point. More often than not, ground intelligence aimed the direction for military and spy satellites to uncover dark truths America's enemies wanted to keep hidden. This was a perfect case in point.

Langdon took a moment to watch the Tiger Ops—two of them, at least—scanning the rugged countryside through sat imagery on their own monitors. One battle-front not on the score card was in the bag. They had done their part, relaying satellite imagery while scanning the AIQ for roving hostiles, aiding and abetting the Phoenix Force–Tiger team as they freed the hostages. No thanks, he thought, to the Tiger Ops leader.

He searched the tent, found CAG—Capricorn Alpha Galaxy—moving through the mosquito netting. Was that a sat phone in the man's hand? he wondered. He had been around long enough, performing black bag services for his country, to know when a player straddled the fence, clinging to his own dark agenda, and CAG felt all wrong. That his men had only set up two workstations pretty much left CAG the day to stroll the island, maybe take a dip, chain-smoke, work on his tan. Two times, he'd caught the man whispering something to one of his commandos. And that sat phone never left his side.

It was time he had a word about CAG's work habits, among other matters.

"I'll be back," Langdon told his men, and plucked up his HK subgun.

Just in case.

For damn sure, something didn't feel right about the setup, as he felt the eyes of the Tiger Ops bore into the back of his head.

"CAN ANYONE TELL ME how or when they think the Iranians came into possession of that beast? How the hell didn't we know about it before now?"

Hal Brognola waited for an answer, watching as Kurtzman shook his head, Tokaido enlarging the sat imagery until the behemoth filled his monitor. At the moment, Price was in her office, working her own NSA sources for whatever intel she could glean that would further improve the chances of the mission's successful outcome. The big Fed found Wethers and Delahunt taking satellite relays from Emerald Base Zero that detailed the quickest and safest flight path away from army border patrols, while working up imagery on al-Namak as fast as they could, relaying layout, enemy positions or suspected hiding places back to McCarter.

And now they were staring down the barrel of a howitzer, one that could blow the entire mission, quite literally, out of the sky. If little else, Brognola was damn glad they had discovered the problem before Phoenix Force–Tiger Ops and their flying armada encroached Iranian airspace.

Brognola washed a cloud of smoke over their heads. "What did you call it, Bear?"

"The Tupolov-160. You're looking at the largest and heaviest bomber the world over, Hal, surpassing even our B-52."

"Ordnance?"

"Well," Kurtzman said, fingers flying over the keyboard, bringing up the specs, "you're talking about a payload of twelve air-launched cruise missiles, or double that number for shorter range attack missiles. And yes, it can carry nukes."

"Akira," Brognola said, stepping up behind Tokaido as the Japanese-American cyberwarrior enhanced the compound. "Crunch some numbers for me on that hardware."

"Whatever this base, it must have been established very recently," Tokaido said, framing vehicles and aircraft while numbers scrolled in the corner of his screen. "We have a list of all Iranian military installations, known and classified, but this one…"

"Come on, come on, I know that."

"Okay. Our people are looking at three Tu-22s, long-range bombers that supposedly are only found in five Russian bases."

"Implying they jealously guard those toys, but they somehow ended up at this base in western Iran."

Tokaido nodded. "Someone in Moscow is not watching their high-tech store."

"You think?" Brognola huffed.

Tokaido cleared his throat. "They have an Ilyushin transport, four T-72 tanks, six BMPs or airborne combat vehicles, ten MiGs…and this," he said, framing for Brognola a missile battery. "Those are SAM-4 'Ganefs' on tracked launchers. Range, seventy kilometers."

"For a number of years now we know the Russians have been selling the Iranians antique ordnance that's been sitting around, getting rusty in warehouses," Kurtzman told Brognola, "but those Tu-22s and the Tupolov are state-of-the-art."

"And your guess as to why the Russians unloaded these high-tech diamonds on the Iranians?"

"Well, with al-Namak about ten klicks south of this base, my guess is that the Grand Ayatollah has far more clout than we originally suspected."

"You mean, he bought that hardware with his own cash, built an entire base complete with MiGs, long-range bombers and SAMs," Brognola said. "For protection?"

"Or to start a war," Tokaido finished.

Brognola feared as much, and knew he had the decision of a career—a lifetime—to make. The covert war against Iran had already begun, with the recovery of the hostages. And the radical cleric had long since openly declared war against American armed forces in the Middle East.

And the Man had left him to make the tough calls.

"Hal," Kurtzman said, "we can't send in our guys with that much enemy firepower sitting around, ready to be called upon at a moment's notice."

Brognola was aware of that grim fact. The mission was launched, the troops ready to plunge the dagger deep into Iran. He read the present situation as a glitch, albeit a big one.

"Bear, run down for me every piece of what Phoenix-Tiger has for air firepower."

Kurtzman did, and Brognola felt himself walk to the edge of the abyss, knowing already the call he would make. He found Kurtzman and Tokaido staring at him, waiting.

The decision of a lifetime.

And Hal Brognola, knowing he was on the verge of starting a war without the congressional seal of approval, told them, "Make sure David understands what they're up against. Make sure all hands, including these Tiger Ops, are on board. Make sure they understand that if it goes south, no one is to be taken alive. When you've done that…have all aircraft at their disposal drop the sky on that base. When it's over, I don't even want to see half of one MiG left standing."

And if it didn't play out the way he envisioned and

hoped, if he had just opened the gates of Hell to a full-blown war between America and Iran...

He hadn't sought out this moment, the grim opportunity to maybe alter the course of world events, but here he was, standing alone in the dark spotlight.

And it hit him right between the eyes that Stony Man Farm had just become that shadow government, all-knowing, all-powerful, the fate of perhaps the entire world, depending on how events shaped up and if it spilled over to other nations, in their hands.

God help him, he thought. God help the Middle East if he had just made the wrong call.

"IT'S BEEN TAKEN care of."

Langdon watched his footing, bypassing slick coral, as he slipped, silent as a ghost, between the palm fronds. HK subgun leading his slow advance, he found CAG, back to him, standing at the edge of a small lagoon.

"Just deliver on your end and all's well."

The tone was guarded, and Langdon kept waiting for the man to speak in some coded language of spookdom, but he stood there, grunting, bobbing his head, smoking.

He stepped out of the brush, sensed the electric jolt hitting CAG as he whirled toward him. The man was good at hiding whatever he was feeling, calm as the blue water in front of him, as he went on, "We'll keep handling their situation on this end, sir. Yes, sir, I understand. One battle does not a war win. I'll be in touch."

Langdon read the subtle change in CAG's expression. He didn't need to see the eyes behind the sunglasses to know the man was weighing the moment, deciding how to proceed. "Something you care to share with the rest of the class?"

The Tiger Ops leader chuckled as he hooked the sat phone to his belt. "If I didn't know better, Commander X, I'd say you were spying on me."

Playing it off. Mr. Cool.

"I have superiors, like yourself, I'm sure, who require frequent updates."

"And you had to come out here for privacy?" Langdon said. "Or for security reasons?"

"Both." The Tiger Ops leader bared his teeth, angry, as he walked away from the lagoon. "And maybe I had to take a dump," he added, brushing past Langdon.

Really? Langdon thought, watching the man sweep through the palm fronds. And heard the voice of bad experience warn him right then they weren't on the same team.

GRAND AYATOLLAH Rafiq Namak believed at least one of his prayers was about to be answered. With the plan to expand his war against the Great Satan, the list of his demands and needs from God seemed to increase exponentially, and each day he found himself imploring for more of everything if only to carry on the jihad, spread the fires of holy war and burn down the infidel wherever he was found.

And he would settle for nothing less than a global war. For that he needed weapons of mass destruction, or, at worst, settle for the time being for newer, deadlier, far more accurate weapons than old AKs and RPGs. Indeed, he needed quality ordnance, where could he strike down his enemies from a great—and safe—distance. Before the sun broke over the barren plain this morning, at least one wish would be granted, and for that he thanked God. Yes, a great battle was about to rage to the southwest, just inside the border, and many of his followers would have to sacrifice themselves in order that he acquire the special ordnance.

The weapons were en route to the village he had named after himself, though the cutout on the other end who had arranged the shipment sounded strange, evasive, questions about the future left hanging, as if he feared someone was eavesdropping. Granted, it wouldn't be the massive shipment he sought, but it was a start, his middleman prepared to hand over cash to the infidels in exchange for what amounted to little more than a sample of the SPLAT weapons system.

Only the beginning, he told himself. More to come, as he had learned from his man in America only an hour ago. And Nurij, faithful servant that he was, had already initiated the steps necessary to transport a far larger shipment than what was already consigned for in the region, months previously.

Sitting cross-legged, AK-47 by his side, he was several hundred feet up the foothills of the Zagros Mountains, perched on an outcrop, taking in the sight of his sprawling encampment. Each day his army grew, as his followers sought out more fighters, bringing them here to the valley from across Iran, Pakistan, Afghanistan, Iraq and Syria, where they trained, planned operations, moved ordnance across the border into Iraq.

After the arrival of the latest group of fighters, he had lost an exact head count but figured the army in front of him reached well into the hundreds. Logistics, such as feeding all those warriors, was a growing problem, but the trucks rolled in on a weekly basis from Tehran, bringing gasoline for all their vehicles, food and water, thanks to certain imams, politicians and intelligence agents who had pledged their undying devotion. Down there, the compound appeared no more than a vast lake of vehicles, tents and a smattering of stone hovels, but this was where he would plan the coming war and cut loose his Army of Armageddon on the world. This was where his greatness and glory would be launched.

He took a deep breath, letting his mind's eye fill with the destruction he craved to wreak on his enemies. It had become a predawn ritual, climbing to this ledge, surrounded by a small contingent of bodyguards, praying while dreaming—envisioning—what would become the greatness of Islam. As he believed himself the last of the twelve imams, the bloodline of the Prophet Mohammed, it was his time to come out of spiritual seclusion, lead all of Islam to victory, prophesied by Shiites since Ali had succeeded the Prophet.

First he saw a vast and bottomless pit, where his hated enemies kept tumbling into the blackness, hurled to the depths by his army, as they marched on, continent to continent, slaying all infidels in front of them. He saw entire city blocks in smoking ruins where his bombs rained down, the dead and dying so many it was a veritable ocean of destruction and mayhem, of wailing and gnashing of teeth. He saw clouds of chemical poison roiling down their streets, the invisible death of a bio agent dropping them by the tens of thousands in agonizing, lingering death.

Fomenting the insurgency in Iraq was but a mere

stepping stone, but he still hoped to place his own man in charge of the country. With each bombing, with every dead foreigner, there was a good chance he would soon control Iraq, if only from the shadows. Soon, he told himself, across the whole Middle East, he would take the war to a newer, higher level. And with the ordnance he would receive he was told he could even strike Israel.

"Your holiness."

Namak looked up and found one of his top lieutenants, Kamal Bajan, standing with a sat phone in his hand, distress in his eyes. His men knew not to disturb him at that time, unless it was an emergency.

"It is Colonel Khatam. He says their base is under an aerial bombardment."

"What? Who?"

"He thinks they are Americans."

Namak jumped up and snatched the sat phone from his lieutenant.

"Look alive, gentlemen."

It was their arranged cue to keep their guard up, be prepared for anything, as Langdon then blinked twice at his men, back turned to the Tiger Ops. They kept their HK subguns within grabbing reach, as they worked their monitors, taking relays—both satellite and radio— and shooting them back to the Farm. He watched the screen light up as Spectre's gun camera relayed the images of the aerial pulverizing that reduced just about every last Iranian aircraft, tank and transport truck to scrap within a few eye blinks, likewise the missile battery going up and away in a blazing Hellfire barrage. It was quite the show, all fire and mass destruction, but he was keeping one eye on CAG, who was back on the sat phone, more intense and grim than ever, hugging the far corner of the tent. Six F-15Es, two Apaches and the leviathan, Spectre, Langdon knew, were razing the clandestine Iranian base on all points of the compass. There were blurry figures, he spied, dashing all over the base, with antlike stick figures sailing away from a marching fusillade of explosions eating up the earth like a giant grinder.

"Sir, I have a satellite phone intercept from the base in question."

Langdon snugged on his headphones, dialed in, in time to hear, *This is because of you, Namak, my entire compound is being reduced to flaming trash by the Americans!*

Do not use my name, you fool! This is not a secured line!

Langdon told his men, "Get that location triangulated," before the next words.

I did not sign on to become your sacrificial lamb!

Then perhaps you have been too amply compensated! Perhaps you have outlived your usefulness if you cannot repel a simple aerial attack!

Simple! If only you were here, you son of a—!

They had their man, somewhere in the general AIQ, he was positive. He hoped Namak and the one he was arguing with—presumably the commander of the base getting shellacked—stayed on long enough for their satellite to intercept the frequency, mark down Namak's exact position.

"What is it?"

Langdon found CAG marching toward him. The sudden interest and the dark expression on the Tiger Ops leader's face raised the hackles on the back of his neck.

"You going to answer me?"

"Namak," Langdon told him, watching carefully as he thought the HK subgun lifted an inch or so in CAG's hands. "We've got him on a sat phone and we're trying to pin down his location. Quiet," he snapped as he heard the thunder of explosions on the other end, then dead silence, followed by static.

So much for whoever the base commander.

"Did you get a position?"

Langdon watched as Mr. Y and Mr. Z worked their keyboards, framing a mountainous region he assumed was somewhere in the Zagros. Then, in the corner of his eye, he saw CAG tell his commandos something, his own HK subgun now rising.

They were going for it. Whatever the plot, whoever they really were and worked for, they had come here from the beginning to commit murder, the rotten sons of—

He thought he beat them to the draw, catching one, maybe two of CAG's thugs, but the bullets were flying back, blasting into the monitor beside him as Langdon bulled into his men, knocking them to the ground.

CHAPTER FOURTEEN

"Omega Base to Commander X, respond."

Brognola tensed as Kurtzman repeatedly tried to raise the relay station. One moment he was standing here, watching the air strike he had called in bring the hammer down on the Iranian base, wreckage, buildings and bodies flying all over the map, and the next, all monitors were threatening to flicker out, until the cyberteam frantically scrambled to keep them up and running, switching back to their own mainframes, severing the connection to the Maldives.

"What the hell's going on?" Brognola demanded.

Shrugging, Kurtzman's expression darkened as he indicated nothing but radio silence from the Maldives. "I don't know, Hal. Our systems are functioning at a hundred percent, but they're shut down on the other end. If it was only a battery…"

"But they have plenty of batteries on reserve. And a generator."

"I have no answers until I can reach our man in the Maldives."

Neither one of them, he knew, wanted to come right and say "sabotage." And why push panic buttons? The big Fed was no technical wizard, but he was sure if he pressed him, Kurtzman could hurl a dozen different plausible explanations off the top of his head.

"What about Phoenix?"

"They're moving in on al-Namak now," Wethers answered.

Delahunt added, "We'll have about a second of time delay, but we can still monitor the action once we tie directly into the satellite they were using in the Maldives."

Brognola muttered a curse. His gut told him there was some major SNAFU on Emerald Base Zero's end, and that it involved Tiger Ops. The big Fed wanted to stand there, watch and will the relay station to come back online, but he saw Price walk up to him. She looked as grim as the cyberteam. "You don't look like good news."

"That all depends."

Brognola was almost afraid to ask, but said, "On what?"

"We need to talk."

Brognola chomped on his cigar. "You know, those are four of the most dreaded words on Earth, and by which I have come to learn in my experience always warn me to be braced for the worst."

HAWKINS HIT THE GROUND running, and came under instant fire. Wielding the big Squad Automatic Weapon, he charged out of the Black Hawk's rotor wash, sighted down on two AK-47s flaming away from the second-floor window of a stone hovel.

This, he knew, triggering the SAW to blast a walking ring of dust and stone shrapnel around the frame as he vectored for a stone wall, wasn't going to be a good day, but few moments in combat ever were, until they walked out the other side and left the dust settling over their enemies. First, the plan to hit al-Namak was full of holes, and he had to lay the blame for this potential disaster on the doorstep of the Tiger Ops leader, who seemed hell-bent on getting his way, even if that meant friendly casualties. They were splitting the teams again, as McCarter and Block had drawn up on the Black Hawk, both sides deaf and blind to the other's movements. Even with com links tying them all in, Hawkins felt his gut warn him the other side wasn't to be trusted, the standing order for radio silence—unless it was a dire emergency—just another pile thrown onto this particular dung heap. Beyond that, he wondered why Commander Block insisted on holding on to his handheld radio, which was dotted with more colored buttons...

Something wasn't right with their supposed teammates. If he didn't know better, he suspected McCarter was locked on to the same train of thought, but letting it play out the way Block wanted. Tightening a noose?

So Tiger Ops was hitting the west side of the village, fighting their way for the north end, while Hawkins and teammates moved up the east edge. A pincers clamp, ostensibly, only this strike was, intel believed, going to end up being a door-to-door fight to the death with hunkered-down militants, some of whom, he was sure, were ready to blow themselves up while taking a few infidels with them. Sat imagery and ground intelligence, he knew, were only as good as the fighting men detailing then enacting the bloody magic of combat, but with enemy numbers here undetermined, the entire village apparently one sprawling trans-shipment point for weapons and terrorists...

Thank God, he thought, they had at least one Apache at their disposal. Grimaldi was at the helm of the Spectre, in charge of the fourteen-man crew, ready to be called in if enemy numbers stacked up in one particular house, tying the whole game up into the knot of a standoff, but for the moment Hawkins suspected all bets were off. Dig in, he told himself, as Encizo grabbed cover on the other side of the wall's opening, McCarter leading James and Manning around the far corner to tackle the next terror haven up the line.

And they came under fire as they vanished around the corner.

The only good news Hawkins could clearly see at the moment was the Multiround Projectile Launcher Encizo lugged as his main piece of killing power. Twelve 40 mm rounds down the chambers, and McCarter, patching through on the com link, put Encizo to work.

Hawkins bobbed his head at his teammate, as return fire chewed the top of the wall into a flying hornet's nest of stone chips and fragments, then the ex-Ranger hit the edge of the corner, pouring out a tempest of 5.56 mm lead, drove the second-story fire team back to cover. Encizo chugged out the first hell bomb, the 40 mm roomsweeper banging out a hole uptop, then he threw another projectile for the front door as two enemy gunners grabbed up a fire point. They unleashed their

Kalashnikovs, good for all of two seconds, before they were little more than a smoking memory.

Hawkins, with Encizo by his side, charged across the short stretch of no-man's land to start clearing out the first house on a list that reached double digits. Which hovel, he briefly wondered, could become one of their personal tombs?

KHAGIL AMHADAN deplored the entire setup. As he heard the shooting break out from the far southern end of the village, he found it strange to the point of suicide that he was being ordered by the Grand Ayatollah to allow the infidels safe passage to his home. The messages he received over his sat phone were encoded, yes, rolling in, one on the heels of the other, setting the stage, but each one only heightened his suspicions and anxiety.

First, Rafiq, mapping out the strategy—kill any infidel not wearing the tiger stripes, since they were the commandos delivering the ordnance Namak was purchasing. Second, a cutout for the commandos in the tiger stripes informing him he was en route, be prepared to ride out in their transport trucks. Or, be ready to head for the hills, as he had told him.

What bothered him last but not least was the age of the combatants Namak had ordered to stand their ground and fight the infidels. All fighters under the age of fifteen were being thrown to the prowling armed wolves, many of them cousins, two sons belonging to his lieutenants. It galled him to hang back, leave the dying and killing to those with little or no experience, while he was supposed to greet the infidels in tiger stripes with open arms, hugs and kisses. Naturally, in the heat of combat, he couldn't guarantee one of the tiger stripes wouldn't be cut down, though he had passed on the orders to his youthful fighters to allow them to pass, unmolested.

As he heard a double peal of thunder in the distance he looked to Ali Samzulah. The boy was hunched behind the wheel of a Russian GAZ-66 transport truck, his brother, Pardin, in the shotgun seat. In the bed was a thousand pounds of C-4, all of it wired to go off at Pardin's touch. If the cutout was correct—or were these tiger-striped commandos playing their own duplicitous game?—the infidels who needed to be taken down would be driving their fight up the east side of the village.

Waving his AK-47, he signaled the boy to move out.

"Go with God!" he called, the truck lurching ahead as he listened to the sound and fury of the battle for the village named after their great leader.

LANGDON HELD BACK on the subgun's trigger. He saw two out of three Tiger Ops going down, ragged holes pocking their chests, as he tumbled over the monitors, seeking cover—if such an absurd notion was even possible, since he was engaged in subgun fire with the Tiger Ops at near point blank range. The monitors were being reduced to flying trash, as he heard CAG howling, taking hits, but firing on, blasting up the whole comm-tracking station, flinging glass and plastic shrapnel in his face. He heard another HK subgun stutter into his line of fire, the converging streams, he spied, chewing up CAG's chest.

And the murdering SOB was falling, subgun blazing on, spraying scrap and sparks all over the tent, shredding camo netting above before he hammered on his back. Then Langdon heard a soft curse, turned, and found Mr. Z kneeling over their teammate. One look at the red ruins of the Stony Man blacksuit's chest and Langdon knew he was dead. A croak from beyond the high-tech garbage mound and he found CAG still clinging to life.

He rose and moved out with pure murder in his heart.

JAMES BLICKTON, a.k.a. Jim Block, saw a golden future at the end of this bloody rainbow. And Mr. M and his comrades weren't part of it. Whoever they were—black ops, he assumed—they were doomed to go down and stay down here in this dusty remote hellhole some twenty miles inside the Iranian border that few even in the intelligence world were aware of, and probably much less cared about, if they did.

This was shit city, rabble central, but it was as good a place as any, he knew, to further uncoil the rope of the big scheme.

It had taken nearly two nerve-racking years to put the pieces in place for this operation, and this was only the beginning of what he knew were several major paydays in the wings. As fate had it, he knew all the right players from the Eagle Nebula from personal service in Delta Force to his country, all like-minded warriors who had turned their backs on the Stars and Stripes, aware the only future available, worth fighting for was their own. They were black ops who commanded more authority in secret than any operative in the American intelligence community, and without them he would have never gotten it this far. Of course, along the way, it helped to blackmail a few of the more uppity types who could aid and abet from their cocoons in the State Department, the DOD and the Pentagon, but he was on track, and rolling now, a few of the "friendly shadows" sure to be terminated soon enough. A few less stooges in Washington, he figured, no one would miss.

Gulf II had provided a web, he knew, where certain operatives could reach out and touch the end-purchaser—in this case, Namak—and offer him the next best thing to a Suitcase from Allah, though the way he heard it that was promised down the line. Beyond that, the chaos of the insurgency in Iraq had helped cover their tracks, those in-the-loop able to play both ends against the middle, putting out certain fires while gathering their own kindling to build their own firestorm into the future. Kill insurgents, make it seem to CENTCOM and the CIA he was doing a damn good job, while grooming contacts to Namak.

Well, the future, he thought, was now.

Hunched, he led his five-man team north, the racket of weaponsfire and the crunch of explosions way off to the east. The bulk of the fighting contained in that direction, so far not a shot was fired at them as they kept on trucking to help land Namak his first shipment of high-tech goodies, HK subgun poised to unload, just in case someone on the terror team hadn't gotten the message, or didn't care who they shot or blew up in the frenzy of combat.

He hadn't made it this far to get waxed when he was so close to the finish line.

Two immediate problems kept him edged out on adrenaline. The first potential glitch was their own air-fire support. He had one Apache on tap all for himself, in the event the winged armada gave chase. Then there was Mr. M and his gang. Say they made it to their pre-arranged link-up where Namak's man was waiting…

Well, he'd tackle that problem if it arose, walking Mr. M and ops into their own firing squad. Either way, his "teammates" weren't walking out of the village. After their untimely demise, round up Namak's cutout and venture out to rendezvous with his Black Hawk. From there, hole up in Iran, maybe Pakistan, until arrangements were ironed out for more deliveries. Sounded like a plan, and all he had to do was keep the faith and his fingers crossed.

He plucked the sat phone off his belt to let their cutout know they were close, and if he wouldn't mind rolling out the red carpet.

Or, in his case, the magic carpet lined with green American currency.

LANGDON SLAPPED CAG's face, reviving the traitor on a groan and a gurgle of blood and spit that trickled down the side of his face. "What was this all about? Talk to me, damn you!"

The Tiger Ops leader made a sound between a croak and a chuckle. "Would you believe…our side taking over…the whole Middle East?"

"Bullshit."

"Believe what you…want…Big Brother…a shadow arm of America…wants to ignite World War III…step in when the smoke clears…take all that oil…I'm just a bit player…"

In some twisted way, considering the state of the Middle East, it made sense to Langdon. The region would always prove a flashpoint, no matter if a so-called democratic American puppet was installed in Baghdad or not. With no end in sight to all the bloodshed, centuries' old hatreds and rivals, with the possibility that someday suicide bombers with tactical nukes would blow themselves up in American cities, he knew the powers-that-be in Washington were damn nervous about the future where the region was concerned. Somehow they wanted to fix the Middle East, meaning reshape it in their own image, no matter who or how many got killed or maimed. Sure, he could see Uncle Sam, or a conspiratorial faction of the intelligence community, looking to seize control of every Islamic country from Pakistan to Turkey, even create a war that would have all Muslims and Israel at one another's throats, the missiles flying until there was little left but ash and cinder.

"Your people, Tiger Ops now inside Iran, what were their orders?"

"Sell…high-tech merch…to Namak…from Eagle Nebula…figure he's the top mullah at the moment…ready to go the distance…"

Langdon stared at the traitor in disbelief. "This is all about selling weapons to a terrorist? This whole thing was a setup? Who ordered it?"

"Never…met the men…Pentagon…DOD…close to the President…trusted…"

"Why us?"

"Already knew…you were going after Namak…"

"So we were sacrificial lambs?"

"Always were…going to take the hard fall…Iran… use covert war…to get the…weapons to Namak…"

"And the men I'm watching are what, unsuspecting tour guides?"

"We needed to watch your people…watch the area…so we could move the merch…couldn't let you kill…our golden goose…"

"You rotten…"

CAG chuckled, then his stare went blank.

"Sir?"

Standing, he found his last commando shaking his head. "Even the sat phones, sir, were shot up. Everything, useless scrap."

A quick check of the enemy dead and he couldn't believe their bad luck. The firefight had shattered their own sat and cell phones to shards. With no spare radio or auxiliary communication of any sort, they were cut off from the Farm, then, no way to warn Phoenix Force. A check of his chronometer and he cursed yet another setback. Their patrol boat, he knew, had already pushed out to sea for its morning recon. It would be another two hours before…

A lifetime for Phoenix Force if he believed the dying words of the traitor.

"THIS IS M TO WILCO APACHE ONE. I need a Hellfire right down Broadway over here! My transponder's on, so get my position marked and hustle up."

The pilot had made a wide circle around the village, ostensibly, McCarter believed, to cover for Tiger Ops when the shooting started. Thus he would be coming in, he had to assume, from the west if he was on the way to clean up his immediate problem.

"Roger that, M."

"What's your position?"

"West side, about midway down the village. Watching my screens for hostiles."

"Any sign of Tiger Ops?"

"Negative, M."

They just vanished? he wondered, but was forced to let it go.

"Get your ass in gear before my bunch start winging out some RPG fire!"

As the pilot copied, McCarter kept hosing down the doorway where three or four fighters were just inside, one of them he was sure, itching to line him up with an RPG, might have lucked out—and still might—unless he kept his stream of autofire pinning them down. They came lurching back, spraying AK-47 autofire, hitting his cover and concealment with one relentless hail of bullets after the other but not before he believed he dropped the RPG man with a round or two to the chest, a lucky tag considering the blanket of lead washing over his position.

Two houses cleared, and McCarter heard yet more autofire one more lair down where Manning and James were engaging a new batch of militants, grenade thunder telling him the big Canadian and the ex-SEAL were lobbing in the lethal steel eggs so they could crash the door. He needed to steal a second to check on Hawkins and Encizo, but told himself no news was good news. And what in bloody hell were Block and mates up to? Assuming he survived, and when he swept the village and found they hadn't fired one shot or nailed one terrorist.

That, he thought, might seal the tomb on what he'd been suspecting about Tiger Ops all along. From the outset, they had thrown all professionalism down the crapper, opting instead to strike out on their own while leaving all the shooting to somebody else. Block and his commandos smelled like a pile of fresh dung, the big Briton certain they were dirty somehow. And if they had some treacherous agenda...

He plucked a frag grenade off his webbing, hugging the face of a retaining wall, ready to go for it on his own, when he heard the familiar buzz of the flying tank killer. The Apache soared in from the west, snapped into a hairpin turn, then hovered as it lined up the terror haven for a Hellfire dusting.

And one Hellfire flamed away from its pod, McCarter eating dirt to ride out the coming big bang.

RETURN FIRE from somewhere in what Hawkins guessed was a living room was ferocious. The ex-Ranger's SAW and Encizo's M-16 would chop down two or three militants, and just as many, if not more, would surge into view, AK-47s flaming like fingers of the damned. Through the boiling smoke, sweeping his SAW, left to right, he nailed a figure with an RPG. He believed the warhead was aimed for the ceiling, as the slight figure toppled back, but roared to Encizo, "Hit the deck, Rafe!"

The blast rocked his senses, as dust, blood and cordite choked into the ex-Ranger's nose.

The wall stayed intact, but Hawkins made out yet more autofire from somewhere inside.

"Finish it, Rafe!"

Going low around the corner, Hawkins pouring out a brief SAW burst, Encizo didn't hesitate as he began unloading the Multiround Projectile Launcher, hitting the interior, right to left, three rolling bands of thunder seeming to want to split the earth beneath Hawkins as they both pulled back to cover. From where he crouched, it sure as hell sounded to Hawkins as if he were sitting on top of the end of the world, as he breathed in the noxious fumes of death, riding out the final few shock waves. It was impossible to scan the ruins, as slabs of rubble kept dropping through the swirling dust storm. Bell rung, Hawkins ventured inside, SAW leading the way, aware they couldn't leave one snake not trampled to rear up on their backside as they forged northward. He clambered over the rubble, the SAW searching for live or wounded combatants. Turning to Encizo, he found his teammate toeing a body, the ringing in his ears muting the curse.

"What is it, Rafe?"

Shaking his head, Encizo vanished through a jagged hole in the far corner of the room for a few moments, then reappeared. "Kids. The ones I can make out so far are all kids. Can't be any more than nine or ten, twelve or thirteen at best."

With all the gore and body parts strewed in front of him, it was near impossible to tell their age, but Hawkins wouldn't put it past the Islamic hatemongers to send out a bunch of teen and preteen boys to meet their martyrdom. It wouldn't be the first time he'd seen Muslim elders use the young to carry out their dirty work of murder and mayhem, while they showcased their radicalism in the mosques or in front of the cameras, inciting yet more young to join their savage ranks.

And Hawkins feared it wouldn't be the last time he encountered such a perversion of life.

NO SOONER HAD the Apache brought the roof down on his shooting problems than McCarter discovered another deathtrap.

A truck bomb, he believed, was rampaging down the street, not more than a hundred yards out, barreling hard, then gathering more speed, it seemed, as if he was the sole source of its murderous fury. He couldn't be sure, but he thought he saw two faces—young faces?—behind the windshield, mouths wide and bellowing their war cry on the way to Paradise. Patching through to his teammates, he shouted, "Find cover, mates! We have a truck bomb in the area!"

Manning and James had already penetrated the next terror nest down, but depending on how much explosive was packed...

McCarter was poised to hold his ground and drop a 40 mm package through the windshield, in the process, he believed, sacrificing his own life when the pilot spoke into com link. "I have them painted, Mr. M. This one's my party."

Have at it, he silently saluted the flyboy as he heard the Apache's 30 mm chain gun roar, caught the first few rounds obliterating the windshield. But McCarter wasn't sticking around to watch the floor show.

The ex-SAS commando was just inside the retaining wall, nosediving, when the payload blew. McCarter covered his head, but a gnawing fear warned him that no matter what, he was going to be buried alive.

And the wall came down.

CHAPTER FIFTEEN

"So, you're telling me the Russians are inviting us in to this Tajikistan weapons factory where high-tech ordnance or schematics for such is believed being shipped to Iran to do what, exactly? Clean up their mess? Wipe off the egg facial for them?"

Hal Brognola already suspected a political angle, and Barbara Price gave it to him as she said, "The read I get from our own sources is, there's major heat building between Washington and Moscow, but the Russians are looking to calm the waters, not further chum them. So, word has it the Russian FSK has made a 'unique offer,' to say the least, for an American black ops team to step in and shut down the factory. No punches pulled, bring the roof down, to quote one of my sources. In that part of the world, it's usually Afghan heroin that creates grief for Moscow, but it seems black market superweapons knowingly falling into the hands of terrorists has them ready to do whatever Washington's bidding. And, from what I hear, Moscow has known for some time they've had corrupt officers and a few black ops at the compound selling ordnance to Iran and who knows else. To answer your question—yes, they're looking at us to wipe the egg off their faces."

Brognola unwrapped a fresh cigar and stuck it in a corner of his mouth. "In other words, they're looking for deniable expendables in case it hits the fan and a bunch of their people—guilty or otherwise—get mowed down in the process."

"That about sums it up. Of course, we would need to pull Phoenix out of Iran and I would have to arrange a DZ where both FSK and CIA agents would meet them."

"And how's this all supposed to shake out? Phoenix marches right in through the front gate and—what? Blows the place off the mountain?"

Price nodded. "Something like that. The FSK has two inside men at the compound, plus an engineer they've turned who have pledged to help. In light of what happened in Vegas—and I take it the White House let Moscow know in no uncertain terms they had their own people involved in killing scores of Americans—the Russian president has agreed to let us handle the matter as we see fit."

"I don't like it. This whole mission has seen turncoats at every corner and what's to keep the Russians from just blasting Phoenix all to hell once they have them inside the compound? Or maybe kidnap them, use them as ransom, threatening to expose an American covert operation for the whole world to see if Washington doesn't sweep their part in the Vegas mess under the rug, all's forgiven?"

Price turned grim. "There's no guarantee that

wouldn't happen." She paused, then added, "The FSK is willing to turn over all documents regarding Jacobs's role in whatever he engineered for them. They also have agreed to hand over their version of Lightning Bat."

"And do what? Just fly out of there with the thing? And what's to say they won't make copies of Jacobs's designs?"

"There's only one way to find out how these questions will get answered."

Brognola studied Price, saw the steely set to her jaw. "You want to do this, don't you?"

"I have a plan and I think it fits into our situation with Namak. This is what I propose to do..."

MCCARTER WAS AMAZED he was still on the planet. Renewed bursts of gunfire, the heavier thunder of what was the Apache's chain gun, broke through the cobwebs, bringing him back to stark reality. Grunting, slipping the com link back in place, he shouldered away a slab of rubble. One look at the wall and he couldn't understand why it was only blown down, front and back, still standing where he'd ducked for cover. Unless, of course, the manner in which the wreckage had been hurled away, or maybe the blast radius somehow...

Stranger cosmic things, he knew, had happened. Why question his good fortune when his troops, it sounded, were alive and kicking?

Or so he hoped all of them were in one piece.

He bulled out of the debris, rising, hauling the M-16 with him as he shuffled up to the jagged fangs of the far edge of the wall. He found the Apache hard at work remodeling a building near the funeral pyre that was the suicide truck. Along the gate, he spotted all four of his teammates throwing rounds and grenades into the Apache's murderous blitzkrieg. Whoever was holed up inside there, he knew, didn't stand a chance.

He gave the narrow street and its stone dwellings a hard search, calling out to Manning, alerting the big Canadian he was on their six. According to intelligence and an inside source, the village was all-male, all-militant. There were other items fanning the flames of his suspicion, but, in due course, he would discover the truth, he was sure of it. At worst, there were no women and children for the terrorists to use as human shields, making their task a little easier, but…

McCarter suddenly thought about Block and company again as the Apache plunged a Hellfire into the next shooting gallery to end the engagement. Too many sirens, too many red flags were clanging and flaring to mind, but he needed to jump back into the game.

March on, and into the belly of the demon.

As dust and rubble cascaded to the street, McCarter told his men, "Listen up, mates. It's about our Mr. Block."

"Yeah," Calvin James retorted. "I know we've been trading bullets with the bad guys for twenty minutes or so, but my hearing isn't that bad. Why haven't I heard any shooting from across town?"

"You're thinking," Encizo said, "our Mr. Block and bad company are dirty."

McCarter waved at the Apache pilot, hand-signaled for him to land, then told his commandos, "I have my suspicions. Here's how we play it…"

JIM BLOCK SUSPECTED the Iranians were light with the cash, saw his hands tremble as anger shot through every limb. Two large duffel bags, about half the size of military body bags, but as he stared down at the hundred-dollar bills, he was pretty sure fifteen million dollars couldn't be squeezed into them.

No way in hell.

Again, under the watchful eyes of the cutout, Khagil…something, he took a bill at random, handed it off to Dutton for inspection. A former U.S. Treasury agent who tossed away his career to join the Marines for Gulf II, Dutton, he knew, could spot a counterfeit bill with a look, a snap, a taste. He did just that, taking his sweet time.

"They are real," he heard the Iranian growl. "Now, can we head for the chopper for our cargo?"

Dutton gave the nod, and Block stood. "Not so fast. I didn't bring my money counter, but I'd say you're short." He paused, read the Iranian's eyes as the militant decided whether to lie. "Well?"

"I was told to deliver half the money. The rest you will receive when we are away from here and have inspected what we are paying for. That includes, we were told, a full and complete demonstration. Complete with access, launch codes, computer mainframes."

"That wasn't the deal." Block gritted his teeth, sizing up the situation. There were twenty-plus fanatics spread out through the small mosque, at least six of them armed with RPGs. He had posted two of his men to stand watch in the courtyards outside, which left him four guns against a dozen inside the inner prayer sanctum.

"Understand our position," the Iranian said, filling his hands with his AK, taking a step closer to Block. "The Ayatollah made these arrangements through middlemen, none of which I have ever seen until now. This is a most unique but unusual and, should I say, troubling situation."

"Dealing with infidels, you mean."

"You said that, I did not. The deal has changed. Accept the terms, or give back the money and leave our country."

"And how would your Grand Ayatollah feel about that, seeing as he went through all this time and trouble to get us here with the first shipment?"

"He trusts my judgment in such matters."

"Really. Are you willing to bet your life on that?"

"If I must."

Block sensed the tension mounting, was considering his options—accept the terms or shoot it out, which was more than likely suicide—when one of his sentries showed in the archway, announcing, "Our friends from the other side are headed this way."

"All of them?"

"I only saw two, Mr. M and Mr. J."

Block looked at the Iranian. "Okay, I accept your conditions, only I have one of my own."

"Let me guess. You wish for myself and my men to help you kill your teammates?"

"That's the one. And they're not my teammates."

MCCARTER TOOK a read on his handheld heat seeker. Two red ghosts, one standing post at ten o'clock, the other sentry holding his position, throwing off body heat at two o'clock. There could be more hardmen, perched and lying in ambush beyond the entrance portals, then there were prayer chambers, antechambers, a main room, with perhaps hidden coves or even a tunnel that would let the rats flee once the shooting started.

Running blind again. But what was new on this mission, where every sinister question only got answered with a body count?

And it was that time again.

Crouched outside the courtyard wall, the big Briton took a moment to cool down as he briefly considered what he'd seen, what he knew and what he suspected. The march north, splitting Manning, Encizo and Hawkins off a narrow side street to seal the west side of the small domed mosque, then a quick sweep of several hovels, and no sign of life, no bodies. Block and team hadn't capped off the first shot. Ugly truth be told, McCarter's hunch was they were expected by the Iranians, allowed free and unmolested course up the west side. Tack on the fact that three waves of fighters had thrown up the lead barrier, confined to the southeast, and McCarter knew it had been mapped out that way in advance, in secret. Finally, he considered the motor pool, Hummers, SUVs, Toyota pickups, the bulk of vehicles confined to the north end of the mosque, where, clearly, a large contingent of jihadists were gathered. Sure, he had noted the obvious during the sat imagery scan while brainstorming with Block on the Black Hawk. But it was then the man had tipped his hand some more. Instead of going straight for the throat, he wanted Mr. M and company dropped off to the deep south, advance from there.

Cannon fodder, as it turned out.

Now McCarter was moments away from staring into the spotlight of the dark truth. Whatever sordid agenda was under way here, McCarter knew it reached back to Washington. Tiger Ops were the President's men, or commandos dumped in his lap from someone close to the Oval Office, but McCarter would simply have to let the figurative hanging go down in its own time on the political scheme of things from Washington's end. Right now, he had snakes in Iran to trample.

The ex-SAS commando gave the street behind a hard but quick scan. Not a militant was stirring. Nothing but flames, black smoke, rubble and strewed terror carcasses. Whoever was inside the mosque was the end of it.

At least in the town built by their Grand Ayatollah.

McCarter gave James the nod, palmed his sound-suppressed Beretta 93-R, then broke through the gate. They came alive, eyes bugging, their AKs coming up to bear, but the Briton pumped one death tap each, between the eyes, dropped them sprawling in the portals. James on his rear, panning the portals with his M-16, McCarter advanced, Beretta searching the gloom for living evil. Hitting the first pillar, he checked the shadowy recesses of the entry corridor, made out voices somewhere inside the main prayer room, or beyond. M-16/M-203 in hand, James covering his flanks and their six, the big Briton hit a crouch beside a pillared archway, edged the assault rifle around the corner and shouted, "Block! It's over! You, your men and your Iranian mates have five seconds to throw down your weapons or we bring down the roof on your sorry

asses!" Dead but tense silence. "You're on the clock!
Four seconds…three…"

DURING THE COURSE of his bloody stint as a Stony Man
warrior, Rafael Encizo had seen enough bad men with
nothing but malice, deceit and murder of heart, who
lived for nothing other than to serve their own gain to
know the shooting would start any second.

That the enemy inside the mosque would go down, to
the last savage. He could live with that, in fact, like the
rest of his teammates, he wouldn't want it any other way.

As he took up a fire point at the edge of the back
courtyard gate, the Multiround Projectile Launcher filling his hands, all chambers slotted with 40 mm room-
sweepers, it was his task to lay waste to any and all
enemy numbers who came running out the back door
once McCarter called in the flying dragon.

He was ready, as he saw the shadows that were Manning and Hawkins chug out 9 mm rounds from their
sound-suppressed Berettas, dusting three roving sentries off their sandals and boots, one of whom he believed belonged to Block.

Shaving odds.

Getting better all the time.

Encizo concurred with McCarter's assessment that
Block had lured them here, hoping they would get
mowed down by the walls of terrorists they had gone
up against to the southeast. The Tiger Ops leader had
some type of deal in the works with the Iranians, only
McCarter was in the dark as to what, or why.

The Phoenix Force leader, he guessed, was about to
get some answers, and maybe the hard way.

Encizo felt the utter stillness around the back portals, beyond and into the shadowy murk that led to the prayer room. Then, from the silence, he made out Block shouting, "Hold on a second, Mr. M. I believe you and me may be able to work something out."

Encizo felt the corners of his lips stretch in a taut smile, could almost imagine McCarter cut a matching wicked grin.

MCCARTER SMILED, but felt cold as ice, head to toe. "The balls of this guy," he told James who was scanning the corridor in both directions for lurking enemy.

"Listen to me, Mr. M. Whoever you are, the crusade is over. Sad truth is, there was never meant to be another crusade. It's all just smoke and mirrors Washington is putting up to cloud the real truth."

"Why, Block?" McCarter yelled back, peeking around the edge and spotting the Tiger Ops leader, flanked by Iranian gunmen, as he moved out of an antechamber.

"You're looking at close to thirty shooters, M," Block said. "Six to one odds. I've seen your work, but nobody's that good." He chuckled. "Have you ever heard of *Hashashiyya?*"

"That's where the word 'assassin' comes from. They were killers, trained and drugged by some old geezer in an Iranian village to search out and destroy both the Crusaders and rival Sunni Muslims about a thousand years ago. What's your point?"

"They came from the valley of the River Alamut, but the folklore shrouded their homeland rep as the Valley of the Assassins. They were the Ninja of their time, could sneak into any so-called impregnable fortress and kill as silent as a ghost."

McCarter felt his adrenaline race as he began searching his flanks, threw a quick look to his rear, aware Block was going somewhere with his recounting of Ismaili assassin history, but taking his time.

"Maybe it's you and your boys who should throw down your weapons, M. Maybe you could be dead before you knew what hit you. To answer your question, it's about this."

McCarter watched as Block chucked a stack of currency across the room. The wad of American hundred-dollar bills landed a few feet in front of the Phoenix Force leader. "That's it? You sold out for money?"

"Who are you trying to bullshit? The majority of the world sells out for money, I just happened to smarten up a little late in the game, but you know what they say about better being late. There's bigger stakes in this part of the world than saving one single country and installing a puppet government-regime to step dance to Uncle Sam's tune, so they can dip into all that oil, while strategically positioning themselves on the Middle East map. We know the truth, and the truth is only a matter of time. Three, four years, maybe less from now, these people over here will have nukes, tactical nukes they can smuggle into western cities. It's going to happen. What you call terrorists, they call freedom fighters, and these freedom fighters are already in possession of chemical and biological agents.

"I want no part of the coming anarchy that is going to descend on America. Hell, Americans start killing each other if they have to wait in line at the gas pump or the grocery store. What do you think will happen when New York or Washington goes up in a ten-kiloton mushroom cloud or hospital emergency rooms are stacked to overflowing from civilians dying from some undetermined bio agent? Banks, postal service, every government and bureaucracy scrambling to put their fingers in the holes of a dike they know is already bursting, the whole damn infrastructure of America collapsing on their heads."

"It won't happen—not if I can help it."

"Don't be a fool. That's ten grand at your feet. You get on board, help me work this arms deal with Namak, you'll be wiping yourself with that much every morning. I need an answer. I'm a busy man."

McCarter let his M-16 answer the traitor as he hit the currency with a 3-round burst.

BLOCK DIDN'T THINK the Briton would sink his teeth into the offer, but he was shocked when the commando blew the wad of paper into flying shreds, fluttering scraps kicked across the prayer room in a minigeyser, bastard showing off he had principles.

The anticipated chaos erupted next as the Iranians began hitting the pillars with streams of autofire, Block hoping three of their shooters had somehow crept into position to outflank what he thought of as the X commandos when he was laying on the stall about the Ismaili assassins. Perhaps some of the Iranians were direct descendants of those feared killers, or maybe his recounting of that time in their history had motivated a group of about ten to prove they could have cut it back then as the rival to the Ninja. They were moving out, either way, hosing down the pillars, dashing apart for outflanking maneuvers. But why was there no return fire?

Whoever the commandos, he knew they were true warriors, perhaps too thick-headed and cemented in place by some sense of morality—all that good-guy-versus-bad-guy nonsense—for their own good, which would seal their doom. In a way he hated to take them down, a part of him hoping they would have jumped to his side of the tracks, though that would have cut into his payday.

The Briton had made his move, didn't want any part of a future paved in dollar bills.

Tough luck for him and his boys.

HK subgun firespraying the pillars, making it look good as he joined the Iranians in a halfhearted show of warrior stand, Block was grabbing up one of the duffel bags when the shooting abruptly stopped. He was falling back, the Iranians checking the outer corridor, barking at each other in Farsi, when he felt a sick feeling drop his stomach into his bowels. He froze, aware the Briton and his comrade were gone.

And knew why they had vacated.

He'd forgotten about the Apache. The clever, devious British SOB was calling in…

Block whirled. He was sprinting for the portals, a few Iranians beating him to the west courtyard when the first Hellfire pounded the front entryways. He didn't need to look back to know the wall was obliterated, along with a contingent of Iranians, since flying rubble and the giant fist of a shock wave was bowling him off his feet.

MCCARTER KNEW the Apache carried a pack of sixteen Hellfires, figured the flying dragon was still in double digits. That was way more plenty enough wallop, he knew, to turn the mosque into a mausoleum for the evil dead.

Crouched at the deep south end of the outer courtyard wall, James hunkered down and, clutching his M-16, McCarter heard two more Hellfires whoosh away, thunderous retorts shaking the ground beneath his boots. He keyed his com link and ordered the pilot to take out the motor pool.

The ex-SAS commando was up and running, wheeling around the courtyard gate in two shakes, James on his heels when he spotted two bloody figures stagger from the smoke. Well, he thought, even the scientists claimed the cockroach would survive a thermonuclear war, and began mopping up enemy mangled, holding back on the trigger of his M-16, James pitching in the autofire right beside him.

ENCIZO BEGAN the turkey shoot with a 40 mm blast into the heart of three walking wounded. Most of the mosque was a heap of rubble, thanks to the vandalizing touch of three Hellfire hammers, but no aerial bombardment he'd ever seen scoffed up every living soul.

A few armed rats always managed to scurry away.

Not here. Not today.

Hawkins and Manning flanking him, standing tall over the top edge of the courtyard barrier, the ex-Army Ranger and the big Canadian unloaded their weapons as they came staggering from the smoke and ruins, screaming and shooting blind. No point in wasting another 40 mm projectile, since the enemy was shocked and reeling senseless, their numbers sure to be shaved to single digits at worst, Encizo unsung his M-16. They were dropping all over the courtyard when a figure came howling from the boiling cloud.

Block.

He was bloodied, scalp to boots, holding on to a duffel bag that was cleaved open, spilling currency as he rolled ahead, cursing like a demon and holding back on the trigger of his HK subgun. Joining his teammates for a burial salvo, Encizo gave the traitor due credit for tenacity, his ability to be able to absorb hits and take the pain while he bulled forward, sweeping the subgun back and forth. He spun, HK still chattering, bills flying in a green cyclone, a few more rounds flaming out from his subgun before their triburst finally toppled him.

"Son of a bitch didn't want to give up the ghost," Hawkins growled.

"Why would he?" Manning said. "Man had a dream."

Encizo took in the slaughter, listening to the Apache unload on the motor pool, what sounded a thundering combo of chain gun and Hellfire demolition. He looked in that direction, as funnels of fire shot for the sky of the coming new day. But for one walk through of the ruins to make sure all enemy bodies were dead and accounted for, Encizo sensed it was a wrap.

CHAPTER SIXTEEN

Ezekiel Jacobs couldn't stop shaking. Beyond fear of the present unknown, he was terrified about the future.

Such as, did he have any tomorrows outside prison walls.

The mere thought of being tossed into a cage with a bunch of savages weakened his knees, threatened to bring on a crippling migraine, squirt bile into his throat. Unless he was placed in solitary confinement or was shipped off to some federal country club with the embezzlers, all ilk of white-collar con artists and so forth, he would never survive the first day. He wasn't a tough guy, or a street fighter, much less a savage who could stand up among criminal rabble and vicious animals, defend himself with fists and sheer brutality. No, he was a gentle, erudite man who had natural ability to create and shape the future of warfare albeit from the isolated safety of a think tank, a connoisseur of the finer things in life, classical music, rare French wine and such. He would never...

A myriad of horrifying and degrading images began

flashing through his mind about all the humiliation that would be inflicted on his body once those bars slammed shut behind him.

Stop it! he told himself. He wasn't there yet, but where on Earth was he?

Backtrack, get whatever bearings he could. A monumental mental chore all by itself, since he had been cuffed and blindfolded when leaving McCarran International, asking questions of his three captors but getting no answers, other than being told to shut his mouth, treated like a common criminal by men of brute force and violence. During the trip, the big one had, however, inquired what he knew regarding the shipment of classified ordnance and documents from Eagle Nebula. He answered them with nothing but the truth, being as he was the one who told them he had hacked into classified Eagle Nebula mainframes on the matter. So he helped, right? Didn't that count for something?

At some point during the terrifying journey of darkness—and how could he track time in the state of shock and panic he was plunged into by events by his control?—he had been handed off to more clawlike hands, digging into the shoulders, manhandling him along, one of the commandos from the Vegas slaughter remarking, "Have a nice life, Doc."

How many hours had actually elapsed since he'd put behind the worst nightmare of his life? Ten? Twelve? A day? Where was he now? It was some sort of installation, he guessed, perhaps a military prison, he feared, since his hands were still bound behind his back, a black hood now dropped over his head, as if…

Oh, God, no. Was he right then being marched to his

own execution? He was still in America, wasn't he? Only in the world of classified operations…well, he had heard the rumors over the years about guilty before being proved innocent.

He willed himself best he could to stay calm as the hands wrapped around his arms kept hauling him forward. If they wanted him dead, surely they would have killed him by now. Or was he being led to a torture chamber? How did this horror befall him? All he wanted was one week in Las Vegas, fun and games, in exchange for what would have proved years of grinding, around-the-clock slavery for the Russians, but at a salary four times what the U.S. government paid him, with promised all-expenses-paid vacations to Monte Carlo, Hong Kong, Paris.

How had this injustice happened to him! How could his whole world come crashing down so fast?

Get control, think. He was positive his situation had something to do with the massacre in Vegas. How, though, could he be held accountable for mass murder perpetrated by other men? After all, for God's sake, he was a simple aerospace engineer, not some steely eyed black ops assassin, or the wild-eyed shooters he'd seen back at the casino. He used his mind, his talent, to create and design prototype weapons and their systems. He was the creator of so much future war technology…

He caught his breath, somehow stopped his mind from racing. There it was. Someone else besides the Russians or the Eagle Nebula assassins wanted to purchase his unique skills. Or did they? Who were the three hard-eyed, grim-faced men from back on the highway of death? He had a suspicion they were involved somehow with law enforcement, since the big one with the mean eyes and wicked tongue was embroiled in such a heated argument back in Vegas in an official-looking building he would have sworn another shoot-out would erupt. If that was true…

No. Say it wasn't so, he heard his mind cry. He was under some type of informal arrest. If that was the case, given he was on the verge of selling classified information and his classified talent to the Russians, he would be branded with treason, a certain life sentence, perhaps charged as a co-conspirator to mass murder, indirectly blamed for the deaths of so many back at the casino, in the street, on the highway, where law-enforcement officers, he knew, had been killed.

Jacobs felt his knees buckle, hands clawing into his arms to jerk him back up and moving. He felt sick to his stomach. Suddenly he found himself wishing…

What? That he was back in North Dakota? Putting in an honest day's work at the Eagle Nebula compound? Safe and snug in the bosom of his wife?

Heaven forbid.

Or would the future skewer him with so much guilt, regret and shame that he would openly weep to return to the simple life of yesterday?

A soft hiss of a pneumatic door and one of them was removing the cuffs. Before he could rub circulation back into his hands, he felt himself shoved into the soft leather of a wing back. The hood came off next, the light piercing his eyes, which hadn't seen anything but darkness for endless hours. Squinting, he spotted what appeared a stocky figure in a dark suit jacket at the end of a long conference table. As he adjusted his vision he found the man chewing on a cigar, which suddenly made him crave one, if only to take the needles out of his nerves. The man looked official, but not in a bureaucratic, nondescript way. His face was grizzled but in a rugged manner, the eyes hard but wise, as if he'd seen the world and all it had to offer and was debating how much of the world he really liked. Whatever the case, whoever he was, Jacobs sensed he was skirting the edge of the abyss.

"Do not ask where you are or who I am."

A voice of authority. Jacobs felt as if he didn't dare even breathe.

"I understand you wanted a deal involving full immunity, relocation in the witness protection program?"

Now how did he answer that? It almost sounded as if the man were digging a pit for him to fall into, kick the dirt over his thrashing body. Jacobs suddenly noticed there was a wall monitor in the room, the man nodding toward the screen, a gesture indicating he should look that way. He did, and recognized the North Strip behind the reporter. Then, the voice authority sounded more like the voice of God as the man listed the number of dead and wounded, projected fatalities from injuries, the missing in the hotel-casinos still buried beneath the rubble from the terrorist attack.

Making it sound as if he was to blame.

This wasn't good. Not good at all.

Somehow, Jacobs found his voice, sensing the man was waiting for him to say something, anything. "What…exactly do you want from me?"

"What about your sweetheart deal?"

"I...don't really care about that anymore. I just want to live."

And Jacobs waited what felt like the longest few seconds of his life, as the man bobbed his head, considered something.

From behind the smoke, the voice of God told him, "Sounds like we can work together."

EAGLE NEBULA Distributions, Inc.

Oh, but they were brazen as the year was long, Carl Lyons had to give the devil—in this instance Orion and men—their due in that regard. Might as well, he thought, crouched at the far northeast corner of the razor-wire-topped chain-link fence, hang out a sign.

Black Ops R' Us. Try us on for size.

Well, Lyons understood, even embraced brazen, hell, figured they could pencil in his name beside the word in Webster's.

Which may or may not work to his advantage at that witching hour along the Chicago River. There was no way, however, he would let another Vegas massacre blow through Chicago, even if the area along South Wacker Drive, inside and beyond the Loop, was a ghost town.

That left the men in blue to contend with, if and when they responded to the coming blitz. In case of just such a 9/11 emergency, Lyons had a number for a direct line to Hal Brognola, but he really didn't want the big Fed to bail them out twice in one mission. One conflict at a time, Lyons told himself, gripping his M-16/M-203 combo, eager to rock and roll.

"C'mon, Gadgets," he urged Schwarz, who was cutting through the fencing with rubber-tipped wire cutters at what felt a pace long enough for another dark nebulosity of gas to evolve into star formations somewhere in deep space. "I got a grandmother who moves faster than this, and she's dead."

Schwarz rumbled something as he kept cutting.

Across the stretch of lot, Lyons found them in agitated high gear. Three eighteen-wheelers were backed up against the warehouse docking platform. Hardmen with shoulder-slung HK subguns were rolling forklifts piled with big wooden crates into the cargo holds. They were moving out, and in a hurry, Lyons certain Orion was feeling the squeeze after his Vegas chorus line had been hooked from the stage. And Lyons figured if the FBI had held them up any longer in Vegas, or Brognola had needed a chain saw coupled with a presidential directive to cut through the web of red tape, the real Feds were suffocating the three of them in.

They were here now, ready to nail Orion and goons, once and for all. And security appeared lax, if not nonexistent, the security force relying solely on its balls, bogus DOD credentials and the power of their guns. Lyons understood something about arrogance, too, but in the enemy's case, it was about to get them waxed.

Lyons hated to admit it, but without Jacobs they would have never found this way station for high-tech ordnance. Even with all the Farm's ultrasophisticated computer hardware, all their hacking and tracking skills, Eagle Nebula Distributions, Inc. was nowhere to be found on any city or national directory of businesses. It was almost as if the place didn't exist. After this mission, Lyons would believe his own government—or the darker elements seeking to run the show from the shadows—was capable of anything. According to Jacobs, from there the cargo was trucked to a freighter ship docked at Calumet Harbor. Manifests were forged, of course, but the ship would chug out a dozen or so miles across Lake Michigan where a seaplane would land, the cargo transferred. After that—and Jacobs fell skimpy on further details here—it arrived in Montreal, stored in a warehouse front for industrial machinery, or so he believed. If Orion was ever asked, Lyons wondered what he'd pass off Eagle Nebula Distribution, Inc. as to the local authorities.

After thirty minutes of watching the store from an adjacent warehouse complex they'd broken into the old-fashioned way—lock pick—Lyons took an enemy head count, best he could, slapped together a plan of attack.

Which was fan out, march straight up the gut, fire and advance.

They hadn't been out of their combat webbing, harnesses and customized windbreakers meant to stow more clips and grenades since Vegas. Lyons was tired, hungry, nicked and scraped from near misses, sore from head to his big toe, but he'd gotten his second wind during the jaunt from Vegas. Adrenaline and cold anger further fueled the tiger caged in his heart.

He could be one-hundred-percent positive Schwarz and Blancanales were likewise good to rock.

Finally, Schwarz sliced away a hole, just big enough for a grown man to squeeze through, but only if he curled himself into a near fetal position. Lyons scowled at Schwarz, who shrugged, the gesture and look all mental telepathy telling his leader he required more time and less mouth to produce sufficient enough space.

Ah, the hell with it. Lyons bent his head, stifling the curse as wire dug into his shoulders and scalp, nearly scraped the com link off his head while tearing at his windbreaker, then he was through, up and rolling, sights fixed on the loading docks. Firing a quick look over his shoulder, he found Schwarz picking up the left wing and vectoring for the motor pool, Blancanales going for the docks, their hardware out and ready to cut loose, Pol sticking to the same HK subgun from Vegas but with pockets stuffed with plenty of extra frag, flash-stun and incendiary grenades.

All set, and Lyons figured no time like the present.

He lifted his combo-blaster, sighted on two forklifts that looked stuck in their own traffic jam and tapped the M-203's trigger.

GABRIEL HORN WAS so angry and so disturbed, he felt disembodied, as if the man inside was about to escape the three-dimensional trappings of the flesh and float, up, up and away to the stars. The walls were closing, the sky was falling, personal doomsday was somewhere in the Chicago night, ready to devour him, a pride of ferocious lions that hadn't seen a meal in weeks. He didn't want to admit it, not even to himself, but he almost wished he was somewhere else besides the planet Earth.

All of these best-laid plans. All the DOD and Company slush funds he'd electronically cleaned out, a thief in cyberspace, dispersed to buy contacts, troops, hardware, small and large. All the extortion or downright threats of get on board his program or die, families included, to get it this far. And now?

Not a clue where it went from here. Except grab what they had removed from Eagle Nebula, flee to parts unknown and dump it all off. Hopefully that would be the Iranians, but he was having his doubts at present on how sincere they were to exchange cold cash for ordnance.

He was shutting down his sat link, felt his empty belly rumbling from tension, a ton of paranoia suddenly dropping square on his shoulders. No word from either of his middlemen overseas, almost as if they had vanished off the face of the planet. Vegas was a wash, all loyal hands and good fighting men dead, but he already figured as much, both from the news accounts of the alleged flying van on I-15, and from the radio silence on Heller's end. If there was good news in that, it meant his cut of the asking price shot like a rocket through the ozone.

Now he was down to six operators, forced to use three of them like common laborers to load the eighteen-wheelers.

He felt the eyes of the Iranian drilling into the back of his head as he sensed the man's presence in the doorway of his office. Without turning, he said, "Don't tell me. You're having second thoughts about my asking price."

"It has been cleared, I have told you. One hundred million American is available, but only once we get the merchandise, complete with computers, all access codes, safely into my country."

And why didn't he care too much for that scenario? Horn wondered, and chuckled to himself.

"Did I say something funny?"

Nurij, he thought, getting cocky now that he believed the brass ring was in his grasp, his Grand Ayatollah giving him the thumbs-up to get the ordnance in country and in his hands. A jaunt inside Iran, though, to trade what he had with the most dangerous extremists on the planet wasn't his idea of just another day at the office. Not unless he could marshal up a small army of his own. He was already in possession of such a fighting force, in fact, but their absence of communication was at the top of his list of nagging concerns.

Horn took up his sat link and HK subgun. "Let's go. We have a long drive to Montreal," he told Nurij, heading for the doorway.

Brushing past the Iranian, Horn was wondering what the hell could possibly go wrong next when—

The explosion seemed to pierce his eyes like a million flares snapping on at once. Blinded for a moment, he turned away on instinct and fear, hit the deck, as the forklifts and their passengers, blown to flying wet flesh and shrapnel, he knew, came banging off his head and shoulders. He heard the rattle of weaponsfire crack slowly through the chiming in his skull, thought he heard Nurij howl and curse from some distant point in his personal galaxy of rage and terror.

And Horn knew what he had to do to survive.

Debris banging the concrete floor around him, Horn jumped to his feet. He found Nurij cowering in the doorway, the stutter of autofire now crystal clear as adrenaline pumped through his veins, drove away the ringing in his ears. Horn fell over the Iranian, who was blubbering, cursing how he felt betrayed, but Orion thought how he hadn't seen anything yet. Who and how many were hitting the warehouse, Horn had no way of knowing, but he was walking out of here, with Nurij in tow. At least one of the eighteen-wheelers, he knew, was loaded, three-quarters, with ordnance. Somehow, some way, he'd make it out of the country.

Or he was dead.

Horn threw an arm around the Iranian's neck, jacked him to his feet.

"What are you doing?"

It was an awkward hold, the sat link heavy in his hand with the arm locked around his human armor's throat, but Horn applied pressure, choking the Iranian into a whimpering silence.

"Just shut up, be still and play it my way! And we may get out of here!"

THE SHOCK ATTACK nearly decapitated the enemy force in the opening shot, if the brief stakeout tallied the enemy numbers for Lyons correctly at around a half dozen, give or take one or two shooters. One 40 mm shellacking, Lyons saw, as he advanced on the eighteen-wheeler, had kicked three of Orion's thugs into a black hole, torn figures plastered on the doorway's floor, sprawled on the dock. From the far side of the big rig line, he heard Schwarz dump another 40 mm grenade into the enemy ranks. How many left standing? How many inside the warehouse? And why weren't Orion and his vaunted shooters venturing to take up positions inside the doorway? Or had they dusted the bulk of his hardforce already?

Running hard, M-16 leading Lyons's rush, Blancanales moving down the platform, cutting loose with his subgun on enemy he couldn't see, the Able Team leader reached the tail end of the eighteen-wheeler, the stink of blood and cordite swarming his senses. Weaponsfire abruptly ceased, but Lyons didn't trust the silence, sensed a presence in the warehouse. He hand-signaled for Blancanales to check the cargo hold. A few moments later Blancanales shot Lyons a thumbs-up, then the Able Team leader pointed at the bay door to the warehouse, patched through to Schwarz. "Gadgets! Are you clear?"

"Clear. I nailed two. Depending on how many you tagged, I think we eighty-sixed all of them."

"Check the other two rigs anyway."

"You out there! I have a hostage!"

Lyons bounded up onto the platform, advancing on Blancanales's backside as his teammate crouched at the edge of the doorway, peeking around the corner.

"It's our buddy, Orion."

"Do tell," Lyons said.

"He's alone," Blancanales said. "But he has a hostage."

"Listen to me," Lyons heard Orion shout. "My hostage is an Iranian middleman for Rafiq Namak. Ever hear of him? The rising mullah star looking to maybe start World War III in the Middle East? Or blow Israel into the Mediterranean? Or bring Iraq and Iran under one Shiite sword? So he sends my boy here to buy some ordnance that was used to topple half of Vegas. Yeah, that was my show, but my boy was there, practically frothing at the mouth, can't wait to get his hands on some Eagle Nebula goodies. By the way, Namak already has some Eagle Nebula ordnance, so maybe we can work something out to get it back."

Lyons took a knee beside Blancanales, heard Schwarz patch through, informing him they were clear. "Take the other side of the doorway, Gadgets. You and Pol cover me when I go in."

"I walk out of here with him, you let me go on my way, out of the country, and I can drop him off for you someplace but only after I know I'm in the clear. I let you know where you can pick him up. What about it?"

Lyons briefly thought about all the innocent blood shed in Vegas, how so many had betrayed their country for a lousy few dollars, and at the risk of starting a war in the Middle East that would only find more countless lives snuffed out at the hands and hatred of a fanatic. He squeezed his eyes shut, took a deep breath, ready now to mete out at least one moment of hard reckoning. Standing, flicking his selector switch to single-shot mode, he wheeled around the corner, M-16 rising, drawing a bead. Shock widened Orion's eyes, his lips moving as he fought to speak.

"We can work something out! I have access to millions of dollars, I have all this cargo that we can sell!"

"You're done," Lyons said, and pumped two rounds into the Iranian's chest.

The corpse went limp, folding like an accordion in his grasp. Orion appeared torn between holding the human shield upright, or dropping him, go for broke as the Able Team leader then saw the fire light his eyes.

And Lyons squeezed the trigger.

Final decision.

CHAPTER SEVENTEEN

Hal Brognola believed the truth in the world in which he lived was either a prison or a door that only opened to a maze of more riddles, questions and lies. Rarely did it set a man free.

Right then—sitting by himself, half listening and watching the cyberteam and its newest but temporary member working up Lightning Bat's specs on a computer with graphics software in a workstation Kurtzman had set up for him next to his own bay—the big Fed felt himself on the verge of plunging into a dark night of the soul.

Even before the start of the campaign, the world felt to Brognola as if it was flying off its axis. Now the entire planet, it seemed in his growing dark mood, was revolving away at light speed, ready to be gobbled up into some black hole where only madness and chaos reigned, forever and into infinity. No sleep, too much caffeine, too much stress. Or so he told himself, fighting to keep the tentacles of depression from reaching out and seizing hold, as he was painfully aware at the moment every flashpoint they doused in blood of the enemy two or more caldrons threatened to bubble over, and with an even more insidious brew.

Speaking of poison, Tiger Ops had shown its true stripes, and Brognola spared a moment to grieve for the blacksuit they'd lost. The only plus he could find in that piece of treachery was that the relay station had managed to mark Namak's location, somewhere within a ten-square-mile radius along the northwest edge of the Zagros Mountains, bounce the signal back to the Farm before the shooting started. Questions were many, too many, in fact, to ponder, he told himself, unless he wished to dangle himself over the threshold of madness, or spiral down into that dark pit of depression.

Which would only prove defeating, for himself and all concerned.

Greed, naturally, was the driving force behind the homefront jackals, he knew, but to move as freely as they had, to create a network of enemy contacts, shipping lanes for Eagle Nebula ordnance, there were snakes somewhere in hiding who had kept the eggs of this viper's brood hatching along. At some point the big Fed knew he would have to confront the President, who might just run for political cover or slip the noose over the man heading up the Sensitive Operations Group. Tiger Ops, after all, had been pawned off by someone on the Man, who, in turn, had dumped them on Phoenix Force with the closest thing to an ultimatum he'd ever received from a sitting President. How the end of that all played out, whose head would roll for the Tiger Ops treason, was anybody's guess.

And now Brognola was shoving Phoenix Force back

into the lion's mouth. They knew the risks they would face when hitting Tajikistan, working with allies who could well turn out to be another shade of Tiger Ops. But everyone was agreed on the plan Price had mapped out.

No other way, Brognola knew, than to suck it up, gut it out. Fingers crossed, offer up a silent prayer, hope for the best but prepare for the worst.

He stood, thought he wanted a cigar, but knew it would only leave a bad taste in his mouth, as he felt the weight of the world on his shoulders. Jacobs, he saw, was working with a frenzy on his keyboard that rivaled Kurtzman's skills. It looked to Brognola the aerospace wizard-sellout was fast piecing together specs on Lightning Bat, inside and out.

"But it is Stealth technology?" Kurtzman asked.

"Based on."

"Meaning what exactly?"

Jacobs shook his head, made a face as if he were talking to an idiot. Kurtzman's scowl indicated to Brognola he was about ready to reach over and smack him on the back of the head.

Jacobs cleared his throat. "There are a few exceptions, such as Lightning Bat is designed for a two-man crew unlike the F-117's lone pilot. I designed cutting-edge avionics especially for this craft, but yes, they are similar to past prototypes, which, I believe, Lightning Bat will—or could—soon make obsolete. You have television-style cathode ray tubes that display all information, but your man had better be sharp and experienced."

"Believe me when I tell you," Kurtzman said, "he is. Don't worry about his end of the deal."

Jacobs grunted as he split his screen, Brognola sensing Kurtzman was anxious for the man to begin detailing the cockpit's nerve center on his monitor. "I essentially gleaned the best of all worlds from the F-117, the B-2, the Blackbird...and Aurora."

Kurtzman looked at Jacobs. "The Aurora Project? I thought that was just some reporter's wild speculation?"

"Nobody knew about Lightning Bat, either, until..." Jacobs fidgeted in his seat, ran a hand through his hair. "Okay, my design has the same subdivisions of triangular and trapezoid facets meant to deflect radar, as you can see here. Its unique shape actually vacuums in enemy radar beams then cuts them down to a mere one to three beams. That the Stealth is invisible is...well," he said, glancing at Kurtzman, "merely some journalist's or ordinary citizen's flight of fancy who has heard one too many Area 51 stories. The goal of Stealth technology is for the pilot to pick up the enemy well in advance before the enemy has detected him by radar. I was looking to further reduce its electromagnetic emissions—which I achieved—advance a higher service ceiling—which I did—with more agility, and the speed I managed with some...well, some help."

"The Divine Alloy," Kurtzman said.

"So, you do know."

Kurtzman cocked a grin at Jacobs. "Consider this place the worst nightmare you ever had about Big Brother."

"Indeed. Now, the alloy is what makes the craft so special, though I still don't fully understand its properties, and because the Russians have not yet been able to adapt it inside a nuclear generator—of which prototype I created—they cannot attain Mach 10 like the American version. Under certain conditions this alloy from space acts as a spent nuclear fuel 'propellant,' with some sort of antigravity property. That is the best way I can describe it. I was working out the properties of this alloy, believed I was a year or less from being able to convert it to a useable and safe fissionable fuel for the nuclear generator whereby a craft could achieve light speed, or even faster. Should I have succeeded in doing that," he said, looking at Kurtzman, eyes glowing behind his spectacles, "deep space travel was well within man's grasp."

Kurtzman nodded, gestured at Jacobs's monitor. "Go on. We'll have plenty of time later to talk about that. And, no," he added with a wry grin, "I won't steal your theories for my shot at the Nobel Prize."

"Indeed. They are more than just theories, as you so glibly put it. And my work was never about glory or any Nobel Prize."

"I gotcha. Let's move on."

Jacobs made a production of clearing his throat again. "You can see my configuration has the same slab-sided fuselage to further reflect away enemy radar, then with the Radar Absorbing Material—"

"I already know all that," Kurtzman cut in.

"Well, excuse me."

"I'm more interested in the cockpit and how my man is going to fly it."

"If you know so much, then you know a very sophisticated network of computers systems fly this bird."

"So, this is what you are trying to tell me," Kurtzman muttered. Not blinking or stopping to catch his breath, the computer wizard rattled off the Stealth digital fly-by-wire control system, tactical cockpit displays, from radar altimeter to Inertial Navigation System, Air Data Computer, listing all display and computer systems so fast Brognola had to strain to catch every word. He heard Laser Radar, though, its narrow beam near impossible to detect as opposed to yesteryear's microwave radar, and with no sidelobes on the LR to leak energy. Digital maps, with the latest TRN— Terrain Reference Navigation—detailing not only ground it flew over but could actually "see" the land well beyond. He was sure LB had bastardized but upgraded versions of GEF404 turbofan engines, only Kurtzman suspected Lightning Bat used some sort of booster before the turbos kicked in, then he rapid-fired onto the internal weapons bay. That Lightning Bat depended on electrooptics for target seeking and acquisition, with UHR—Ultra-High Resolution—for target recognition, and that LB couldn't carry external missiles or it would not be classified as Stealth.

Jacobs frowned. "You know it all. So, what do you need me for?"

"A lot," Kurtzman returned. "Work up the control and weapons system you designed, and, for your sake, I hope the Russian version is close…"

"I built it for them," Jacobs said, his voice rising in sudden anger. "Unless they made changes I am unaware of, it is an exact replica of what I designed for Eagle Nebula."

Brognola stepped up to Jacobs. "What I think he's asking is, can our man fly it?"

"If he's ever flown a Stealth, he can."

Brognola washed a cloud of smoke over Jacobs's workstation. "He's flown everything, including a shuttle."

"Then he should have no problem."

"But you, Dr. Jacobs," Brognola said, "need to pick up the pace. I need all specs and schematics faxed to our man ASAP, complete with thorough detail on all navigation and weapons systems. You have thirty minutes."

"I can manage that."

"Further, you do understand, since our man does not speak or read Russian, you will be in constant communication with him as soon as he takes his seat in Lightning Bat."

"I believe you already made that clear."

"This is not a threat, it's a promise. If our man goes down because of either neglect on your part or if you fail to perform at the top of your game or deliver all we need to get him up then back on the ground, you're going to crash before he does."

Jacobs nodded. "I understand. If he knows the craft, as expertly as you say he does, and can follow my instructions to the letter, he will succeed. Trust me."

Brognola cocked an eyebrow, managed to keep the grin off his lips but hit Jacobs in the face with a cloud. Message delivered. "What about the Four Points weapons system?"

"What about them?" Jacobs said, a little snippy.

"Are you prepared to walk him through it when he tells you to?"

"So, this is about more than just stealing the craft from the Russians?"

"Answer me."

"I am at your dispo...I am at your service."

"Hal."

"Keep working. Twenty-nine minutes and counting," Brognola told Jacobs, then walked over to Tokaido who was monitoring what they believed was Namak's largest terror camp in Iran.

"That's a..."

"A Black Hawk," Brognola said. "Enlarge that."

While Tokaido enhanced the image to near kissing-close, Brognola watched as a figure bounded out of the chopper. He wasn't seeing the figure in living color, but he could tell the man was wearing tiger-striped camous. Brognola muttered an oath.

"A few of them must have slipped the net on Phoenix," Tokaido said.

"Keep an eye on the area and keep me apprised of any unusual developments," Brognola said, then turned to Wethers and Delahunt, who were imaging the region around the Zagros Mountains. "Any luck on a Namak sighting?"

"We have movement," Wethers said, while Delahunt shook her head. "Looks like five, maybe six, armed men. But they just dropped into a ravine. I'll have to wait until they come out."

"If it's Namak, I want him tracked. Wherever he goes. Whatever you have to do."

Brognola left them all to it, checking his watch, mentally ticking down the numbers until Phoenix was dropped by a C-130 to Tajikistan soil. Hours still. He saw Price walk into the Computer Room with what he hoped was a fresh batch of intel. He met her halfway. "Is Phoenix set to go?"

"They are. Only the CIA special ops and the FSK have insisted on a little tinkering with the original plan."

Brognola sounded off a grim chuckle. "Why am I not surprised?"

CHUCK AVALON KNEW that, in CIA parlance, he was considered an A Specialist. That meant he was number one operator, viewed by peers and superiors alike as the best of the best in every area of combat, from hand-to-hand to sniping to manning a 155 mm piece to arming a backpack nuke, down to the nuts and bolts of tactics and leading commandos on through to successful operational execution. Surviving under any conditions, man-made or natural, was a given.

At the moment his survival was far from guaranteed.

As he watched about two, maybe three, hundred armed extremists run up to the Black Hawk, shouting in a babble of Arabic, Farsi and broken English for him, Cheevers and Solstice to drop their weapons and throw their hands up, he didn't feel so special.

Not in the least.

Briefly, as he threw away his M-16/M-203 combo and raised his arms, he considered the insanity of the moment. Tiger Ops, as he had seen from a distance, had most likely been found out and waxed by their X commando counterparts. Couple that with radio silence and the mosque avalanching on all the home-team players he knew had been inside the domed so-called holy ground when the Apache brought the roof down with some Hellfires…

The three of them were on their own. That was his call, and anybody who didn't like it could feel free to hop off and walk back to the border. His teammates had stayed on board.

What choice was there, after all?

Going back to Base Boomerang—and how was that for irony? he thought—was out of the question. Low on fuel anyway, there was CENTCOM, with their own special ops who still shrouded themselves in the Stars and Stripes to factor into what would be certain execution if they went into the bag, now that Tiger Ops was blown. So he'd struck out on his own, hoping to save his payday, maybe square the moment with Namak, map out a new future. From the moment he'd signed on with Gabriel Horn to be a point man for delivery of the ordnance, he'd known he was way past the point of no return anyway.

Avalon looked at the wall of terrorists. He had to admit they were a damn spooky sight, armed to the gills, AKs, RPGs, LMGs, what looked a Stinger. Most of them kept their faces concealed, a smattering of black hoods, with kaffiyehs wrapped around the lower part of their faces, sunglasses hiding the eyes. And he could feel their rage rise up the murder meter.

"Settle down, fellas! I'm here to speak with your Grand Ayatollah! I have a special gift for Namak!"

That calmed some of the fanatics, he saw, at least the ones who understood English. A bearded man wearing a turban, decked out in what looked like baggy black sultan pants and purple tunic, holding a Russian RPK-74 LMG nearly as long as he was tall, parted the crowd.

"You Namak?"

"I am Salidin Ahmed Tujuourez. I am lieutenant of operations. What is this gift?"

A large group had already swept past, pilfering the Black Hawk, so Avalon jerked a thumb over his shoulder. "What they got their hands all over? That's what your boss ordered. First shipment. All of it. Can you get a message to him?"

Tujuourez stopped, inches from Avalon's face. "I am not so sure he wishes to speak with you."

Avalon kept a straight face, grateful his eyes were shielded from both the blast furnace that was the sun and to hide any flicker of the true ill will and contempt he felt toward this rabble. He was aware of the lethal trouble his people had encountered at al-Namak, figured Namak was likewise up to speed.

"Is there a problem?" Avalon asked.

"You might say."

"Telling me the deal's off? That you're just going to shoot me and my men and take the stuff anyway?"

"Give me a reason not to."

"How about a shipment of warheads with chemical or bio agents? How about maybe—depending on how things shape up in the near future—I can land you a few artillery shells with a five-kiloton wallop?"

Avalon saw the fanatic thinking hard about his next move, then the Iranian gestured for him to follow. He lit up a cigarette, keeping it casual all around as he ran a look over the sea of hostile faces, his men falling in behind. For as far as he could see, it was tents, stone hovels, vehicles, both military and civilian. Not even an antiaircraft piece, and even if they had a few Stingers, he knew, more than likely, they were deadweight, juice in the batteries long since dried up. An air assault, even a half-assed one, would squash this camp like a squirrel run over by an eighteen-wheeler. East, where the Zagros rose from the plateau in a series of black fangs, he figured Namak was perched in a cubbyhole, maybe watching the action through field glasses.

Roughly a hundred yards farther along, and he found the Iranian lieutenant holding back the flap to a GAZ-66 transport truck. Avalon wandered at his stare over the stacks of artillery shells. They were 155 mms, stacked on top of one another in the bed, about six or seven high. Then he spotted a pile of vests with fixed canisters to one side. For some time, the rumor mill from the Company whispered to those in-the-loop that Namak and his followers were planning to ship out a new breed of suicide bombers, martyrs blowing themselves up with chem or bio agents. The world, he thought, had truly become one strange, screwed-up mess, and he was glad—if his own plan worked out—to be stepping out of the black ops game, hopefully with a few duffels of cold, hard cash. Finally he noted the Russian markings, whistled, as if admiring the cache.

"Is that what I think it is?"

"What do you think it is?"

Avalon blew smoke over the shells. "Artillery shells with nerve, maybe bio agents."

"Yes. Courtesy of the Syrians, and the former Iraqi dictator's Republican Guard who were looking for fast cash in order to flee before your people invaded and occupied the country. So, you see we already have Sarin, VX and botulin," the Iranian said, the tone striking Avalon like a father showing off his firstborn. "We can get what we want from the Russians, if necessary."

"Not what I can give you, and for a far more reasonable price, I'm sure, than what Mother Russia wants."

The Iranian lieutenant dropped the flap. "Convince me then."

Avalon smoked, took his time. "I have a very special cannon your Ayatollah ordered. Computerized. Can hit a target within three meters from a long, long way out. Four long-range missiles with a special package for a warhead. Your troops over there breaking those crates open like they're breaking open a box of candy?" Avalon said, chuckling as he pointed his cigarette toward the Black Hawk where the militants were breaking open the crates with rifle butts. "That's some sensitive ordnance. I would tell them to back off before they break something your boss is paying for."

Avalon puffed, laughing again, as the lieutenant shouted in Farsi at the vandals. They cleared out, he thought, like roaches in the dark being hit by a sudden burst of light.

The Iranian bobbed his turban. "You do know I can take what I want, if I so desire."

"Then that ordnance will be useless scrap to you. You need me more than I need you, Hadji. See, you're going to need training on how to use the stuff I brought. Like I said, it's all computerized ordnance, complete with access codes, which I have," Avalon said, tapping the side of his head, "all up here. And I would forget the Russians, since I know they don't have anything close to SPLAT. What they unloaded on you probably dates back to the start of their Afghan war. If I check these shells, I bet I find rust, a few cracks make you and the others run for the mountain." He watched the lieutenant's eyes, militant thinking hard. "I have chemical shells, brand-new and clean, and an Unmanned Aerial Vehicle, with a warhead, I might add, already stuffed with a VX package."

"And how long would it take for us to learn how to operate this ordnance?"

"That all depends," Avalon said, smiling, "on how quick a study you and your boys are."

"And I assume you want money?"

"That's what brought me here."

A dark look fell over the Iranian's face. "What if I tell you we already paid for this merchandise. That fighters we had sent to al-Namak to meet with you Americans have been assassinated."

Avalon balked, felt his heart skip a beat. "Then you know what happened. But before you get your undies all in a knot, I had nothing to do with that. I lost comrades back there, too, men who were in this deal with Namak. There was another team attached to this operation but unaware of our operation. They were supposed to be the fall guys, but it didn't quite work out the way we'd hoped. What I'm saying, is, me and my men here are on our own. We're the last infidels you have to deal with. You want to do business, I have contacts and connections that can deliver all the special merchandise you can pay for."

"But you understand we cannot pay you any more for this shipment?"

Avalon bit down the curse. "How about we work out a price? For showing you how it all works, give you the access codes?"

The Iranian thought hard about something, then nodded. "It is not up to me, you understand."

"Then let's go talk to the Grand Ayatollah."

"Wait here."

Avalon felt the heat rise, inside and out, as he watched the Iranian lieutenant walk away, a group of six militants falling in to seal the three of them in a ring of potential death. Soon, he knew, their fate would be decided, one way or the other. He had a good feeling, though, the Grand Ayatollah would play ball. Or so he hoped.

McCARTER BEGAN to take a head count of his teammates as soon as he shed his parachute.

Insertion inside Tajikistan—or any hostile territory—would normally, he knew, be considered the most dangerous part of the mission. There was radar detection, for starters, though he'd been assured that was being handled by FSK agents inside the compound. Then there were heavy machine guns, antiaircraft guns, shoulder-fired missiles, surface-to-air missiles, any of which could have blown them out of the sky. The safest ceiling for air insertion, he knew, was 50,000 feet. But all that "could have, should have, would have" blather, he decided, was best left to journalists and talking heads, where Monday-morning quarterbacking was their field of expertise.

It was his call, a six-hundred-foot combat jump, and visibility above their hop off the C-130 was less than zero. Plus, there was wind drift, with gusts their Doppler radar measured at plus-20 knots, then the mountainous terrain to consider where deep ravines could swallow one of them and bog down the mission for hours with a search. Thus the shorter the fall under the conditions they faced, the better.

The easy part was over.

A hundred-and-one monkey wrenches, he thought, could be hurled into this leg of the campaign, and before the CIA-FSK retrieval team even picked them up. Roving Russian patrols and Tajik guerrillas, though, could prove the least of their obstacles.

Unbooting his M-16/M-203 combo, he slipped on his night-vision goggles. There. Two figures at the far edge of the clearing, having just barely landed inside the treeline. All six of them, he knew, were togged in whitesuits, boots to gloves to hoods, with thermals beneath to help ward off the bitter cold, as they were some three-thousand-plus feet high on the plateau. Combat vests, slotted with grenades and extra clips, M-16/M-203, with Hawkins the odd commando out, toting the SAW with its box mag of two hundred 5.56 mm rounds, Encizo to go in armed with the Multiround Projectile Launcher for quick killing duty. McCarter wondered, considering the task they faced, if they had enough firepower. Soon, he'd find out.

Grabbing up his chute, intending to sterilize the DZ best he could, he tromped through about six inches of snow.

The Farm had given him the choice of whether to accept the mission. After Price and Brognola laid it out, and he discussed it with his mates, they had agreed—despite the glaring potential for another giant knife to plunge between their shoulder blades—to breach the Russian weapons factory. The star of this particular show was Jack Grimaldi, and McCarter found himself admiring the mission controller's guts for what she had in mind. Naturally, it was their grim chore to pull off what seemed like the impossible.

A quick check of his GPS module and he found they were just outside fourteen kilometers of the target. The red homing beacon on the handset flashing, looking at the digital readout and gauging the distance, and he figured their pickup should be there within fifteen, twenty minutes, tops.

McCarter began skirting the edge of the treeline, weapon out and fanning the green murk for any sign of hostiles, any figure, that wasn't clad in whitesuit. He fastened the com link around his head, as three then four whitesuits advanced.

"Call off," he whispered as they crouched inside the trees, the troops naming themselves by initial.

Manning was missing.

McCarter keyed his com link. "G? Respond, G."

"On the way. I got into a wrestling match with some trees. I think I'm about a hundred yards northeast of where you landed."

McCarter moved them out, hustling, double-time on a vector to where he hoped to find Manning in one piece. They found Manning, on the ground, sheathing his commando dagger, his canopy fluttering in the wind, about twenty feet up.

"I'm good," Manning said.

McCarter checked his GPS, the second red dot marking their retrieval team closing fast.

And the Phoenix Force leader led them through the woods. He recalled what Brognola had told him when he'd accepted the mission, something about sending them into the lion's mouth. McCarter clung to grim hope those jaws weren't about to snap shut.

CHAPTER EIGHTEEN

The Tajik rebel was dead. His scientists—one of whom was a former medical examiner for the Moscow police—explained away the phenomenon as death by slow radiation poisoning. There had been high fever, chills, nausea, all the symptoms, yes, of death by exposure to lethal doses of radioactive material. Only what Colonel Ytri Kolinko now viewed from beyond the reinforced glass of the quarantine bubble didn't sufficiently explain whatever the bizarre truth.

The Hazmat team was finished now with its preliminary examination, except for one last sweep of a Geiger counter over the corpse. Kolinko saw the needle waver up, what appeared a measurable read, indicating the body was still hot. Incredibly, it took only one spacesuit to lift a fully grown man over the gurney, where he would be wheeled away for a complete autopsy, which, he hoped, would learn more about the cause of death.

It was as if the corpse weighed little more than a feather, as the spacesuit laid it on the gurney, but one of his scientists had already informed him the Tajik had no skeletal mass. Once he had begun to—what, come down to Earth in this cell?—his whole appearance had drastically changed. There was the flesh, white as the snow beyond the compound, but appearing to glow, near bright enough that Kolinko believed the corpse was...

What? Shining? Transparent?

Next, the eyes. They had turned into what he could only describe as two large black marbles. Then the fingers and toes. They seemed to have grown together.

He turned away, checking his watch.

For he had far weightier concerns than the unexplained death of a Tajik fighter.

It would be a quarter-mile march and then some by the time he made the hangar. With any luck he would miss the event altogether, but his presence had been deemed critical, since he was to be the one to essentially set the bird free. Suspecting how this event would come to pass, he touched the butt of his hip-holstered Makarov, veered left down another grim-looking, narrow, white-walled hall. When dealing with the FSK and special ops, it was best to go to a potential gunfight with bullets to spare. The armory was on the way, and he suspected he would need far more than a pistol for the showdown. He no longer even trusted his own Red Lightning commandos. In truth, he believed some, if not all, belonged to Military Intelligence Specialists from the GRU, the Main Intelligence Directorate.

The better part of him—the loyal soldier to the Motherland—was glad it was over. The isolation, for one matter, could grind down the inner man all by itself, until all he wanted to do was remain secluded in his quarters and swill vodka, day and night. Then there was guerrilla war with the Tajik rebels. He wasn't opposed to getting his hands wet with blood, but this was a land that would never be tamed, and there was something unsettling, perhaps even depressing about existence in a land where he was fiercely hated by the locals. Beyond that, he never knew when a corrupt officer would come to him with a bribe to either work with the drug dealers or—

Enough. One way or the other, his post here was finished.

That he had been contacted by the Ministry of Defense personally, informed of the coming event, signaled him he wasn't destined for the gulag or a bullet behind the ear. If he wanted to salvage his career and save his life, he had pledged cooperation, betraying what he knew about the special operatives, which, in and of itself, meant he could be marked for death at some future point. Since day one of his command, the men in black came and went on a frequent basis, arrived without warning, then often malingered for days, armed with directives from the GRU. For some time he had suspected they were stealing ordnance from the warehouse, smuggling small and large arms, along with chemical and biological artillery shells that were supposed to have been destroyed long ago in an agreement between his country and America. They presented him with manifests that declared removal of WMD for this or that incinerator in the Ukraine.

Little more than mercenaries in his mind, they believed themselves clever.

Reaching the steel door to the armory, he began punching in the access code. The door was sliding back when the pager on his hip vibrated.

It was beginning.

CALVIN JAMES FELT as if he was on the longest forced march of his life.

They were inside—or, rather, beneath—the weapons factory, perhaps a mile or more due south, if he had gotten his bearings correct outside. One of the spooks—Russian, he assumed—had accessed the keypad to a door that was at the end of a deep but narrow ravine where the mountains seemed to shoot straight up and through the clouds. Now they were being led through a series of tunnels, the mountain rock braced by steel walls, mounted bulbs, staggered at hundred foot or so intervals, barely enough light to catch a potential armed shadow ahead. Each narrow, dimly lit labyrinth seemed to go forever, and James kept expecting a large fighting force to come around each and every corner, assault rifles blazing.

End of game.

Gripping his M-16/M-203 combo tight in white-gloved hands, James had already taken a head count, just in case. There were ten of them, equally divided, front and rear, Russian and CIA, split down the middle, all armed with AK-74s.

Hemmed in by the spook squad.

The ex-SEAL didn't like the set up in the least, knew that if it went to hell, the six of them would either fight their way out or die here in this mountain compound in a region of the world few people in the West had ever heard of.

According to the CIA, the six of them were American mercenary-terrorists, or at least that would be the cover story issued by Moscow should they be captured or killed. As for the CIA, they declared the Russians were handing them over some alloy that had allegedly fallen from space and contaminated parts of Tajikistan. No more elaboration on this space ore, other than the CIA would scoop it up for themselves, but James knew the Company often spoke out of both sides of its mouth anyway.

Trust no one.

They could well be there looking to abscond with a few backpack nukes, or the latest biological genie, for all he knew. Whatever was down in Level Four was off limits to the six of them.

The hangar where Lightning Bat was parked was their battlefront.

Oddly enough, he found no posted sentries, no clue they were being watched by surveillance cameras.

Listening to bootheels drumming over concrete, the sound seemed to accelerate his adrenaline rush. This wouldn't be the first time, he knew, that Phoenix Force was summoned by the Russians to clean up what was to Moscow an embarrassing mess. All of them knew from the Farm's brief about the attack on Las Vegas, that Russian operatives somehow had plunged a bloody hand into what was a major terrorist attack on American soil.

Like the others, James could be sure they seethed

when they thought about the Vegas attack. Scores of innocent lives had been lost, and still counting. Families left behind to grieve the loss of loved ones, gaping holes in lives never again to be filled. And a nation once again gripped in shock, horror, anguish, with rage and the call to vengeance and arms not far behind.

Calvin James figured to do his avenging part, aware that those primarily responsible were still perched in the wings, scheming murder and mayhem, about two thousand miles to the southwest.

A few hundred militants on the back burner, but not for long.

First, the theft of what they hoped would clean their clocks.

He found they were closing on a wide steel door at the end of yet another tunnel. When they reached the door, the Russian working the numbers on the keypad, one of the CIA men told Grimaldi, "You're on."

James watched as Grimaldi shed the whitesuit, the nylon fabric tearing down both sides, shoulders to ankles. The ace pilot stepped out in his pilot's jumpsuit, black, the color of this compound's flight crew, a red star over his left breast. He ripped off the white hood, delved into his nylon bag, produced his helmet with visor and fixed oxygen hose, snugged it over his head.

Suddenly, as the doors parted, revealing a large elevator shaft, it felt too easy to James. Then again, why go through all this trouble, the Russians handing over a prototype fighter jet, working with the CIA, just to set the six of them up? Maybe, for once, there was no subterfuge. Maybe...

He piled in with his teammates, the spook squad

cramming in beside them. One of the Russians punched a button, the doors closed and they were rising.

NIKOLEI DYNORCHIK had lured enough enemies into traps over his years of service for the GRU to know when a pit was being dug. It was something in the way the other man moved, a tightness about the shoulders, for example, a sheen of sweat brought on from a racing pulse, the fear and paranoia he might be found out causing him to move a little more quickly than normal. Eye contact was another giveaway, the opponent laying the ambush unable to look directly into his own eyes or to hold his stare.

Colonel Kolinko displayed all those symptoms, he decided, of a man with something to hide as he worked whatever his own agenda.

But did he not have his own scheme in the works? Perhaps that was why Kolinko was acting so strangely? Perhaps Kolinko knew, had sounded the alarm to those of authority beyond the Main Intelligence Directorate? If that was true, then there was much to fear.

That he and his GRU comrades were smuggling ordnance, including chemical and biological agents, out of the compound, purchased by Iranian militants, should be of no great concern for Kolinko. The deal had already been approved by his superiors in the GRU. Kolinko, however, need not be privy to the details, as his service record, complete with psychological profile, indicated the colonel would never accept such intrigue, tainted with the appearance of probable treason.

In the beginning, his superiors, Dynorchik recalled, had explained the business transaction with the Iranians as matter of national security, that a rearmed Iran, flush with WMD, was necessary to preserve their own crumbling, volatile borders. Plus, Moscow didn't want to see another Islamic nation fall to the Americans.

And what gave the Americans the right to anoint themselves the world's policemen?

Should America—bitter rivals still, he knew, despite their propaganda about a free and democratic Russia—occupy another oil-rich Muslim nation, there was no telling how far and wide they would attempt to extend their power by military force. Who would be next to get stomped under the bootheel of American imperialist colonialism? Uzbekistan? Chechnya? Tajikistan? They were having trouble enough, as it stood, with the breakaway so-called satellite states. Why should his country fear American occupation on its very border?

Not on his watch.

The fact that he and his colleagues were turning more money in one deal than they would see in a lifetime of service to their country… Well, after twenty years of risking his life in service to the security of his nation, he figured he owed himself—the country owed him—more than wasting away in a drab apartment in Moscow when he retired.

AK-74 in hand, he led his four-man team into the command and control center.

And he discovered only two operators at the banks of monitors. He read the fear in their expressions as he marched toward them. "Where are the others? There should be at least eight men in here at all times! Speak!"

Their lips were moving, as croaking sounds struggled to emerge.

He flew down the banks of monitors, inspecting every square yard of the facility displayed to him. Spacesuits down in Level Four, working with their centrifuges and vials, fiddling with dials on various panels, or sitting at their computers. Normal routine. The perimeter in front of the compound, north to south, looked quiet enough, sentries at post in the towers. He focused next on Hangar 2 where they were building another Lightning Bat, engineers spread down the spars, tools in hand, lab coats in bays working on computer graphics. He was about to demand where Colonel Kolinko was when he spotted him on the last monitor. Why was he in the main hangar? he wondered. The colonel was waving off the sentries posted around the hangar, as he clearly moved with purpose for the main door, AK-74 in hand. Dynorchik was looking toward the arrow-shaped fighter jet when he spotted the pilot in full jumpsuit and helmet heading straight for Lightning Bat. And why were the ramp ladders in place, allowing him a quick climb into the cockpit? There was no test flight scheduled. A moment later and another figure in jumpsuit and helmet emerged, but coming from the wrong direction, the quarters of all flight crews located…

They were stealing Lightning Bat!

He whirled on the two young operators, then one of his own intelligence officers barked something about the hangar doors opening. True, he found Kolinko beside the keypad, the doors parting.

"What are they doing?" he roared at the operators. "Talk or die!"

"Sir, it's the colonel's orders. We were ordered to let in a team from Z Entrance, but we know nothing else!"

Dynorchik cursed, spittle flying from his lips, spattering the closest operator's expression of terror. "You are lying! You sat here all along and allowed intruders into this compound to steal a prototype aircraft that belongs to our country. That amounts to no less than treason!" He lifted his AK-74, stepped back. "I will save the state the cost of having to try to execute you!" he bellowed.

And hit the trigger.

JACK GRIMALDI THOUGHT he could hear the wardrum of his heartbeat pounding inside his helmet. This was the craziest damn thing, he thought, he'd ever done, no exceptions. Sure, he'd flown just about every type of aircraft built by human hands, Stealth, included, but manning the helm of Lightning Bat was far from his greatest, darkest worry. With the specs he'd pored over, faxed to him by the Farm, committing to memory all vital displays and control systems, Lightning Bat should be no problem to handle.

Provided, of course, the six of them weren't being corralled for slaughter.

Adrenaline searing through his veins, the list of everything that could go wrong shot like lightning bolts through his head. Going in blind didn't even rank the classic understatement of his life.

Teaming up with a Russian pilot, dumped on him at the last minute by the Company, Russian operatives allegedly paving the road in and out. Lightning Bat supposedly given a thorough preflight rundown already by his Russian counterpart, the bird ostensibly his pride and joy, Grimaldi was told the man knew every nut and bolt and wire, stem to stern. Told also by the Company that the Four Points missiles were already loaded in the weapons bay. Hangar doors and front gate would be opened by an inside man. Runway was just beyond the front gate, a five-thousand-yard stretch of hard-packed earth.

Insane?

Let the madness begin, Grimaldi decided as he marched out into open ground, spotted his counterpart moving swiftly to starboard. Coincidence or perfect timing? he wondered. The Russian threw him a thumbs-up, left hand, Grimaldi matching the code sign but with his right thumb in the air. There was a wide, metallic walkway directly above, suspended on poles, not wire like the standard catwalk.

And he heard boots drumming up there.

Then he heard a clank and grind as he closed on the tail of the big bird they would commandeer out. The doors were opening.

Up, up and away. Oh, man, his gut warned him that was so far easier said than done.

Well, they'd all gotten the craziness that far.

Go for it.

Visor down, but the M-16, held low by his side, just in case the Russian pilot was a human adder, the duffel bag with his sat link in the other hand, and Grimaldi heard his breath whistle out tightly compressed lips, echo through his helmet as he fell in behind Lightning Bat's port. He was hidden from the view of sentries up on the catwalks to the north, west and east, his potential snipers spread around the massive hangar, but he kept waiting for the hammer to drop.

It was going so easy, as he heard the pilot bounding up the ramp, beating him into the cockpit—

And he heard a voice, shouting in Russian. He didn't know the language but, as he felt his heart leap into his throat, he was pretty sure the barker was yelling "Stop!"

Or, "Shoot them!"

"FEEL FREE TO SHOOT anyone who shoots at you."

David McCarter briefly remembered those solemn words issued by the Company man who'd given them the final brief right before they were excused back at their Iraqi base. When he'd heard those farewell words, he'd wanted to chuckle at what he perceived as the man having a talent for stating the obvious.

He wasn't laughing now.

It was going to hell fast in the hangar, as he heard Russian voices hollering, autofire breaking out from various undetermined points beyond the doors. The joint American-Russian operatives had, it seemed, begrudged them the blueprints to what they were told was their target area. It was mentally mapped, but McCarter had to wonder just how raw and bloody it could all get if the fighting spilled into other areas of the complex.

No point, he knew, fretting about a future that may never come.

He ordered Hawkins and James to peel off for a narrow corridor that paralleled the length of the hangar. Shooters were clearly already out in open territory, winging bullets at Grimaldi or the bird of the ages or both, and the ex-Ranger and ex-SEAL knew, without his telling them, it was their bloody task to hit their blindside. The CIA-FSK detachment, McCarter then saw, throwing a look over his shoulder, were splitting off for what appeared a hallway to his deep six, gone to do whatever their spook duties. Part of their job, or so he was told, was to secure the antiaircraft batteries that, assuming Grimaldi and his Russian flyboy counterpart rolled out of the gate, could blow them to smithereens before they were wheels up.

McCarter led Manning and Encizo through the double metal doors, shouldering his way, all bull, all adrenaline, and found the layout matched the blueprints.

Maybe they were being told the truth for once?

The passageway was a twenty-foot charge, then the ex-SAS commando hit the corner, took in the uniformed guards on the catwalk downrange. Several of them were frozen uptop, uncertain who or what to shoot, as a blacksuit with an AK-74 led a squad away from the chopper pool to the deep north end, shrieking in Russian at the armed statues. Autofire, he heard, blistered the air from the hangar doors, parted wide now to reveal the compound wall beyond.

Despite the sudden eruption of autofire, so far the CIA-FSK ops looked true to their word.

So far.

But Grimaldi was taking fire, he found, halfway up his ramp, the ace pilot sweeping his M-16 back and forth at however enemy troops were above.

"Rafe!" McCarter shouted at Encizo, pointing at the walkway directly ahead.

Encizo flying past, the Multiround Projectile Launcher filling his hands, McCarter wheeled around the corner, Manning on his right wing. Then both

Phoenix Force commandos unleashed their M-16s on the enemy pack headed for Lightning Bat.

GRIMALDI NAILED two soldiers up top with his opening M-16 burst, the chest fronts of uniforms chewed to red tatters by the 5.56 mm blizzard as they pitched back, out of sight. That left four more AK-74s, the stragglers now charging down the walkway, drawing beads with their assault rifles, two, maybe three, lines of autofire cutting loose.

Dammit! Where was the cavalry?

Sparks blazing off the ramp, he heard rounds drum over Lightning Bat's hull, the Russian shouting something from inside the cockpit. The turbofans shrieking to life was hardly music to his ears, but Encizo breaking out into the open below, the Multiround Projectile Launcher spitting smoke and flame to bring down the ceiling on the four shooters, was like the singing of angels.

And Grimaldi, so jacked on adrenaline, felt as if he was being lifted on divine wings as he flew up the rest of the ramp, the thunder of the explosions above slamming shock waves into his backside. The clam-shell canopy dropping, he jumped down into his seat, felt the fighter jet lurch ahead, wrenching away from its ramps, as he dumped his weapon and bag on the narrow space between pilot and copilot chair. Strapping himself in, he was ready to rumble, grab the side-arm controller when he noticed the display and control panels were all lit up in red.

Indicating nothing but danger!

He didn't know whether to curse, crap or go blind.

Lightning Bat was malfunctioning so far into the danger zone...

"I am Yuri."

Grimaldi looked at the handsome face inside the helmet as the fighter jet gathered speed. "Why is our instrument panel all red instead of green?"

"No worry. Everything normal."

"Red tells me we're in the crapper."

"Red, yes, good. Remember. It is Russian jet."

YTRI KOLINKO KNEW he wouldn't make it through the night, but determined he would reach the gate, even if he was shot down, forced to drag himself the rest of the distance, trailing blood and guts. If he was going to die, then it wouldn't be in vain. At the very least he would defeat the GRU traitors by freeing Lighting Bat from their clutches.

The battle was raging to another crescendo of weaponsfire, it seemed, as he plucked his handheld radio off his belt. They were dark shadows up in the three towers, he spied, immobilized by the uncertainty of the moment, but he had to try to reach them before they opened fire.

Running hard, he was on the verge of patching through when the first heavy machine gun began thundering from the closest tower. But, of course, he thought.

The GRU man had alerted the sentries.

A fresh clip fed to his AK-74, he held back on the trigger, sprinting on, closing, fifty feet or so, as he blasted out the window behind the sentry. The heavy machine gun fell silent as the guard vanished. He was beyond any decent field of fire from the other two towers but...

Twenty feet. Ten.

The heavy machine gun roared back and Kolinko screamed as the round tore into his thigh. He was spinning, falling, but somehow he managed the strength to return fire, the earth ground up around him in a series of divots.

Close.

And he thought he glimpsed the sentry jerk, the flaming nose of the big gun swinging for the dark Tajik sky.

Would his luck hold?

Would he bleed out before...

He collapsed beside the gate, the world spinning. There was a whine, what he distinguished from the din of weaponsfire as turbofans winding up to jettison the craft.

Gasping for air, the light fading from his eyes, he knew he was hit bad, bleeding out quick, shock about to paralyze him. He shimmied up on his good leg, threw his hand against the wall, bracing himself.

Willed his fingers to work.

He tapped in the first two numbers...

CHAPTER NINETEEN

Rafiq Namak couldn't sleep. The infidel situation was troublesome enough, and he had been in counsel with eight of his top lieutenants at length. Questions, rife with concern and laced with worries over the sincerity of the American commandos, had taken up the better part of an hour. Did they do business with these Americans, and after the failure of the first group he had been put into contact with? Could the Americans get their hands on more of this SPLAT ordnance? A tactical nuke even? Were they telling the truth, or simply stringing him along, for money, to spare their lives? That they didn't trust the Americans went without saying, and he sensed several of his lieutenants would just as soon execute the infidels than attempt to purchase another shipment. Already two major attacks, one on his village near the border and the aerial bombardment on al-Sadq, had decimated his forces, and now, without air support...

And then there was the dream.

Three nights now the dream—so lifelike he was

left shaken, drenched in cold sweat when he'd come lurching, gasping, to a breathless awakening—had invaded his mind just as he'd fallen asleep. In that dream—no, nightmare—he had seen giant vultures, but birds of prey dropping missiles and guided bombs from their talons. In that dream, the same living vision, he had seen the camp go up in flames, his holy fighters, shrieking human torches, thrashing all over the ground. He had stood, the Grand Ayatollah on the mountain, watching the horror in front of him, frozen in place before hitting his knees, crying out to God, demanding, "Why?"

And then the armed shadows were coming for him.

They wielded axes, swords instead of small arms. As they moved near, he saw they weren't human. Rather, they had the faces of demons, red eyes burning with rage, fangs dripping blood, their flesh covered in oozing sores, with maggots spewing from their mouths. He would fire upon them, but the bullets seemed to core right through them, as if their flesh were made of water. Then, as they descended upon him, these silent demons who then appeared more animal than human, hacking away at his hands, feet...

He shuddered, willing the image to vanish from his mind's eye.

It was time to take action. He would see the night through, sleep or not, and in the morning there would be a massive call to arms. It was time to ship out the great jihad, one wave of suicide bombers with the WMD vests after another. Iraq, Israel, it was time to scorch the Earth. If the infidels chose not to give him the access codes, then he knew drastic measures would prove necessary. He didn't think they would capitulate under torture, but if he took his sword to one of them...

It was worth a try. Surely in all the land he could find, purchase, the services of a computer hack.

His handheld radio crackled with the voice of Tuju-ourez. "Yes."

"The Americans, your Holiness, they will not give us the access codes."

They wanted money, which he intended not to give them. Yes, he would promise them payment once they handed over the access codes, then...

Or perhaps not. Say they could land him more ord-nance? If so, they would have to prove that they could before they received another payment.

He took his field glasses, switched them to infrared. He found the group in question, about fifty yards north of the two Russian transport trucks. The cannon had been put together, erected near the pod with its four Eagle Nebula cruise missiles, the UAV on the ground beside the launch rail.

Decision time.

"Tell them to take the night and sleep on their deci-sion. Then bring them up here to me before the sun rises."

When his lieutenant confirmed the order, Namak searched the length of the camp on all points, then looked up at the dark, moonlit sky. He decided to pray, if for nothing else, that God would grant him a night's sleep, free of the terrifying vision of his gruesome death.

MCCARTER SHOT from the hip as he charted his fight-ing course for the hangar door, tagging one, then two,

Russian hardmen charging from the chopper pool. They all knew the towers housed heavy machine guns, and right then he was more worried about Lightning Bat getting blasted off the ground than the fighting force downrange, which Hawkins and James appeared to have under bloody control. The Briton saw Hawkins and James hitting the enemy backside with a blizzard of rounds, hardmen and those Red Lightning commandos giving up the ghost as they spun, toppled like dominoes. The catwalk shooters were in the process of taking hits from Manning, swan-diving to concrete, crash-landing with a sickening crack of broken bones, as wild return rounds came screaming their way, whining off the hangar floor.

Aware of the consequences of ultimate mission failure, McCarter found Encizo taking the lead as he burst onto open ground beyond the hangar doors. Something was wrong near the gate, McCarter saw, a figure struggling to stay on its feet, hand punching at the keypad. Assume he was their contact...

He was lining up one of the three towers, heavy machine guns blistering the air, when Encizo beat him to it, chugging away two hell bombs. The explosions lit up the night, silenced those big man-eaters, McCarter cursing, willing the gate to open as the fighter jet appeared to halt then the figure collapsed.

"Son of a..."

He was running in that direction, ready to pulverize the gate, when it began to part.

And Grimaldi gave the bird ignition as the turbofans screamed. The ex-SAS commando briefly admired the ace pilot's brazen style, the fighter jet streaking away, wings clearing the gate with two or three feet to spare. Scouting the open ground around him, withering fire hitting his backside from the hangar, and McCarter was grateful when no cavalry charged into the night. He saw Lightning Bat shrink as Grimaldi and his Russian copilot hit full throttle, tearing down the runway, lifting next, rising...

Then shooting for the sky, swallowed within seconds by thick, low cloud cover.

Mission accomplished.

Now, he thought, all they had to do was find out if their CIA counterparts would live up to their promise of trucking them to a waiting Gulfstream.

A curtain call was due before dawn. He checked his watch. Factor in travel time back to base in Iraq, and if their air armada was refueling and re-upping the hardware as Brognola and Price had informed they would...

Hardly the homestretch.

But it was getting better by the minute.

Every enemy they dropped from here on would make the world a little kinder, gentler place.

McCarter took his handheld radio and raised the Company man. "The bird has flown," he told the CIA man. "Now. How about that ride out of here you promised?"

BROGNOLA SAW Price give him the thumbs-up as she walked away from the sat link.

"Jack's clear of Tajik airspace," the mission controller said. "They came under fire on the way out, but he says he doesn't think anything was damaged. He'll know more when he gets back to our Iraq base and can give Lightning Bat a thorough check. His Russian counterpart went over all systems again."

"Let me guess," Brognola said, working on a cup of coffee. "He aced the test."

"He says it's actually no more difficult than your standard F-117. There's no nuclear reactor, no Divine Alloy to worry about with this version, which, I suppose, under the circumstances, is a plus."

"I'll take all the pluses I can get right now."

"David called. Phoenix is on the way out, pretty much in Jack's exhaust."

"Which means," Brognola said, checking his watch, "they could still hit Namak before dawn."

"We'll use the same air firepower support as before."

Brognola heaved a breath. For once, something was going right. For once, someone had played it straight with them. "Hunt and Carmen think that Namak may be sitting on some special ordnance in camp."

"Those Russian transports you mentioned?"

"Yeah. I don't want our guys setting foot in that camp. I never liked the idea of our troops running around in Hazmat suits anyway. Too damn cumbersome and confining, you ask me. So let the place get burned down from above, whoever scurries out of there we'll get another day."

"And Namak is still perched on his roost in the mountain?"

Brognola nodded. "About three hundred or so feet up, facing toward his Army of Armageddon, which, I hope, will soon be the Army of the Damned."

"So, you want Phoenix to take Namak and whatever lieutenants he has with him on the mountain?"

"That's the plan. Get all pertinent imagery faxed to

David. I need to go have a quick talk with our aerospace superstar."

Brognola walked up to where Jacobs and Kurtzman were going over the grip map of Namak's camp. "How's it going, Bear?"

"Ask the good doctor."

"After all your insistence I would prove so critical to getting your man in the air," Jacobs squawked, "and you had a Russian pilot with him all along."

"It was last minute, and we still need you to calibrate those missiles for my man."

"Should be simple enough," Jacobs said, fingers working the keyboard. "It will be a fairly straight drop, and he'll have to calibrate the missiles with the degree bearings…I'm working on it now. You said he'll be strafing from five thousand feet?"

"Yes," Brognola said.

"Four hundred knots?"

"Yes."

"The calibration will have to coincide with a delay shutdown valve for the missile rocket fuel. That way, they'll drop at the degrees I will give him, hit and skim. He'll have to rotate the spindle according to the bearings I send on."

"Don't let me standing here stop you. Get it done. You have fifteen minutes."

"Slave driver, aren't we?"

Brognola ignored Jacobs and walked away for a moment of silence. None of them was in the clear yet, but the big Fed was beginning to see daylight. Whatever mess, political or otherwise, lay ahead, he'd deal with the fallout when the time came.

This was his show.

And this was one war Phoenix Force and Grimaldi were meant to take to the finish line.

AVALON KNEW it was over. The Iranians wanted the codes, and he didn't need to hear the "or else" to know they were about to kill the three of them.

He found the Grand Ayatollah sitting, Indian-style on the ledge, an odd smile on his lips as he stared at the sprawling mass of his camp. They were getting ready for something down there, Avalon surmised, armed jihadists piling into vehicles, about two hundred or so in the heart of the camp, truck engines grinding to life, the distant babble of excited chatter reaching his ears. Heading out, he believed, for Iraq, ready to kill a bunch of innocent people. And he was sure Namak was about to put the ultimatum to him.

Screw it all. If that was the case...

Avalon decided to play it cool, lighting up a cigarette. He took in the setup, having already told Cheevers and Solstice to be braced to go for broke, throats, eyes, nuts, whatever was necessary to take one down and grab a weapon, start spraying but spare Namak, if possible. Ten militants, though, would prove a tough match, unless he got his hands on an AK with his first strike. One Iranian just to his left, eyes boring into him, assault rifle aimed off his body, though, for the moment. If he couldn't get money, then he could at least survive, figure out his next move once he was back in Iraq. He still had a few contacts in the Company, men who had fought beside him, proved loyal, were perhaps of like mind when it came to turning a buck.

Avalon checked the sky, a dirty gray smudge, the dawn of a new day less than an hour off.

A new day, but with very little promise.

"Don't you worry about an air attack?"

Namak took his time answering. "If it was going to happen, it would have already happened."

Avalon grunted. Not necessarily, he thought, wondering why his nerves were getting torqued up the longer he watched the skies.

"You will give us the access codes."

Avalon chuckled. There it was. "What about our money?"

"The men who, you claim, were killed in the village, were already paid for this shipment."

"It's no claim. They're history. Money or no codes and that UAV stays grounded without them."

"I see."

Avalon pitched away his cigarette. "I don't think you do."

He thought he heard a faint buzzing to the south, was searching the horizon in that direction when—

The first line of thundering explosions tore through the heart of the camp, jolting Avalon with cold fear.

Now, he knew, it was over. Those were cluster bombs, as he watched one wave of brilliant flashes after another marching in lines, all points of the compass, massive explosions erasing any object in their paths. The transports, with their gruesome payloads were ignited, flung into the air, as more blasts sheared them apart, stick figures skyrocketing from wreckage winging out in all directions. A quick look skyward and he believed he made out the batwing shape of a Stealth, several thousand feet up, and soaring over the mountain. And in the distant west he spotted the air strike coming in to mop up whatever was left down there, fleeing for its life. Fighter jets, and what he believed was the girth of a Spectre, coming in low and hard, dropping the hammer.

Avalon wheeled on the closest Iranian, clawed his hand into his throat, choking the shout back down the jihad's yap as he squeezed. The Iranian began dancing, holding back on the trigger of his assault rifle, Avalon glimpsing two then three of his fellow extremists absorbing rounds, tumbling as the autofire blazed on.

And Avalon ripped his throat out, flung the bloody flesh away as he plucked the AK from limp hands. Now where was Namak? he wondered, and found the Iranian running down a gully, a few lieutenants on his heels.

"Let's go get our man with the money," Avalon told Cheevers, who was checking Solstice for a pulse. "Forget him, he's gone. Our money, though, is running away."

MCCARTER WANTED a DNA sample from the terror lord of the year. No double, no ringer was going to muck up the mission, now that he sensed they were snapping the jaws of death shut.

He led the hop off the Black Hawk, M-16/M-203 filling his hands for the finishing touches, his Apache gunship swinging out to the north, gone to search for enemy blood. No Hellfires, no extended chain-gun barrage unless he gave the order. He didn't need to spend two days scooping up blood and gristle and guts just for some CIA guy back in Iraq to tell him it wasn't Namak.

There were five of them, he spotted, and heading right in their direction.

Blind, and straight into their guns.

According to the Farm's sat stake, the black turban belonged to Namak. He hand-signaled his troops to grab a fire point, twenty yards or so where the armed group would run right into them. They appeared more concerned about the Apache, as they began spraying autofire at the war bird, but it was like shooting spitballs at the gunship's armored skin. He stole a second to take in the air bombardment eating up the camp. Grimaldi had done his part, dumping the Four Points cluster missiles, dead center, where they had puked away countless payloads to rip the guts out of the epicenter.

Now their part.

McCarter hit a crouch behind a boulder, drew a bead with his M-16, waiting as they came around a bend in the gully. "Fire at will!" he shouted.

And Phoenix Force cut loose in unison. Holding back on his trigger, McCarter hit who he believed was Namak with a long burst of M-16 autofire, rounds chewing up his chest as the mullah who would be Shiite king of the Middle East flailed, his AK stuttering impotent rounds at the sky.

"Hey! You up there! Listen to me! I got a proposition!"

McCarter climbed for higher ground, leading his men to a promontory, homed in on the direction of the voice. His Apache pilot patched through on his com link, informing him there were two hostiles, tiger stripes, marking their position.

"I'll handle it."

He almost couldn't wait to hear the man's deal, but knew how he'd answer.

They were about twenty feet below, two heads and shoulders above a ring of boulders.

"You! There's money in this, you get us out of here! Millions, if you let me get in touch with my people back in the States! I know a classified base, they make all kinds of high-tech merchandise! We work together with my people in the States, you'll be a rich man! There's plenty of Namaks in these parts! Won't be any problem unloading the stuff! I see you up there!"

"Throw down your weapon! It's over!" McCarter shouted.

"Kiss my ass. It's never over!"

"Rafe," McCarter told Encizo, "finish them off."

Encizo unsung the Multiround Projectile Launcher, began chugging away the final answer. McCarter counted three explosions, possibly four, but it was more than enough to blow two traitors off the mountain.

EPILOGUE

"Congratulations are in order, my Justice Department friend. I should have brought champagne, but you strike me more as a whiskey man, not some wine-bibbing, sissy-fied Frog or yuppy tea-totaler we have swarming all over this fair city of ours. Look at yourself. If I could hug you, I would. You are the man, you took on Iran, declared a war, albeit covert, all on your own pair, no White House, no Congress. Barely a peep from that part of the world, not even a sound bite from al-Jazeera, and there you sit. King Kong, Godzilla, that twenty-five-footer from Jaws can't compare to you. You have this Administration running for cover, the President and all his little men all in a bitch snit. You are the Man. Never in my life…"

And neither had Hal Brognola. If this was the Shadow Man's way of praising him for a job nobody else wanted well done…

So, why did he feel like weeping? Why did he feel as though he was still trapped in a dark night of the soul?

He was back in the spook van, staring at himself in

the one-way glass. Something inside him had changed, though he wasn't sure what the metamorphosis. He only knew he was different. Somehow. Forever.

Hitting his reflection with a blast of smoke, he wasn't sure he liked what he saw. Older by a decade in the span of a few short but eternal days. Haggard. Soul all fragmented.

He, like the Shadow Man, had seen the future, and it wasn't bright.

But it was duty, what he did, always had been, always would be, and tomorrow would thrust another Namak, more Tiger Ops in his face.

Who are you? Who are you really? he wondered, staring hard at his reflection.

Husband? Father? Protector of national security? One more finger plugging a hole in the dike?

The big Fed wasn't sure if he silently asked himself the questions, or the entity behind the glass. He heaved a breath, wondered if his soul wasn't right then flying toward his image.

"Where's it all headed? Where's the world going?" The disembodied voice sounded pleased with itself. Whoever the entity, Brognola knew he wielded big-time clout. Questions about the Farm's security lingered, but...

The Entity spoke. "You look exhausted, depressed perhaps, but I can understand, man of your position and power, secret as it might be. You want depressed? Allow me to tell you where it's all headed, my friend..."

He had been fairly summoned, a FedEx package deposited on his desk, with a simple but ominous, "We need to talk."

Different P.O. Box return address this time, different name…

It was all Brognola could do to focus on the moment. How long since he'd seen his wife? Oh, but how badly he wanted, needed, to return to the simple life of sanity, with someone who knew…or did she really know him at all?

"Near future worst case," the Entity said, "a suitcase nuke is detonated in the heart of Washington. Congress. Senate in full session. President and all his important men under the White House. Bang. Poof. All gone. The entire seat of our government is wiped out, anarchy sweeps the country. It's been stopped twice already, but there will be a third attempt. And who knows? Maybe this time they succeed. Could be more Tiger Ops out there in the bush. Selling out. Smuggling in the Suitcase from Allah. Setting the table for the enemy. Skipping off to Tahiti with numbered accounts so fat…"

Brognola was too damn tired for doomsday prattle. All he wanted was a double whiskey or two—alone. Listen to some music—alone.

Alone.

Carrying the truth of the world in which they lived in his heart.

"You said you might have something for me."

"Indeed," the Entity said. "My man will give you the package when you leave. First, house is in the process of being cleaned. Pentagon. DOD. The State Department. The NSA."

"Trying to tell me the jackals who thought they were safe are in the process of being executed."

"A crude way of stating the truth, but yes, they are being systematically eliminated."

"And the Eagle Nebula?"

"It will be cleaned likewise. Relocated. Restructured. Reclassified. Too much cutting-edge work was going on there. We can't afford to just drop all the projects they were working on. As for Ezekiel Jacobs, I heard the Justice Department will be getting a visit soon."

Brognola chuckled. "Someone will show up at my office, you mean, make me and him an offer we can't refuse?"

"More or less. Jacobs will get immunity and a deal— sort of."

"Spell that out, if you don't mind."

"He'll spend the rest of his life under house arrest."

"While he jumps through hoops for the government and goes on creating the future of warfare."

"Something along those lines."

The Entity was pretty typical of a Washington intelligence insider, he thought. Talking but not saying much. Evasive. Double-tongued. Always leaving an escape hatch open.

"The Russians aren't happy, I understand, about losing Lightning Bat, but I would surmise they kept enough blueprints to build another, only our side retrieved all of their Divine Alloy."

"Small price to keep world peace."

"The cold war never ended, my friend."

"Tell me something I don't already know."

"If only I were in that position."

"Are we finished?"

"For now. Again, congratulations."

One of the Entity's men opened the door on cue. Brognola stepped out, and held his ground for a long moment.

Wondering.

Another battle, he knew, was won. For the moment at least. Tomorrow…

God only knew, he thought, what tomorrow would bring. More critical mass building somewhere in the country, on the planet, he was sure. But he would be there, ready to go the distance, perform his duty.

It was who he was. It was all he knew.

∴ James Axler
Outlanders

The war for control of Earth enters a new dimension...

REFUGE

UNANSWERABLE POWER

The war to free postapocalyptic Earth from the grasp of its oppressors slips into uncharted territory as the fully restored race of the former ruling barons are reborn to fearsome power. Facing a virulent phase of a dangerous conflict and galvanized by forces they have yet to fully understand, the Cerberus rebels prepare to battle an unfathomable enemy as the shifting sands of world domination continue to chart their uncertain destiny...

DEADLY SANCTUARY

As their stronghold becomes vulnerable to attack, an exploratory expedition to an alternate Earth puts Kane and his companions in a strange place of charming Victoriana and dark violence. Here the laws of physics have been transmuted and a global alliance against otherwordly invaders has collapsed. Kane, Brigid, Grant and Domi are separated and tossed into the alienated factions of a deceptively deadly world; one from which there may be no return.

Available at your favorite retailer.

TAKE 'EM FREE

2 action-packed novels plus a mystery bonus

NO RISK

NO OBLIGATION TO BUY